FREEZE

A WEEK WITH MR. HOPKINS

VOLUME ONE

ELLIS KROSS

E/K

...

First Edition, July 2014
Written by Ellis Kross
Edited by Sidonie Lailler

PUBLISHED BY ELLIS/KROSS

ISBN: 978-0-9894376-6-0
Kross, Ellis, 1983—
Freeze: A Week With Mr. Hopkins
I. Title. Fiction. Mystery/Thriller

ISBN: 978-0-9894376-6-0 pbk.

Jellyfish Cover

Story by Ellis Kross
Book Design by Izzy
Interior Photograph by Collage_Best (istockphoto.com)
Front Cover Artwork by Yuriy Kovtun (istockphoto.com) and Natalia Churzina (istockphoto.com)

This is a work of fiction.
Names, characters, places, and incidents are the products of the author's imagination.
Any resemblance to actual persons, living or dead, is entirely coincidental.

Written at the Crow's Nest.

Printed in the United States
10 9 8 7 6 5 **4** 3 2 1

...

A Week with Mr. Hopkins

Freeze Volume 1

P R O L O G U E

IF the bullet was given eyes to see, it would've hit the same couch that she leaped behind.

If the bullet was given a mouth to speak, more than likely it wouldn't have said anything—not even a wiz, whoosh, or whistle—for it would've been in too much shock to comment on her unusual quickness.

And if the bullet was given a pair of wings to help it curve around the couch, it would've *still* missed its target for it carried a great deal of respect for her.

As Anne peeked over the couch, she saw a glimpse of the shooter's red face drifting into the darkness of the living room.

With her senses enhanced—the smell of gunpowder hovering in the air and the vibrations of tendons tightening throughout her fists—she crouched behind the couch while the shooter reloaded the machine gun.

A streak of light suddenly flashed through the living room and highlighted the shooter's whereabouts.

She was still waiting behind the chewed up couch when a light flickered across her range of vision. She carefully moved her eyes toward the living room window. There, she noticed a police car cruising by the house. Once more, the cruiser's spotlight crossed the living room and highlighted the shooter's face and his weapon.

Next, Anne heard footsteps, this time trailing farther away from her.

Another *squeak* across the living room!

Then, she steadily glanced over the couch.

The shooter was no longer there.

More footsteps now!

Anne tracked the footsteps, which were now coming from the kitchen. She quickly scurried from the living room before the other intruder could locate her. She sneaked down a narrow hallway and approached him from behind like a predator to a prey. The intruder made it to the kitchen, but the intruder *wasn't* alone. Unlike the two intruders, her footsteps were as silent as a ghost.

Holding a knife in one hand, she approached the intruder. Just inches away now. . . He spun around, only to be greeted by a flying arm. Dodging the blow before Anne could make contact, he fired two shots at her, but she remarkably bent herself around each bullet. Anne made another attack: a swift kick to his arm. The pistol dropped from his sweaty grip, leaving him vulnerable now. He swung at Anne three times, each punch and slap methodically redirected and followed by Anne pouncing onto the countertop and flipping over the intruder. Now, behind the intruder, Anne plunged the knife into his neck before he could strike again. Juvenile noises exited from his throat: a fizzle and then a gurgle. Then, his red face slackened into a gaping expression. His fists uncurled in surrender and fell to his side.

Anne pulled out the blade from his throat, causing a stream of blood to spurt over her face and chest.

Police sirens blared from outside!

The front of her house lit up with bright colors, mainly reds and blues.

As the intruder bled out on the kitchen floor, she couldn't help but notice a tiny glare right next to his pocket. The glare, Anne saw, begging for attention.

She reached down and carefully patted his pocket. Another object, Anne realized. She pulled out both a silver necklace and a USB flash drive. She examined the necklace first and then the flash drive. However, Anne brought her eyes back to that one necklace. So familiar, she thought—*similar*—if not, the exact same one that she ordered online a week ago. . .

PART ONE
DAY AND NIGHT

CHAPTER 1

THREE o'clock in the afternoon: a special time for Anne when all of the morning caffeine from the two rounds of coffee—three if it was a long night—had worn off (this, of course, was what the telemarketers at Universal Satellite Radio called being "tired," but to Anne, she knew it as the "three o'clock feeling," which, in the end, turned out not to be much of a feeling at all but more or less a lack of feeling, a state of emptiness and then, finally, one finds himself or herself asking the inevitable question: *Why do I keep coming back here*, here, at this prison we called USR, trapped, confined, and alone in this nutshell of a cubicle? Surely, it wasn't because of the money or the hundred and sixty hours of vacation each employee received per year. Then, what was it? Self-torment? The common question: Was I a prisoner of my own design? As many questions followed, as they almost always did, the answers would never come, as they almost never did). But like most employees at USR, including Anne, the only thing keeping their engines running was only one thing: *routine*. Anne was, as with most at USR, one who lived and died by routine. And that was what she dreaded the most about the job: not only routine, but also the predictability.

Except for Friday and Saturday nights (Sunday being the only day she could really get her beauty sleep), Anne set her alarm to seven-thirty every night after she brushed and flossed her teeth, and then every morning after she climbed from her tedious dreams—driving a car without brakes, going to work naked, an army of cheeseheads invading the office, that sort of thing—she rolled out of bed, literally.

By the time Anne gathered herself, it was around seven forty-five—this was after hammering the snooze button with her fist a couple of times and giving the little pest a run for its money.

At the pace she was going, she was going to break the world record for most broken alarm clocks—she kept breaking them as if it was never going out of style and then she kept forking out the money to buy them. Once, Anne tried the built-in alarm on her smartphone, an Ellipse 4G, customized with the standard bells and whistles: Bluetooth, GPS, Internet. You name it. It had it. But as with the other alarm clocks, Anne ended up breaking the Ellipse, which ended up costing her a pretty penny. So, she decided to stick with the cheapos that ran about fifteen bucks a pop at the nearest Big Mart store. On some mornings, Anne shed about five minutes from picking up the leftover fragments from a shattered alarm clock. Now, she was already going on three alarm clocks this month, one higher than her monthly two.

7:46 AM

THE chirp of an alarm clock, or what was left of an alarm clock, fizzled out into a soft whisper.

On the way down, her feet managed to catch the fall as they always did.

As she staggered around the bed, one of her feet accidentally kicked a battery, which was previously ejected from the clock. The battery skated across the hardwood floor until it came to rest at the doorway.

After one mighty stretch, occasionally wiping the crust from her eyes, Anne inserted each contact into her eyes, the first eye being the hardest and most difficult. A framed painting was mounted to the right of where she was standing. She blinked several times and focused her eyes on the contemplative painting, which she had bought at a thrift shop about a year ago. The painting by local artist, Sue Vanguard, was called _Death Row: The Last Walk Before I Die_. Every morning after Anne inserted her contacts, she would take a minute of her time to stare at the black and white painting: a long, narrow, and weathered dock stretching out into a foggy lake.

Before she could lose herself in the painting, Anne pulled herself from the vacant stare and shuffled her way through the living room and into the kitchen where she brewed a coffee packet in her single-serving coffee maker, a gift from her foster dad last Hanukkah. Anne stuck with the hardcore stuff, not that weak _Dippin' Donuts_ bullshit that everybody and his uncle drank every morning. Instead, she bought packets of gourmet coffee, _Richer Beans_, a robust blend of French roast, tucked away from the big brands in the very back of the aisle. She drank the stuff with no cream or sugar. When asked, she retorted, "I'm already sweet as it is," which Anne was, but she never really showed that side to anyone except for the people in her circle. She was hard on the outside, soft on the inside. A man's woman who enjoyed drinking her coffee all the way black. Just a single whiff of the stuff while it was brewing got her bowels moving like a pissed off racehorse.

7:50 AM

IT didn't take too long for Anne to go.

Not much pushing was involved. She wiped three times and then flushed the toilet without looking down into the toilet bowl.

By the time she slipped back into her clothes, her bottom was clean enough to eat off, but for Anne, there wasn't much eating going on, or whatever the kids were calling it these days, when it came to that department. Her boyfriend, Michael, an accountant, wasn't much of a caretaker per se. He didn't like going down on Anne, which, at times, made Anne question his sexuality. Not to mention: always hanging out with "the guys." Said that he didn't like the taste and that it made him gag. He was more of a receiver than a giver, obviously. And Anne, on the contrary, was more of the giver than the receiver; however, she wished Michael pleasured her more often.

Lately, though, there wasn't much pleasuring going around, nor any giving *or* receiving for that matter.

7:54 AM

THE comb that Anne used for her hair had been with her ever since she could remember. Her foster mom, Molly, passed down the comb to Anne. It was quite an ugly thing. From a distance, the comb looked like a cross between a porcupine and a dead squirrel that had been flattened by a car. Nonetheless, it got the job done. Anne wasn't thorough with her hair. She mostly primped. For about a minute or two, she ran the comb through her dirty blonde hair, and then, after she patted down the remaining rogue hairs with a sheet of fabric softener—a little trick a girlfriend taught her a couple of years ago—she wrapped it in a ponytail with a black barrette.

Next, she washed her face with cleansing cream while she worked her way through her first cup of coffee.

For Anne, the whole point was to stay awake. If there was a moment when she closed her eyes, then there was a chance she would fall back asleep, which would've been detrimental to her health.

Now was the most crucial part of Anne's morning routine: sip coffee, keep eyes open, *move.*

7:59 AM

Two different outfits that Anne had collected from the closet lay on the edge of the bed. She did the whole eeny, meeny, miny, moe thing. Since USR promoted a relaxed environment, the dress code was very casual; but Anne enjoyed looking good every time she stepped out into the public. Both of her foster parents were nice dressers. Harold always wore khakis with a sweater. Molly something chic. Very old fashioned people.

After about a minute of displaying the outfit in front of the standing mirror, Anne went with the navy blue blouse underneath a black sweater and a pair of black pants. She dressed like she drank her coffee: black.

8:15 AM

Once Anne was dressed, she applied makeup to her face. She didn't put on much makeup; in fact, there was no need. Anne was an attractive woman, narrow face and hazel eyes, innocent and yet fierce at the same time. She wasn't too liberal on the makeup, whereas a lot of women around the office used about as much makeup as a mortician. Anne was subtle, though, a little bit of dark shadow around both of her eyes, a dash of powder on her sunken cheeks to cover up the dim freckles, a generous amount of mascara, and then, to top it off, glossy pink lipstick.

Anne checked the time on her phone.

The time read: 8:22.

"I'm going to be late," she whispered to herself.

8:23 AM

ON the way out, Anne grabbed a ripe banana, as well as a lite snack from the pantry, usually a granola bar or cereal bar, which was low in carbs, low in fat, not a lot of sugar, and then poured the rest of the coffee in a silver thermos from the row of cleaned dishes that she did the night before. She did one final check around the kitchen and made sure everything was turned off, including the coffee maker, and then exited the house.

8:30 AM

ANNE was out the door. She locked the door behind her and grabbed the morning newspaper from the WELCOME mat. USR was about ten minutes away, but morning traffic always doubled the ride. It took about three minutes to get her used 2000 Honda Civic warmed up. The car had about 87, 000 miles on it, and was a pothole away from blowing its trans-mission. Other than that, like her mom's comb, it got the job done.

While the car was warming up, she picked out a CD for the road. Most of the music Anne listened to was sung by a dude with jet black hair combed over one side of his gaunt face, black eyeliner, bitter as hell, witchy voice—the genre of music was what the little headbangers called "screamo," which was apparently a subgenre of emo.

8:34 AM

THE traffic was starting to get congested near Wiltshire Avenue where Anne waited in the turn lane to Seventh Street. Most of the cars behind Anne changed lanes and skipped in front of the line, while Anne, as always, waited there patiently. She didn't hit the heavy traffic until she reached Seventh Street, which ran into College Street, which took her directly to USR. On the way, she saw the same traffic everyday, same people, same faces, same cars, each one headed to a company or an office or, like Anne, a cubicle. Most of the faces she saw carried the same expressions, long and tired.

8:53 AM

AFTER cutting in and around traffic and nearly getting sideswiped as she made a sharp right into the USR employee parking lot, Anne parked in her favorite spot underneath the maple tree, which had already started to change from green to a mixture of orange, red, and yellow. She did one last primp before exiting the car. Lastly, she reached into her purse, pulled out a medicine bottle, and downed her prescription drug Paxil with the rest of the coffee from the thermos. It took a few minutes for the Paxil to work its magic—usually by the time she entered the office. In the reflection of the driver's side window, Anne did yet another last minute adjustment, this time rearranging the gray scarf around her neck.

With only five minutes left (technically, the clock-in device gave an employee seven minutes of leeway, before and after the scheduled time), Anne rode the elevator to the fifth floor, USR, one of the many companies in America whose jobs were outsourced to India. Most of the employees had been laid off and left to suffer in the feeble economy and then, later, replaced by machines, the Siri-type fuckers; however, after President Shaw's reelection in 2012, the jobs were brought back to the humans of America (but this, of course, was after President Shaw failed to create *and* sustain new energy jobs, as he had campaigned during his reelection).

Anne stepped from the elevator and greeted the receptionist, Mary, on her way into the office.

At the clock-in device, she punched in her nine digit social security number two minutes before her scheduled time, 9:00, and then did her daily bump-in with her friend, Jamie Vasquez, who shared a double-wide cubicle with another employee, a couple of feet away from the break room. By the time she made eye contact with Jamie, the nerves leftover from the morning routine were washed away like a footprint in the sand after a high tide. Her friend, Jamie, was seven years older, thin body, healthy-looking face, short curly hair with orange highlights. Her fashion tastes were not too far off from Anne's—only Jamie wore more jewelry. Bracelets were her thing. Each day, she wore a different bracelet, maybe gold, silver, tiger's eye, or beaded, to match whatever outfit she was wearing that day.

"Hey there, stranger," Anne said as she stuck her head inside the cubicle.

Jamie turned away from the computer and noticed Anne standing over her shoulder.

"Hey, girl," Jamie said, her voice drawn out with excitement.

Anne asked, "Did you get that picture I sent you last night?"

"I was meaning to ask you, but I ended up passing out early," Jamie said. "Where did you get that dress? That was like some *Bazaar* type getup! Seriously!"

A hint of red painted over Anne's cheeks.

"Stop it," she said.

"I'm serious," Jamie said cheerfully. "Girl, if you sent that picture to every single man in Lansford, then you would have men throwing themselves at you. One by one, they would be dropping to their knees, asking for your hand in marriage."

Anne chortled.

"Serious," Jamie said. "So, where did you get that thing?"

"I bought it from Milanos last week," Anne said. "It's been so cold out. I haven't had a chance to wear it."

"What about Michael?"

"*What* about him?"

"Well, has he seen it yet?"

"Yeah," Anne said closer now, "but get this. He said I look like I'm going to a funeral."

"Get outta here!" Jamie blurted out. "No he didn't!"

"Can you believe that?"

"Well, that man has no sense of style," Jamie said, her voice trailing off. "I mean, you *would* think he would." She raised her eyebrows. "You know."

"Don't go there, Jamie."

"I'm just saying," Jamie returned. "I think you can do much better." She shrugged her shoulders. "For what it's worth, I thought you looked great."

"Thanks," Anne said, again, her cheeks turning red. "So, we still on for lunch?"

"I'm a little backed up right now," Jamie said. "But I'll let you know."

"Text me."

"You bet," Jamie said, smiling.

On the way to her cubicle, which was at the other end of the office, Anne said her friendly "good morning(s)" to the employees who acknowledged her, mainly women, one of them being Susanne Marshall Culpepper, or soon-to-be Susanne Marshall, a voluptuous woman who, like Anne, had struggled with a severe weight problem, only hers being from having two children. As for the men who worked at USR, there were a couple of them who acknowledged Anne and not just her ass. There was Lester, also known as "What-A-Mess-Less," who complained how much he hated his job and how, for years, he had been telling folks around the office, including Anne, that he was going to move to Montana and become a park ranger. Then, not too far off: Stephen Bagger, who preferred to go by Stevie, a name he picked up after his favorite pop singer, Stevie Wonder. The employees had a better name for Stephen: Mr. Monotone, named after his flat, turtle-speed voice, as well as the trite conversations he would try to jump-start in the break room. Like What-A-Mess-Less, Mr. Monotone was always giving his two cents about the job. And like most, if not *all* employees around at USR, they either talked about how much they hated the job or hid their heads behind their cubicles like a bunch of moles, except for Tom Swearinger, also known as the "King of Sales," or better yet, the "Office Prick," the douche bag who bragged about the many sales he made, which, he did. He had quite the silver tongue on the phone. See, Anne figured out after a year into the job, a term like *brown-nosing* didn't exactly mean a thing in the corporate world; and Tom, well, he took full advantage. Had the track record to prove it. He was the guy many employees, mainly men, loved to hate, not only because he was the King of Sales and held the most sales within the department, but also most of the employees, especially the women, couldn't resist his charm and handsome looks. Anne wasn't a fan. Tom was well aware of how much Anne despised him; and as a result, every time Tom bumped into Anne, Tom would be super-duper nice to her. For most employees, each selling style was different. Jamie was a go-getter who customers either enjoyed or despised: enjoyed, because she was extremely personable and easy to talk to; or despised, because she didn't take no for an answer, which, consequently, led to an earful from the customer and then a swift *click* on the other end. Stan, on the other hand, Anne's neighbor, was very passive and made most of his sales from older customers. Tom, however, was a master manipulator who would tell customers *exactly* what they wanted to hear and even lie to them to make a sale.

Anne passed Tom, who was wearing that same ole shit-eating grin on his face, as well as that same ole red tie around his neck.

If only murder was legal. . .

"Good morning, Annie," Tom said in an overly friendly manner.

"Morning," Anne said and kept walking.

Tom said to himself but loud enough for Anne to hear, "Looks like someone woke up on the wrong side of the bed."

Anne ignored Tom and mentally told herself to keep walking.

And that she did.

One foot in front of the next.

9:05 AM

"LET me guess," a delicate Southern voice said from Anne's right side. "Bad case of the Mondays, Anne?"

Stan, Anne's colleague in the neighboring cubicle, slowly rose from the chair as Anne settled into her cubicle.

Inside, she had various knickknacks around the desk: a Teddy bear holding a cup of pens and pencils, a giant smiley face button that said, "Have a nice day," a couple of Happy Meal toys all stationed in tactical positions, a black and white poster of Gene Kelly from the film, *Singin' in the Rain,* and a couple of clippings from the comic, *Dilbert,* tacked on the walls of her cubicle.

Stan, short and wide like a tree stump, who wore Buddy Holly glasses and a short-sleeve shirt with a blue tie everyday, waited for Anne to respond.

Instead, she jokingly rolled her eyes.

Stan said softly, "You know I'm just teasing you, Anne."

"I know you are, Stan," she said with a sigh. "How's it going?"

"Can't complain," he said with a smile on his round face.

"You're looking quite merry today, more so than your usual self."

Anne glanced around the office. She found herself looking toward the break room. Her eyes came across Jamie, who was standing from her cubicle and looking toward Anne's direction. They both shared a smile and then Jamie sank back into her cubicle.

"Well," Stan drawled, displaying the dimples on each side of his face, "I had a fantastic weekend!"

Anne pulled her eyes from Jamie.

"You did?"

Stan bobbed his head while Anne placed her coat on the hanger on the cubicle wall.

"Melissa and I spent Friday night and all day Saturday at Mayberry Valley and then came back Sunday morning," Stan said and leaned forward. "I tell you what. I am ex-*ha*-usted."

"You and Melissa, huh?" Anne said strangely as she placed the newspaper on the desk. "You've been seeing her for how long now?"

"About nineteen days."

"Wow," Anne said quietly. "Isn't it a little too soon to be going to Mayberry Valley after nine days?"

"Nine*teen* days, Anne," Stan corrected, emphasizing the teen in nineteen.

"Whatever."

"Well, we both like each other, both enjoy each other's company," he said. "I think, well, I don't want to rush into anything too fast because I know that only fools rush in," Stan placed his hand over his mouth and said behind his hand, "get it. . . "

Anne got the joke, but she didn't show an inkling of amusement on her face.

"And I'm no fool. . . anyway, I know it's way too soon but I think she could be. . . you know. . . "

"Let me guess, Stan," Anne said bluntly. "She let you fuck her. Right?"

"Potty mouth!"

"Am I right?"

"Well. . . "

Stan chuckled.

"Don't be shy, Stan."

"I'm not," he said in a high pitch voice. "I just think it's a private matter. I am a gentleman. And gentleman don't kiss and tell."

Stan tried to conceal his smile, but the smile eventually broke through his face.

"I hate to say it, Stan, but nothing's private anymore."

"Well. . . "

"I'm happy for you, Stan," Anne said as she carefully cleared her throat. "I wish I had a guy like you, Stan, a guy who treats me nice, takes me to romantic places. Forget about jewelry and all that. I just want some attention."

"Who doesn't?"

"What can I say?" Anne said as she leaned over the cubicle. "I envy you, Stan."

."So, how's it going with you and Michael?"

"Going straight to hell," Anne said flatly. "That's where it's going."

"Anne, you know what?" Stan said. "I say the heck with him." Then, he noticed the supervisor, Dave Fuller, six foot five inches tall, body shaped like Big Bird, roaming the aisles with a clipboard in his hand. Stan hunkered back into his cubicle and whispered to Anne, "Looks like the wolf is out on the hunt." Anne drew her eyes across the office and carefully eyed Dave, his slouched body moving as if it was attached to an assembly line.

Before Stan slipped back into his cubicle, he said to Anne, "Have a good day. . . "

"Yeah," Anne said in a trance-like state and then sat down in her chair. "You too."

After a minute went by, she pulled out her phone and texted, "So how was Melissa?"

Stan received a text message from Anne.

> SweetStan: What u mean?

Anne received the reply from SweetStan (Stan) and then texted back.

> DirtyTill30: Was she good in bed?
> DirtyTill30: Doggystyle? Missionary? Reverse Cowgirl?
> SweetStan: LOL! Ur crazy girl!!!
> DirtyTill30: I want details
> SweetStan: Sorry, Anne. Ur gonna hav 2 use that imagina-tion of urs
> DirtyTill30: You're no fun :(
> SweetStan: Maybe at lunch.
> DirtyTill30: ???
> SweetStan: MAYBE I'LL TELL U AT LUNCH!!
> DirtyTill30: Hahahahahahaaa, TELL ME NOW!
> SweetStan: Nuff CAPS
> DirtyTill30: LOL
> SweetStan: Wolf Alert!

Anne removed the phone from her face, stood up from the chair, and cautiously poked her head out of the cubicle like a jittery mouse poking its head from a hole.

Her supervisor, Dave, was making his way down their aisle—closer now.

Anne quickly sank back into her cubicle and texted Stan.

> DirtyTill30: Fine. We'll talk later. . .
> SweetStan: K

As Dave slowly made his way past Anne's cubicle, she placed the phone back in her purse. She checked the calendar, week of October 20th through 26th, and checked out what the week had in store for her. There wasn't much of anything going on: Monday, cardio @ 5:30, Necklace!!! *The End Zone* @ 9; Tues-day, Pick Up Dry Cleaners @ 1:00, workout, Doctor's Apt. @ 3:45, *Blood Diaries* @ 10; Wednesday, morning cardio, Dinner w/ M @ 7:30; Thursday, Talk w/ HR, Mandatory Meeting @ 4:00, WORKOUT (arms and shoulders) Pizza Night! *Wicked @ 10*; Friday, cardio; Saturday, groceries, make list, new vacuum; Sunday, Lazy Day.

For about a minute, she piddled around the cubicle, doing minimal tasks such as reading her zodiac sign, Aquarius, from the daily horoscopes, as she did every morning (today, her sign read, BE ON THE LOOKOUT! YOU HAVE A SECRET ADMIRER, which was immediately followed with her mumbling the words *yeah right*), or organizing the pens and pencils or tidying up the little knickknacks around the desk before she logged into her computer. To the right of ID, she typed her name, ANNE ROTH. Underneath ID, and to the right of the word *Password*, she typed ALCATRAZ123, therefore bringing forth the one unavoidable question later in the day during her moment of reflection, that special place in time, three o'clock.

Next, she pulled up the list of customers (most, of course, being customers who discontinued their services).

After Anne was all situated, she made the calls. The first call was to a recent divorcee named Ms. Susan Corset, a mother of two, USR customer for about two years until she had to cut expenses, including cable, landline, and magazine subscriptions to name a few, in order to provide for her two children. So, she decided to cut USR services and go back to listening to her old CD's, as well as the local AM/FM radio.

When Ms. Corset answered the phone call, Anne started with "Hello, may I speak to Ms. Corset?"

"Speaking. . . "

"My name is Anne Roth, and I'm calling from Universal Satellite Radio," Anne said. "How are you doing today, Ms. Corset?"

"Fine," Ms. Corset said sharply.

"Wonderful," Anne said, almost robotically. "I promise this will only take a second. The reason I'm calling you today is that we've noticed that you canceled your subscription to Universal Satellite Radio and, at this time, we would like to offer you a special six month package for only twenty-four dollars and ninety-five cents—"

As the customers always did, they usually interrupted Anne whenever money was brought into the conversation.

Anne listened closely.

She heard Ms. Corset breathing heavily on the phone.

Then, a sudden burst. . .

"What. . . what do you want from me?" Ms. Corset shouted.

Of all the responses Anne had heard in her two years of working at USR, she had never heard that question before. Usually, she got the typical "Not interested" or "Call back another time" or "I can't talk right now," but a response like "What do you want from me" sounded like, to Anne, that this woman, Ms. Corset, was at the end of her rope and even when she tried to escape the world, the world wouldn't let her.

"We, at USR," Anne stuttered, "have enjoyed your business, Ms. Corset, and would like to have you back as a customer—"

"Why?" Ms. Corset cried.

Anne could hear the tension in Ms. Corset's voice.

"Well," she said carefully, "we're running a special deal that you can't get anywhere else. Now, we have over a thousand channels to choose from, including *Newstalk*—"

"You know," Ms. Corset interrupted, "this is the fourth time this month you people have called me. I tell you time and time again that I'm not interested and yet you keep calling me. Do you people enjoy doing this for a living, harassing people because that's what you're doing? This is harassment and if you call back here one more time, I swear to God I will call the police. . . ."

"I apologize, Ms. Corset."

"You apologize?" Ms. Corset chuckled. "Now, you apologize? What is your name?"

Anne hesitated.

"Anne," she said, her voice slightly trembling.

"Anne," Ms. Corset said mockingly. "Anne what?"

"Anne Roth."

Ms. Corset laughed again, but this time at the name, Anne Roth, and said under her voice, "Typical." Her voice suddenly spiked like an amplifier. "How about this Anne *Roth*?" Ms. Corset quickly followed, exaggerating the *Roth* in Anne Roth. "I'm not buying whatever you're selling, Anne *Roth*. So please, why don't you do me, as well as everybody else a favor, and just leave us alone? Is that too hard to ask? Huh? Anne Roth?"

A sharp *click* on her headset!

Anne disconnected.

She sighed and removed the headset from her head.

"That didn't go so well," she said to herself.

It wasn't unusual for Anne to get about halfway through the pitch before she was interrupted. Like Ms. Corset, a lot of the customers were fed up with the numerous calls; however, most of them didn't go as far as Ms. Corset and attack the actual telemarketer. Anne didn't mind the bluntness; in fact, she enjoyed talking to people throughout the day despite how rude or curt they were to her. The one thing that Anne hated the most about the job was the hangups. Sometimes she would be almost done with the pitch when she would hear the *click* on the other end. Other times she went through the whole pitch and then there was nothing but silence on the other end as if she was talking to a ghost. From the dozen calls she had made so far, most of them being hang-ups, she made one potential sell, which was to an older man named Daryl Finney, a retiree who talked to Anne for about twenty minutes on the phone. Half of the conversation wasn't even about USR or whatever Anne was selling. Mr. Finney did most of the talking; however, whenever Anne spoke, Mr. Finney would follow up with more questions, more stories. He mainly talked about his three kids and then his kids' kids, his grandchildren—seven of them, Anne only remembered two of their names, Bradley and then Tanya. Bradley was into playing games on the eTab, whereas Tanya was more into playing dress up with her sisters. Anne didn't mind talking about family affairs with Mr. Finney. She enjoyed getting away from the standard pitch even if it was only for a short while. This was the only highlight of her day—that moment where she felt as if she belonged.

9:48 AM

AFTER eight calls into her day, Anne decided it was time for her to stretch her legs and walk a lap around the office.

The mission at USR was to provide a safe and stress-free working environment, a so-called "*greener*" company, which was its way of saying that they wanted to promote a healthy way of life for USR employees, despite the frequent celebratory gatherings around the office, and recommend that each employee take a break every thirty to forty-five minutes to stretch his or her legs. USR provided a couple of designated rooms, one called the Workout Room, which had several treadmills and elliptical machines, always there and ready for the employees' disposal, and another room with soundproof walls called the Vent Room, which received most of the attention throughout the day. There was even a weight chart in the break room for those who were counting calories on a daily basis. The employees who participated in the weekly Wednesday Weigh-In received a free five-dollar gift card to Smoothie Paradise. And the winner who ended up losing the most weight at the end of the ninety-day contest received a one-year membership to the popular water park, Slide-Or-Dive. Even though USR promoted these greener options for its employees, the company practically celebrated everything from birthdays to whatever was considered a holiday, which was pretty much anything. There was even a day called Boss Appreciation Day. So, what better comfort food to enjoy on celebrations than cake? About two months ago, the people upstairs decided to add healthier options such as gluten-free snacks and low fat cookies, which, to Anne, tasted like tree bark; but, if Anne had the guts, she would tell the people upstairs where they could stick their gluten-free snacks and low fat cookies.

10:37 AM

ANNE was wrapping up a call with a recent graduate, Kyle, who was extremely interested in USR but couldn't afford the service due to loans and a tight budget, when a stabbing pain in her eyes forced her to disconnect with the potential customer. She removed her headset and hurried to the ladies restroom where she splashed her face with cold water. While doing so, one of her contacts came out. She quickly shut off the water and plugged the sink before the contact fell into the drain. She ran her finger across the sink until she came across a round object. She picked up the object and held it close to her good eye, the right one. She squinted her left eye and focused with the right. The contact wasn't flimsy as before; instead, it was hard like glass. Anne placed the contact between her fingers, index and thumb, which caused the contact to break in half. The sudden break pricked her thumb, drawing a drop of blood. Nearly blinded, she went to the break room and grabbed a Band-Aid from the first aid kit and placed it over her thumb. She managed to find her way back to her cubicle with one eye. Then, she used a pair of backup glasses that she kept in her desk drawer. She removed the other contact in her eye and used the glasses for the rest of the day.

12:03 PM

AFTER Anne finished her final call before lunch, her phone suddenly chirped inside her purse!

She pulled out her phone and read the text, "In the mood for Indian food?" She pressed her thumb against the fingerprint icon on the screen and then opened the TextYou app from the menu.

> DirtyTill30: You trying to get me in trouble??? You know I'm watching my weight.
> Jamie: How about El Rio's? They have salads. Yum!
> DirtyTill30: Too filling. I can go for sum Freak right about now. Met Café?

DirtyTill30: Greek*
Jamie: Sure. That sounds great. You ready now?!?
DirtyTill30: Give me a sec
Jamie: Okay ☺

Anne removed the headset and stretched, sneaking a peak inside the neighboring cubicle.

Stan's head was held down into his smartphone.

"Intrude much," he said, not making any eye contact with Anne.

"Whatever," Anne said. "Be like that then."

"I'm texting Melissa."

"Isn't that sweet," she said. "Do you guys ever, you know, like talk on the phone."

"Talk on the phone?" Stan replied with a grin. "Who does that anymore?" He finished writing his last text and did so with a smile on his face. "So, did you hear the news?"

"I think someone's in love."

"Don't go there," Stan waved his hand and placed the phone into his pocket. He noticed Anne's glasses. "Whoa! Nice look, poser."

"Very funny."

"So, did you hear?"

"Hear what?"

"They're bringing in a cake this afternoon," he said cheerfully. "It's going to be chocolate. Your favorite. . . "

"Whose birthday?"

"Bob Fleming from HR."

"Jesus," Anne said abruptly. "That's like the fourth one this month."

"I think the Almighty is testing your patience."

"Tell me about it."

Stan asked, "So, what are you doing for lunch?"

"Jamie and I are gonna grab something across the street." Anne nodded at Stan. "Wanna join? Oh!"

Anne said suddenly. "That's right!" Her eyes crossed a flattened brown bag on Stan's desk and then a half-eaten wedge from a peanut butter and jelly sandwich next to it. "I forgot your PB&J."

"Man's greatest creation."

"Well," Anne said and gathered her things, including her scarf, coat, and purse, "have a nice lunch."

"You too," Stan said and took a bite from the wedge.

12:29 PM

BOTH Anne and Jamie managed to find a booth in the back of the restaurant, Met Café, away from the line, which was now wrapped around the building. They snacked from a basket of pita bread and hummus and, after Jamie ordered the chicken gyro, they talked about the rules of being a vegetarian (Jamie, who called herself a vegetarian, not a strict vegan, which Anne retorted by calling Jamie a "hypocrite," argued that chicken wasn't really considered meat in her native country) for about five minutes until their meals finally arrived. The waitress arrived at the table with a smile on one side of her face. She placed both the Greek salad and then the chicken gyro with a side of lemon fries on the table. They thanked the waitress, who, in return, told the two to enjoy their meals.

"Keep *that* away from me," Anne said, pointing at the chicken gyro.

Jamie spread the tzatziki sauce over the gyro and then held out the gyro in front of Anne.

"Just one bite. . . " she said, ". . . it's borderline orgasmic."

"I wouldn't go that far now, Jamie," Anne said, her voice drawn out. "It looks like a sandwich made from road kill."

"Trust me," Jamie said closely. "This is *much* much better than road kill."

"I'm telling you, Jamie," Anne replied and held out her hand. "I'm on maintenance right now. I can't have over twelve hundred calories a day. You know this."

"Oh come on," Jamie persisted. "What's one bite going to do?"

"I'm telling you," Anne said louder. "I can't!"

"Fine," Jamie trailed off as she unfolded the aluminum foil and stuffed the end of the gyro into her mouth. Her eyes rolled back into her head.

"You okay over there?"

Jamie quickly followed with one side of her mouth full, "You're missing out."

"No, thank you." Anne poured the vinaigrette dressing over her salad. "I'm just fine here with my salad. Besides, I don't see how you eat that kind of stuff and never put on a single pound. Not unless you throw it all back up."

"Ugh!" Jamie slapped the side of the table. "Don't talk like that when I'm eating."

Anne laughed.

"Sorry."

"You know I have a high metabolism."

"Well, you're lucky," Anne said. "Some people would kill to have your metabolism. *Seriously*."

Jamie finished the rest of the bite.

"So, how much longer do you have on 'maintenance'?"

"Well, it's been five weeks now," she answered. "So, one more week and then I'm all good to go."

"You've come so far, Anne," Jamie said sympathetically as she tilted her head to the side. "I mean it. You really have. Me, I couldn't do what you do everyday, stick a needle into your stomach. That's pretty intense."

"It's only for the first forty-two days."

"Still," Jamie chuckled, "I couldn't even do that for a day."

"Wuss," Anne said and took a bite of salad.

"Call me what you like, Anne, but I have a low tolerance for pain," Jamie said. "I know you're doing it for all the right reasons, but I just don't understand why some people enjoy the pain."

"It's not *so* bad."

"Yeah, but it hurts. Right?"

Anne shrugged.

"A little," she said. "But you get used to it."

"I don't see how."

"It's not like I get off from it," Anne said, "like some people do with BDSM."

"BDSM?"

"Like that bondage stuff."

"Yikes!" Jamie exclaimed as she checked a message from her phone. "How can someone get off on pain?"

"You'd be surprised nowadays."

"To me, it makes no sense whatsoever," Jamie said with her head down. "Weird times."

Anne said quietly, "Tell me about it."

"It's starting to feel like the Twilight Zone, and our whole fabric of society is rewiring itself."

Anne couldn't help but look at what Jamie was doing.

"Jamie?"

"Yeah," Jamie continued with her head down.

"Are you talking to me or the phone?"

Jamie pulled her eyes from the phone.

"I'm talking to you," she said, chuckling. "Duh!"

"Who are you texting?"

"Geez," she said. "I'm just checking my email, Anne."

"You know I don't like that kind of stuff when I'm eating."

"Why?"

"For one, it's rude."

"Okay, Ms. Moral Authority," Jamie said. "So, talking about puking is acceptable?"

"You know what I mean."

"*Anyway*," a sigh, "I got an email from Rebecca. She's interested in buying that one piece."

"Which one?"

"The one I showed you the other day," Jamie said, "the one with the man and the child."

"That's a nice piece," Anne said. "Congrats."

"Thanks," she replied. "It's gonna be hard giving it away, though. It's become like my own baby."

"I don't see how you don't get rabies from working with all that rusted metal," Anne said. "I would be afraid to even touch it."

"Hence why I wear gloves," Jamie replied, as she took another bite of the gyro. "I did get cut once, though. Had to get a tetanus shot. Definitely do not want to go through that whole ordeal ever again. What a nightmare!"

"You know," Anne said and sipped from the glass of water, "I heard that's how Edgar Allan Poe went out."

"From rabies?"

"Yeah," Anne said. "They found him in an alleyway."

"I doubt he was making sculptures with old junkyard parts, but I guess it comes with the territory,"

Jamie said. "Me, I love it. I couldn't see myself doing anything else."

"I need to find a hobby like that," Anne said quietly, "something that I'm passionate about. Lately, all I've been good at is drinking an entire bottle of wine by myself. Perhaps I could be one of those guinea pigs who sits on the couch every night with a bottle of wine and watches television for hours at a time until I pass out."

"I didn't know they had such a thing." Jamie's eyes lit up. "We should go to a movie! We haven't done that in a long time!"

"There's nothing really out," Anne said. "Same ole crap."

"So, what about you and Michael?"

"What about us?"

Anne took another bite of her salad and tried to ignore the question.

Jamie sighed.

"It's these shots you're taking? Isn't it?"

"No," Anne said. "That's not it."

"Then what, Anne?" Jamie leaned forward. "I like hanging out with you, even if it's just going out to lunch. We're friends. Right?"

Anne didn't respond.

"I know sometimes you want to be alone. I understand that."

Anne said, "I'm *not* alone."

Jamie smacked her gums.

"Please, Anne," she said. "Every time I go on MyCircle, you're online. It's okay. There's nothing wrong with that."

"Whoever said there was?"

"I'm just saying, Anne."

"What are you saying?"

"I'm saying there's nothing wrong with going on MyCircle," Jamie said and pointed at herself. "I do it too."

"Then, why are you judging me?"

"No," Jamie said, reaching over the table. "I'm not judging you. If there's anybody who should be judged, it's me. Trust me." Jamie pushed aside the plate. "What do you really want, Anne?"

"I don't know. . . "

"Of course, you do," Jamie said. "There's no shame in admitting it, Anne."

"I don't know," she said, her voice shaking. "I want a man who tells me I'm beautiful, not some narcissistic asshole who cares more about his job or the way he looks than his own. . . girlfriend. Is it wrong for me to want a man who will tell me those things?"

"Absolutely not," Jamie said as she placed her hand over Anne's hand. "You are beautiful, Anne?"

Anne replied with her head down, "I can't even get a nibble on FindYourRomeo to save my life."

"Why do you still mess around with that site?"

"I don't know." Anne shrugged. "Probably because I can't find a decent man during the day. For example, like in the grocery store or at the gym, I hardly get guys to approach me. And I see so many hot guys in the store. Do they approach me? No. They're too busy staring at their phones. But at bars, though, it's different. It's like I can't brush them off quick enough."

"It's because they've already had one or two drinks," Jamie said. "That's why. You know, liquid courage. By then, all they want is sex. Nothing serious. It's like after these men drink they got nothing to lose. Most men don't have the *cojones* to approach women anymore. Sober, I mean."

"I know I'm not going to find a decent man at a bar."

"Then, why even try?" Jamie said bitterly. "Why exactly are you still with Michael? Shouldn't you find someone—I don't know—more like you?"

"What is that supposed to mean?"

"I'm not saying that because he's black or whatever, but shouldn't you be with someone who you actually enjoy being with or someone who you at least share a common interest with?"

"He takes me shopping and stuff."

"Anne, really," Jamie said sharply. "You two just don't seem like a really good fit. I mean, if you're always on the lookout for another man—which I know you are—then that tells me right there your heart is not into Michael. I mean, I would end it the first chance I get and be with someone who shares the same interests. You would save a lot of time, not only for yourself, but for him as well. Then, you could focus on finding a better match for yourself."

"You're right," Anne said quietly.

"What's preventing you from being like," her voice went from her normal voice to a rough impersonation of Anne's, "Hey, I'm sorry, dude. But this thing here, I'm sorry but it's not working out between us. I think it's best for the both of us if we go our separates w-a-y-s."

"You mean ways?"

Jamie rolled her eyes.

"You know what I mean." She leaned in closer to Anne. "If I were you, Anne, I wouldn't get so caught-up with the whole online dating thing." She sat back in her seat. "I tried it once. Talk about a *real* nightmare! It was almost like playing Russian roulette. There are some real creepos that go on there."

"But still," Anne said, "that wasn't FindYourRo-meo."

"The way I look at, Anne," Jamie said. "It's all the same, really."

"I've seen some really cute guys on there."

"Yeah," Jamie said shortly. "And most of those pictures either, one, were stolen, or two, were taken like ten years ago when they had a head full of hair and not a sandbag for a belly." She dropped her head in thought. Her eyes flicked up at Anne. "The first time we met. . . do you remember?"

"Yeah," she said. "You were having trouble with the vending machine."

"And you came over like it was no big deal and gave the vending machine a smack to the side," she said. "My Dark Bar dropped to the bottom like it was nothing."

"Thanks," Anne said despairingly.

"I'm teasing," Jamie returned. "After that, we instantly became friends. And look at you now. You're literally half the woman you were when I met you."

"You know I always wasn't like that."

"Hey," Jamie said, "it's hard to believe but I used to be pretty big myself."

"You?" Anne returned. "Get out of here!"

"People made fun of me for my weight," Jamie followed. "Then, when high school came along. . . I don't know. . . " Jamie shrugged, ". . . I stretched out like a piece of gum. Now, look at me. I got the body of a high school boy."

Anne laughed a little.

Jamie said, "You were, and still are, that same gorgeous woman not just on the outside, Anne, but on the inside. However—"

"—I know you're trying to make me feel better," Anne interrupted, "but I've been feeling this way for some time now."

"It's about Michael," Jamie said. "Isn't it?" A sudden pause and then a faint gasp spilled from her lips. "Think about this, Anne. He didn't even talk to you when you were, you know, 'bigger.' The guy even forgot about your birthday. Come on!"

"His brother was in town that day."

Jamie rolled her eyes.

"The thing is, Anne," she said abruptly, "you're not that woman anymore and yet, at times, you still carry around her same self esteem. It's just sometimes you sell yourself too short. That's all."

"I know," Anne said and pushed around the romaine lettuce in her salad. "Maybe I still think he can change." Anne naturally shrugged her shoulders. "I mean, I did. So, why can't he?"

"Anne," Jamie paused once more in thought, "I just think now you should stop caring about what other people think about you and just accept you for who you are. When you get to that point, then that skin you're in, Anne, it will be like a force field against all the haters out there."

"Maybe you're right."

Jamie said, "This is just my opinion. I think you deserve so much better. All Michael cares about is Michael."

"Yeah," Anne said. "I know. It's just. . . " Anne paused, ". . . I feel like my clock is ticking right now, and if I don't find someone soon, then there might be a chance I will never have a family."

"I thought you didn't want to have children, Ms. *DirtyTill30*."

Anne shook her head.

"I don't," Anne hesitated, "I mean, maybe I do one day. I don't know."

"With Michael?"

"I don't know," Anne said. "He's already told me that he doesn't want kids."

"But Anne," Jamie said, "you got at least six years until you run into all sorts of problems."

"I can't imagine myself being thirty years old and single. I don't see how you do it."

"I enjoy my independence," Jamie said and sipped from her drink. "I will never get back those three years I spent with Trevor. He really screwed me up in the head when he came back from Iraq. He was a liar, manipulator, had no feelings at all. He wasn't the man I fell in love with. Honestly, I don't know if I'll ever be the same, the way he treated me, all the mind games, it was like living with Dr. Jekyll and Mr. Hyde. After Trevor, I will never be able to trust anybody ever again."

Anne said, "Least you once had somebody. Me, I've had nobody. I've been alone my entire life. . . "

"Have you ever thought that maybe some people are just meant to be alone?" Jamie said quietly. "Or, maybe, they just choose to be alone."

They finished the rest of the their lunch, mostly in silence.

1:16 PM

ANNE was exiting the break room when Jamie suddenly said from behind, "Thanks for lunch."

She turned her shoulder and said, "Thank you."

"You're very welcome," Jamie said and found herself struggling whether or not she wanted to continue the conversation or depart with Anne. "Anyway," she said finally, "I'll see you around."

"Yeah," Anne said and smiled. "See ya." She nodded to her cubicle. "Now, it's back to the penitentiary."

Jamie chuckled.

"Say," she said. "We should catch a flick at my house sometime. We haven't done that in a while. Maybe one day later in the week."

"Yeah," Anne replied. "I would like that."

"Okay," Jamie said. "I'll talk to you later."

Anne said, "Later."

She walked back to her cubicle where Stan was on the phone, talking to a potential customer. He noticed Anne in the corner of his eye. He gave her a quick nod as she entered her cubicle. She placed her things around the cubicle and got back to work. She made more calls from the list of customers. She experienced more rejections, more hang-ups, and more irritated responses. The customers—Anne knew from having worked here for several years—were less bold in the afternoon for a couple of reasons: one, they were too busy to talk or in the middle of doing something; and two, they were—for most part—well beyond the early morning blues.

1:42 PM

ANNE excused herself from the cubicle and went to the ladies restroom where she relieved herself.

While washing her hands in the sink, she received a text from Michael.

> Michael: Hey you
> DirtyTill30: Hey! How's it going?
> Michael: Good. Just taking break, thinking about you
> DirtyTill30: That's sweet ;)
> Michael: Gtg. Talk to you later
> DirtyTill30: Sure

DirtyTill30: I wish this day was over already. . .

No response.

2:13 PM

FOR the longest time, Anne got used to staring at that weight chart every afternoon. Then, the weight came off. And then, she stopped staring. However, every once and a while, she would find herself looking in the vicinity of the weight chart. The chart, nonetheless, was a simple reminder of how far she had come.

2:59 PM

The minute passed before she could even prepare herself for the feeling, or better yet, the lack of feeling to come. Then, once Anne removed the headset from her head, she pulled her eyes from the screen and found herself staring at the clock across the office, which brought her to here everyday, to three o'clock, a specific place in time where time didn't exist at all. The caffeine, which propelled her through the job as if both her mind and body ran on autopilot, was tapered down to a dull tingle. The job, which had occupied most, if not all of her time, was three-fourths finished. Then, that strange feeling came over her, the emptiness, heavier now. Her limbs were first to go dead and then the joints, now as stiff as a pecker in the morning, and then, finally, her eyes, now as heavy as Droopy. For most around the office, it was an easy fix: a trip to the bathroom (James from two cubicles down carried a *Playboy* disguised underneath the Living Section of the *Lansford Tribune* to the men's restroom everyday where he would rub one off until his knuckles turned white. And if he didn't have a *Playboy* handy that day—James had a tendency to pass around the mags like trading cards around the office and usually, if he got them back in one piece, the pages were all stuck together—he resorted to a fail-safe: his smartphone, which had over a dozen porno-graphic videos, mostly POVs), a mental vacation (one time Anne caught Dave, her supervisor, *the wolf*, flip-ping through photos of an exotic paradise on his tab-let), or a visit to the vending machine (Deborah Bor-ough, or "Debby," as most called her, another tele-marketer like Anne, grabbed a bag of fried pork skins everyday to fill the void inside her stomach). But Anne knew all too well that these people weren't just searching for a quick release from reality, an "instant gratification," or even filling their stomachs with food. They were trying to fill a void inside them, literally, not that hunger. Throughout the entire workday, Anne felt like a puppet being strung around through the calls, through the office, bodies like holograms passing her by; but when Anne found herself at the grip of three o'clock, the strings were gone. She stopped what she was doing, took a look around the office, and realized how miserable her life was. At three o'clock, Anne became an observer, the wander-ing eyes of the office, gathering various habits, man-nerisms, ticks, and escapes, analyzing them in her own thoughts. She was good at reading other people, their mannerisms and habits. The only thing she wasn't good at was reading her own self. Even when she looked in the mirror, she didn't know who was looking back at her.

Then, once three o'clock passed, and that same feeling, or lack of, was left lingering around, Anne searched, like many, for a release from the daily grind. She found that release here on MyCircle, a website, which, like many other social networking websites such as FriendCloud or eContacts, allowed friends to follow or share or post all sorts of info about themselves, photographs—mostly selfies—comments (trolls not allowed after the recent Anti-Bullying Act, which was passed last February), personal feelings, thoughts, or inspirational quotes from their favorite authors, philosophers, musicians (she currently had eighty-nine followers in her circle, seven of them Anne had known from the workplace, including Jamie, whereas the other eighty-two followers she had never met or seen in person before), and here, on FindYourRomeo, a dating website for single women searching for a man, or Romeo. Like other social networking websites, FindYourRomeo used "nibbles," which was the same thing as "follows" or "winks," only nibbles left it up to the person who was being nibbled at to nibble back, which, if he/she did, the nibblee was interested in getting to know the nibbler, which, inevitably, led to a date. As for Michael, he was unaware of Anne's FindYourRomeo account, and Anne planned on keeping it that way. If Michael ever found out about her account (which most likely he wouldn't for *two* reasons: one, he wasn't in the market for a single man; and two, he wasn't the type who stalked his girlfriend on the Internet or kept tabs on what she was posting or writing), Anne always had the "it's an old-account" excuse.

3:34 PM

THE office was chattering in clicks, sharp and dainty, and ranging in pitch like a boundless swarm of locusts in a fertile pasture, the swarm migrating from cubicle to machine, machine to cubicle, hundreds and thousands of human fingertips tapping along the hollow, block-shaped keys as each and every letter formed into a word, the words formed into a sentence, hundreds of voices strong, eyes staring drunkenly into the hazy electronic white landscape of computer screens glowing faintly from the viscera of every cubicle. The pale light shined on the dead faces of dazed telemarketers, hypnotized and paralyzed, from staring blindly into the screens all day. Their glassy eyes were bloated and fatigued. Ten fingers stronger and faster and harder out of the thousands tucked behind those concealed cubicles, Anne finished her second sale of the day, Darren Blunt, a retiree who canceled his USR services three years ago, and now, after Anne's long pitch, decided to rekindle his business with USR. The rough and callused tips of Anne's fingers were like diminutive doorways, and every single time in a variable rhythm or beat, she pressed them against the letters on the keyboard, and just like that, a sale was born.

"Piece of cake," she said with relief.

The harsh ambience around the office dimmed a little, and then Anne heard the sound of a massive exodus moving closer to the break room. She poked her head from the cubicle, only to find the staff gathering around the break room.

Stan rose from his cubicle and glanced at Anne.

"You know I can't, Stan," Anne said depressingly as she filled in the rest of Mr. Blunt's information. "Just the smell of it would send me over the edge."

"I'll make sure to bring you back a piece," Stan said and winked at Anne.

"You better not."

Stan grinned.

"I'm joking."

"You better be."

Stan pushed his chair back into the desk and joined the other employees in the break room.

While Anne sat in her cubicle, she overheard her colleagues singing the song, "Happy Birthday," to Bob Fleming, a father of two, who, after the applause, blew out all thirty-nine candles on the birthday cake.

There was another applause, Anne heard.

As the applause faded out, Anne's cheeks suddenly turned fiery red. Sweat beads formed over her fore-head and other regions of her body. To the right of the computer was a small portable fan. She switched it on and then reached around her desk and pulled out a photograph from the bottom drawer. The pho-tograph was taken three years ago at Anne's college graduation. Harold and Molly were standing on each side of her. The woman who was dressed in the pur-ple graduation gown and standing between Harold and Molly didn't look a thing like Anne; in fact, the woman was nothing more than a stranger to Anne. From a distance, Anne could hear the vulgar names being yelled out from a crowd of jocks and cheerlead-ers as if she was standing outside a cave and the fellow students were screaming at her from inside the dark hollows. Nicknames like "Cow," followed by *moos* or "Here Comes The Walrus, " followed by *goo goo goo joob* or "Miss Piggy," followed by *snorts* and high pitch voices—all punch lines: "Where's your boyfriend Kermit?" or even worse, that one name, "Fat Ass," all could be heard inside the recesses of her mind, and then that smile, *his* smile, the creature's smile, as sharp and pointy as a trowel, a hideous thing that always went unforgotten, always bending and stretching across the murkiest corners of her mind, revealed itself inside the dark hollow. She remembered hearing those two words, *Fat Ass*, all throughout the tail end of high school, mainly her junior and senior year, and then running to the bathroom where she hid inside a stall and cried for hours at a time. Those six or seven years, even the first year at USR, were extremely rough for Anne; and if she didn't do anything about it and shed the weight, then the insults would've eventually gotten the best of her. But they didn't. Anne decided enough was enough! It was time for a change. The tipping point was on the day the elevator broke and she had to climb five flights of stairs. When she reached her floor, the fifth floor, she could hardly catch her breath. To top it all off: witnessing a pink turd in the women's restroom after Jane Fisher's birthday. The thing was floating there and gaping at Anne as if it had eyes and mouth, that mouth saying, "Flush me! You're pathetic!" After that day, Anne stopped flocking to the frequent office gatherings like the ones Stan went to, placed her name on the weight chart, and played along. The goal for the first week was to lose five pounds, which, to Anne, didn't seem like much. She first started by running a mile a day, but as much as she would burn off during the day, she would equally gain back at night. So, she stopped eating at night. "Portion control" was what the trainer told Anne. However, after three weeks of eating healthy, three square meals a day, yummy salads, no bread, lean meats, fruits, and vegetables, Anne *still* wasn't seeing the results that she wanted. So, she tried the whole diet thing. There was the Atkins diet, the South Beach diet, the so-called "LA diet," which Anne would *not* recommend, Jenny Craig, and then Weightwatchers. Anne lost the weight, especially after the LA diet; but, a week later, Anne was hospitalized after an overdose of cocaine. Altogether, she lost about fifty pounds, which put her right at two hundred and twenty-four pounds. *Still*, it wasn't enough. Then, a friend told her about *HCG*, short for Human Chorionic Gonadotropin. The diet was fairly complex, legal, of course; however, when Anne went to her doctor with the idea of trying HCG, he told her that she would have to endure many shots. Otherwise, if she could withstand being poked everyday with a needle, then she would see great results and it would be well worth her time. "Guaranteed fifteen pounds," was what he told her. For the first forty-two days, Anne thought she would become a raging horny bitch (after all, the doctor was injecting hormones into her stomach), but, on the contrary, she didn't feel that way at all. Strangely, the shots made Anne feel slightly. . . euphoric. During those first forty-two days, she had to maintain her diet to five hundred calories a day, no more, no less, and then after the first forty-two days, she was on this thing called "maintenance," for six weeks, which, during that time, Anne had to maintain her diet to no more than twelve hundred calories a day. Then, for the first six months, including the first forty-two days of hormonal shots, Anne received two shots once a week—one shot was a fat buster and then the next was a B12 shot, which were both taken in the hip. After the first round of HCG, Anne lost about thirty-five pounds. However, Anne wanted to lose more. So, she did another round just like before, but, instead of six weeks of maintenance, it was eight weeks, and then, depending on the results, if she continued a third round, which more than likely she wouldn't, then it would be ten weeks of maintenance. After the second round, Anne lost a whopping forty-four pounds. She was greatly satisfied with the results and decided to lose another ten more, which would put her around the same weight when she was a sophomore in high school, around one hundred and thirty-five pounds, but, of course, she would have to do it on her own and not with HCG. During the diet, she thought men would approach her more, as she shed the weight.

For Anne, that wasn't the case at all. There were a few one-night stands while she was on the HCG diet: one of the guys, whom she met at a club, having a shy turtle head for a dick, and the other one, a banker, decent size, talked a lot of game and yet, while in bed with Anne, he was about as erratic as a buoy in a turbulent ocean—no rhythm whatsoever, and then another, a string bean, acted as if he was having seizures during sex, and like the guy before him, lacking any rhythm whatsoever. Of all the awkward hook-ups, there was only one guy who paid her the most attention, her boyfriend, Michael, who was introduced to her through Shane, a coworker from Advertising, during a night out for drinks. However, as with the diets and the weight loss, the attention Anne received from Michael wasn't enough.

4:38 PM

FOR the past ten minutes, Anne couldn't keep her eyes off the clock. She made a few more calls before the hour hand finally struck five and then called it a day. She made sure to log out from the computer.

In the cubicle next to her, Stan was packing up his things.

"Thank God this day is finally over," he groaned, moving the strap to his bag over his shoulder.

Anne returned, "That bad?"

"Melissa and I just got into a fight on the phone."

"What happened?"

"I asked her if she wanted to come over tonight and she got all mad."

"Really?" she said. "That doesn't make any sense."

"Well, she worked a double last night and she said she was dead tired."

"So, she got mad at you because you wanted to see her?"

"Here," Stan pulled up the conversation from the phone, "read for yourself."

He handed Anne the phone.

Anne read the text out loud, "Why don't u cum over? Sounds like u need a release." Anne handed the phone back to Stan. "Sorry, buddy," she said. "That sounds like a booty call."

"That's not what I meant," Stan said angrily.

"Then, what exactly did you mean by 'release'?" Anne asked. "Also the way you spelled come. You're kind of sending a mixed message."

"I meant like watch a movie or do something fun," Stan explained. "Release can mean anything—a release from the job, a release from reality. . . "

"I get it, Stan," Anne said. "Booty call or not. You wanted to spend time with her. Right?"

"Exactly."

"Well, maybe she wants some space."

"She could've just told me that instead of using what I said and turning it against me. . . "

"Just give her some time," Anne said. "And don't text her. *Call* her. Let her hear your voice. You can really tell how she feels by the sound of her voice."

"How do you know all of this?"

"I'm a woman, Stan," Anne said. "That's how."

Stan hung his head.

"Stan," Anne said, "if it's not meant to be then it's not meant to be. Things like this either bring couples closer or pull them apart."

"I can't think about this right now," Stan said and paced around the cubicle. "I have to get out of here."

"Are you okay?"

"Yeah," Stan stuttered, "I just. . . I need to go. . . "

Stan exited the cubicle.

"See you tomorrow," Anne said as Stan walked away, not even saying goodbye to Anne.

5:06 PM

ON the way out of the break room, Anne stopped at Jamie's cubicle. Inside, Jamie still had her headset on. Jamie, rolling her eyes, held her hand as if it was a gun, placed her index finger into her mouth, and pulled the hammer, which, in this case, was her thumb. Anne laughed to herself and then motioned to Jamie: her hand shaped like a phone and pressed against her ear, mouthing the words *call me*.

5:25 PM

"*GYM rat,*" were the words Anne used whenever any discussion of exercise was brought up in a conversation. She didn't mind calling herself a gym rat. Molly hated the name; in fact, she couldn't stand the name. After about a year into her daily regimen, gym rat became a nickname for Anne. The weightlifters, even runners, would refer to Anne as gym rat to fellow members—you know, that awfully cute shy girl who used to be as wide as a tractor trailer, comes in here all the freaking time and works out by herself, you know, gym rat.

About three times a week (four if she didn't have much going on Saturday afternoon), Anne drove to the neighborhood gym, Fitness City—a membership cost thirty-two dollars a month with a free guest once a week. Since Anne didn't live in an apartment complex or an organized community with a fitness center, she didn't mind forking out the money every month. In addition, the gym offered a whole range of equipment, as well as its own personal trainers, which was

all included in a monthly package. Most of the trainers, unfortunately for Anne, were homosexuals. Nice
guys. But totally gay. That went for most of the guys
who had a membership. However, she didn't mind.
She had a decent gaydar as well. It was the gladiator-
type guys spending hours staring in the mirror at the
muscles on their finely sculpted bodies while lifting
weights who really threw Anne for a loop. In the two
years Anne had been coming to Fitness City, she had
only been approached by three men, two of them
were gay, and the other one was her math teacher
from her senior year, Mr. Lawrence, and he was going through what he called a "midlife crisis."

Anne finished her protein shake in the parking lot
before heading into the gym. She said hello to a couple of frequent members, changed from her work attire in the locker room, and did a quick five-minute
stretch before hitting the dumbbells first and then the
machines. Anne's workout consisted of mostly arms,
shoulders, chest, and abs, basically her entire upper
body.

6:40 PM

As she always did after an intense workout, Anne
waited in the hallway, mostly surfing the Internet or
checking emails on her phone, until the showers were
completely empty before entering the locker room.

6:43 PM

THERE was only one girl a few years older than Anne
in the locker room, and she was applying deodorant
to each one of her armpits.

Anne waited until she left before undressing. She
brought three things with her to the shower: a bottle

of body wash, a bottle of shampoo, and the second towel from a stack of fresh towels. She switched the water to warm and washed herself underneath the last shower faucet tucked away in the very back of the locker room.

While washing the shampoo from her head, she suddenly heard the *squeak* of the locker room door!

Anne pulled her attention toward the opposite end of the locker room, toward the row of navy blue lockers, and peered through the clouds of steam.

Next, she heard yet another *squeak*, sharper now like two hinges grating against one another. Her heart began to race. She switched off the warm water, shielded one hand over her groin while she grabbed the towel from the hanger with the other hand, and then wrapped it around her torso. She saw, or at least she thought she saw two shadows dancing across the distant wall. Anne wasn't wearing her contact lenses (the only pair Anne had were discarded at USR) or her glasses, which were resting on top of a porcelain soap holder; and yet, she saw those two shadows on the wall as clearly as the letter E on a Snellen chart. Anne carefully honed in, all senses enhanced. A single drop of water cast from a faucet pulled her wide eyes toward the set of mirrors across the locker room. Her reflection was distorted, she noticed. The steam from the showers had fogged up all mirrors expect for one. Her body was much thinner, ghastly, the skin scaly. Anne reached around to the wall and blindly grabbed the glasses from the holder and placed them on her face. She heard the piercing sound of rattle. The right side of the frame cracked and then the mirror, in which her reflection stood, suddenly split in half, causing Anne to slip over the wet tile. She landed on the left side of her body, which made a loud *smack* against the tile. During the impact, her left wrist caught most of the fall. Even moving it an inch sent a stabbing pain up her entire arm.

6:57 PM

WITH her gym bag in one hand, her good one—the pair of broken glasses inside the pocket—Anne, who was dressed in her previous work clothes, squinted her way to Gregory, a trainer who was closing up a session. Gregory's eyes shot to Anne's wrist, which was held still and upright.

"Oh my god!" Gregory blurted out. "What happened, Anne?"

"I fell," Anne muttered.

"Come," Gregory said and walked Anne into his office.

7:04 PM

DESPITE having a body shaped like Hercules, pecks like two granite rocks, no neck, and forearms as big as Anne's thighs, Gregory had extremely gentle hands— no Lennie and the rabbits here. He finished wrapping Anne's wrist with his massive paws and did so tenderly as if he was picking petals from a flower. When it was all said and done, Anne was left with a sense of great bliss. It was just too bad Gregory was gay and that he had a partner whom he was madly in love with. Once, Anne thought about bringing Gregory over to her side of the team, but in Gregory's defense, as he explained to Anne, he was too emotionally involved with another person who turned out to be another man. Anne never brought up the matter while the trainer was wrapping her wrist. Instead, she smiled respectfully and thanked him for his assistance.

Before she left, Gregory specifically told Anne to ice the wrist with a bag of ice or anything cold she could find in the refrigerator such as a bag of frozen peas for about twenty minutes (and make sure she kept on the wrap while doing so), and then keep the wrist elevated for the rest of the night until the swelling went down.

7:28 PM

As Anne pulled out of Fitness City's parking lot, a car followed behind her.

She didn't think anything of it, of the car, at least not yet.

7:37 PM

TWO headlights suddenly appeared in the rear view mirror. The car was too dark to make out from the darkness of night and the lack of streetlights—a sedan, she guessed—although, she did recognize the headlights, the left headlight slightly dimmed as if it was about to burn out while the other one, the right one, was bright and blinding—same as before.

Anne made a right onto her street and then the mysterious car behind her took a right as well.

With her eyes squinted, Anne checked the rear view mirror once more.

The strange car was still there, although it was keeping its distance from Anne, which made her even more suspicious.

A block away from her house, the car eased back.

She finally arrived at her house.

As Anne pulled into the driveway, the strange car slowed down in front of her house, nearly stopped next to the mailbox, and then drove away into the night.

7:47 PM

SINCE Anne couldn't see much without her contacts and wasn't in the mood to pick up any food, she decided to throw a TV dinner into the microwave—one of those low fat cordon bleus with a side of green beans, which had been sitting in the freezer for about six months.

While the dinner was cooking, she dressed in more appropriate attire: a long white tee that stretched halfway down her thighs. She fished out an old pair of reading glasses from the nightstand. They were ugly things, very how-would-she-say, "old fashioned," but they did the trick. Anne went back into the kitchen where she watched the timer on the microwave count down until it finally reached zero.

For Anne, most nights during the weekday consisted of takeout food (there was a local Chinese place, family-owned, not too far from her house called The Golden Panda, which Anne frequented at least twice a week; and every time Anne called, they knew exactly who it was on the phone and what she wanted to eat—kung pao chicken, gleaming with MSG, and a side of edamames). Normally, she ate about half of the dinner and saved the rest for leftovers the next day. Again, it was all about portion control—especially at night. It was the sweets that really got Anne into trouble. As for her source of entertainment, if her favorite shows weren't playing that night (tonight was *The End Zone*, a popular sci-fi drama, at nine o'clock, along with a glass of red wine and one Percocet, and her wrist iced with a bag of frozen peas that she dug out from the bottom of the freezer and then elevated as Gregory had instructed her), then most nights consisted of Korean horror flicks, as well as martial art flicks (*Old Boy*—the original one that is—being one of her favorites), maybe an occasional romantic flick—usually a box of tissues handy, depending how depressing her day was—dates with Ambien, and if she was out of Ambien, she resorted to hard alcohol, mainly rum or vodka, the flavored kind, pineapple or mango, anything she could get her hands on around the house. Nonetheless, she didn't have much of a problem sleeping, more or less passing out. She got about seven solid hours of sleep every night, all, of course, done with some sort of aid, either it be pills or booze. Most nights were spent passed out on the couch; however, if she didn't drink or take a pill to help her sleep or exercise that day, then she usually spent the night tossing and turning in her bed or watching late night television until she finally dozed off. Tonight, Anne didn't have too much of a problem sleeping.

10:03 PM

THE phone *chirped* on the coffee table!

Startled, Anne bolted upright from the couch and checked the message on the phone.

It was a text message from Michael.

Michael: Where u at???

Anne rolled her eyes and let out a sigh.

"No booty call for you," she said to herself as she silenced the phone.

She fell back into that same comfortable position on the couch, rested both feet on the edge of the coffee table, and elevated her wrist on a stack of pillows.

At her final peak of comfort, she wrestled through the cushions and checked her phone once more.

"Fuck it," she groaned.

There was no message; however, she picked up the phone and got through four words, *do you want to*, before she turned off the phone and settled back onto the couch where she eventually fell asleep.

10:23 PM

TWO men, both as dark as night, quietly sat inside the black car parked outside Anne's house.

The man in the passenger seat, thin face, high cheekbones, eyes like marbles in the faint moonlight, glanced down at the flip phone, which suddenly lit up. He flipped open the phone and answered before the phone had a chance to vibrate, "Everything is going according to plan, sir."

A resonant voice on the other end: "*The package will arrive tomorrow.*"

"What do we do until then?" he asked.

"*Wait until further instruction.*"

"Yes, sir."

The other end of the phone went dead silent.

"Sir," the man in the passenger seat said, finally realizing the call had ended after he glanced down at the screen of the phone, which was flashing 00:00:12.

"He's not much of a talker," the man in the driver's seat said. "Is he?"

The other man didn't answer; instead, he pulled his eyes toward Anne's house and watched carefully for any sign of movement.

CHAPTER 2

THE last two images before Anne climbed from her dreams were of a strange pale girl screaming to the top of her lungs and then a round brilliant light bearing down on her. That girl was Anne, but Anne knew nothing of this until the brilliant light filled her eyes. She was ten years old, give or take. There she was, Anne saw behind her eyelids, the young girl standing on the side of a desolate road in the middle of the night with two bright headlights of a truck bearing down on her. The girl's hair was wet and stringy, her body malnourished, eyes strung out, and both of her stick-like arms were erected outward in front of her puny body; and the girl was screaming, violently. A loud screech of tires coming from behind the light pierced through her ears like an air horn with bronchitis; and there, at the moment, Anne found herself in the body of the young girl, the very same one she watched from a safe distance standing on the side of the road. Her arms were erected outward in similar fashion, voice cut with terror. Then, that brilliant light filled her eyes!

Anne opened her heavy eyes, only to find another woman, much older, quite burly, screaming as she waddled toward the camera. Anne flinched and came to and, after a couple of seconds, realized that the burly woman wasn't waddling toward Anne but to another woman who had apparently called her a "bitter, flabby-lipped skank" off screen. Anne grabbed the remote, which was wedged between two cushions, and turned down the volume from the late night reality TV show, *Reality Check*.

Still in a daze, Anne checked the time on the cable box.

The time read: 4:23.

She turned off the television, picked up the damp bag of peas, which was completely thawed out now, from the armrest of the couch, carried it back to the kitchen, and tossed it into the freezer.

Next, she stumbled her way into the bathroom where she did all the things that she normally would've done before she went to bed at around ten forty-five, except for flossing her teeth or weighing herself on the scale or washing the makeup from her face. All she really accomplished was brushing her teeth and even that was a task all by itself, as she did so in a drunken state.

After Anne brushed her teeth, she sipped from the faucet, rinsed her mouth, and squinted her way to the doorway where she made three attempts at cutting off the lights.

Once the lights were out and the bedroom was left cold and dark like the inside of a tomb, Anne staggered over to the window and peeked through the blinds. There, she saw a car parked outside, possibly the same one as before with the dim headlight. Inside, there were two men, she witnessed, both as shifty as wall shadows. She closed the blinds and slipped underneath the bed sheets and swaddled her body with a comforter. She didn't think too much about the car parked outside or the two men sitting inside— at least not long enough for it to occupy her mind. Anne was too tired to think, too tired to worry. So, she closed her eyes and went to sleep.

8:23 AM

THE sunrays cut across Anne's eyelids.

The distant dreams, which faded into the recesses of her mind, washed over with a glowing orange and then red color as she awakened.

The warmness of the sun was familiar, a feeling she would often experience on a Saturday morning, *not* a weekday.

Anne briskly opened her eyes and rose from the cool pillow with a sudden sense of urgency.

Startled, she turned her shoulder and checked the alarm clock on the nightstand.

Her face lit up.

"Shit!" she blurted out.

She grabbed a backup pair of glasses from the nightstand and put them on.

For about a minute, she wandered through the bedroom: first, to the closet where she grabbed the first thing that she set her eyes on, a black sweater; secondly, to the dresser where she grabbed a pair of skinny jeans; and lastly, from the top drawer, a pair of wool socks.

She undressed from her sleeping clothes and then redressed into her working clothes.

She ignored the faint pain in her wrist and darted into the bathroom where she rushed through her daily morning routine: wash the face, do the hair, which she wasn't so diligent about—Anne just threw it in a ponytail—gargle mouthwash, and apply deodorant.

When she was all clean and ready to go to work, it was already a quarter till nine.

Anne ended up skipping the meticulous steps of the morning ritual, which had kept her balanced day in and day out, including breakfast along with coffee—those sorts of things she could grab at work—as well as doing her makeup—that, she could do in the car while sitting in traffic—and jetted out the door.

8:46 AM

As Anne inserted the car key into the lock, her eyes crossed her shoes, which were two different colors. One was brown, and the other was black.

"Damn it," Anne said to herself.

She turned on the car, warmed up the engine, switched on the heat to the medium setting—warming both the inside of the car, as well as defrosting the windshield—and then rushed back into the house where she couldn't help but check the time on the microwave.

"Shit," she hissed. "I don't have time. . . "

Instead of changing her shoes, she rushed back to the car.

8:49 AM

Anne was back in the car with the same two different colored shoes she started out with. Half of the windshield was now defrosted while the other half was still covered in frost. She turned on the wipers a couple of times, which, eventually, cleared away the remaining frost on the windshield.

Right before she drove off, she glanced down at the dashboard. The red bar was hovering just above the E. If things couldn't get any worse. . .

"Damn it," Anne whispered as she slammed the gear in R and reversed from the driveway.

Halfway down the driveway, Anne realized that she never picked up the mail from yesterday. She parked the car, made sure the brake was all the way up from the slight incline of the driveway, and hurried to the mailbox.

Anne checked the mailbox, but there was no mail inside, which, to Anne, was unusual. There wasn't a holiday yesterday, at least not to her knowledge; however, on the other hand, she wondered, the way holidays, appreciation days, or whatever days popped up every year, she wasn't the least surprised if the mail didn't come because it offended somebody or interfered with another person's beliefs.

She hurried back to her car. She switched the gear to reverse; and then, the second she pressed her shoe against the gas pedal, a potent waft of funk came over her like a fart in a crowded city bus. Yet again, she switched the gear in P and sniffed the inside of the car, the vents, the steering wheel, and then her hands, her crotch, and lastly. . . her armpits. The horrendous smell came from none of those places, even her armpits. Then, it hit her like a punch to the face. She peeled her brown shoe from the brake and lifted up her ankle, only to find a lump of dog shit on the sole of her shoe, a fresh turd as round as a smashed nugget.

"*Shit*," Anne seethed intensely, as she pointed out the obvious, that she stepped in a piece of dog shit in the front lawn (which could've come from any of her neighbors, since most of the neighbors had dogs and walked their dogs on the sidewalk, most of the time without their little shit baggies). At this point Anne's outrage was burning like hellfire.

8:55 AM

WHILE Anne was applying the lipstick across her upper lip, a car horn suddenly blared out from behind! She pulled her eyes from the overhead mirror and without knowing it, smeared the lipstick across one side of her entire cheek. Then, the traffic began to part. The car behind her cut into the next lane, raced around Anne, and then cut back into her lane. Anne proceeded forward; however, the traffic slowed once more, which now left Anne behind the *same* car that had pulled out in front of her.

Then, the traffic moved again, yet Anne remained at a standstill. The man who was in the car in front of her was looking down into his lap. A couple of car horns blared from behind Anne. The man in front of her pulled his head from his lap, raised a phone, and held it against his ear. Once the man realized that *he* was responsible for holding up traffic, he proceeded forward, but not as aggressively as before.

8:58 AM

WITHOUT a minute to spare, she made a pit stop at the nearest gas station, Pearl Gas, where she filled the tank with regular. She only put ten dollars in the tank (enough to make it to work and then back home).

As Anne grabbed the receipt from the pump, she heard a sudden *splat* near her feet and then an ice cube struck the side of her ankle. A stocky man, who was dressed in khaki shorts, red baseball cap, and strolling away from Anne, had missed the trashcan nearest her pump by *at least* four feet. Not even a brick or a bank shot. Still, the man continued at his leisurely pace—a steady penguin toddle—and didn't bother picking up his trash.

Anne's eyes crossed the ice cube, the little bit of soda left behind on her pants.

With her teeth now clenched and the upper part of her cheeks filled with a shade of carmine red, Anne glanced below at the plastic 48 oz. cup, as well as the scattered ice cubes, inches away from her back right tire. She directed her narrow eyes toward the litter-bug, who didn't even acknowledge what he had done, and yet, he kept strolling back to his car as if he was a man strolling through a park.

Anne reached down, picked up the cup from the ground, tossed the trash into its rightful place, ripped the receipt from the pump, stormed back to the car, and slammed the door behind her.

9:03 AM

AFTER Anne parked, she did a once over in the reflection of the driver side window and saw the lipstick on the side of her cheek.

"You gotta be kidding me," she said, as she leaned toward the driver's side mirror, licked her fingers, and wiped away the lipstick from her cheek.

Lastly, Anne checked her shoes, first in the reflection of the car and then, secondly, side to side with a long gaze. *Doesn't look that bad*, she thought as she tried to extend her gaze from another perspective, from vertical to horizontal, which, physically, seemed impossible to pull off. When does a person look at another person's shoes?

Either way, it was going to be that kind of day.

Anne just hoped the worst was behind her.

9:06 AM

WITH one minute to spare, Anne arrived at USR.

She rushed through the cube farm and into the break room where she clocked in with a couple of seconds to go.

As her hand swept across her forehead, Anne said to herself, "Buzzer beater."

Once Anne clocked in, she grabbed something to eat from the vending machine—one of those healthy bars that tasted like cardboard—and then fixed a cup of coffee in the break room. She passed Jamie on the way to her cubicle. She said good morning to Jamie, but Jamie was already on the phone with a customer. In return, Jamie nodded at Anne, mouthed the word *hey*, glanced down at the time on her phone, and then rubbed the top of her index finger with her other index finger, a gesture of "shame on you," only done in a joking way.

"I know," Anne repeated and hurried through the office.

In the neighboring cubicle, Stan, like Jamie and the rest of the employees, was on the telephone with a customer.

Anne arrived at her cubicle.

As she placed her purse on the desk, her phone chirped twice!

She checked the two messages from Stan.

SweetStan: Good morning, Sunshine
SweetStan: Ur late.
DirtyTill30: Forgot to set alarm *___*
SweetStan: Don't worry. I covered for u. Told Dave u were having a lil car troubles.
DirtyTill30: Awww. . . That's nice of you. Thanks, Stan :)
SweetStan: Np.

9:18 AM

BEFORE Anne made her first call of the day, she received another text on the phone.

She rolled her eyes, and hoped it wasn't Stan again.

It wasn't.

The sight of the name on the text caught her by surprise.

> Michael: Are you ignoring me???
> DirtyTill30: What is that supposed to mean?
> Michael: I texted you last night
> DirtyTill30: Sorry. I got it just now. Went to bed super early last night. So exhausted. Plus my alarm never went off this morning so I was in straight panic mode all morning :(

Anne waited for Michael to text her back, and did so for about ten minutes (spending most of time surfing the Internet, skimming through the recent headlines on her homepage, checking her email, logging onto FindYourRomeo where she had 0 nibbles) until she finally decided to get to work.

9:57 AM

NOT too long after the second cup of coffee was finished, Anne could feel the morning turd making a last-second escape. She stopped what she was doing and went to the bathroom to relieve herself.

Once Anne was relieved, she removed the glasses from her face and massaged her wrist for about a minute. Then, after the massage, she washed up, her hands first and then her face. The touch of cool water against her sore eyes felt pleasing.

As she pulled her hands from her cheeks, a coarse material brushed along her fingertips. She quickly put on her glasses and looked down at her hand. In her fingers was a piece of what looked like skin. The sliver was no larger than a fingernail, however, soft and squishy from the water. Anne looked in the mirror and examined her face, her cheeks. She didn't have any marks or discoloration, not even a single cut or bruise on her face.

Anne dried her hands and then her face and went back to her cubicle where she made more telephone calls.

11:45 AM

A head manifested in the corner of Anne's eye.

She turned her shoulder and spotted Stan's upper body dangling over the cubicle.

"How's it going, Anne?" he asked.

With a sigh, she said, "It's going. . . "

Stan studied Anne's face, the paleness of her skin, and the dark circles around both of her eyes.

He asked, "Are you feeling okay?"

"Fine."

"Are you sure?"

She rotated her weary eyes at Stan and then turned away.

"It's my eyes," Anne mumbled and grimaced as she removed the glasses from her face. "They've been killing me."

"Have you seen a doctor?"

"I'm going this afternoon."

"Does Dave know?"

"Not yet," Anne said as she rubbed the corners of her eyes, "but it's the only time I can go. So," Anne paused, "if Dave has a problem, then Dave can kiss my ass."

"Anne. . . " Stan said quietly.

Anne moved her eyes toward Stan and looked at him directly in the eyes.

"Yeah."

Stan suddenly paused!

His face went slack and expressionless.

"Stan?"

Anne tilted her head in confusion.

Again, Stan remained still and expressionless.

"Did I say something?"

With a sudden gasp, Stan jerked his head back and forth.

Anne asked, "What was *that* about?"

Stan said confusedly, "What was what about?"

"You looked like your cheese slipped from your cracker."

"Cheese?"

Stan froze from that word *cheese*. Strangely, so did Anne after the word unexpectedly rolled from the edge of her tongue.

"It's like ah. . . " she said slowly, ". . . you know, an expression."

"Oh."

Anne leaned closer.

"You're not going *loco* on me, Stan. Are you?"

"It's. . . " Stan drawled. "I don't know. That was weird. I just. . . just. . . I don't know." Stan furrowed his brows. "I guess I just forgot what I was going to say."

"Happens to all of us," Anne said.

"Yeah," Stan mumbled, shot a sharp glance at Anne, and then timidly sat back down in his chair. "Right."

Anne rolled her eyes, placed the glasses on her face, and made a couple of calls.

12:20 PM

TEN minutes before taking a lunch break, Anne mostly piddled around the cubicle. She thought about giving Michael a call. Then, she remembered that he wasn't a fan of talking on the phone. For him, it was easier to text. She came up with three texts (*Hey there*, then erased it, *Wanna grab a bite*, then erased it, *Are you busy*, then erased it) until she finally settled on: *Hey, Michael. I was going to grab some lunch, wondering if you wanted to join?*

> Michael: I would love to, but I have a meeting
> DirtyTill30: Some other time then.
> Michael: How about we get together after my meeting?
> DirtyTill30: I have a doctor's apt at 3:45.
> Michael: How does 2 sound?
> DirtyTill30: Sounds perfect
> Michael: I'll text you when I get out
> DirtyTill30: Ok.

12:25 PM

AS her supervisor, Dave, was heading out the door for lunch, Anne informed him about the doctor's appointment at "two o'clock," and instead of letting her take a lunch, he told her to clock out around a quarter till two and take off the rest of the day. Anne agreed. Not like she had any choice in the matter. She made herself a cup of green tea in the break room and took it back to her cubicle where she mostly played the popular app, *Angry Ducks*, on her smartphone for the next twenty minutes.

1:37 PM

THE desk suddenly vibrated!

ELLIS KROSS

"I appreciate your time, Ms. Connolly," Anne said to the former customer, Jennifer Connolly. "Have a nice day."

Anne removed the headset from her head and answered her vibrating phone.

"Hello," she said.

"Ms. Roth, this Pam from Cherry Blossom Dry Cleaners."

Anne gasped.

"I completely forgot," she said nervously.

"That's all right," Pam said. "I call to let you know coat is ready for pickup."

"Thank you," she said with relief and then paused. "I actually can't pick it up until later."

"You pick up later?"

"Of course," she said.

"What time?"

"What time do you close?"

"We close six o'clock."

"Thank you," Anne said. "I'll pick it up before six. And thanks for calling."

"You're welcome," the lady said. "Bye."

2:07 PM

SEVEN minutes passed, and still no text from Michael.

While she was waiting on Michael's text, she decided to clock out and pick up her coat from the dry cleaners.

On the way to Cherry Blossom, she received a text from Michael.

Michael: Just got out of meeting. Wanna meet me at Yellow Fin in 10 minutes?

"Yellow Fin?" Anne said with mild disgust. "He knows I got food poisoning the last time we went there." She let out a sigh and said to herself, "Whatever."

DirtyTill30: Ok. See u there.

Anne stopped at the next intersection and did a U-turn. Yellow Fin was about fifteen minutes away, but Anne could make it there in ten.

2:18 PM

MICHAEL'S car wasn't in the parking lot when Anne pulled up to Yellow Fin. She did a last minute primp in the rear view mirror and waited on the sidewalk in front of the restaurant and searched for Michael's car for about five minutes until she finally pulled her phone from her purse.

Halfway through the text (Anne typing the words *where* and *are* on the keypad of her phone), she heard the rattle of a trunk from a bass system. She pulled her eyes from the phone and spotted Michael parking his black M3 BMW across two parking spaces near the back of the parking lot. He waited inside the car for about two minutes, but Anne couldn't see what Michael was doing behind the tinted windows, which were not even considered street legal. He finally stepped out of the vehicle.

During his walk through the parking lot, he was texting on the phone. For a second, Anne thought he was texting her. So, naturally, she glanced down at her phone but received no text. She placed her phone back into her purse and waited for Michael, who was taking his time. He finally arrived at the sidewalk where Anne was waiting with her arms folded over her chest. He shot his head up at Anne, which was the first acknowledgement from the moment he arrived at Yellow Fin, and then forced a smile.

"Hi, babe," he said and kissed Anne on the cheek.

"Hey," Anne replied as she slipped her hand down by Michael's side and intertwined her fingers between his, and together, they entered Yellow Fin.

2:40 PM

THEY grabbed a seat in front of the sushi bar, which, believe it or not, was fairly crowded considering the lunch crowd usually flowed in around noon and didn't let up until a quarter after one. Most of the patrons were younger, hipsters and students who attended Western Madison University, which was a walking distance away from the restaurant. Instead of watching the chef prepare the sushi, Anne squared herself to Michael and devoted most of her attention to him. She asked him how the meeting went, which he replied, "Boring as usual." Michael did most of the talking, mostly about himself, his colleagues, and not once, did he ask how Anne was doing. Right before they ordered California rolls, Michael received a text on the phone. Then, seconds later, his phone rang.

As Anne opened her mouth to speak, Michael held up his finger and said, "Hold that thought."

He turned away from Anne and answered the phone.

For about a minute, he talked business and then mixed in a little pleasure with his colleague. Most of the conversation on the phone consisted of Michael bashing his new boss, who was a woman, and calling her derogatory names; and he even had the audacity to attack his boss's character right in front of Anne—saying she was an anal you-know-what and that she needed to get a man in her life, a man who would you-know-what to her. Anne could only catch the word *anal*, which immediately caught her attention. She focused on Michael, what he was saying on the phone, and then him beaming and laughing while she drifted into a daze. Anne tried to focus on the words that projected from his mouth, but they were all disjointed and muddled together. Even the ambience around the sushi bar was muffled.

Michael motioned to Anne, whispering the words, *"I'll be back."*

With a vacant expression, Anne nodded her head as Michael stood up from his chair. He didn't wander too far from Anne, not enough to where Anne couldn't make out what he was saying, but even then, she still couldn't comprehend a single word throughout the restaurant. She suddenly pulled herself from her thoughts, the volume clarifying in her ears. She took a sip of water, grabbed her purse, and darted toward the exit.

As Anne swung open the door and stepped outside, a firm hand grabbed her by the forearm and pulled her back into the restaurant. She spun around, only to witness Michael standing there. He released his hand from her arm.

"You mad?" he asked confusedly.

Anne cleared her throat.

"Michael," she said, "I can't do this anymore with you."

"Do what?"

Her eyes widened.

"This!"

"What was I supposed to do?" He innocently shrugged. "I had to take a phone call. And now, what, you're getting all mad at me?"

"You act like I don't even exist, Michael."

"You know I've been busy with work."

"Then, why do you have a girlfriend, Michael?" Anne's voice rose. "What am I even doing here?"

"I can make more time for you," Michael said quietly. "Anne, please." He glanced around the restaurant, hoping nobody was looking at them. "You're making a scene."

"You're making a scene, Michael!" she blurted out. "This thing is supposed to go two ways!"

"And it will get back to that," he said and stepped forward but Anne took another step back, closer to the door. "It's just now, I've been busy. . . "

"I know," Anne said scornfully. "You said that already."

Michael sighed greatly.

Before he had a chance to reply, Anne stormed out of the restaurant.

"Where you going?"

"I have a doctor's appointment," she said over her shoulder. "Remember?"

"I thought that wasn't until four."

Anne paused, turned her shoulder, and then stormed back to Michael, who was standing at the edge of the sidewalk.

"Here's one thing to think about," she said sharply. "I want you to tell me one good thing you've done for me in the past month and then see if it amounts to half the bullshit I've done for you! Go on! Tell me, Michael!"

Michael childishly rolled his eyes, sighed, and then turned away.

"That's what I thought," Anne said coldly and walked away.

Michael callously waved her off and said under his breath, "Forget your ass."

As Michael walked back into Yellow Fin, Anne was already getting into her car. She slammed the door behind her and dropped her head into her hands and cried deeply.

"Why is he doing this to me?" she whined, the tears racing from her eyes.

The feel of the tears on her cheeks seemed strange. Many times, especially while she was going through weight problems, she had cried. But not like this. Something was off, not with the emotion, but from what resulted in the emotion. She carefully fingered her cheek and then pulled her fingers away. She held her hands inches away from her face. The tears were thick, almost slimy to touch. When she pulled her wet fingers apart, a thick string pulled along with her fingers.

"Oh God," she said suddenly and rubbed her fingers together.

The tears had the consistency of glue, only less sticky.

She reached into the glove compartment and found a napkin. She used the napkin to wipe the tears from her hands and then her face. She placed the damp napkin into her purse, wondering whether or not to give it to the ophthalmologist.

Finally, after about a minute of taking in deep breaths, slowly through her nose and then exhaling through her mouth, she stared into the rear view mirror where she cleaned the smudge of mascara from her face, as well as the phlegm from her nose with another napkin. Her eyes glazed over, and at that moment, all emotion emptied from Anne's face.

3:20 PM

ANNE got through the first two songs on the CD that she had ripped from the Internet (the compact disc being Mona's Arch sophomore album, *Machine Mistress*, including an unreleased track from the Japanese release) before gathering enough nerve to turn off the car.

She pulled the mp3 player from an adapter, which was connected to the auxiliary input of the stereo interface, and exited the car.

3:34 PM

AFTER Anne handled all of the basic procedures of signing in, which, in fact, didn't require a signature from Anne at all but a scan of her palm and then a proof of insurance, she was asked to take a seat in the waiting room.

Despite the fact that there were only four other people in the waiting room, she waited for about twenty minutes until the nurse finally called her name and escorted her to her room. She was asked the standard questions: So, what brings you in today? How long have your eyes been hurting you? On a scale of one to ten, one being the least and ten being the worst, how would you rank your pain? Are you taking any medications for the pain? If so, which ones? Are you taking any over the counter medications? Are you allergic to any medications?

After the round of questions, the nurse exited the room and suggested Anne read a magazine while she waited for the ophthalmologist, Doctor Sanders. Anne didn't read from the stack of magazines. Instead, she waited there on the table in that stale room and stared at a diagram showing the different parts

and workings of the eye. Ten minutes later, the doctor finally entered the room. He was a thin man with
little expression on his face. He greeted Anne with a
handshake and then skimmed over Anne's chart as he
washed his hands in the sink. The doctor followed
along with the same questions that the nurse had
asked Anne prior to his entry. From there, he examined Anne's eyes with a scope. Anne told the doctor
about the tears and how thick they were; and she even
showed him the napkin that she carried in her purse.
However, the doctor didn't appear too interested in
the napkin. He told Anne that it could've been from
allergies or the change in seasons. A couple of patients before him had complained about the same
matter, at least that was what he told Anne. Then,
she was tested on several strange devices, one being a
phoropter and then another being a tonometry, which
checked fluid pressure in Anne's eye. Then, she read
the letters from the Snellen chart on the far wall, starting from the biggest to the smallest letters. Anne read
them off perfectly, which, more or less, baffled Doctor
Sanders. He asked Anne if she had ever been
through laser correctness surgery, and the reason, the
doctor noted, was that Anne's vision was actually
much improved from her 20/40 vision; in fact, she
was now on the fringe of 20/20, which meant she
didn't need any contacts or prescription glasses. The
doctor asked more questions: Is there any change in
your diet? What kind of foods do you eat on a daily
basis? Doctor Sanders insisted that nothing was
wrong with Anne; in fact, it was the artificial correc-
tors like the contacts *and* the glasses that were causing
the pain in her eyes, which, to Anne, seemed more or
less. . . bizarre. Anne was prescribed a pair of glasses
(pretty much reading glasses, which was about the

lowest lens there was), and sent home with a clean bill of health.

5:47 PM

ON the way to Cherry Blossom, Anne ran into heavy traffic on the interstate. The entire time in the car, she watched every minute pass on the dashboard. When the time reached 5:54, and she had only moved about two miles in the time span of seven minutes, she knew she was going to be late.

By the time Anne reached the dry cleaners, it was ten minutes past six.

Frustrated, she checked the front door, but it was locked. She peeked inside, but nobody was around.

On the way back to her car, Anne pulled out her phone.

> DirtyTill30: Wanna grab a drink?
> Jamie: Absolutely!
> DirtyTill30: It's been a long day. I sure as hell could go for something stiff right now ;)
> Jamie: Shouldn't Michael be helping you out in that department?
> DirtyTill30: I mean a drink silly
> Jamie: I'm teasing, Anne. Where do you want to go?
> DirtyTill30: Happy Hour at Red Roxx?
> Jamie: Yes!
> Jamie: What time?
> DirtyTill30: Can you meet me there at 6 30?
> Jamie: I'll be there! ☺
> DirtyTill30: :)

6:33 PM

WHEN Anne pulled up to Red Roxx, Jamie was already there.

"Hey, girl," Jamie said.

Anne replied, "Hey. You got here fast."

"Yeah," Jamie said and pointed to the east of Park Road, "I was actually in the area. So, when you texted me, I was literally five minutes away. How are you?"

Anne groaned.

"It's a long story," she said. "First, I need a drink."

Jamie smiled and said, "You and me both."

6:36 PM

THEY sat at the end of the bar, sipped from their glasses of Vodka and club soda with a dash of lime, and checked out prospects around the bar. Anne was doing most of the scoping (her type being the thin ones but not sickly-thin like the ones in Lansford's historic art district, North End, but a lean cultured man with a little gel in his hair who could at least bench his own body weight), which, to Jamie, was a clear sign that things weren't going too well between her and Michael. However, Jamie never asked why she was scoping for men, mainly thin with dark hair, a little gel but not too much. She wasn't one to cramp one's style. Anne mentally noted that there *wasn't* much potential; however, there was this one guy, she saw, tall and handsome, but he was with another girl. Other than that, it was the same crowd: middle-aged men, most, if not all married, catching the tail end of happy hour before they went home to the misses.

Jamie first started off the conversation with a question.

"So, how did your doctor's visit go?" she asked and sipped from her drink.

She grimaced from the taste of the drink and then flagged down the bartender and asked him if she could have another lime to put in her drink.

"You won't even believe me if I tell you," Anne said without a single trace of excitement in her voice, despite the good news.

Jamie said teasingly, "Try me on for size."

Anne furrowed her brows.

Then, she said, "He said my vision is better."

"Better?" Jamie said and jerked back her head. "Better how?"

"Like twenty-twenty better."

"Really?" Jamie said, her voice higher. "How is that even possible?"

"I have no idea, Jamie."

Jamie pointed at Anne's eyes.

"Are you wearing your contacts?"

"No."

"How do you see right now?"

Anne briefly looked around the bar.

"I see fine," she said surprisingly. "Just like I did in high school."

"That is freaky," Jamie said, sipping from her drink.

She smacked her lips together and nodded in satisfaction.

"How's the drink?"

"Delicious."

Anne sipped from the drink.

"Not bad," she said with a grimace.

"So, tell me more about this visit," Jamie said.

"I did all the tests," she replied, "read the letters on the chart. When I took off my glasses, the pain in my eyes was gone."

"Are you serious?"

"Totally," Anne said and took another sip from her drink.

"You've been wearing contacts ever since I've known you and you've never had a problem."

"I've only had them for about four or five years," Anne said. "I mean, before, my vision was normal. And now, well, I don't know, it's kind of hard to explain. It's fine, I guess."

"Well," Jamie said as she raised her glass, "some things aren't meant to be understood." She toasted her glass against Anne's glass. "Here's to our eyes and keeping them beautiful."

They both gulped from their drinks, Jamie killing hers and Anne leaving a little bit left.

"I thought I had a long day," Anne said, noticing the empty drink in front of Jamie.

"And it's only Tuesday."

"I know, right?" Anne replied and finished the rest of her drink. "I can't wait for the weekend."

"I'm the same way."

"Lately, it seems like every week I get more and more ready for the weekend," Anne said to Jamie. "I mean, there's been times when I've walked through those doors on Monday and been like, oh my God, is it Friday yet."

"I know," Jamie said giddily.

"It's like every week is getting longer and longer," she said. "It's like I'm in a time warp."

Jamie made a high pitch "Oh-we-you" noise with her mouth.

Then, said: "You're in the *Twilight Zone*."

Anne said from the side of her mouth, "Funny."

Jamie giggled a little.

"Hate to say it, Anne, but," she said, more flatly now, "I've learned that the job is the only thing carrying me through the week. That," a grin inched its way across her face, "and watching Taylor bend over to grab his Dark Bar from the vending machine. I swear, that man has an ass like a model. He should be an ass model."

Anne shrugged.

"Euh," she said.

"You don't think so."

"He's not that attractive."

"I never said ass models were attractive," Jamie said and sucked on a piece of ice from her empty glass. "They got a nice ass. That's all. Hints: ass model. I mean, Anne. . . they wouldn't be ass models if they didn't have a nice ass. Now, would they?"

"No," Anne said. "They wouldn't."

The bartender chimed in, "Would you ladies like another?"

"Yes," Jamie said, "please."

As the bartender went to prepare their drinks, Jamie suddenly blurted out, "Wait a second!"

The bartender strolled back to the bar.

Jamie said to Anne, "How about cherry bombs!"

"Cherry bombs?" Anne said with a cringe. "You know, we do have to work tomorrow."

Jamie shrugged and did so with a grin on her face and a mischievous twinkle in her eye.

"It's still early," she said quietly. "Besides, tonight is a night of celebration. Tonight is for you, gorgeous."

Anne sighed.

"All right," Anne said, as Jamie ordered two cherry bombs, "but if I'm hungover tomorrow, I'm going to. . ."

Jamie turned away from the bartender, who was now preparing their drinks.

She said sassily, "You're going to what?"

"I'm going to kick your ass," Anne said. "That's what I'm going to do."

Jamie laughed.

"Girl, I like to see you try!"

"Hey," Anne said louder, "just because I'm now a skinny bitch doesn't mean I can't still throw some bows. I got a mean right hook, Jamie. Ask David Sherman."

"Well," Jamie said closer now, "I don't know who David Sherman is, but I'm sure you kicked his ass."

Anne sipped from the melted ice in the glass and said with a smirk worn on one side of her face, "Ex boyfriend. We went out in ninth grade and then I found out he cheated on me with this slut, a senior who was on the cheerleading squad. Gave him a black eye."

"Get outta here!"

"Hey," Anne said. "If you don't believe me, then ask David. . . ."

"I got it," Jamie repeated, smiling. "Ask David Sherman."

8:50 PM

IT usually didn't pick up until around ten o'clock and yet it was fairly crowded for "Ladies Night," as it was known at Red Roxx, which they had every Tuesday and Thursday night, Thursday being the busiest night of the week. On these two particular nights women received half-price on all drinks, even the fancy, color-ful kind, which, for both Anne and Jamie, either worked *for* or *against* their convenience: for, meaning they didn't have to fork out a lot of their hard-earned money for drinks, even the fancy kind; or against, meaning it attracted a bunch of double-s-assholes who were trying to take full advantage of the ladies. That's Stingy-Sleazy for those who were asking, "What the hell is a SS asshole?" The worst nights especially for Anne: Thursday nights, which attracted SSHD a-holes—Stingy-Sleazy-Horny-Dopey. Anne didn't have to worry too much about a barfly playing the trump card on her. There weren't many douche bags around, at least none who could quite fit up to her standards. She tamed her gaze and decided to eat before the night got out of hand. Both she and Jamie soaked up the alcohol with an order of two appetizers, Red Roxx's famous southwestern egg rolls and then a plate of Korean barbeque with lettuce wraps—the lettuce wraps being for Anne. They finished their appetizers in swift form and nursed a lite beer.

When most of the patrons who were there only for the food had left and then a much younger crowd who was there only for the drinks and the music had funneled in, one of Anne's favorite songs came on. The song, "Wax Sculpture," by none other than Mona's Arch, debuted fifteen years ago, thus making it what Anne called an oldie, despite the song having only been fifteen years old. Every now and then, at Red Roxx or any other bar or club for that matter, the DJ would play an old gem like "Wax Sculpture" if the dance floor was sparse, provoking the ineluctable "Oh my God! That's my song!" line from at least one person in the crowd. Classic ruse used by DJs. From there, all it took was one person to hit the dance floor. After that, others would eventually gather around and test the waters. Then, not too long after, the place was jumping like a flea over dry hide.

Before Anne and Jamie went back to the bar, they picked out a guy who wasn't doing much dancing at all, mostly people-watching, and asked him to take their picture, one Anne could post on MyCircle. The guy was more than pleased to take the picture. Unfortunately for Anne, he just so happened to take the picture when Anne was complaining to him about how slow it was taking him to take the picture. He took two pictures without a stutter and handed Anne back her phone. What the guy had taken was beyond posting, Anne saw as the guy disappeared in the crowd. In the picture, Jamie looked good as always, keeping to her gleaming smile as the guy yelled out, "Say cheese!" Anne, on the other hand, had an ugly face, one eye squinted, teethed bared like a rabid dog, ugly.

9:24 PM

AT the bar, they hammered their way through three more rounds of shots, not the cherry bombs but three shots of a pineapple-flavored vodka, and then followed with a lite beer. Despite having eaten about an hour ago, Anne started to feel the effects of the alcohol and clearly showed it in her behavior.

Anne closed one eye and with the other, she peered at the older man in the sports coat sitting at the other end of the bar.

"There you go, Jamie," Anne said, nodding in the vicinity of the older man. "What do you think of that guy? He's kind of cute."

Jamie finally acknowledged the man who was staring down at his phone.

"No thank you," she said aloofly. "He looks like he's been clinging onto that suit for the past ten years."

"So what," Anne slurred. "He's cute."

"Probably married."

"Prolly," Anne replied and looked closer. "I don't see a ring."

Jamie sipped from her beer.

"For one," she said, "he's twice your age, Anne."

"So," Anne blurted out.

"And he has a flip phone," Jamie returned. "Come on. Really? It's not the nineties."

"You wouldn't go out with a guy who has a flip phone?"

Jamie shook her head.

"No," she said. "Would you?"

"Really, Jamie," Anne said surprisingly. "You think I'm that. . . *that* conceited. If two people love each other. . . "

"Wow, Anne," Jamie said quietly. "You haven't even met the man and you're talking about love." Her eyes widened. "*Wow*."

"In general," Anne corrected. "It doesn't matter what kind of phone they own or what car they drive or what clothes they wear. I don't want to be with a man who always puts himself first, a man who thinks that buying gifts will make up for how bad he really treats you." She shrugged one shoulder, left the other one deflated. "Gifts are nice. I can't complain."

"Sure," Jamie drawled.

"I don't know, Jamie," Anne said over Jamie. "Maybe I don't want gifts and jewelry and roses or chocolate. I don't care about the money, Jamie. For all I care, that guy over there could be a garbage man who owns one nice suit."

"A garbage man?" Jamie said, her eyes narrowing. "Really, Anne? You've reduced yourself to garbage men?"

"I just want a man who has my back," Anne said, "and I had that with Michael, at least when we first started going out. Now, he can hardly even look me in the freaking eye. I want a man who actually *sees* me, Jamie. Materials," she shrugged once more, now both shoulders, "materials are things that disguise who we really are. And if you strip them away, then all you have is yourself."

"I mean, Anne," Jamie said, "it's not like we're living in prehistoric days where we walk around with a club and a piece of road kill for underwear."

"We're almost there," she said grumpily, "at the rate society is going. . . "

"Don't be like that," Jamie said over Anne's voice. "Materials are what set us apart from those people on the side of the street begging for money. That's just the way it is now. You can either except it or join the guy with the cardboard sign. You know he could always use the company."

Anne lowered her chin, brows furrowed into a V.

"That's harsh, Jamie," she said.

As Anne did, Jamie harmlessly shrugged her shoulders.

Anne chugged her beer, leaving mostly head at the bottom.

Jamie said foolishly, "It's reality." She focused more on Anne, the defeat in her face, as well as in her voice. "I say forget about guys for now. That means Michael as well. Concentrate on work." She leaned closer to Anne. "That's exactly what I do when I can't find a decent man. I focus on work and I keep climbing my way to the top."

"That's the difference between you and me, Jamie," Anne said and then motioned to the young bartender for another beer. Without saying a word, he pulled out a bottle of beer from the cooler of ice, opened it, and then placed it in front of Anne. "Thanks," Anne said to the bartender and then directed her attention back to Jamie. "I can care less about moving my way up the corporate ladder. You really want to be doing what Dave does? Really, Jamie? Longer hours. Not much more pay. . . "

"That's not what I'm saying, Anne," Jamie emphasized as Anne gulped from her fresh beer. "I say *you* stroll into USR tomorrow and whop Tim's ass in sales. I'm serious. Put his lame ass to shame."

Anne hung her head and mumbled, "I don't know."

As Anne went to rest the beer, she spotted Susanne across the bar. She threw a nod toward Susanne's way. In return, Susanne, who was sitting next to a younger man, mid-twenties, wearing a dark Polo shirt with blue jeans as tight as his skin, acknowledged Anne with a discreet wave. Susanne finished her Jack and Coke and then split with the young man after he paid the tab.

Jamie followed Anne's eyes.

"Is that Susanne?" Jamie asked, peering closer. "With a guy who could pass as her son?"

"Don't judge."

"Uh," Jamie stuttered. "I'm not."

Anne waved around the bar.

"Judge-free zone."

"Right," Jamie said, a strange tension building in her voice. "I'm not going to judge a forty-three year old mother with two children who goes to bars every week and picks up young guys." Jamie paused suddenly. "And it's not even a weekend. . . "

"So what, Jamie," Anne said. "A woman has needs. *We* have needs. Right?"

"Of course," Jamie said in return, but this time with a high voice. "But she has children to look after."

"Did you ever think that maybe she has a baby sitter?" Anne asked. "Or maybe her ex has the kids this week?"

"Maybe," Jamie said quietly and then her voice rose with excitement, "I don't understand women who get married and then, when things get tough, they bail. Where I'm from marriage is sacred. Sure.

I know times have changed. Marriage is a lot broader than the past, which," she expanded her arms in demonstration, doing a lot of talking with her hands as well, "I'm totally cool with," Jamie said casually as she shifted her weight closer to Anne. She sat upright on the stool and then squared herself to the bar. "Once you tie the knot, then that's it. It's done. That is your partner for life. If things get tough, you learn how to work through your issues, especially if you have kids."

"Yeah," Anne said defensively, "but, Jamie, what if you're *not* happy, then you have every right to leave."

Jamie shrugged.

"Tough," she said.

"The way I look at it. . . marriage—in a way—is. . . is. . . " she searched for the right words, which was like panning for gold in a creek—given Anne's drunken state, ". . . it's filled with certain. . . " there it was, *that* word, glimmering in the sieve, ". . . certain compromises."

"Absolutely," Jamie said in return. "I agree."

"But if he can't compromise or change," Anne said, "then what's the point?"

Jamie never responded to Anne's question.

They both sipped from their beers, Anne killing hers.

"It's sad to say," Jamie said quietly, "but today, you don't even need a man anymore to have a family."

"What do you mean?"

"You know," Jamie said, "the whole artificial insemination thing."

Anne said sardonically, "Where's the fun in that?"

"I know right?"

Jamie laughed awkwardly; however, Anne kept to her somber state.

Then, a silence swelled over the conversation.

"You okay, Anne?" Jamie asked as she studied her friend.

"I'm a little," Anne said loosely, her left eye squinting a bit, "a little off-kilter."

"Are you gonna be straight to drive?"

"I don't mean like that, Jamie," Anne said with her head held down.

"Then, what do you mean?"

"Not setting my alarm last night," Anne listed, "waking up late this morning, skipping lunch, having that fight with Michael. . . you know how I am. . . "

"Yes," Jamie said as she sipped from the beer. "I know, creature of habit. That's unlike you to show up late like that."

"Well," Anne said, "it wasn't like I was an hour late. I was only like ten minutes late."

"Yeah, but still, that's unlike you." Jamie leaned closer. "Are you feeling well? Are you on drugs?"

"Stop it," Anne said seriously.

"Because if you're not," Jamie said mischievously, "then I got some pretty sweet drugs in my car that—trust me—will make you feel a whole lot better. If you know what I mean."

Anne cracked a smile, wounded.

"That's the smile I was looking for," Jamie said closely as she studied the smile on Anne's face. "I knew it was buried deep somewhere in that face of yours."

"Thanks," Anne said, "but not now, not tonight."

"Okay."

Anne paused in thought.

"Do you ever feel like you're trapped in someone else's body? Like. . . "

"Like. . . "

"You know like. . . "

"Like what, Anne?"

"Like a robot?"

"A robot?"

"No," Anne corrected. "Like a clone or something."

"A clone?"

"Yeah."

Jamie chuckled.

"I'm serious," Anne said over Jamie's laughter. "Do you ever feel like your body is like... I don't know... like you're attached to this giant string, and all you're doing is... is drifting along through life with no movement whatsoever, floating around like ah... like... like this ghost?"

"So, now you're a ghost *and* a clone?"

Anne's face went expressionless.

"I can't keep doing this to myself, Jamie," Anne said, her tone sharp and steady. "I don't see how you do it everyday. You say the job is what carries you through the day, but, to me, I don't know, it's the job that's making me worse." Anne sighed. "I'm just sick and tired."

"Sick and tired of what, Anne?"

"Of coming to these same ole freaking places," she said. "Why do we keep coming here?"

"You mean Red Roxx?"

Anne said bitterly, "Where else would I be talking about?"

"Okay," Jamie said as she eased away from Anne, "retract the claws, Anne."

Anne paused for a moment.

"All I'm saying," Anne hesitated, "this place is a black hole."

Jamie furrowed her brows.

"How so?"

"Don't you get sick and tired of coming here all the time, seeing the same tired faces, bumping into the same douche bags. . . "

Jamie shot a glance at the bartender, who was shaking his head with a sense of amusement rather than disgust.

She whispered to him, "*Sorry.*"

". . . and yet," Anne continued, "we keep coming back like this is the last place left on earth and we're trapped in a fucking loop. Like a black hole, sucking us in every time we come here and spitting us out for shits and giggles."

"Anne," Jamie said sincerely, "you keep coming back here because you're looking for him."

"Him?"

"Yeah," Jamie said. "*Him*, you know, Mr. Right. Your knight in shining armor. Prince Charming."

"Jamie, I'm not going to find Prince Charming in a place like this," she said. "Besides, I think I'm in the wrong city. I know it and yet, it's like, I can't leave even if I try."

"What's wrong with Lansford?" Jamie asked. "You practically got everything you need here. . . "

"Lansford is a transplant city," she said. "All that live here is a bunch of stuck-up wannabes pretending to be someone they're not."

"So. . . "

"So?" Anne mimicked.

"They're not all like that."

"All people care about around here is work," Anne said bitterly. "That's all it is. And if it's not work, then it's 'who can I fuck after I get off work?'"

Jamie slowly rotated her head toward Anne.

"Sounds like someone I know."

"Whatever."

"Thought we were in the 'judge-free zone,' Anne."

"We are," she said dourly. "It's just. . . I don't know. . . it gets old. That's all."

"But where else are you gonna find a man—like a really *good* man—at this hour of the night?" Jamie asked loudly. "If it were me, I'd start by looking in bookstores, coffee shops, or festivals. Those kinds of things. Not now, but you know, sometime during the day."

"I work all day," Anne said coldly. "Remember?"

"I'm talking about the weekends," Jamie replied. "I mean, if you really want 'It' at night, it's only lust. If you want 'It' during the day and everyday and every hour, every second of your life with that one person who you think about all day, well, it's love."

"*Well*," Anne said closely, "I could use 'It' right now. Not just 'It,' but I'm talking about the *It* of the century, the kind of 'It' where you can't walk straight for the next three days. You can call it whatever you want. . . lust. . . *love*. . . "

"I'm telling you, Anne," Jamie said. "That's only going to make it worse. If you're really looking for a man to settle down with, which," she leaned closer for a moment, "I know you are, then for one, it'll happened if it's supposed to happen, and two, I wouldn't look in a bar, and three, I wouldn't be sleeping around with every guy who acknowledges me."

"What are you talking about?"

"Two weeks ago," Jamie said. "Remember?"

Anne didn't respond.

"Does Michael know?"

"That wasn't my fault, Jamie," Anne said. "I was wasted."

"That guy totally took advantage of you," Jamie said. "If he didn't pull that shady shit, saying that you two were going outside for a smoke, then that little excursion never would've happened. I'm not one to cock block, but damn, Anne, that guy was a complete mess. . . "

Anne remained quiet.

"Sorry," Jamie said softly.

"I'm confused, Jamie." The tears swelled within Anne's eyes. "I. . . I don't even know who I am or what I'm doing anymore. By the time I reach thirty, my face is going to look like an old catcher's mitt. Who the hell would want me by then? Who would want to go out with a face like that? Let's face it." She sniffled up the phlegm in her nose. "I'm gonna be alone for the rest of my life."

"Don't talk like that, Anne."

"I mean it," Anne said, louder, "I just. . . I just want to *feel the smile on my face*, Jamie, *to know that it's real*. That's all."

"Do you want to be alone, Anne?"

"No," she said. "I don't, but. . . "

"But what, Anne?" Jamie said, leaning closer to Anne. "Don't act like the world has turned its back on you, Anne, because it hasn't. Maybe you want it to, Anne. Only you choose whether or not you want to be alone. *You*, Anne."

"I mean, don't you. . . I don't know. . . don't you ever think about leaving. . . "

"Leaving where?"

"I don't know," she stuttered, "like somewhere exotic, somewhere where people speak a different language. . . "

"Anne," Jamie said expressionlessly, "now you're starting to sound like a crazy person."

"Call me crazy," she said aggressively. "Call me whatever you like. I'm sick and tired, Jamie. I'm sick of going through the motions. I'm tired of the constant abuse day in and day out, people treating me like I'm a fucking doormat. I've had enough of it!"

"Aw, Anne," Jamie said as she rubbed the back of Anne's shoulder. "I'm sorry you feel like that." Jamie momentarily drifted into thought. "You know, I always wanted to move to a small town where everybody knows each other by their first name. Open up my own hair salon. Every single woman in town would come to my salon. I'd give them all different kinds of haircuts, each one different from the next. Then, I," Jamie cracked a smile, "when the women in the town would ask where they got their haircuts, they would always mention my name. . . " Jamie bobbed her head, ". . . now, I'd like that, Anne." She turned her attention toward Anne. "It's fantasy. All I know is the present, the *now*. I can't go running off to a small town and open up my own hair salon. I wouldn't even know where to start." Jamie sighed. "This is where you're at right now. Instead of trying to find whatever you're looking for elsewhere, you have to open your eyes, Anne, and accept the hand you've been dealt."

Anne sipped from the empty beer.

"One day," she said, calmer now, "you're going to stop by my cubicle and there's going be nothing left of me but a pool of blood."

"Don't say that."

"It's true, Jamie," she said solemnly. "This job is turning me into a zombie, in the afternoons. . . Thank God for the gym. If I didn't have the gym. . . "

Jamie leaned back, her face lit up with eureka.

"Ah-ha!" Jamie blurted out. "You're talking about that three o'clock feeling. Aren't you?"

"Yeah!"

"Like you just want to melt in your chair like the Wicked Witch of the West?"

"Yeah!" Anne's voice rose higher. Her face lit as well. "Exactly!"

"It's called six-hour energy," she said and reached into her purse on the stool next to her. "I take them every day after lunch and it keeps me focused for the rest of the day."

"That crap makes me twitchy."

Jamie displayed the tiny bottle to Anne.

"Not this stuff," she said. "No side-effects. No crash. . ."

"So, exactly how much are they paying you to advertise that stuff?"

"I'm serious," Jamie said. "I felt the same exact way before I took this. . . " Jamie rattled the bottle and then winked at Anne, ". . . works like a charm."

Anne let out a yawn.

"Am I boring you?"

"No," she followed. "I don't think a pill can cure the way I feel."

"Sure it can," Jamie said bluntly as she squared herself to Anne. "You're only twenty-four years old, Anne. You're still young. People make career changes all the time. Hell! I know a guy who's in his late-thirties, and he gave up engineering to work in retail. A grocery store, Anne! Now, he owns a small organic store off Cameron Avenue. He doesn't make that much money, but he's happy, Anne. And in today's world, that's all that matters. It doesn't matter what you do. Remember that, Anne."

"Says the woman who was bashing garbage men."

Jamie smacked her gums and rolled her eyes, as an adolescent would do.

"All that matters is what makes *you* happy." Jamie finished her beer. "The question you should be asking yourself: What makes you happy?"

10:38 PM

BEFORE the overhead lights came on throughout Red Roxx and spotlighted the poor, desperate souls clinging onto last call—twelve o'clock during the weekdays, two o'clock during weekends—both Anne and Jamie staggered from the bar.

Parked along the curb was a taxi van with the phone number 777-7777 written along the side of the door, which made it easy to remember, especially after a late night of drinking—just hit one number a bunch of times until there was a ring.

As Anne's heel caught the edge of the curb, she stumbled forward. She reached out to grab Jamie before the fall, but accidentally grabbed Jamie's chest.

In return, Jamie grabbed Anne, removed the hand from her breast, and balanced Anne upright.

"Whoa there," Jamie said, laughing. "Rounding second base. Are we?"

"Sorry," Anne said innocently. "I couldn't help myself."

Jamie leaned forward and studied Anne's face, the dark bags underneath her glossy, red eyes.

"Are you okay to drive?"

"I'm fine," Anne slurred and sipped from the bottle of water. "I swear. I've driven under worse conditions."

"Are you sure?"

"Yeah," she said, louder this time. "I'm fine. I don't even feel that drunk."

Anne waved off Jamie and reached into her purse. The purse slipped from her hands and fell to the ground. Jamie kneeled down and picked up the purse, as well as the contents from inside the purse, which included a tube of mascara and a bottle of Paxil that had spilled onto the sidewalk.

Jamie read the drug on the bottle.

"Paxil?"

"Yeah," Anne said with deflation. "My crazy pills."

"Anne," Jamie said seriously, "you didn't drink while taking these. Did you?"

Anne frowned.

"Of course not."

"Okay," Jamie said as she cautiously handed the purse to Anne. "Just be careful."

"Always am."

Anne glanced around the quiet street, and as she pulled her eyes back to Jamie, she spotted the same exact car from last night, the one following her from the gym, parked across the street. She looked twice, and did so without fully turning her head toward the car's direction.

"What's wrong?" Jamie asked. "Anne?"

Anne's face went blank and sober.

"Do you mind following me home?" she asked. "Make sure I get home okay?"

"Yeah," Jamie said. "I don't mind at all."

"Are you sure?"

"I'll follow you home," Jamie said clearly.

Anne paused once more on the way to her car, which wasn't parked too far from the bar.

"Jamie?"

Anne turned around and faced Jamie.

"Wassup?"

She hung her head for a moment and then glanced around the empty street. Her red eyes shifted into thought. Stilled. Then, she moved her eyes back to Jamie.

"Don't follow too close," she said finally.

"Sure thing, Anne," Jamie said with a smile and strolled away. "I'll see you bright and early in the morning!" Jamie walked farther away. "And you better be at work!"

Anne thinking: *work, why did she have to bring up work?*

For a moment, as brief as it was, the thought of USR was the farthest thing from her mind, and yet, once the word *work* was mentioned, that feeling came over Anne again, that sinking feeling, the one Anne knew all too well.

10:47 PM

"YOU got a flat tire. . ." a raspy voice said from over Anne's shoulder as she inserted the key into the door.

She removed the key from the door and turned her shoulder, only to find an older black man, well into his sixties, possibly seventies, skinny, standing like a wilted daisy on the side of the alleyway, with a scanty white beard, red eyes hidden behind a pair of murky glasses, and a brown bag covering a whiskey bottle in his right hand, cigarette smoked down to the filter in the other. He was wearing a yellow fedora and a dark leather jacket, which appeared as if it was family heirloom, sections of the sleeves cracked like chapped lips.

With caution, Anne stepped back from the car and glanced down at each tire on her car, all inflated, *not* flat.

"Nah, Baby Girl," the old man said once more. "You got a flat tire."

"Excuse me," Anne said, taking a step closer to the strange old man.

"You not listenin'," he said with a soft lisp as he flicked the ash, which was about as long as the cigarette itself. "Your soul has a flat tire. So, Baby Girl, what do you do when you got a flat tire?"

Anne shrugged.

"You fix it?"

"There you go!" he said jubilantly. "You fix it!"

He beamed from one side of his face to the other, exposing his coffee stained teeth, as tiny as woodchips.

A bright light flashed in the corner of Anne's eye, which pulled her attention from the old man. She faced the light, squinted from the two headlights of a burgundy car, and then peered through the light where Jamie was waiting behind the steering wheel.

"Let's go, Anne," she said from the cracked window. "It's getting late."

"What's your name?" Anne said as she rotated her shoulder.

The old man was nowhere around.

Anne searched the side alleyway, but, just like that, he was gone.

11:12 PM

As Jamie drove away, Anne extended her hand from the driver's side window and waved goodbye as she pulled the car into the garage. She safely parked the car and walked to the mailbox. There was no mail in the mailbox. Then, she checked the neighbor's mailbox, which always had the red flag up; however, the red flag was down, *not* up. She checked the inside of the mailbox again, thinking that maybe her weary eyes were fooling her. She blindly reached her hand inside the mailbox, but there was nothing.

Another holiday, Anne wondered. Who knows?

On the way to the house, Anne heard a car approaching from behind her.

She turned to the car.

Before she could make out the car, mainly the headlights, the car suddenly took a left onto another street and vanished into the night darkness.

"Get a grip, Anne," she said to herself and walked into the house via the front door.

She locked both locks on the door and peeped through the curtains.

The street was still and quiet, not a car on the road.

11:24 PM

AFTER grabbing a snack from the pantry and downing two glasses of water, Anne undressed and prepared a warm bath. While doing so, she began to feel nauseous. So, Anne did something that Jamie had taught her a while back, which helped cure Anne's nausea, and that was running her fingers under warm water. She did this for about three minutes until the nausea faded a little. She checked the time, and then, having realized the time, turned on the television. The show, *Blood Diaries*, was replaying on air for those who missed the ten o'clock show. Anne was about halfway into the show, precisely twenty-seven minutes. For the sake of spoilers, she skipped the rest of the show and planned on staying off the blogs until she caught a rerun on the Internet later in the week.

Discouraged, she turned off the television and ambled to the bathroom where the water was almost done filling the tub.

11:36 PM

ANNE removed each layer of clothes, starting from her torso and then making her way down to her legs and feet, lastly her wool socks, until she was as bare as the day she was born. Her pale body caught her eye in the reflection of the mirror. She stumbled over to the mirror, that pale reflection—both of her eyes bloodshot from the alcohol—and leaned over the sink with languid movement.

The question came without a second's thought: "Who am I?"

In the mirror, she looked over the old scars on her body, a long and pink and jagged one that stretched all the way up the right side of her ribcage, and then a vertical scar, as narrow as a blade, along her upper abdomen from where she ruptured her diaphragm in an accident she had no memory of, only the flashes of a distant nightmare which had haunted her whenever she closed her eyes to sleep.

11:49 PM

ANNE eased herself into the warm, bubbly water and lit a couple of scented candles on the edge of the tub, mostly eucalyptus.

As she oozed farther down into the tub, she lifted one leg from the water and applied shaving cream to the leg, starting from her ankle to her thigh. She used the razor, which she kept on the lip of the tub, and slid the blade along her leg the same way she applied the shaving cream: from her ankle to her thigh.

Each stroke ran farther up her thigh, close to her pubic hair.

While running the blade around her knee, she felt a sudden tug of the blade and then a pinch over her skin. The blade popped from the mount and fell into the water. She sat upright and caressed her knee.

When Anne pulled her hand from the soapy water, she pulled something else in return. She pulled her hand closer to her face. *The same* as in the bathroom, Anne thought as she studied the piece of skin between her fingertips.

The sliver of skin was the same exact size as the one before, the size of a fingernail, hard like a fingernail too.

Almost, she wondered, *like a snake's scale*.

"What in the. . . " Anne drawled as she cringed in disgust.

She lifted her leg from the water and checked her skin. There was no bruise, no cut, *no* blood, no mark on her body. Nothing whatsoever.

Letting out a sharp *yuck*, Anne waggled her fingers until they were clean and then searched for the razor blade at the bottom of the tub. She finally came across the tiny blade. Instead of trying to pick up the blade, which could've resulted in further injury, she pressed the blade against the tub and slid the tiny thing against the side of the tub.

Once the blade was free from the water, she finally got her two fingers around the blade. For the longest time, Anne stared at that glistening blade—part of it speckling with froths of soap—and contemplated the one thought that had been cooped up in the recesses of her mind. Anne wondered about them, them as in her colleagues at USR, and whether or not they would miss her. Would they ridicule her even after she was gone? How about her foster parents? What would they think? She couldn't possibly put such a burden on them—especially after all they had done for her. But then again. . .

As Anne gently pressed the blade against her pale wrist, she heard a car door slam shut from outside!

PART TWO
TRIAL AND ERROR

CHAPTER 3

THE question finally came to him: *What have I become?*
Not who, but what?

The detective peered into the mirror as if the mirror itself was an entity peering right back at him. The question had been lingering with him all day and well into the night hours; and when the question finally spilled from his lips, the answer was written all over his face. Funny how that works, how a piece of glass can answer the questions to any man's troubles. The mirror didn't exactly answer in spoken tongue, yet it answered with pictures. At that moment of clarity, it showed him the answer to the *what* he had become: just another old dog. He watched it happen to Corpus, his former partner. Surely, he wondered, it was never going to happen to me. Never. *But it did*, the mirror showed, as much as he didn't want to admit it. In all his years on the force, he never understood how a person could become so jaded, at least not until this very moment. The detective studied the lines on his face, the dark bags underneath his weary eyes, and the pouch of a belly, which hung over his belt buckle.

He turned toward his coat, which was lying on the top of the sink, reached into the pocket, pulled out an airplane bottle of Jack Daniels, and downed the bottle until there wasn't a single drop left.

"Hey, Merrotti!" said a stern voice of a woman behind the door.

A *pound* at the door followed!

Merrotti wiped the liquor from the corner of his lip and barked back, "Yeah!"

"Come on," she said. "It's time to roll out!"

He checked his watch.

The time read: 12:53.

"Just," the detective said softly, his voice trailing off and then sputtering, "give me a minute. Will you?"

A strain in her voice: "You okay in there?"

"Fine," he replied and inserted a stick of gum into his mouth.

1:12 AM

MERROTTI and his partner, Pamela Florence, drove through the city without speaking a word to one another. Florence had her reasons why her partner was so quiet. The gum was what really gave it away.

"Can I ask you a question," Florence said finally, "but you promise me not to get offended?"

Finally, Merrotti thought, after all these years.

"No guarantees, Florence," Merrotti said, moving his eyes from the dark road and then shooting a glare at his partner in the passenger seat. "If you think it's going to offend me, then it's probably best you keep it to yourself."

A tense silence. . .

Then, Merrotti cut right through the silence with a question of his own.

"So, where we going?"

"Name: Diana Hailey Roth," Florence informed. "Your everyday B&E gone bad."

"How many bodies?"

"Just one."

"The girl?"

"Nope," Florence replied. "Surprisingly enough, she survived." She shot her eyes at Merrotti. "Us women ain't like we used to be during your time."

"You pick up that attitude during your narco days?"

"No," Florence said teasingly. "Just from hangin' around *you* all these years."

"Geez, Pam," he replied. "You make me sound like I'm a dinosaur."

"Well, you kind of are."

Merrotti cracked a smile.

Then, Florence followed with a shrug, "No offense."

Merrotti said under his voice, "None taken."

1:18 AM

THE only detail the police officer had written down from Anne's statement was that the other intruder was a male (possibly black from his dark complexion, but Anne wasn't quite sure), standing roughly six feet in height, slender frame, and as with the dead man lying over a puddle of blood, dressed in all black—not like a ninja but more like the "rough-looking" type, as she explained—black leather jacket with black jeans, scraggly hair, and a thin beard, or what fashionistas call "designer shave." However, she knew these men were anything but chic or pristine. They were, indeed, the real deal. The intruder also had a pistol. That, Anne *was* certain of. The gun was much larger than the John Doe's pistol, which was later tagged by investigators as a SIG Pro, bullet untraceable—the investigator's professional opinion was that it was sold on the black markets (the serial number had been etched away as well)—but Anne knew nothing about that or the two weapons other than what she had seen from flipping channels. "Like the ones in the movies," she told the officer. The officer responded, "You mean a machine gun?" Then, Anne: "Yeah," she said. "Like a machine gun." Other than that, the clothes, the profile, and the weapons, she remembered nothing more about the previous events. A red haze, Anne saw. In that haze were two men, as she explained to the officer, both dressed in dark clothes, both lurking through the shadows of the night.

Since Anne was still in a mild state of shock (her symptoms had become even more evident to everyone at the crime scene: pallid, clammy skin, irregular breathing, and dilated pupils), the young officer, Officer Dwayne Lawson, dispatched an ambulance and told Anne to relax while they waited for the paramedics to arrive.

1:26 AM

WHILE the ambulance was parking in the front of Anne's house, the detectives arrived at 1875 Tuttle Drive.

Inside the house, an investigator from the crime lab took several pictures of Anne's hands, both covered with bloodstains, and then the cutoff tee shirt, which was mostly damp around the upper part of her back from where her wet hair rested, and like the hands, covered in blood.

"I'm going to have to ask you to remove your clothes," the investigator said through his monotone voice.

Anne didn't budge a hair.

"Ma'am?"

Finally, she snapped from her daze.

"My colleague here will escort you to the restroom where you can change."

His colleague, a tall lady with thin brunette hair who was around the same age as the investigator, had already picked out a change of clothes for Anne.

In a quick survey, Anne eyed the gray sweater, as well as the pair of folded blue jeans, in the older lady's gloved hands.

"Will these do?" she asked. "I can grab something else if you like."

Anne didn't respond.

Instead, she acknowledged the investigator with a blank expression.

"Let me help you," she said and guided Anne to the bathroom.

After a brief struggle, she lunged forward and peeled away the shirt from her gummy skin. She rested the shirt on the sink and glanced at the bathtub, which was still full of soapy water, and then the dark outlines of her footprints exiting the bathroom. An image flashed through her mind: darkness first and then the soft glow from a candlelight burning behind her eyelids. Where there were images, Anne realized, there were sounds. The slowly moving water sent Anne into a state of relaxation, same with the faint smell of incense in the moist air.

If it wasn't for that car door outside, Anne thought vaguely, *then. . .*

Was Anne really going to do it?

She returned to the recent events.

The sudden *squeak* of the front door pulled Anne from her tranquility in the bathtub.

Then, she snapped open her eyes, dropped the razor blade from her hand, and then peered through the dimly lit bathroom, only to witness a lanky shadow sidling across the living room wall. . .

(*Would you like some help, ma'am*)

. . . A slender man dressed in all black creeping through the dark living room. . . a gun held in his right hand. . .

(*Ma'am*)

Anne pulled herself from her trance and moved her eyes to the mirror where she saw the investigator standing behind her with her back turned.

She said, "I can leave the room if you like."

With her breasts covered, Anne bobbed her head.

"Yes," she mumbled and then slipped into the sweater.

Then, without the investigator looking, Anne reached into her underwear and pulled out a USB flash drive.

One by one, she guided her legs into the jeans.

Once Anne was changed into more comfortable clothes, she secretively placed the flash drive into her pant's pocket, handed the bloody shirt to the investigator, and then exited the bathroom.

"Thank you," the investigator said as she placed the shirt inside a plastic evidence bag.

As the other police officers on the scene escorted Anne through the house and outside to the ambulance where the paramedics treated Anne on site (taking her blood pressure and checking her vitals), the two detectives approached the house.

Before the two had a chance to question Anne, the ambulance drove her to Madison Memorial.

1:29 AM

MERROTTI and his partner greeted the investigators on the front porch of Anne's house.

Merrotti was first to speak.

"What do we got?" he asked.

First, the investigator acknowledged Merrotti's exhausted state and then, secondly, without any questions, walked the two detectives through the house.

"It's a mess," the investigator said.

Merrotti: "Any witnesses?"

"No," he answered. "Well, neighbors said they heard gunfire. One neighbor across the street said she saw a man dressed in black."

"Man in black, huh?" Merrotti uttered. "Sounds like she cracked the case."

"The woman could hardly speak a word of English."

Another investigator: "Why in the hell do they live in this country if they can't even speak English? I mean, if I went to their country, I would at least *try* to learn how to speak Spanish." The investigator pointed at his chest and then shrugged. "That's me."

With a wide grin, Officer Lori Chavez said from behind, "Yeah right, Walker. Did you ever think they do know how to speak English? They just don't act like it in front of *pendejos* like you."

"Ouch," said another officer, who was also grinning.

"That'd be something," the investigator replied. "Now, wouldn't it?"

The two detectives ignored the chatter from behind and tiptoed around the debris on the hardwood floor: shards of ceramic glass from a broken vase, tiny pieces of glass from a hallway mirror, cotton balls from the couch, and fragments of aged wood and drywall from where the bullets had cut through the living room.

Merrotti examined the bead-like holes drawn like a tidal wave across the pale blue walls.

"Who exactly is this woman again?" he asked the investigator.

"Anne Roth," the investigator answered. "She's in sales."

"What kind of sales?"

"Telemarketer at USR."

"USR?" Merrotti said. "You mean like the. . . "

Florence: "Satellite Radio."

"That's the one," the investigator said with a sigh.

"Impressive," Merrotti said as he closely eyed the bullet holes in the wall.

His partner cut in once more, "Either she was one lucky woman or she has amazing survival instincts."

Then, Merrotti followed, "I'd say she had a guardian angel watching over her."

"Didn't think you believed in that kind of stuff, Merrotti."

"I don't."

The investigator led the two detectives to the body where a young police officer was patting the corpse's pants.

"Excuse me, Officer," Merrotti said with frustration. "What exactly do you think you're doing?"

The officer sprung upright.

"Uh. . . " he stuttered, ". . . I was. . . I was just checking to see if the perp had any sharp objects on him."

"He's dead, son."

Merrotti glanced at his partner in bafflement.

His partner, Florence, was baffled as well.

"Give the kid a break, Merrotti," she said to him.

Merrotti looked around the kitchen.

"Would someone get this moron out of here before he ruins our crime scene?" he said to another much older officer.

The remaining police officers exited the house while Merrotti whispered to himself, "Fucking amateurs."

The investigator kneeled down with the other detective, Florence, peeled back the corpse's sleeve, and showed her the strange tattoo on the corpse's wrist: a capital letter, **E**, which was rotated horizontally, with the letter, **v**, written on top of the spine of the letter E, which, to the naked eye, appeared like an E with antennas.

"Interesting tattoo," Florence said, thinking. "Local gang?"

"Could be," the investigator said, thinking as well.

Merrotti said quietly, "Does it matter whether it's a gang or not?"

The investigator ignored Merrotti and said to Florence, "Never seen one like this before." He shrugged. "But who knows? I'll run it through the database and we'll see what comes up." Then, he pointed at the corpse's neck. "Check out what our victim did."

Merrotti glanced around the ruined house, the overturned coffee table in the living room, the debris on the floor, the bullet holes.

He said under his breath, "They certainly screwed with the wrong girl," and then, somehow, his weary eyes mistakenly crossed his partner.

"You okay?" Florence said.

Merrotti didn't answer.

The investigator interrupted the momentary silence, "The crazy thing is, Detectives, besides her old battle wounds, she didn't even have a mark on her."

"Battle wounds?" Merrotti said suddenly. "What kind of battle wounds?"

"Don't know," the investigator said. "Maybe from a car accident?"

Merrotti stepped closer to the investigator.

"Who did you say this woman was again?"

"Telemarketer," he returned. "You know, the people who call you up during suppertime and bug the shit out of you. Those kind."

"Wouldn't know anything about that."

"Sure you wouldn't, Detective."

"Maybe she knows something," Florence said.

Merrotti drew his eyes to the corpse below.

"Maybe," Merrotti mumbled as he carefully examined the laceration around the corpse's neck.

2:49 AM

TO be safe, the doctors treated her accordingly: plenty of oxygen with a round of intravenous fluids.

Anne started to doze off when she suddenly heard a commotion coming from behind the curtain.

"Anne!" an older man cried out, his voice sharp and penetrating. "Where's my Anne!"

The next sound: footsteps, now getting closer.

Her foster parent, Harold, who was dressed in his daily sky blue dress shirt, no tie, and newspaper gray sports coat, peeked around the curtain and found his Anne resting on the hospital bed. His wife, Molly, wasn't too far behind.

They embraced Anne, Harold first and then his wife, Molly, a bloated face woman with short colored hair.

In a state of panic, Harold asked, "How are you, sweetie?"

"I'm fine," Anne said tiredly.

"Oh!" he said with relief. "Thank God!"

"I'm just. . . just a little shaken up," she said as she cleared the tears from her eyes. "That's about it."

Now standing a couple of feet away from Harold, Molly said, "What happened, dear?"

"I. . ."

"You can tell us."

"I don't know. . ."

"Those men who broke into your house, did they touch you?"

Anne said abruptly, "No."

"Molly," Harold said patiently, "please." He ran his hand over Anne's forearm and tightly gripped her bruised hand. "We're so glad you're okay." With his other hand, he patted the top of Anne's hand. "We'll get through this, Anne."

Once more, Anne's eyes swelled with tears.

"It's okay, sweetie," Harold said and then hugged Anne. "We're here for you. Whatever you need."

4:15 AM

HAROLD pulled up to the two-story stucco house located in Madison Hills.

Anne was riding shotgun, whereas Molly was sitting in the backseat.

Harold parked the silver Mercedes in the driveway, shut off the ignition, and hurried to the passenger side before Anne could step out. He helped Anne from the car.

"No place like home," he said merrily to Anne.

Not so merry, Anne returned, "Thanks, Dad."

"No need to thank me, Anne," Harold chirped. "You just go inside and get yourself some rest."

"Yeah," Anne mumbled as she walked with Harold to the house.

As before, Molly wasn't too far behind.

4:32 AM

THE touch of warm water running down Anne's face eased the pain behind her eyes.

Whenever the numbness kicked in, Anne would occasionally rotate her head and then let the water run down the backside of her neck. For a moment, the recent memory of what happened ceased to exist; and it was just Anne and the running water, the sound of it, the feel, the calmness. No one would reach her in here, her temple. Then, a tiny *squeak* from where her bare foot slid across the slick tub triggered a sequence of images in her mind's eye: the sudden *squeak* coming from the living room forced her narrow eyes from the razor blade between her fingertips to the bathroom door; she placed the blade onto the lip of the tub and eased herself from the soapy water; her prune feet inched across the cold bathroom tile, now wet from where the water dripped from her naked body. The sound of running water grew harsher now. More images sent her into a state of frenzy: Anne grabbed the pink towel from the holder and patted the sides of her neck and then her abdomen. Footsteps, Anne heard. She suddenly dropped the towel, threw on a pair of underwear, as well as a raggedy cutoff tee, grabbed her smartphone from the edge of the sink, and dialed Michael's number. Nobody answered. Instead, she got his voicemail, but she never left a message. Anne dialed 911 on the touchpad. "911," the operator said, "Please state your emergency?" Anne whispered to the operator, "There's someone in my house." Then, the operator: "I'm sorry. You're gonna have to speak up." Anne whispered, now sharply, "There's a person inside my house!" The lights in the bathroom suddenly cut off followed by the slow hum from the air conditioner.

The house was pitch black, and left in a globe of loud silence. Anne hung up the phone and ducked into the guest room as the strange man in black crept through the dining area. She clenched her teeth. Jaw tightened. Her heart pounded like a kick drum beating throughout her entire body, the ripples of each beat sending trembles down her arms and legs. The strange man made his way into her bedroom. Anne sidled behind him while, at a distance, she heard the sounds of water beating down on the porcelain behind her, a steady stream of noise cast from real time. She crept to the kitchen where her only means of protection awaited: a knife; in fact, a large one that could really do some damage. She returned to the running water, her temple. The blood in her veins boiled from the warmness of the water. Anne ignored the water and kept close to the images in her mind. She removed the knife from the holder and heard another *squeak*, this time inches away. She jerked her head to the left and witnessed another strange man entering through the back door. As Anne darted through the living room, the strange man in black drew his gun. Bright flares of gunfire suddenly flashed through the living room, briefly highlighting the shooter's face— the sight alone of the man's shadowy face raced uncontrollably through her mind, rapid flickers of his cringed face, his bared teeth, the flexed muscles protruding from his jaw line, his marbled eyes, all expressions and surroundings turning the color red in her mind's eye; and then, the shooter's perspective: the pale outline of a svelte woman gracefully leaping behind the couch, the bullets running like a zip line over her head. In her reminiscence, Anne's memories came to her in full bloom. In the flickers of gunfire, Anne recalled, his face was revealed. What stood out the most from his features was a scar on the right side of his eyebrow. The man had gotten the scar when he was not a man at all, but only a child—five years old, actually. He slipped over a bar of soap and smacked the side of his face on the faucet, which resulted in him getting twenty stitches, as well as a balloon and a lollipop to show how careless children could be. If asked about the scar, the man spoke of other legends. The story was always different. Once, he got the scar when he was sixteen while boxing. Another time, he got grazed by a stray bullet and nearly lost his eye. Anne knew absolutely nothing about these stories or who the man might have been, but she did know his face. That, she *was* certain of. . .

Anne pulled her face from the showerhead to the curtain, which slowly started to stir as if someone, not the water, had moved it.

A sharp sting of panic penetrated her insides, mostly stomach.

She carefully unfolded the edge of the curtain, only to witness her own reflection in the mirror.

Startled, she carefully stepped from the shower and locked the bathroom door. Then, she placed her face back underneath the showerhead and let the warm water run down her eyes.

4:51 AM

As both of her hands began to prune like raisins, Anne switched off the water and opened the curtains. She grabbed a towel from the holder and wrapped it around her breasts. She went directly to her smartphone, which was lying on the edge of the sink, and called Michael from the contact list.

The phone rang four times before his answering machine came on: *"Hi, you've reached Michael. Leave a message after the beep and I'll call you back as soon as I can. Thanks and have a great day.*"

This time, Anne decided to leave a message on his voicemail.

"Michael, it's me again," she said while sniffling. "Please call me. . . I. . . " a sudden pause, ". . . just call me back. I'm at my parents' house."

Anne ended the call and then sent Michael a text message.

DirtyTill30: Where are you? I need to see you right now!!!

5:02 AM

NOW that Anne was mostly dry, she put on a black tank top and a pair of purple sweatpants with the words CAN'T TOUCH THIS written over the rear of the pants.

With her dirty blonde hair dark and stringy from the recent shower, she ambled to the dresser where she picked up the USB flash drive next to a picture frame of her foster parents, Harold and Molly. Behind the picture frame, there was a collage of both men and women models and celebrities—all, of course, borderline nude—tacked on the wall. Most of the pictures were cut from girly magazines like *Seventeen* or *Cosmo* or *Vogue*. And most of the people in the pictures were actors and actresses, all standing or lying or posing in risqué positions. On the opposite side of the bedroom, she had a poster of the lead singer from Mona's Arch, Henry the Fif', who was wearing his patent black blazer with chain mail underneath, standing at a slant, one half of his mouth raised in an arch, while displaying the Fif' sign with his hand. Next to the poster was a desk with an older mac, 2006 actually, considered a prehistoric thing, even though, till this day, it ran like an old Chevy.

A sudden tap on the bedroom door sent Anne scurrying toward her bed where she quickly placed the flash drive in the drawer of the nightstand.

"Anne, sweetie," a soft voice said from behind the door.

"Come in," Anne said and squared herself to the door.

The door slowly cracked open.

"Am I interrupting?" Harold asked as he stood at the doorway.

"Just got out of the shower," she said as Harold entered the bedroom.

Nostalgically, he gazed around Anne's bedroom, at the framed pictures on the dresser from when Anne was in high school, mostly the ones where Anne was thinner, mainly during her freshmen and sophomore year, before he sat down on the edge of the bed.

Anne sat next to Harold and said, "What's up?"

"A week after Molly and I adopted you, there was a man who visited the house," he said mindfully. "He didn't look like he was from the agency. He asked about you. I asked how he knew your name. He told me he was a friend of your father's and that he wanted to make sure you were doing okay and that you were taken care of. Then, like that, the man left, never to be seen ever again."

She furrowed her brows, slid closer to Harold, and asked, "Why are you telling me this?"

"I don't know," he said with his head down. "Ever since you left, Molly has gotten worse. The drinking. The pills. It's like she can't go out in public without them."

"Has she seen a doctor?"

"Doctors can't help her," he said solemnly. "She acts like she's trapped here, Anne, like she's given up on life."

"What?" Anne's voice shifted. "Because of me?"

"No, Anne, sweetie," Harold said and touched the top of Anne's hand. "It's because. . . it's because she hates me."

"She doesn't hate you."

Harold followed, "Yes," he said. "She does." He paused in reflection. "Molly was barren." He turned to Anne for a moment. "You know this."

"Of course," Anne said.

"When the two of us were high school sweethearts, all we talked about was starting a family together," he said. "When Molly found out that she couldn't have children, I was devastated. The one woman I loved was the one woman I couldn't create life with. I knew that, if we kept trying, though, then it would work out. For years, Anne, sweetie, we tried, and each time we tried, it was pulling us apart." He let out a sigh. "Trying to raise a family was the one thing that was hurting our relationship the most. Then, out of the blue, we got a call. They found somebody, a girl. By the time we found you, Anne, it was already too late. Molly and I," another sigh, "we were already heading in opposite directions. It took me years to finally see the red flags, the signs. I remember," a shadow of a smile glimmered across his face, "that one day, the day the agency called and told us about you. Molly and I decided to give it another shot and work through our issues." The smile grew and lifted across his face, his eyes glazing over. "That day was one of the happiest days of my life, of our lives, finding you. The moment I laid eyes on you, I knew that you were special and I was the luckiest man in the world."

"Awww," Anne said, her voice cracking like a teen-ager. "Thanks, Dad."

Harold suddenly laughed, quietly though.

"You," he said, his eyes brimming with tears, "you used to make this face when you got upset." He tried to mimic the facial expression: his head held forward, slightly lowered, with his eyes squinted and his eye-brows formed into the shape of the letter V. "I re-member we would stop what we were doing and just watch you. Then, I would copy your face. We would have these stare offs. You would always win. Then, we would laugh, as if. . . as if the troubles Molly and I had were gone, even for a moment. You've come so far, Anne," Harold said closely. "We've come so far."

"I know we have," Anne said quietly.

"I don't want you to think that you had something to do with Molly and I," he said. "There was always something brewing between us. We thought having a child would make it all better. Who were we kidding? We were only delaying the inevitable."

"People can change," Anne said and shrugged her shoulders. "I guess. When you get older you either grow apart or grow closer."

Harold patted Anne on the top of her hand.

"I couldn't agree more," he replied. "But don't you worry about us. What's important now is you getting rest and trying to forget about what happened tonight."

Anne cried, "How can I forget?"

"Because you have to," Harold said seriously.

She cracked a smile and rolled her eyes up at Har-old.

"I love you, sweetie," he said and wrapped his arm around Anne. "I will never let anything bad happen to you. *Ever.*"

Anne hugged Harold.

She said into his shoulder, "I love you too, Dad."

Harold got up from Anne's bed and walked to the doorway where he stood.

"Is there anything you need?" he asked. "Anything?"

"No," Anne said, thinking. "Well," she paused, "my coat. I need to pick up my coat from the dry cleaners."

"Done," Harold said. "I'll take care of it. Anything else?"

Anne thought briefly.

"I also need to call my supervisor and tell him I'm not going to make it to work tomorrow."

"I'm on it," he said. "I'll call your supervisor first thing in the morning. Anything else?"

Then, she shook her head.

"No," Anne said. "That's about it."

"If you think of anything else, you let me know."

"Okay," she said. "I will."

"Goodnight, sweetie," he said and closed the door behind him.

"Goodnight," Anne said.

She stood by the window and scanned the neighborhood for any suspicious vehicles. There were none. The street was dead quiet, the night too.

5:49 AM

IN a dark alleyway in the projects of uptown Lansford, a man dressed in a black suit was standing in the shadows outside the orange beam of a floodlight. He was fairly short for an average man, only standing five feet seven inches; but what he lacked in height, he equally compensated with other characteristics.

The intruder who shot up Anne's house was lurking through the alleyway, searching for a man whom they called, "The Voice." He was a slender man, the intruder, as Anne described to the officers, however, *not* black. He was Latino with long curly hair and a five o'clock shadow on his face.

As the intruder paced around the alley, he sensed a presence sneaking up behind him.

He spun around and then flinched from the sight of the strange man.

A *gasp* sliced through the eerie darkness!

"The Voice?" he whispered. "It's really you? Isn't it?"

In a resonant voice, like his body, cloaked in sheer darkness, this so-called Voice interrupted, "Did she receive the package?"

The intruder quickly bobbed his head.

"I think so," he said, his voice trembling.

"You think so?"

"Cabrera said it wasn't on Martinez when he patted him down," he replied. "So, yeah. She found it. Yes!"

"How sure are you?" the Voice said as he strolled around the frightened intruder.

"A hundred percent."

"Good," the Voice said, his right hand, which was covered with a black leather glove, slowly crept over the intruder's shoulder. "It's unfortunate we lost our good friend, Martinez. He was dedicated."

"His death won't be for nothing, sir," the intruder replied. "There's no question. He sacrificed himself."

"Yes," the Voice said from behind. "A sacrifice. Well put."

"So, am I in?"

"I'm afraid there's one last thing he would like you to do before your initiation is complete."

"I'll do anything, sir," the intruder said confidently.

His gloved hand fell to his side.

"Good," the Voice said.

Without the intruder looking, he pulled out two wooden handles, which were both connected to piano wire, from his pocket.

10:23 AM

THE sound of distant sirens filled her eyes and then a loud croak from a man's throat. . .

Letting out a sudden gasp, she bolted through the recent memories and found herself on her old bed.

The light was bright in her eyes, not reds or blues, but a soft morning light, which was warm on her face, as well as the sheets around her body.

She gathered her surroundings and checked the time on the nightstand.

The time read: 10:24.

The ringing in her ears was still there, though.

She turned toward the desk and noticed the screen on her phone lighting up in two-second intervals. She rolled out of bed, picked up the phone, and read the name on the screen. She pressed the IGNORE button, which immediately silenced the ring, and then, after another thought, decided to answer the call.

"Hello," she said, rubbing away the thick crust from the inner part of her eye.

"Anne," Jamie said with a worried tone in her voice. "I just spoke to Dave. Are you okay?"

"Yeah," Anne drawled. "I was trying to get some rest."

Jamie asked, "What happened, Anne?"

Anne fought back to tears.

"After you left," she said and cleared her parched throat, "I was taking a bath when suddenly I heard a noise in the living room. When I got out, the power went out. It was dark and next thing I know. . . I see these. . . these. . . two. . . men in the living room."

"Oh my God," Jamie said. "How did they get inside your house?"

"I don't know, Jamie," Anne said. "I locked the door after you left. The police found no signs of forced entry."

Jamie asked, "Did you call the police?"

"Yeah," Anne answered, "but they didn't get there till afterwards."

"After what?" Jamie said carefully, "Anne, they didn't. . . "

"No," Anne said suddenly. "No, Jamie. One of them shot at me. I managed to get out of the way. From there, it was really all a blur. One of them left, but there was still another one in the house." She sighed, but loudly. "I did what I had to, Jamie. He was going to kill me."

"Oh, Anne," Jamie said. "I'm so sorry. . . "

Anne cried, "There was so much blood. . . "

"Anne," Jamie interrupted, "I'm sorry. Did the police find the other person?"

Once more, Anne cleared her throat.

"No."

"Where are you right now?"

"I'm at my parents' house."

"Is there anything I can do for you?" Jamie asked. "Can I bring you something to eat?"

"No," she said. "I'm fine."

"Are you sure?"

"Yeah," Anne said. "I'm fine. Really."

"Anything you need, Anne," Jamie said sternly now. "You know I'm here for you."

"I know you are," she said, the trembling easing from her voice. "You've been a good friend, Jamie. Thank you."

"I'm gonna let you go now," Jamie said. "Please, get some rest. And I'll give you a call when I get outta here."

"Okay."

"And remember, Anne, anything you need," Jamie said. "Don't hesitate to call. Okay?"

"I will."

"Okay," Jamie said. "Talk to you later."

Anne said, "Bye."

She ended the call and then checked her voice-mail.

No messages.

Next, she checked her text messages to see if Michael had texted her. As with the voicemail, she had no messages.

10:47 AM

OFFICER Lawson was only two blocks away when he received the dispatch. Second to arrive at the scene were Merrotti and Florence.

"What do we got, Officer?" Merrotti asked as he and Florence stepped from the Crown Vic and made their way to the side alleyway between the two buildings, one a Chinese restaurant and the other an apartment complex.

"The owner of Flying Wok, Mr. Chow, said he found the body while he was taking out the trash," Officer Lawson informed. "From the looks of it, he appears to have died from strangulation."

"We'll be the judge of that," Merrotti said as he nodded at the officer. "Thank you, Officer."

"No problem, sir," he said as Merrotti raised the caution tape for Florence.

She entered the crime scene and then Merrotti.

"What a gentleman," Florence said coyly and smirked at Merrotti.

He replied, "I have my moments."

The two detectives put on their gloves and approached the body, which was lying next to a dumpster. There was a thin red line around the corpse's neck from where he had been strangled to death.

"Don't see any other wounds on the body besides this one right here," Merrotti said as he pointed at the neck. "Whoever did this more than likely knew him."

"What makes you say that?"

Merrotti gazed around the gloomy alleyway.

"This place gets pretty quiet around nighttime," he said. "It would take a ghost to be able to sneak up on a man like this, especially in the middle of the night." Merrotti directed his attention back to the corpse. He squinted his eyes as he peered at the corpse's mouth. "Hold on a sec," he said abruptly and cracked open the corpse's lips. The teeth were all brown and decayed, like wood chips. The detective's face furrowed in repulsion. He said to Florence, "Meth mouth."

"Hispanic like our other perp and dressed in black and, apparently, a junkie."

Merrotti noticed the gunpowder residue on the corpse's hands. He kneeled farther down and smelled his hands.

"What are you saying, Detective?" he asked.

"Just saying." She threw a nod at Merrotti. "Gunpowder?"

"Yeah," he said, stood up, and examined the alleyway for any clues while Florence peeled back the corpse's sleeve and inspected the corpse's hands and wrists. Unlike the previous body from last night, there weren't any gang tattoos or markings on either wrist.

"What is it?" Merrotti asked Florence.

Florence shrugged her shoulders and said, "Nothing." She stood up as well and checked the alleyway with her partner. "It's nothing," she said and scanned around the dumpster.

As the two detectives came up short with any other clues that could pinpoint the murderer, other than the victim was killed by some kind of wire or string and that the victim was possibly a gang banger from the residue of gunpowder on his hands, the young officer called out from behind the caution tape, "Think I found the victim's car!"

"You check it out," Merrotti said to Florence. "I'll hang around here."

Florence left the crime scene while Merrotti hung back.

The officer walked with Florence to the victim's car.

"I typed in the license plate number in the computers," Officer Lawson said to Florence as they walked through the empty parking lot. "The plates are bogus. However, I did check the VIN on the windshield. The car belonged to Edward Jones. Mr. Jones was murdered two weeks ago. His body found outside a convenient store in Madison. Multiple stab wounds."

"And the perp?"

"The case went cold," he informed. "Never found the killer." The officer pointed at the car. "But we found the car."

They arrived at the stolen, now abandoned car.

"Hey, Lawson," Florence said, grinning. "The department could use a guy like you. Ever put any thought into becoming a detective?"

"I have a life, Florence," Lawson said optimistically. "No offense. It's just. . . " the officer shrugged, ". . . I don't think I can put in the hours you guys put in. Lately, it seems like Weathers is running you guys into the ground."

"It's not so bad," Florence said as she paced around the car.

"I do have a family, Detective."

"Well, the payoff is much better," she said flatly. "More mouths to feed."

The officer chuckled.

"Two's enough for me."

"I hear you, Lawson," Florence said as she opened the driver's side door. She removed a small flashlight from her pocket and swept the inside of the car. There were a lot of plastic wrappers on the floor mats, mostly from potato chips and other cheap snacks. She made her way to the backseat and found an empty box underneath the seat. She shone the light on the name and then the address on the delivery box: *"Anne Roth,"* the name read on the box. The address: *"1875 Tuttle Drive, Lansford, MO, 63098."* She opened the box, only to find a balled up sheet of bubble wrap and a crumbled receipt from a retail store, Jewelry Nook. On the receipt were Anne's name and address, as well as the last four digits of her credit card—the others starred out—and the words *thanks for your business* written at the bottom.

"Hey, Lawson," Florence said over her shoulder.

"Yes, Detective."

"Would you be a dear and grab my partner for me?"

"Yes, ma'am," Officer Lawson said and hurried to the alleyway where Merrotti was going through the corpse's wallet. He checked the name on the driver's license. The name read, "Jonathan Denmark," but to the detective, the corpse looked nothing like a Johnnie or a Denmark. So, Merrotti removed the driver's license from the holder and then scratched away the photograph, which revealed the *real* Jonathan Denmark, white male, glasses, definitely not a match to the victim, or, considering the discovery, the perp.

A voice from behind: "Detective?"

Merrotti stood up from his kneeled position.

"Hey, Lawson," the detective said. "Get my partner for me. Would you?"

"Funny," Officer Lawson said. "She said the same thing."

2:07 PM

THE shut of a door downstairs caused Anne to wake from her sleep.

She lay in bed for about four minutes, literally staring at the ceiling above, until she finally rolled out of bed and did the one thing that she swore she would never do while dating Michael. She didn't want to be the type—the psycho bitch always keeping tabs on her man. It wasn't that Anne didn't care what Michael did on his personal time. She respected his privacy, and with Michael, vice versa. Sort of "Whatever happens on MyCircle stays on MyCircle." She logged into the computer, pulled up the Internet, and hacked into Michael's MyCircle page. The password easy: his date of birth. She skimmed through his latest posts, mainly ranting about Lansford's awful baseball team, the Archers, or quoting lines from popular movies. What really caught Anne's eye was a couple of photographs at the bottom of the page. The first one was taken at a coffee shop, Beret. Michael and another girl, a blonde with tits twice the size as Anne's and a face that looked as if it was painted by Picasso, were sitting together on the patio and sipping from their coffee. Her body was a nine or ten, Anne deemed, but her face was a three or four at best. Anne looked yet again at the photograph and realized, after spotting the mole on the side of her cheek and her lazy eye, she knew the girl. She had seen her numerous times at the Drunken Monkey, a frequent nightclub she and Michael had visited—or at least *used* to visit. They hadn't been back since last spring. Every time they did go, they always bumped into this one blonde in particular, Ms. Party Pants, either hanging all over some desperate schmuck or a dude who had enough money to buy the entire nightclub. That one blonde, Anne didn't know her name. All Anne knew was that she was your run-of-the-mill barfly who clung onto wealthy men after a few drinks. In the blonde's case, a third royal flush. And it wasn't just her, the blonde. It was the same for each and every one of them. They got what they wanted like a free drink or a wet smooch or something else and then shooed you away like the fly you were. Anne felt herself getting the clap by just looking at her.

Anne composed her thoughts—*possible friend at work*, she thought, or even a *girl he knew from childhood*— and scrolled through other photos on MyCircle. All it took was the next three photos, which were both posted last night at 10:37 PM, to send her into another state of frenzy. The first photo was of Michael and that same blonde from Beret. They were at the same nightclub, the Drunken Monkey, posing together in front of the bar, Michael's hand grabbing the blonde's left breast and licking the side of her cheek. The second: the two inside Michael's BMW, both of their faces mashed together into a drunken kiss. The third: a hickey that Michael had left on the girl's neck, like a signature. The theme remained consistent with each photograph: Michael with the same girl, the blonde, doing physical activities together. Anne was so disgusted with the photos that she didn't even bother looking at the others, mainly taken with other girls, and logged off the computer.

4:37 PM

THE bedroom door cracked open, which caused Anne to stir in the bed.

She slowly came to and found Harold standing at the edge of the doorway.

"I didn't mean to wake you," he said as he stepped back into the hallway.

"No," Anne said as she sat upright. "I couldn't sleep." She scratched the corners of her eyes. Then, after the blur ran free from her eyes, she noticed something in Harold's hands. She asked, "What is that?"

"Your friend, Jamie, I believe," Harold said.

"Yeah," Anne said. "How did you know?"

With a bowl of soup in one hand and a cup of water in the other, Harold stepped into the bedroom.

"She stopped by the house and brought this over for you," Harold said, showing Anne the bowl of soup. "It smells delicious."

"What is it?"

"It's called ah *sopa de. . . de lima. . .* " he said carefully and then paused, ". . . I think."

"Yeah," Anne said. "It's a Spanish dish."

"She said she made it all by herself," Harold said. "A recipe that was passed down from her grandmother."

"She didn't have to do that."

"She's a sweet woman. . . and beautiful."

"Yeah," Anne said as she propped the pillows behind her back. "She's half Ecuador, half French."

"Half French, huh?" he said, his voice trailing off. "Interesting."

Anne tilted her head in dismay.

"Really, Dad?" she drawled.

Harold said, now in a high pitch voice, "What?" Next, he placed the food, as well as the drink underneath an old newspaper that he had brought from downstairs on the nightstand. "Here," he said, "get some food in you and I guarantee you'll be feeling much better."

"Thanks," Anne said and arched her head over the bowl of soup. "You're right. It does smell good."

"You eat now," he said and walked away. "Let me know if you need anything."

"I will," Anne said as she grabbed the spoon from the bowl and pushed around the shredded chicken inside the broth. "Thanks, Dad."

"You're very welcome," he said and cracked the bedroom door behind him.

4:41 PM

DURING the entire flight from LaGuardia to the Bangor International Airport, Edie Cohen, senior editor at *Flashback* magazine, stared at the last two text messages on her phone. The flight was approximately an hour and a half, but to Edie it felt like twice that. The first text message read, "See you soon." Like most editors who had been in the game for many years, Edie had gotten that warm and fuzzy feeling inside her gut once Renny broke the news to her last week. The story was going to be huge, Edie knew, like the reunion of Mona's Arch-huge. Then, the second text, which was sent last Monday morning, had thrown

Edie a wicked curveball. She had no idea what Renny meant when he texted, "I'm in danger." Was he really being serious? Or was it a joke? Writers lived and died by their words. However, Renny hardly told jokes. It wasn't because he didn't enjoy a good laugh here or there. He was never good at telling them. So, when Edie received the text, she knew Renny was in danger. Then, he ended the text with the word *please*. She wondered if he meant to text more. *Please what*, she thought. Please help?

Edie finally arrived in the small town of Whisperfront after hailing a cab outside the Bangor airport.

"Ahrighty now," the taxi driver said and parked the yellow cab outside the local sheriff's office. "We here."

Edie packed lightly, only an oversized purse that carried a change of clothes, as well as all of her makeup and stuff. She paid the taxi driver and thanked him for the ride. The temperature outside was not too different from what it was in Manhattan. Still, it was cold enough for a light jacket. Edie walked into the sheriff's office and asked to speak to the man in charge, which was none other than the sheriff of Whisperfront, Lucas Navarro, an even-tempered man who had a face shaped like a chunk of granite stone, also described around the office as a Man of Little Words. Edie explained the dire situation to the rugged sheriff, told him about one of her contributors, Renny Jacobson, and how she hadn't heard from him in several days and thought that *maybe* Renny's life was in danger. The sheriff acted as if the situation wasn't so dire as Edie had trumped it out to be. To further convince the sheriff, she even showed him the text she received from Renny on Monday. If that wasn't enough to convince the sheriff to take her to Leatherby Manor, Edie thought about the last resort. She hoped not to go there, to be so forthright and say what was really on her mind. After all, the only reason she flew all the way out here was for *him* and him only. Either they would believe her or they wouldn't or they didn't even know who *he* was. It's been so many years. . . Most people had probably forgotten about him. The worse case scenario (that was if they knew who she was talking about): they would peg her as a bloody loon.

Edie was about to change her mind and tell the local deputies the truth when the sheriff said, "I'll drive you up there, if it makes you happy."

Edie agreed, but it didn't make her happy.

4:56 PM

WHILE Anne was watching a rerun from *Blood Diaries* on the Internet and sipping from the broth of the soup, her phone quietly chirped.

She placed the bowl aside and checked the phone.

It was a text from Stan.

SweetStan: I heard the news from Dave. If there's anything u need or if there's anything I can do for u, get your mail, take out ur trash, if u want me to bring food to the house, whatever, please let me know. Hang in there, Anne!

Anne texted back.

DirtyTill30: Thanks, Stan. I appreciate that.

5:06 PM

ANNE received another text on the phone.

The sight of the text released a groan from her chest.

Michael: We still on for tonight?

Anne stared at the text on the phone for the longest time. She finally decided to ignore the text. She placed the phone aside and finished watching the rerun on the Internet.

5:18 PM

WHAT kind of sheriff has tattoos, Edie thought as she eyed the strange tattoo on the sheriff's wrist.

The sheriff found Edie's eyes fixed on his wrist. He discreetly moved his hand from the steering wheel and steered with the other one.

"We're almost there," he told Edie.

5:23 PM

WHEN they arrived at Leatherby Manor, the sheriff escorted Edie to the front door.

Sheriff Navarro knocked twice, but nobody answered.

"Looks like nobody's home," he said to Edie.

"That's bullshit," she said angrily. "He's here. I know it."

The sheriff furrowed his brows as he placed his hands over his hips.

"Is there something you're not telling me, miss?"

Edie shook her head.

"What do you mean?" she asked.

"I mean why you came all this way to a place like this?"

"And what kind of *place* is this?"

The sheriff gazed around the area, mainly the dark woods surrounding Leatherby Manor.

"Sometimes, I find myself asking the same question," he mumbled.

The sheriff still waited for an answer to his previous question.

"I told you," Edie said defensively. "My friend may be in danger."

"I got that part," he said. "But why by yourself?"

"Because maybe I'm the only person who gives a rat's ass about him," she replied, her voice sharper. "That's why. . . "

The sheriff asked curiously, "And do you know who lives here?"

"Yes," Edie hesitated. "Mr. Hopkins."

"Right," the sheriff said with a faint grin. "Do you know Mr. Hopkins?"

"No," she said with hesitation.

"Then, you wouldn't know that he's a sick man and he doesn't like to be disturbed."

"Are you going to help me or not?" Edie said to the sheriff. "All I'm asking for is a little gratitude. I'm not leaving here without my friend. He texted me and told me he was staying here. Then, days later, he texted again and told me he was in danger. Now if you don't help me sort this thing out, then I will find someone who will."

Sheriff Navarro smiled strangely.

"As you wish, Ms. Cohen," he said and knocked again.

As before, nobody answered.

The sheriff reached down and untwisted the doorknob.

"Would you look at that?" he mumbled.

The door opened.

A loud *creak* cut through the dead air. . .

First, the sheriff entered the dimly lit mansion.

Edie stayed behind.

"It's the sheriff!" Sheriff Navarro shouted out, his resonant voice carrying throughout the mansion. He turned around to Edie who hadn't moved an inch from the doorway. Then, he asked, "You coming or not?"

Edie finally stepped inside.

They searched through the entire downstairs but couldn't find any sign of Renny.

As Edie was about to call off the search, she found a trail of dried blood against the bottom of the baseboard. She kneeled down and felt a cool draft coming from a slit in the wall. She checked behind her. The sheriff was nowhere around. Just seconds ago, he was right behind her; and now, he was gone as if he was never there to begin with. Edie called out, "Sheriff Navarro." Then, when Edie received no response, she directed her attention to the baseboard. Since she had gotten this far all on her own, there was no reason to turn back now.

Intrigued by the draft, Edie ran her finger across the slit in the wall.

"You gotta be kidding me," Edie mumbled as she pressed her shoulder against the wall.

A hidden door sprung open from the wall and revealed another room, which was no larger than a walk-in closet.

Edie followed the blood trail to a computer station. Next to the computer were a wireless router, as well as a modem, and a spool of wires running into a large conduit.

She stepped farther inside and found another desk. There, she found a mobile jammer, which she hadn't seen in years. She wondered why in the hell a sick old man would want a mobile jammer in a place like this, which probably didn't even have good reception (Edie checked her phone and noticed one bar over her signal, barely flickering). Most importantly, she wondered why in the hell would he have a secret room.

As Edie walked around, she came across a phone, Renny's phone, as well as his laptop! The two had been smashed to bits.

"What happened here?" she asked herself.

The answer never came to her.

Instead, something else did. . .

As soon as Edie rotated toward the open doorway, a plastic bag was suddenly forced over her head. The only thing she could make out was a black glove. Two of them, she saw, balled into fists pressed against both of her cheeks. Edie struggled and kicked and gasped for oxygen, but the man in black was too powerful for her.

5:36 PM

As Anne picked up the newspaper with two wet rings, one from the bowl of sopa de lima and the other from the glass of water, she found herself eyeing the drawer. She placed the newspaper, as well as the dirty dishes aside, and opened the drawer. There, she found the USB flash drive. She stared at the flash drive for what felt like the longest time. A drop of blood, which was now dry and nearly black, was caked on the side of the drive. *What does this mean?* Not the blood, but the flash drive in her hand. And what about *the necklace?* But most importantly, Anne thought, *why this?* Anne slid the switch upward from the housing of the drive, which revealed the USB connector.

She stood up from the bed and went to the bathroom where she wiped away the dried blood with a damp piece of toilet paper.

Once the USB flash drive was clean, she decided to insert the connector into the port on the backside of her computer. Having done this, the computer suddenly woke with a noisy *click* and then a steady and yet quiet hum. The screen lit, revealing the desktop image of what was known as the "Devil's Throat," part of the Iguazu Falls located in Argentina.

A small icon of a USB flash drive labeled RENNY popped up on the bottom of the screen.

With the mouse in her hand, she moved the cursor over the name, RENNY, and double-clicked on the icon.

There, in the Finder window, two blue folders, one named STACEY'S STORY and the other named A WEEK WITH MR. HOPKINS, appeared before Anne's eyes.

Anne double-clicked on the very first folder, *Stacey's Story*, and skimmed through the notes and interviews inside the word documents. The Stacey in the story was the same Stacey who was reported missing a couple of years ago, Stacey Dilworth. Any person who watched TV or read the newspaper knew as much about Stacey Dilworth as her own two parents. However, there were always two nagging questions people asked: What was real? What was false? Anne remembered watching the constant reports and updates on the news, wondering whether they were true or false. Ten-year old girl disappeared on her way home from school. That, of course, was *true*. No question. The rest was in the air. All cops found were a bloody shoe and a barrette from Stacey's hair, which both matched Stacey's DNA. For weeks, the residents of the town, Hillsboro, Colorado, as well as cops and volunteers, combed the entire state of Colorado; but after the trail went cold, the case went cold and people just stopped searching for young Stacey Dilworth.

Anne closed the folder and directed her attention to the other one.

"*Mr. Hopkins. . .* " Anne said to herself.

She highlighted the folder and hit the quick key shortcut, Command + I (I, meaning *Information*), on the keyboard. Another much smaller window popped up on the left-hand side of the screen, revealing the info within the folder: Kind – folder, Size – 12.3 GB, Created – Sunday, October 12, 2014 10:23 PM, Modified – Monday, October 20, 2014 9:48 AM.

Anne closed the information window and double-clicked on the folder.

> A Week With Mr. Hopkins
>> Journal Notes
>> Tape Recordings
>> Photos
>> Miscellaneous

Anne double-clicked on the folder, *Journal Notes*.

> Journal Notes
>> The Email
>> Thoughts
>> Journal Entry 10.13.2014.doc
>> Journal Entry 10.14.2014.doc
>> Journal Entry 10.15.2014.doc
>> Journal Entry 10.16.2014.doc
>> Journal Entry 10.17.2014.doc
>> Journal Entry 10.18.2014.doc
>> Journal Entry 10.19.2014.doc
>> Journal Entry 10.20.2014.doc

Intrigued and yet, at the same time, somewhat confused, she moved the cursor over the drive's icon and read the name below.

"Renny," Anne whispered. *Renny.* "Where have I heard that name before?"

She double-clicked on the last journal entry, *Journal Entry 10.20.2014*.

The word document opened.

Anne skimmed through the first part of the entry:

Woke up extra early to finish our final interview. I finally asked him who this Anne girl was.

Anne paused for a moment.

Read.

At first, he acted as if he didn't know what I was talking about. Then, I told him that I overheard Diego talking on the phone. Leon came clean, and what he told me completely blew my mind. Ready the presses. I got a story to tell! I can't wait to get back home where I can finalize this baby and hand it over to Edie. Somehow, I need to find a way to email her the story in case anything happens to me.

Anne decided to close the document.

Next, she double-clicked on the first document, *Thoughts*.

Closing up shop when I received an email from a man named Marcus Hopkins. . . it can't be, not him, not *The* Marcus Hopkins. Sure enough, it was him.

The email, Anne thought.

She closed the document and opened up another, which turned out to be *not* a document but a 33KB JPEG image, which had been taken as a snapshot from Renny's computer screen. He later renamed the file from Screen shot 2014-10-12 9.34.02 PM to *The Email*.

Anne double-clicked on the JPEG. . .

From: thejs@idiscover.dot
Date: Sunday, October 12 9:13 PM
To: rjacobson1@flashbackmagazine.dot
Subject: Invitation

Dear Mr. Jacobson,

You do not personally know me, but I assume you have heard of me. My name is Marcus Hopkins. I have been following your work for some time now and have come to the conclusion that you are the right person for the job. For twenty-six years, as you may already know, I have worked for an organization known as JeneCorp. During my time at JeneCorp, I developed a special relationship with a gifted individual who needs no further explanation. That individual was named Leon Dorsey, but you may know him as Freeze. The reason for my email is that I would like to tell the real story about my dearest friend, Mr. Dorsey, for the sake of bringing to light all of the false allegations. There have been many speculations in the past, mainly negative or hearsay, which have forced me into a life of solitude. Now is the time to put those rumors to an end, Mr. Jacobson, and I want you to be the person to bring forth *the truth*. Will you be the one to finally tell Freeze's story?

The choice is yours, Mr. Jacobson.

Anne removed her eyes from the computer screen.

"Renny Jacobson?" Anne said as she checked the drawers of the desk. "The writer?"

She hastily stood up from the chair and scrambled around the bedroom for the magazine. There was this one, Anne remembered, it had to be in here somewhere. *If it wasn't here*, Anne thought as she searched through her closet, *then it was back at the house*. She tossed old clothes out of the way, but came up short. She checked the top shelf of the closet, but she mostly found old shoeboxes and game systems, which had been collecting years of dust. She moved her search underneath the bed, but didn't have any luck. She decided to end the search exactly where she started. She sat back down in the chair and focused her attention on the screen.

"Okay, Renny," she said to the computer, "let's find out who you really are."

Anne minimized the document and launched the Internet from the dock.

Firstly, she googled the name *Renny Jacobson* on the search engine. There were tons of Renny Jacobsons—mostly has-beens on MyCircle, a couple of doctors, Dr. Jacobson from Pittsburg and then another Dr. Jacobson, a cardiologist from Lansford, but only Renny Jacobson caught her eye: contributing editor for *Flashback* magazine. Anne moved the cursor to the top of the page and clicked on the link of the first site in the search engine:

www.flashbackmagazine.dot/contributors/renny-jacobson

On the website, Anne found many articles that Renny had written, mostly about celebrities, throughout his brief career with *Flashback*. There were a couple of television show reviews, specifically on certain episodes. His most recent work was about true crime stories, mainly strange murders, massacres, and, as reported with the Stacey Dilworth story, abductions. She exited the website and opened the following website, which was Renny's MyCircle page. There, Anne found Renny's personal interests, his "FAVS." Below his profile was a list of his fav TV shows, including *Blood Diaries* and *Wicked*. His fav food was Thai food, which happened to be Anne's fav food! He also enjoyed watching Korean movies, which, you guessed it, happened to be Anne's fav. She continued to read through Renny's favs, most of them close, if not, identical to Anne's favs.

Next, Anne checked out a couple of photos, mostly selfies. Renny wasn't a GQ model, but he was a fairly handsome man with a crew cut, fairly thin, the kind of man who—Anne assumed—didn't have much trouble with the ladies.

After Anne spent a couple of minutes on Renny's MyCircle page, mostly checking out his photos, she opened up his Chatterz page. There, he had 23,000 chirps, 28,000 stalking, and 38,000 stalkers.

Anne read Renny's latest chirp:

> Renny Jacobson
> @RenJacobson
>
> @FlashFan13 Doesn't get any better than this. . . sipping on gin and tonics, eating lamb shanks, and watching clouds
> pic.chatterz.dot/wm3EUdJA
> 3:02 PM – 13 Oct 2014
> **28** RECHIRPS **17** FAVORITES

Anne noticed Renny had posted a picture on his Chatterz page. She clicked on the link. The picture was taken with Renny's smartphone. It was of him holding an empty glass of gin and tonic and a plate of lamb shanks and what looked like a side of asparagus on a tray next to his lap. Behind him was a breathtaking view from his airplane window: a blanket of clouds with the fading sun casting a shade of pink across the horizon.

7:37 PM

ANNE was making her way downstairs when she heard the clinking and clanking sounds from the dishes and silverware being loaded into the dishwater. She arrived at the edge of the kitchen, only to find Harold loading dirty plates into the dishwater and then Molly, as suspected, polishing off her second glass of red wine at the table.

After Molly finished the rest of the bottle by pouring herself another glass of wine, Anne inched into the kitchen.

Harold caught Anne in the corner of his eye.

"There she is, Sleeping Beauty," Harold said gladly as he turned away from the sink. He pointed to the plate of spaghetti and slices of garlic bread on the counter. "I made you a plate, if you're hungry."

Anne held her hand over her stomach.

"No thanks," she said, displaying a look of disgust over her face. "I'm still a little full from earlier."

"Well," Molly said, the volume of her voice higher than average, "we can just wrap it up and stick it in the refrigerator if you like and you can eat it later whenever you get hungry."

"Yeah," Anne said with a smirk. "Sure."

Molly got up from the table and approached Anne. "Did you sleep well, dear?"

"I did," she said.

Molly rubbed Anne's shoulder.

"That's good."

Anne motioned to the porch outside.

"I'm going grab some fresh air," she said.

"You might wanna grab a coat, Anne," Molly declared, her voice still raised. "It's pretty nippy out there. Last thing you wanna do is catch a cold. . . "

"I got it," she said with hostility as she walked away from the kitchen.

She grabbed an old coat from the hallway closet and exited through the front door. She walked around the side of the house while lighting up a joint that she had found in the bottom of her drawer. The joint was roughly around a year old, and the weed inside was about as dry and brittle as the autumn leaves scattered around the backyard. Anne coughed a couple of times from the first drag, but then acquired the taste.

While staring down at her phone, checking her emails and text messages (wondering if Michael was *ever* going to text her back), surfing FindYourRomeo for any nibbles, she wandered blindly around the deck in the backyard until the joint was halfway smoked.

A *squeak* from the house!

The backdoor closed.

Anne immediately slipped the phone inside her pocket and concealed the joint behind her back.

"So, when did you start smoking?" Harold asked as he stepped outside.

Anne replied, "What do you mean?"

"I can smell that junk a mile away," he said, rubbing the sides of his arms.

Anne glanced down at the tightly rolled joint cupped in her hand.

"Only smoke when I'm stressed out," she said, her body shrinking. "Don't tell, Mom."

"Don't worry," he said. "I won't."

"It's not like I'm a stoner."

"I know you're not, Anne."

"I'm *really* stressed out," she said. "With everything that's happened, with last night, work. I'm just stressed out. . ."

"Well," Harold said as he walked over to Anne, "I guess you have every reason to be." He held out his hand. "May I?"

"May you what?"

"I promise I won't tell your mother," he said and winked at Anne. "Our little secret."

Anne smirked, this time wider.

"Really?"

"You're not the only one around here who's stressed out."

"Where's my dad and what did you do to him?"

"Anne," Harold said, lowering his head.

Anne handed Harold the joint.

He took a long drag.

As with Anne, he coughed a little after he exhaled.

"Where did you get this stuff?" he asked as he sniffed the end of the joint.

"It's pretty old," Anne said, laughing. "I found it upstairs in my bedroom."

Harold handed the joint back to Anne.

"I shouldn't be smoking this," Harold said. "Your mother would kill me, especially after me getting all over her case the other day for, you know, the pills. She's a different person when she takes them, Anne. And, lately, she's been mixing them with alcohol, which does *not* help."

Anne asked, "Have you tried to help her?"

"I hid her pills once," Harold said. "It wasn't a pretty sight."

"You have to," Anne said, "otherwise, she's going to destroy herself."

"I know," Harold said, sighing.

He bundled up from the chilly weather and gazed out into the bright sky, the stars. He directed his attention to Anne, who, after a minute of thought, put out the joint on the side of the deck.

"Anne," he said.

Anne turned her attention to Harold.

"Yeah," she said.

"Are you happy?"

"What do you mean?"

"I mean, are you happy," he repeated, "you know, with your life?"

Anne turned away.

"I don't know," she said. "I mean, not really."

"Let me put in a word with Roger," Harold said closely. "You could be making twice as much, less hours." He leaned even closer. "Plus, you don't have to deal with people, especially a bunch of jerks all day. I know how people can be."

"I told you, Dad," Anne said sternly. "I don't need your help. Besides, it beats flipping burgers."

"But it's an opportunity, Anne," he said louder. "There are a lot handsome guys who work there. And they're good guys too, Anne."

"Thanks, but I'm still with Michael."

"You are?"

"Yeah," she said. "I am."

Harold raised his hands in surrender.

"I didn't mean to pry," he said. "I'm just trying to help. If you don't want my help, then I completely understand. I respect that. You're a grown woman." A tense silence filled the conversation. Harold sighed once more. "I'm gonna finish up inside."

Anne didn't respond.

Yet, she stood there staring into the dark woods behind the house.

"You know you can stay here as long as you like," Harold said from behind. "This is your home too, Anne."

He attempted to hug Anne, but then eased away from her and walked off.

As he approached the back door, Harold turned his shoulder.

"By the way," he said, "the man who visited you when you were younger, his name came to me while Molly and I were eating dinner. Hopkins," Harold said.   "His name was Marcus Hopkins.   Thought you'd like to know."

10:49 PM

ANNE thinking: *Marcus Hopkins.*

Where have I heard that name before?

As Anne tossed and turned in her bed, the sheets coiling around her body like a spring, she thought more about the Marcus Hopkins on the USB flash drive and then that one strange name, *Freeze.* Surely, she wondered, they couldn't be related. There were a lot of people named Marcus Hopkins out there.

What are the odds?

She rolled out of bed and woke up her computer.

After Anne logged into the computer, she pulled up the Internet. She typed the name Marcus Hopkins in the search bar. As she thought, there were a lot of people named Marcus Hopkins, none of whom had caught her eye. There was even a Marcus Hopkins on MyCircle, but he was a couple of years younger than Anne. Based on mere assumption, the Marcus Hopkins Anne was looking for was probably in his forties or fifties. She decided to log off the computer.

As Anne slid back underneath the bed sheets, her phone suddenly chirped!

She reached across the bed and picked up the phone from the nightstand.

Anne read the text message, "I'm outside."

As before with Michael's text message, she thought about whether or not she should respond.

Anne texted back.

DirtyTill30: I'm not at my house.
Michael: I know

She quickly rolled out of bed and checked the bedroom window. She cut off the nightlight and peered out the window. There, in the backyard, she saw Michael standing slouched with his eyes aimed directly at her window.

Michael: Can I see you?

Slightly flustered, she walked away from the window.

DirtyTill30: Give me a minute

Anne threw on some sweatpants and a sweater and crept downstairs where she found Michael standing outside on the porch. He was wearing a white collared shirt, top two buttons unbuttoned, with the sleeves rolled up his forearms. He peeked inside the house and then, once he saw Anne making her way to the backdoor, he took a couple of steps back and gradually eased his hand up in a wave.

Anne didn't wave back.

Instead, she carefully opened the backdoor.

"I went by your house," Michael was first to speak. "Your neighbor told me what happened."

He stepped inside the house and hugged Anne.

"Are you okay?" he said into her shoulder.

His mouth ran up the side of her neck, and then, once he reached her chin, he made an attempt to kiss her on the lips.

In return, Anne immediately retracted from the smell of alcohol and cigarette smoke on his breath.

"Where have you been, Michael?" Anne interrupted. "I called you like a dozen times."

Michael replied, "My phone hasn't rung once."

He reached his hand in his pocket to pull out his phone.

"You reek," Anne said sharply.

"After I stopped by your house and found out you weren't there, I talked to your neighbor and she said she thought you were staying with your folks," Michael explained. Every now and then a slur would slip into his voice, especially after an s, like *she said she* or *staying*. "I figure you probably didn't want to be disturbed. Then, my boys, Todd and Jonah, called me up and they wanted to know if I wanted to grab a drink," he said, this time louder. "I only had like two drinks, baby." He ran his hand over her cheek. "But how are you?"

Anne puckered her face in disgust.

"You're going to wake up my parents."

"Sorry," he whispered. "Anne, baby, what happened to you? Your neighbor said they took you to the hospital." He scanned her body and checked for any visible injuries. "Are you hurt?"

"I'm fine, Michael," she said coldly.

Michael stepped in closer.

"You mad at me," he said.

Anne didn't answer.

"What did I do?"

She folded her arms across her chest.

"That's the problem, Michael," she said. "You didn't *do* anything. I was here alone when I needed you the most. And you were nowhere around. You were too busy getting loaded with your friends."

"Anne," Michael returned, "what about you? We scheduled this dinner a week ago and when I texted you earlier you ignored me."

"I was resting, *Michael*," Anne said, trying to restrain her voice. "Do you know why? Because I didn't sleep at all last night because two men broke into my house and nearly killed me!" Louder now. "That's why! So sorry I upset you by not responding to your text! It's not like you haven't done it before. . . ."

Michael tried to speak, but Anne quickly cut him off.

"What are you doing, Michael?"

"What do you mean?"

"What do you want from me?" she asked. "You think you can just show up here at eleven o'clock at night and just hang out with me. What do I look like to you? A hooker? Is that what you think I am? A hooker you can just call up whenever you like. . . fuck whenever you want to fuck? Because to me that's what it's starting to seem like, Michael." She shrugged. "You don't even call me anymore."

"That's not true," Michael announced. "I text you."

"Right," she said sarcastically. "You text me. What if I don't want you to text me?"

"Then, what do *you* want?"

"It's not about what I want anymore," Anne said angrily. "It's about you. If you really want to be with me, then *you* have to prove it to me. Do you know how little you make me feel, Michael? Like I'm just someone you hang out with whenever you have nothing better to do than get drunk and watch football with your friends." She leaned in closer, close enough for Michael to see the tears forming around her eyes. "I *needed* you, Michael."

"Anne. . . ."

"Do you even know what happened?"

"I asked you?"

Michael touched Anne on the arm.

In return, she moved her arm away from his grip.

"Don't do this to me, Anne," he said. "Don't shut me out now. Please tell me."

"I. . . " she struggled to catch her breath, ". . . I want you to leave."

"Please, Anne. . . "

With the anger carefully restrained in her voice, Anne said deeply, "I don't have to explain anything to you anymore."

"Anne. . . "

Her eyes sharpened.

"Leave!"

"Anne, sweetie?" Harold said from behind Anne and stepped into the kitchen, "Is there a problem here?"

"No problem," Anne said to Harold. "Michael was just leaving."

Michael leaned forward to kiss Anne on the lips, which caused her to tense up in her stance. She closed her eyes, not acknowledging Michael, as the tears ran down her cheeks.

Harold moved farther into the kitchen, forcing Michael out the door.

"What was that all about?" Harold asked and locked the door behind Michael.

"I don't want to talk about it," she said, sniffling.

Harold turned to Anne.

"Here," he said and reached in his pocket. "I stole this from your mother's purse. It'll help you sleep."

Anne grabbed the Xanax and washed it down with a glass of water.

As she rested the glass on the countertop, a sudden pain rippled across her eyes.

Harold couldn't help but notice Anne's obvious discomfort: the crow's feet digging alongside the corners of her eyes; her fingers caressing the backside of her eyelids; and then, finally, a long, dreadful sigh escaping from somewhere wet and murky inside her chest.

"Are your contacts hurting you again?" Harold asked.

"I'm not wearing them," she answered. "I left them at the house."

"Take these then," he said and grabbed the reading glasses from the breast pocket on his bathrobe. "I got an extra pair upstairs. You know me. Without my glasses, I'm as blind as a bat."

"I'm fine. . . " she said, ". . . really."

"Are you sure?"

"Yeah."

Harold inserted the glasses back into the breast pocket.

"I just need to get some sleep."

Harold leaned forward and kissed Anne on the forehead.

"Sweet dreams," he said and exited the kitchen.

As Harold made his way halfway upstairs, Anne said from the base of the staircase, "Dad?"

Harold turned around.

"Yes, sweetie."

"That guy, the one you talked about. . . " Anne said unsteadily, ". . . who visited you. . . "

"What guy?"

"Hopkins?"

"Yes," he said curiously. "What about him, Anne?"

"Do you remember what he looked like?"

Harold drifted into thought.

"Ah let's see," he said slowly. "I remember he was a tall man, well-dressed."

"Was he white?"

"No," Harold said as he took one step farther downstairs. "He was black. Why do you ask, Anne?"

"Just curious," Anne said as she shrugged her shoulders. "I guess."

"Well, if you're thinking about looking him up on the computer, then don't even bother."

"Why?"

"I tried many times," he said. "The man's a ghost." He smiled at Anne. "Save yourself the trouble and get some rest, Anne. Will you?"

Anne bobbed her head in agreement as Harold walked up the stairs.

CHAPTER 4

THURSDAY, OCTOBER 23, 2014

NINE hours later, Anne woke from her vacant dreams with warm rays of sunlight glistening over the side of her face. Her dreams were exactly that, vacant. Nine hours ago, the bar of Xanax that Harold gave her hit her like a swift smack to the backside of her head while she was brushing her teeth. Anne didn't remember a thing from the time she left the bathroom to the time she stumbled into bed. The second Anne's face hit the pillow she was out. Then, nine hours later, Anne woke without carrying a single dream or thought inside her head—not even a memory. First, Anne witnessed, there was a calm ocean of darkness. Seconds later, the light came on like an old incandescent light bulb past the blurry horizon. The light brightened ever so brightly. A yellow ray of sunlight shining over the black sea revealed the stony faces of models and celebrities posted on the walls of her bedroom. There was one model in particular: a bearded man with hair like cauliflower. The strange man's face faded from her eyes, which left Anne in a state of wonder. *Amazing*, she thought as she stretched her arms to the ceiling, how a single pill could teleport one's body from one time period to another—time travel, in substandard form. Anne was now refreshed like a spring chicken, not groggy, as she might have predicted. The bottom part of her lip was partially caked with dried toothpaste from the night before. She moistened the toothpaste with her tongue and then licked it away until her chin was clean. Her senses slowly came back to her: first, the sight of girly posters displayed around the bedroom; second, that taste of peppermint on the tip of her tongue; third, the feel of warm shag carpet between her toes; fourth, the smell of rich coffee lingering in the air; and finally, Anne's fifth sense, the sound of two dogs barking across the street. And for a moment, things were okay—*back to normal*, she thought to herself. Then, she pulled herself from her current environment and ventured into her thoughts. The thought of yesterday as well as the night before—Anne killing another person in self-defense—and then most importantly, the information on the USB flash drive, stirred a sense of panic throughout her body. Anne didn't feel the least disconcerted from killing the intruder, although in the back of her mind Anne knew somehow the dead man was now going to be a part of her life like a tumor, only growing in size if she let it. He might've had a family who loved him or even a woman who was the sole purpose for his existence. Hell, a couple of rug rats. He might've had a pastime besides killing—but Anne didn't care the least about any of that. He might've had a favorite color that he sported on Sundays—Anne doubted it. When Anne thought of him, the dead man, all she saw through her mind's eye was the color crimson red; first, a single drop of it dribbling from an open wound and then an endless stream of red drowning her thoughts. He remained as a poster child of death, and how close it was to access; and it was up to Anne to determine whether or not his legacy would consume her entire thinking.

She scrambled toward the nightstand and found the flash drive sitting there on a stack of owner's manuals for the computer and other electronic devices.

Pushing aside the dead man in her thoughts, she picked up the USB flash drive and eyed it closely in her hand.

Then, as Anne ambled toward the computer, the doorbell *chimed* with a sunny melody.

Anne carefully inserted the flash drive inside a music box that Molly had given her when she was younger and listened to the front door opening downstairs.

"Can I help, you gentlemen?" Harold said from below.

She sauntered from her bedroom and made it to the landing where she saw what looked like two detectives, a man and a woman, standing on the front porch. Both detectives were nicely dressed. One was a white man with a lot of years on his face who was wearing a beige trench coat that looked like something out of a J.C. Penney catalogue; and the other one, a black woman, dressed in a black pea coat, much younger—at least ten to fifteen years younger— her hair parted to one side of her scalp, cute and yet modest. Both of them were holding out their wallets and displaying badges for Harold to see. The two certainly didn't look as if they were going anywhere any time soon, Anne realized, as she peeked over the banister. Then, she heard the man refer to himself as "Detective," which immediately confirmed her suspicion. Anne listened closer by extending her body past the banister, head arched like a giraffe over the staircase. She thought she heard Harold say something

like: "She's *asleep right now. . .* " and then, ". . . if you would, *please come back* at a later time. . . "

The detective responded, "It's vital that we talk to your daughter, Mr. Roth. We'll take only a minute of her time. We promise."

Harold stuck his left foot behind the door, Anne saw.

Then, the conversation faded slightly, their voices muffled from the door.

Anne walked back to her bedroom and glanced through the window at the unmarked cruiser parked in front of the house. Not too far from the house, she saw two news vans drive past another car, long and black like a Cadillac or Crown Victoria, parked along the curb. Anne didn't know what kind of car it was, the black car, but she had seen similar ones in the movies, like the ones the special agents drove, that kind. There was only one agent she could think of, but she wondered why *that* kind of agent would be parked on the street. She counted two men inside the black car. The men didn't look a thing like the agents she was thinking of; in fact, she swore the two men were wearing police uniforms. Anne peered closer. The driver's side window was cracked far enough for the eyes to see through. And the eyes, Anne realized, were staring precisely at her (at least that was what she thought), even though the bedroom window had a reflective tint over the glass.

Startled from the strange men parked outside, she walked back to the landing where she heard Harold still talking below. He was still standing in front of the doorway, left foot wedged behind the door, which was still cracked far enough for Anne to see the two detectives standing outside.

"*Do you know. . . any enemies, Mr. Roth?*" one of the detectives asked.

"*Not. . . I'm aware. . .*" Harold responded as Anne listened closer. "*She's. . . good girl. . . went through a rough patch before we adopted* . . . Nobody wanted her." Anne took a couple of steps down the staircase and listened closer to the conversation. "She went through two other families before us. They couldn't handle her. They said she was too much of a problem for them. Never talked. Very shy. Unsociable. Short temper. One day, police found her on the street. Alone. She had no birth certificate, no social security number. It's like the world had abandoned her. We tried to track down one of foster parents, but it was a dead end. Whoever he was, he ah. . . " Harold paused, ". . . ah he did a number on her."

"Care to explain?"

"He abused her," he explained as, not too far away, Anne's face turned pale from the story. She inched farther down the stairs and listened even closer. "When my wife and I first met Diana, we were unsure whether or not there was a chance for her, but we decided to raise her anyway. The first year was extremely tough. My wife found a couple of hypnotherapists online who dealt with children coping with past traumas, but, after the first consultations, they told us that the only way to help her was through more extreme measures. . . "

"What kind of trauma?"

A bedroom door suddenly opened from above!

Anne turned her shoulder and found Molly waddling toward her old bedroom.

She walked back up the stairs.

"Mom?" Anne said with a rattle in her voice.

"*Oh,*" Molly said abruptly. "You're up early."

Harold heard the distant commotion upstairs, mainly the conversation between his wife and adopted daughter. Molly's voice had a way of traveling like a cave echo throughout the house. For many years, Harold had gotten accustomed to that voice. *But,* he wondered, *did they hear her voice?* He put aside the suspicion and asked the detectives if they could come back later, of course, when Anne was awake.

From above, Anne made out what Harold said to the detectives, his raised voice signifying an end to the conversation.

She suddenly blurted out, "Dad!"

The detectives rotated back around.

Harold tentatively glanced into the house before closing the door.

Anne poked her head through the crack.

She asked, "You two are detectives?"

"We are," Merrotti said. "You must be Anne Roth."

"That's right," she said as Harold stepped out of the way.

"If you don't mind, we would like to ask you a couple of questions," Merrotti said. "It will only take a couple of minutes."

"Sure," Anne said.

Harold opened the door, wider this time.

He said, "Come on in, I guess."

9:13 AM

HAROLD carried two mugs of coffee, one with lots of cream and lots of sugar and the other black, into the living room where the three were sitting, the two detectives, Merrotti and Florence, on the couch and Anne in the chair across from the couch. He set the warm mugs of coffee on the coffee table.

"Thank you, Mr. Roth," Florence said.

Then, Merrotti: "Thanks."

"You're welcome," he said and then gestured to Anne.

"Yes," she said. "Please."

Harold walked back into the kitchen and brought Anne a mug of coffee as well.

"If you need anything else. . . " he said as he rubbed Anne on the shoulder.

"I will," she interrupted as Florence carefully watched the interaction between Anne and Harold. "Thanks."

"So, Anne," Merrotti said as Harold exited the room, "we know how hard these past couple of days have been for you, so we'll be as brief as possible." He turned to Florence and nodded. His partner pulled out a folder and placed it on the coffee table. "Do any of these men look familiar to you?"

Next, he pulled out two photographs, one being a photograph taken from a crime scene—a close-up on the man Anne had murdered, this "Martinez" guy whom the strange men had spoken of in the alleyway (there was a yellow sticky note covering the gaping hole in his neck)—and the other being a mug shot of the man who was found dead in the alleyway next to the Flying Wok.

"Start with this one," Merrotti said as he placed the mug shot on the coffee table in front of Anne. "Was this the man who was at your house on Tuesday night?"

Anne leaned forward and studied the face in the mug shot.

Right off the bat, Anne noticed the scar on the side of his face. How could she forget such a scar? In her mind's eye, she witnessed the shooter's face flickering in the bright flashes of gunfire. Each flash revealed a feature on the shooter's face. One flash: his mad eyes.

Another: both his sharp grimace and his wide grill. Lastly: *that* scar, same one in the mug shot.

"No," she said finally as she cleared her throat with a swallow. "I mean he doesn't look familiar. It was dark."

The detective studied Anne's blank face.

"Are you sure?" he asked her.

"Yeah," she answered. "I'm sure."

"His name is Raymond Santiago, also known as the *Stingray* on the streets."

"Stingray?" Anne returned. "What kind of name is Stingray?"

"Raymond enjoyed sneaking up on bystanders," Merrotti said as he squared his body to Anne. "He would stab them in the back with a switchblade and steal their money. To Raymond, it was easier than robbing a convenient store. He was a petty thug, Anne. He got involved with a local gang called the Blacktops. One day, Raymond here got caught sneaking up on the wrong bystander, an undercover cop. He did a few years behind bars. We think he might have been involved in another gang besides the Blacktops—"

Florence interrupted, "We don't really know that yet."

"Well, not exactly," Merrotti said. "All we *do* know was that this man here, Raymond Santiago, was found Wednesday morning eleven miles from your residence." The detective's face went grim, Anne witnessed. "He was strangled to death," he said to Anne. "So, may I ask you where you were Wednesday morning?"

Anne picked up the mug shot.

"This man is dead?"

"Yes," Merrotti said. Then, he followed up with the same question as before. "Where were you Wednesday morning around six o'clock?"

"I was here," Anne said innocently.

"Can you prove that?"

Anne placed the mug shot back on the table.

Harold couldn't help but overhear the conversation.

"Of course she can," he said bitterly as he stepped into the living room. "I picked Anne up at the hospital and we came directly to the house. She hasn't left the house since."

Merrotti returned with a shrug.

"I just had to ask, Mr. Roth," he said.

Harold pointed to the mug shot on the table. "You think my Anne had something to do with this man's death?"

"That's not what we're saying," Merrotti said patiently. "We're crossing off any potential suspects. I assure you. We want to catch this guy as much as you do."

Harold turned to Anne.

"Are you sure this wasn't the guy who was at your house?" he asked her.

"Yes," Anne said loudly. "I'm positive."

"How about this other guy?" Harold asked the detectives.

Anne's eyes mistakenly crossed the photo of the other guy on the coffee table. All Anne could see was a dying man lying before her, a hole in his neck, him taking his last breaths, the blood being wringed from his veins by gravity.

(*We're still working on identifying the suspect*)

The detective's voice pulled Anne from her deep thoughts.

Then, Florence said, "For now, all we know is that he was illegally living here."

Merrotti: "I have to ask you, Anne. Did you have any beef with anyone? Anybody who might've had a grudge?"

Anne shook her head.

"No," she said.

"Anyone on the street?"

Anne shook her head once more.

"In your workplace?"

Again, Anne shook her head.

Harold asked, "What kind of person would want to hurt Anne?"

"Well, if these men were a part of a gang, then more than likely it was an initiation and Anne was targeted."

"Initiation?" Harold asked confusedly as he stood behind Anne. "What kind of initiation? Like a cult?"

"Most of the time with gangs we're looking at robbery, but every now and then, especially with these types of characters, we're dealing with murder."

Harold's face went long, his eyes glazed.

"*Murder*. . . Oh geez."

"I know it's hard to take in, but those two men were there to kill your daughter," Merrotti said. "For what reason, we don't know yet."

Florence: "Ms. Roth, is there anything else you can tell us that may help us with our investigation?"

Anne hung her head.

"I don't know," she said toward the floor, "it was like, I don't know, I just wanted to live. That's all. I didn't want to die, especially in my own house." She raised her head and looked the detectives in the eyes. "I just wanted to live."

"Of course," Merrotti said with a nod.

Harold asked, "Do you think she will be safe to go back to her house?"

"We think so," he replied. "Yes. Have you ever thought about buying a security system?"

"No," Anne said. "I haven't."

"I don't see the point in that," Harold said. "She lives in a safe neighborhood."

"Nowadays," the detective said. "Who knows? But for now, it's probably best you hang around here for a couple of days. When you feel comfortable, then you can go back to your house. If you have a friend you can call. Maybe someone who can keep you company. Other than that, I think we're about done here."

Harold stepped forward and shook the detectives' hands, first Florence's hand and then Merrotti's.

"Thanks for coming by," he said and showed the detectives the door.

9:39 AM

BEFORE Harold said goodbye to the detectives, they gave him a number where Anne could reach them. Harold closed the door behind the detectives and made sure to lock both locks. He turned around, only to find Anne standing by the living room doorway.

Molly poked her head over the banister.

She asked, "Who's at the door, Harold?"

Then, Anne said quietly, "Police."

"Police?"

"They're gone."

Molly walked to the landing.

"They just had a few questions for Anne."

Anne glanced out the front window and saw the car driving off.

Molly marched downstairs.

"Haven't they bothered Anne enough?" she asked sourly. "What else do they want from her?"

"Molly," Harold said seriously, "they just wanted to ask her some questions about the other night."

"Well, couldn't they at least let her rest?"

Harold said over his wife's voice, "How about breakfast?" Then, he nodded at Anne. "Eggs and pancakes?"

Anne thought for a moment.

"Waffles?" she said vacantly.

Harold smiled greatly and said, "Waffles it is."

10:06 AM

ANNE placed the plate of waffles on the kitchen table and sat down next to Molly.

Harold asked Anne, "So, did you sleep well?"

"Yeah," she said as she drizzled the maple syrup over the waffle.

"How about your eyes?"

"What about them?"

Anne took a bite of the waffle and washed it down with a couple of sips of orange juice.

"Thought you said they were bothering you last night," he said. "Are they feeling any better?"

Anne bobbed her head *yes*.

"That's good to hear," he said hesitantly and then stopped Anne from taking another bite. "Anne," Harold said over a sudden thought, "I have to ask you this, and it's okay if you didn't feel comfortable telling the police, but do you have *any* enemies? Do you *know* anybody who'd want to hurt you or get back at you? Something you did? Someone who *looked* at you the wrong way? Anyone?"

Anne shook her head *no*.

"No," she uttered.

"Try to think, Anne."

"There's a guy at work," Anne said. "I don't get along too well with him, but he would never go so far as to hire a couple of men to kill me. . . "

"Anne," Harold said abruptly, "these men weren't just any ordinary men."

"Maybe they saw an attractive girl and thought they could take advantage of her," Molly said and then sipped from her coffee. "I mean she lives all by herself, Harold."

"Maybe," Harold said and held onto Anne's hand. "Right now, all we do know is that you're safe. . . "

The doorbell suddenly *rang* out!

"Again!" Molly groaned as she slammed her mug against the kitchen table. "For God's sake! Don't they ever give up?"

"I'll get it," Harold said and got up from the chair.

"Don't answer it," Anne said as she grabbed Harold by the arm.

"It might be one of those reporters," he said and touched Anne's hand. "I think I saw one of their vans driving around here this morning."

"Please don't go," Anne begged.

"It's all right, sweetie," Harold said reassuringly. "Soon, it'll pass. Then, they'll find someone else to bother."

Harold smiled down at Anne.

She reinforced her grip around Harold's arm.

"Tell them that we're busy eating breakfast."

"I'll tell you what," Harold said. "I'll grab my broom and I'll shoo them away."

He left the kitchen and walked to the front door.

At the front window, he saw two police officers standing on the front porch.

Hesitant, he answered the door.

"My daughter can't talk right now," Harold said bluntly.

As Harold was about to close the door, one of the officers pulled out a pistol with a silencer from behind his back and aimed the pistol at Harold.

A soft *chirp* from the hallway. . .

From the kitchen, both Molly and Anne heard the sound of a muffled gunshot and then the loud thud of Harold falling onto the floor, but Molly had no idea what the sounds were or where they could be coming from.

With her face pale and blank, Anne dropped the fork onto her plate as Molly stood up from the chair and hurried down the hallway.

In the hallway, Molly saw Harold lying on the floor (his red hands clutching his chest, the blood pooling beneath his curled body).

She suddenly cried out, "Harold!"

Then, with their pistols drawn, the two officers stormed inside the house.

Molly's cries changed to screams of sheer horror. "Anne!" she screamed. "Hurry! Come quick! There's someone inside the house!"

The two officers spotted Molly staggering down the hallway.

From the kitchen, Anne heard two more chirps followed by a blaring crash in the hallway.

Before Anne darted from the kitchen and into the hallway, she found Molly's arm, as well as the top part of her forehead, behind the panel of the kitchen doorway. Anne inched closer for a better look. Next to Molly's lifeless body were scattered picture frames and novelties, which had fallen from the foyer table.

Anne immediately covered her mouth and gasped in great terror. Then, she heard footsteps. Louder! She scurried from the kitchen and up the side staircase located in the back of the house before the two officers spotted her.

When Anne arrived upstairs, she could still hear the footsteps, but this time in a less frantic manner. She tiptoed toward her bedroom. On the way, she peeked over the banister and found the shooter creeping up the stairs. From what she gathered in her brief survey, the man appeared like a police officer, even though he didn't look like any ordinary officer. He looked foreign, Anne noticed, *not* American.

As the strange man crept up the stairs, Anne went to her bedroom. She wondered why they were after her: What reason! What purpose! The men from early Wednesday morning were most likely part of a gang, as the detectives had informed her only minutes ago. These men right here—except for the outfits— were much different, she realized, more professional looking. Hired guns like in the movies. What were they after? What did they want? Then, Anne's eyes crossed the music box. She hurried to the box and grabbed the USB flash drive from inside before the music could play.

A sudden *creak* outside the bedroom!

Anne pocketed the flash drive and exited through the bedroom window. She only had two options: up or down. Anne could climb up the roof and hide behind a chimney until the men left (maybe the neighbors heard the gunshots and now the cavalry was on the way! *But* what if these men are police officers?). Or the other way: she could climb down the gutter and make a run for it!

At the very last second, she decided to climb up the roof. The man was closing in on her bedroom when she thought of a plan of diversion. Anne kicked the side of the gutter and loosened it from the mount and then scuttled up the roof and hid behind the chimney as the strange man was entering the bedroom. The first thing he acknowledged: curtains flapping around like a weightless mane of hair and then the open window. He stuck his head halfway out the window and then looked to his left, up the roof where Anne was currently hiding, and then to his right, at the gutter. He stuck his right foot outside and made an attempt to climb up the roof when he came to a sudden halt from the single notion of *the plan*. And like that, the strange man returned to the bedroom, noticing the gutter and how it was crooked and on the verge of falling from the house.

He hurried back to the hallway and yelled out from above, "Francisco! Outside!"

In the foyer, the other man, Francisco, met his partner.

"She couldn't have gotten far," he said, his foreign accent thick and yet difficult to pick up from where Anne was cowering.

Anne waited behind the chimney until she heard the car peeling away down the street.

Shaking uncontrollably, she glanced around the chimney and saw the same black car speeding away.

10:28 AM

By the time Anne reached Molly in the hallway, she was already dead. A bullet had penetrated her heart, instantly killing her.

Anne checked the pulse on the side of Molly's neck to be sure, but she couldn't find one.

From across the hallway: "*Annnnnn. . .* "

Anne turned toward the moan.

"Dad!" Anne cried out and then ran to Harold, who was taking his final breaths.

She grabbed Harold by the hand while the blood filled his lungs, which resulted in a steady flow of blood from his mouth and nostrils. The thought of crimson red flooded her thoughts, but she ignored the dead man at her house and focused on Harold's needs.

"Where's. . . where's y. . . mother?"

Anne wiped the strings of blood from Harold's chin and then shook her head. She slid her arm around his neck and prompted his head upright as she turned the upper part of his body over on its side.

"She. . . " Anne said, her voice now trembling. ". . . She didn't. . . "

Harold extended his bloody hand.

Anne grabbed a hold of his hand and tightened her grip.

"Please, hang on," she cried. "Dad!"

Anne attempted to flee toward the phone in the kitchen. Harold reinforced his grip around Anne and pulled her back down to the floor.

"Don't. . . " he uttered as the blood choked his every breath, ". . . stay. . . "

"I'll call an ambulance. . . "

Harold was shaking his head.

"Nooo. . . "

Anne kneeled beside Harold and, as demanded, stayed with him till he took his final breath.

"You can't!"

"I. . . "

"You can't leave me like this!"

"Yo're ah. . . stron. . . " the blood came in waves, gushing from his mouth, ". . . w'man. . . "

"Why did they do this to you?" she cried, the tears racing from her eyes. "Please tell me! Why?"

Harold trembled. His eyes, like Anne's, were filled with tears.

"Find him. . . Anne. . . " he uttered, his bloody hand gripping tighter around Anne's hand.

"Find *him*?" Anne said urgently. "Find who?"

Harold's hand loosened.

"You must. . . " Harold gasped suddenly and then gargled, ". . . *you*. . . "

Harold's hand went limp. His eyes drifted from Anne's and then fixated on the lawn outside.

"Dad?" Anne shook Harold. "Dad? Please. . . "

She sat with Harold in her arms for a couple of minutes, the blood acting like adhesive over his skin, binding the two together. Anne pulled her eyes from her gummy hands and stared into Harold's still eyes. At that moment, she finally realized that Harold had passed away, that the life that once thrived inside his body had traveled somewhere else, *not* here but elsewhere, to a place that Anne knew little about. She had traveled there before, a long time ago. So long ago that she couldn't remember what it had felt or looked like. It was cold, she remembered, so cold. Then, there were hundreds and thousands of lights glistening over a hazy darkness—each light different from the next. Some small and brilliant while others big and colorful. Then, from the darkness, something else came to her, something unearthly; and when it did, it slid across her body like a cool shroud. How familiar it was, *that* feeling, a stinging presence birthed from the womb of an intangible existence, the great feeling switching over into something cold, inhuman, a creature that was once buried deep in the darkness; and now, it was alive again, rampaging throughout her body like the angry bitch it was. The ripple cast from this strange thing spread over her face, her mad eyes. Then, the shock was gone. . . she knew all too well about the shock, for she had felt the effects of it from the day before. This peculiar presence, however, was something ugly, a mere relative of rage; and it gripped Anne tightly and sunk its jagged hooks into her loins.

Before this creature could take hold, Anne unglued herself from Harold and focused on the next course of action. Anne rushed toward the kitchen and grabbed the phone from the counter. She dialed the first two numbers, 9 and then 1. She hesitated before dialing the very last number, the number 1. *What if those two men really did work for the police, or even worse, the Feds? Would I be inviting these bastards back to the house? Would I make it* that *easy for them? What if they were impostors?*

After careful consideration, Anne went ahead and dialed the number 1.

10:41 AM

IT didn't take long for the police to arrive. There were twice as many cops as last night, as well as a helicopter, which had been called to the scene, hovering in circles above the Roth's residence. Then, there were different news channels—all local—news vans, Anne noticed, as a young officer escorted her to his cruiser. Three channels, she counted. *No.* Four? Before the reporters had a chance to bombard Anne, the officer eased Anne into the back of his cruiser and drove her back to the precinct where she waited in the interrogation room for nearly an hour until the two detectives arrived.

Anne tried to visualize the shooter's face as she glanced down at all of the blood on her hands and clothes, but all she received was a stark image of Harold taking his final breaths before her. She blocked out the shade of red and focused on the unruffled moments prior to the shooting—the waffles. Now, a string of blood drizzling over her plate. . . she cringed in horror. She kept coming back to *the red*. Where there was red, there was a face, long and tanned. He was strikingly handsome, Anne remembered, possibly Spanish from the accent. He also had an aura about him—European? Definitely *not* from around here. He had dark hair, dark skin but *not* black, tall, slender and yet fit, and a long beak of a nose. *That*, she remembered, the nose and how long and pointy it was. Even the way the man moved around the house, she also remembered, fluid like a dancer. He definitely wasn't your ordinary gangster like the one from Tuesday night. Could've been a trained assassin?

A resonant and yet distant voice pulled her from the daydream.

Leaning over the table, Merrotti said, "Ms. Roth?"

Anne carefully studied the two detectives' faces in front of her, especially Merrotti's heavily scarred mien. She couldn't match the face with the one she witnessed after her dad and mom were gunned down, the one with the long and pointy nose; and even so, if Anne discovered a similar trait from the list of suspects, like that beak of a nose or a dimpled chin or even a distinct feature that remotely came close to the one on the shooter's face, she was prepared to sink her claws into his face and then make a cute balloon animal with the fleshy remains.

Merrotti nodded at the empty cup of coffee on the table.

"Would you like another?"

With her head held down, Anne said softly, "No."

Then, Florence said from behind, "Can you tell us what happened after we left, Ms. Roth?"

Merrotti shifted his chair closer to Anne.

"You said these two men were dressed like cops."

No response from Anne.

Again, Merrotti: "Anne? Is that right?"

Anne sniffled and bobbed her head.

"Yeah," she mumbled.

"Are you sure they were police outfits?"

"I'm sure," Anne said, her voice louder as she moved her eyes to the other detective. "I know what I saw. We were," she caught her breath, "we were eating breakfast. The doorbell rang." Her eyes flared at the detective. "I told him *not* to answer the door. But he did any—"

"Why did you tell your father not to answer the door?"

"Because that's what happens when you're involved in a crime that makes the headlines on the front page," Anne said tearfully. "And they don't stop coming. They keep harassing you. They might as well pull the trigger themselves. Because that's what they're doing. They're killing you."

"Who's killing you, Anne?"

"The news reporters, journalists," Anne listed as the anger cut through her voice, "people like you. I *never* asked for two men to break into my house and try to kill me. I *never* asked for my parents to be murdered. I *never asked* for any of this!" Anne wiped away the tears with a tissue, which wasn't too far from arm's reach. "All I know is that you two came by this morning and not too long after you left, two men dressed in police uniforms barged into the house and shot my dad dead and then my mom."

Florence crossed her arms.

"We didn't see anybody on the premises, Ms. Roth."

Anne sighed angrily.

"So, what?" Anne blurted out. "You don't believe me? Is that what you're saying?"

Florence uncrossed her arms. "We're just trying to get the story straight, Ms. Roth," she said. "That's all."

"What story?" Anne snapped. "Two cops murdered my parents! You catch 'em! You lock 'em up! *End* of a story!"

"Please listen to me, Anne," Merrotti said, as patiently as a saint. "If what you're saying is true, and what happened on Tuesday night is connected with what happened today, then we need to know why these people are after you. Maybe they know you. Maybe you have something they want."

"Like what?" Anne shrugged. "There's nothing special about me." She seethed, "I'm a lousy telemarketer who gets treated like shit every fucking day of her life." Anne laughed, which trailed off into a sob. "Why do I keep coming back? You ask me?" She pointed at the two detectives. "It's because I like it," Anne cried. "I like the abuse! I like being treated like shit! It's the whole fucking reason why I get up in the morning!"

"Take it easy, Anne," Merrotti said patiently.

"I won't take it easy," Anne seethed. "My parents were murdered right in front of me. And you're telling me to take it easy. If I wasn't here talking to you, then my ass would be out there looking for the sons of bitches who did this. . . " the tears ran down Anne's eyes, heavy sobs and gasps following, ". . . why are you here? *Why* are you talking to me when you could be out there right now trying to find these. . . "

"We're doing all we can, Ms. Roth," Florence said calmly as Anne's words crumbled into muffled gasps and then moans. "Trust us. We want to find the people who did this as much as you do."

Anne grabbed another tissue and wiped away the phlegm from her nose.

"This is what I deserve," she said quietly, "to be miserable, for the people who I love to be taken away from me because that's who I am and that's who I'll *always* be."

Florence said closely, "And why exactly do you deserve to be miserable, Ms. Roth?"

With her eyes red and glossy from all the crying, she stared vacantly into Florence's eyes and said, "I don't know." She cleared her throat. "All I know is that it has to do. . . "

"Has to do with what, Anne?"

Anne shrugged.

"My past," she mumbled. "*But I can't,*" her voice cracked, "I can't remember. ANYTHING! Do you understand?"

Florence glanced at her partner and then directed her attention toward Anne.

"Can you give us a minute?"

Anne didn't respond.

Florence motioned to her partner, and they walked out of the interrogation room together.

"Devon, she's hiding something," Florence said to Merrotti. "I know it. I *feel* it. For all we know, she could've paid off those men to kill her parents."

"And why in Sam Hill would she do that, Pamela?" Merrotti said, almost with frustration. "You've seen her record. She's clean as a bell. Ordinary girl with a cubicle job."

"The will," Florence whispered, scanning around the quiet hallways of the precinct. "Think about it for a second. She gets all the assets when her foster parents die. It's not like her parents don't have money. Her father, the Vice President for Central Reserve. Her mother, former hot shot real estate agent. Seen it hundreds of times, Devon."

Merrotti sighed sharply.

"Thought you ladies had each other's back."

"Don't even try to pull the sexist card bullshit."

Merrotti copied Florence's previous gestures. "Then, how do you explain the two missing uniforms?"

"You know how unies get misplaced all the time around here."

"Pam, you're stretching it," Merrotti said as he shifted his weight to one side of his body. "All of a sudden she decides to put a hit on her parents. She's got a decent job, despite all the shit she said in there, a nice house. Why would she give all that away?"

"Bigger house," she said with a shrug, "better job."

"Do you know how absurd that sounds?"

"Not *that* absurd," she said. "It's just a thought, Devon. Right now, we need to have an open mind on this thing and exhaust every avenue we have because, right now, Devon, we don't have much to work with."

Merrotti thought to himself, of course, out loud as he had a tendency to do from time to time.

"Local gang bangers and possibly hired guns," he said in a trance. "You're looking at it the wrong way. What if these guys are after the money? Kill the closest heir, which is Anne Roth. Doesn't work out as planned. One of them dies in the process. Then, another one winds up dead in an alley. Whoever's running this ship doesn't like the sloppy work. So he takes care of the problem, brings up a couple of pros, only to find out they have a bigger problem on their hands."

"You ever think she might've been lying about Raymond Santiago?"

"Lying?" he said. "Why?"

"Revenge."

"So, first she puts a hit on her foster parents and now it's revenge," Merrotti said closely. "What do you have against this girl?"

"I'm just saying," Florence said defensively. "Man tries to kill her. And then, hours later, he winds up dead. Then, they retaliate and kill her foster parents. What are the odds?"

"You're saying she killed Santiago?"

"No," Florence said. "But what if she was involved? I do believe, though, someone is trying to tie up loose ends."

"Someone," he said. "*Yes*. But not her."

"What makes you so sure, Devon?"

He held down his head and pinched the bridge of his nose and then ran his fingers across his sore eyes.

Florence studied her partner, his diminishing state.

"So, what do we do?" she said, carefully eyeing Merrotti.

"It's probably best that we keep a unit on her," he said as he reached into his pocket and pulled out a bottle of aspirin. He shook out two pills into his palm and washed them down with a sip of water from the nearest fountain.

Florence asked, "What's wrong?"

"Must be the change in weather," Merrotti said and wiped away the water from the corner of his mouth with the edge of his sleeve.

"Right," Florence said as she rolled her eyes. The action, of course, went unnoticed. "So," she said, crossing her arms, "then what?"

"Watch her every move," Merrotti said, "for her protection if she is telling the truth. If not, we'll see what she's up to. But if you're wrong, Pamela, and these guys do come after her, we'll catch these sons of bitches in the act. That's all we can do right now."

11:39 AM

JAMIE exited the elevator and turned her head left and then right and then left one more time as if she was crossing traffic.

On her second survey, Jamie found Anne sitting on a bench outside the homicide department.

"Anne," she said solemnly as she marched through the hallway.

Anne stood up from the bench, the sight of Jamie causing the tears to come, slowly at first and then an all-out downpour.

Jamie embraced Anne and said into her shoulder, "I was so worried about you. How are you holding up?"

Anne wept into Jamie's shoulder.

"That's okay," Jamie said and stroked Anne's hair. "You don't have to explain."

"What do I do now?" Anne said unsteadily.

"We take it one step at a time."

Anne whined, "I can't. . . "

"Sure you can," Jamie said as she rubbed Anne's back. "In the meantime, you stay with me."

She pulled her face from Jamie's shoulder as wet gobs and strings of tears and phlegm and saliva stained over her jacket.

Anne asked, "Are you sure?"

"Of course," Jamie said. "That's what friends are for."

12:47 PM

"APPARENTLY you didn't look close enough at Diana Roth's record," Florence said dourly as she showed the old photograph to her partner. "Pulled a picture from the databases. I decided to print it out because I know how much dinosaurs like to hold onto old stuff."

Merrotti smirked from the comment.

"Funny," he said as he glanced down at the photo. "This our girl?"

"Yep," she said. "That's her. Can you believe it?"

The photograph was taken many years ago. She was only twelve years old at the time. Her hair was long and greasy. Her face long and empty. Still had freckles too. Anne looked like one of those missing girls one would find on the back of a milk carton, lost and alone, as if they didn't exist in real life and all that remained of them was a sad photograph.

"Hard to believe that's the same girl," he said as he studied the photograph.

"Cops found her with bite marks all over her legs," Florence informed. "She hadn't eaten in weeks. She had bruises around her genitals."

"The father said something about him and his wife seeking treatment for Anne when she was younger."

"Yeah," Florence said as she handed her partner the doctor's files and clinical notes on Anne. "That's right. Psychiatric hospital, Mercy Mental, where they zapped her brain."

"Poor girl," Merrotti said as he pushed aside the files and studied that one photograph of young Anne.

2:12 PM

JAMIE parked her 2012 Ford Taurus in front of Anne's house, which was exactly the same as Anne last left it, only without a swarm of officers and para-medics and coroners and news reporters.

"Are the cops necessary?" Jamie said as she glared at the two cruisers in the rear view mirror.

"It's either them or me being held up in some secret location."

"What do you mean?" Jamie said foolishly. "Like protective custody?"

"Something like that."

"Wow," Jamie said under her breath. Then, she turned to Anne and said in her normal voice, "How can we trust these people now after what you said?"

"They weren't cops."

Jamie asked, "How do you know?"

"I just know, Jamie."

Anne turned away from Jamie and stared out the passenger window.

"Listen to me, Anne," Jamie said carefully. "If any lowlife lays a hand on you, then they're gonna have to go through me first."

Before Anne exited the car, she turned back around. "Jamie," she said, "thanks for doing this."

"You can stay with me as long as you like." She reached over the console and placed her hand over Anne's thigh. "It's no problem. You'd do the same for me."

Anne bobbed her head and wiped the tears from her eyes.

"Besides Michael, you're like the only family I have right now."

Jamie grabbed Anne by the hand.

She asked, "Have you talked to him?"

Anne shook her head *no*.

"He doesn't know yet," she said. "We had a bad fight last night."

"Forget about him, Anne," Jamie said as she turned off the ignition. "I promise I'll look after you. Okay?"

Once more, Anne bobbed her head.

"Come on," she said as she stepped out of the car. "Let's go get your things."

Jamie walked with Anne to the house.

The inside of the house was still covered in debris. The two police officers lingered around the front porch and stood guard while Anne and Jamie strolled inside.

"This might take a second," Anne said to Jamie, who was standing by the front doorway.

"Take your time," Jamie replied. "I'll be right here."

Anne shuffled around the broken glass in the hallway. She went into her bedroom and grabbed as much as she could from the closet, mostly sweaters and dresses, as well as a few pairs of blue jeans, shirts, and underwear from the drawers, and stuffed everything inside a large pink suitcase.

Next, Anne moved to the dresser and picked out several bracelets and necklaces and rings that matched each outfit and placed them in the side pouch before closing the suitcase.

Lastly, she grabbed her electronic mp3 player, a pair of ear buds to go along with it, an electronic tablet—pretty much anything with the letter *e* in front of it—as well as her laptop from the desk, and placed them on top of the suitcase.

After Anne was done with the bedroom, she went into the bathroom where she filled a handbag with all sorts of things: hair products, makeup, shampoo, conditioners, lotion, toothbrush, toothpaste, mouthwash, and tampons.

On the way out, her eyes crossed the dry puddle of blood inside the kitchen. She paused for a minute and stared at the puddle, as well as the mental flashes of a man who once stood over that very same tile floor before his blood had escaped his body. A faint echo of gasps and gurgles from a desperate man choking on his own blood plagued her ears, unavoidably resulting in the erection of hairs over the gooseflesh of her arms.

Anne shook the chills from her body and turned to Jamie, who was waiting patiently at the doorway.

As she made an attempt toward the front door, her eyes suddenly crossed another piece of debris left behind from the chaos: a magazine. The magazines had been ripped from the coffee table, which was nothing more than chewed up wood and glass. *But* that one magazine, which lay openly over the living room floor, caught Anne's eye the most.

She motioned to Jamie.

In return, Jamie grabbed the pink suitcase and handbag from Anne's hands and carried them to the car while Anne ambled through the ruined living room. She placed the laptop aside and picked up the glossy magazine, *Flashback*. She brushed away tiny shards of broken glass with the backside of her hand and then skimmed through the magazine.

On page 49, she came across a feature called PAST THE FAÇADE. She remembered reading the feature in the break room at work: a gripping story about an architect named Philippe Benot, born in France, who moved to the States when he was eight years old; and by the time he reached the age of twenty-three, he was one of the most famous architects in the entire world. Philippe's work was extremely popular in the late 1970's and well into the 80's. There were others like Van Garr, Tomas, and Le Peep, and then there was Philippe Benot, the man known for reshaping the East Coast with his "gothic meets modern classical style." However, what made Philippe's story so interesting was that, by 1989, he was flat out broke—not a single penny to his name. Then, years later, he was involved in a string of murders but later found not guilty. Although never proven, there was even a theory floating around that his rivals framed him for murder. . .

Anne looked at the writer's name underneath that title.

"Renny Jacobson. . . " she said out loud.

She reached into her pocket and pulled out the USB flash drive.

Couldn't be a coincidence, she wondered.

"Are you ready, Anne?" Jamie said from behind.

"Yeah," she said in a trance-like state.

"Don't worry about food," Jamie said. "I got plenty at the house."

Anne inserted the flash drive into her pocket, grabbed the laptop and then the magazine.

"I have to grab one more thing," Anne said to Jamie as she arrived in the kitchen.

Without Jamie looking, she grabbed a steak knife from the knife holder and carefully slipped it inside the side pocket of the laptop case.

Jamie from the doorway: "You all set?"

"Yeah," she said. "All set."

Anne exited the kitchen and then the house.

2:43 PM

THEY didn't say much during the ride to Jamie's house. Anne was not only still grieving from the recent death of her foster parents, but was also in a state of bafflement from that one name, *Renny Jacobson*, and why the intruder had Renny's USB flash drive in his pocket.

2:53 PM

THEY arrived at a suburb called Greenway Valley, three miles from the projects. Each house on Jamie's street was different from the next. Jamie's house, which was built in the late sixties when the population of Lansford was half the size it is today, was a little bit bigger than Anne's house—only a couple hundred square feet—spacious backyard with a charcoal grill, an elevated porch, dark green siding with burgundy trim, an open living room and kitchen, and three bedrooms: one a guest, another an office, and the third, Jamie's room, with a raised ceiling. Just across the street was an impassable wall of shrubbery and uncut grass, which was one of the many agendas on the city's list. Higher population meant bigger budgets, which meant bigger lists, which included building more houses and paving more roads. Past the overgrown vegetation stretched a mile full of woods, which, like most areas of untouched land in and around Lansford, was scheduled to be cleared out in order to make room for cheaper houses.

Jamie helped Anne carry her luggage to the front porch.

As soon as she closed the front door of the house and set Anne's things on the floor, the two were instantly greeted by a jubilant black Labrador.

Jamie rubbed the side of the Labrador's neck.

"I missed you so much, Harley," she said, her voice sounding like a mother talking to a baby.

The dog wagged his tail back and forth, even more jubilant than before.

Next, the dog frolicked toward Anne.

In return, Anne placed her laptop aside and petted the dog on top of the head.

"As you can tell," Jamie said to Anne, "spoiled as ever."

Anne kneeled down to Harley's level where she moved her hand down the side of his face.

Harley shook like a turbine, ropes of drool flinging from his gaping mouth.

Anne jarred back a little and wiped a few black hairs from her sweater.

"Please forgive Harley," Jamie said, kneeling down as well. "He's been shedding a lot lately."

Anne's facial expression went long and empty—*shedding*, she thought.

"It's okay," Anne said flatly and stared into the dog's dark eyes. "He's just a sweet dog who wants to be loved."

Harley stopped panting.

The wagging stopped as well.

Suddenly, the dog moaned and scampered behind Jamie.

"What's a matter, Harley?" she said. "Its just Anne. You remember Anne. Don't you, boy?"

Harley darted into the kitchen where he escaped through the doggy door.

Dumfounded from Harley's reaction to Anne's presence, she said quietly, "That's strange." Then, she stood up. Anne stood as well. "I've never seen him do that before."

"I see you redecorated," Anne said as she strolled toward an aquarium with plecostomus, or pleco fish, various kinds of crowntail bettas, an albino tiger oscar cichild—most notably known as an oscar fish—a red swordtail, and a couple of lyretail guppys. She looked closely at the fish inside. The pleco fish, which was hanging around the bottom of the tank, slowly eased back into the dark recesses of a driftwood ornament.

"Are you hungry?" Jamie asked from behind.

Anne stared even closer at the pleco fish, which was now motionless.

"I can fix you anything," she said again. "I make a killer mac' n cheese. . . "

Anne didn't respond.

(*Something wrong?*)

Anne stepped away from the aquarium.

"Fine," she said, her eyes glazing over. "I need to use the restroom."

"Sure," Jamie said curiously. She pointed at the hallway. "Second door on the left."

With her head down, Anne hurried to the bathroom and closed the door behind her. She looked in the mirror and cried, but this time the tears burned in her eyes as if her tears were seasoned with a hint of cayenne pepper. And even when they ran down her cheeks, the tears, they burned her cheeks as well.

Jamie pressed her ear against the door and heard Anne crying from inside.

"Anne," she said, "can I come in?"

Anne cried harder, louder.

Jamie tapped on the door before cracking it open and entered the bathroom.

Anne was seated on the tile floor with her back against the wall and her head held into her lap.

"I'm *so* sorry, Anne," Jamie said as she eased onto the floor and embraced Anne in her arms. "*We* will get through this. Okay?"

"I couldn't. . . " Anne struggled to breath, ". . . I couldn't say goodbye, Jamie."

"What do you mean?"

"He died," Anne cried, "right. . . right in my arms. . . but I couldn't say goodbye to him, Jamie. I just couldn't." Anne reached deep inside, the words flowing freely, honing like a blade. "I know somehow I will see him again, Jamie, maybe not here, but I. . . I *know* that I will be with them again. Every inch of me just *knows*." She sniffled the phlegm from the tip of her nose. "I don't know why this is happening to me. We were having. . . having break. . . fast. Next thing I know, I hear these. . . these gunshots. . . but it wasn't. . . it wasn't like a normal gunshot."

Jamie asked, "What are you talking about, Anne?"

"It. . . it had one of those. . . long things on the end. . . "

"End of what?" Jamie said confusedly. "The barrel?"

Anne bobbed her head.

"You mean like a silencer?"

Again, Anne bobbed her head, but this time much more quickly.

"Yes. . . "

She paused for a moment and traced her thoughts back to the silencer and why a person would want to use one. She knew that the average gangster wouldn't use a silencer. Why would they? Every time in the news there was always a witness or a neighbor talking about a gang shooting. There was always someone who explained to a reporter what happened, and they were always taking about "hearing" gunshots. With Anne, there were *no* gunshots, at least not the ones that could be heard from a distance. The only thing she could think about when it came to silencers were hit men or hired guns, the kind of people who knew exactly what they were doing, *not* amateurs, she knew, *not* gangsters or thugs, but fuckers whose job was specifically for one purpose: to kill.

Anne cried out, "They're going to kill me. . . "

"Anne," Jamie said, holding Anne tighter, "who's going to kill you?"

"I don't know, but I know it, Jamie. . . "

"Don't talk like that," Jamie said angrily. "Nobody is going to kill you. Besides, if these people who did this to your parents come after you, then they'll have to deal with the police and then they'll have to deal with me." Jamie's eyes narrowed as she grabbed Anne's chin and directed Anne's bloodshot eyes into her eyes. "Anne," Jamie said, peering closer now, "I'm not going to let anything happen to you."

Once again, Anne bobbed her head.

Jamie used the vanity to help herself stand up.

"What you need now is some food in your stomach and a good night's sleep," she said and stepped into the hallway.

While Jamie went to the kitchen to make Anne something to eat, Anne pulled out the USB flash drive from her pocket and stared at it closely. . .

4:04 PM

WHILE Jamie prepared the food in the kitchen, Anne wandered around the downstairs. She came across a door at the end of the hallway and decided to open it. The blood suddenly raced throughout her body, leaving her limbs—mostly legs—as stiff as roots. For a moment, Anne found herself in the face of a group of men, as gangly as aliens with elongated limbs and torsos, standing in bizarre postures. At first glance, they appeared like dark silhouettes through the faint sunlight cast from the bed sheets pinned over the garage windows.

Startled, Anne remained like the alien men, still. It took a few moments for her eyes to finally adjust to the darkness of the garage and realize that these celestial-like beings were nothing more than a collection of sculptures that Jamie had sculpted from rusted metal and scraps like old cable wires and mangled car parts gathered from local junkyards.

In fascination, Anne flipped on the garage light, revealing the sculptures. She wandered around the metallic creatures, some posed in tormented postures, others disturbing. Nonetheless, all of them—five of them, she counted, all varying in shapes and sizes—painted a graphic scene of struggle and violence and yet, on the other hand, of love and nourishment.

A voice from behind: *What do you think?*

The sound of Jamie's voice caused Anne's blood to race even faster through her veins, her heart skipping a beat, literally.

Anne grabbed hold of her chest.

"Jesus, Jamie," Anne said, catching her breath. "Don't do that."

"Sorry," she said innocently. "Didn't mean to scare you."

"I was just looking for something to drink."

Jamie nodded at the refrigerator to the left.

"There's soda in the fridge," she said.

Anne checked out the fridge. There weren't many drinks inside, only a few grape sodas, a half-gallon of 2% milk, which was past its due date, and a six-pack of beer imported from Mexico.

"Grab me a cerveza," Jamie said. "Will you?"

"Sure." Anne grabbed two drinks, a grape soda for herself and a beer for Jamie. "Are you going to work tomorrow?"

"Nah," Jamie said. "I'm taking the day off."

"You don't have to worry about me," Anne said. "I'll be fine. Really."

"No way," Jamie said as she grabbed the beer from Anne's grip. "Besides, I got so many freaking sick days I don't even know what to do with them."

"Thanks," Anne said sincerely.

Jamie cracked open the cerveza and nodded at the sculpture.

"What do you think?" she asked.

"I like it," Anne replied. "Did you do all of this?"

Jamie bobbed her head as she sipped from the beer.

"It's a modern spin on *Laocoön and His Sons*."

"Laocoön?"

"He was a priest from Troy." Jamie pointed at the lanky sculpture in the very middle and then the two smaller ones on either side. Entangled around the three sculptures, one the father and the other his two children, were these two subterranean-like creatures, which were made from PVC pipe and broken glass. "Laocoön and his two sons were killed by two giant sea serpents after Laocoön warned the Trojans about the Greeks and the wooden horse."

"Interesting," Anne said vaguely.

Jamie placed her hand over Anne's shoulder. "Come," she said. "Your food's getting cold."

5:02 PM

AFTER Anne grabbed a bite to eat—homemade macaroni and cheese and then a shot of NyQuil to follow, of course, to help her sleep (it was either that or the bottle of Peach Schnapps in the refrigerator)— she retired to the guest room.

For about twenty minutes, Anne lay with her eyes closed but didn't get much sleep at all. She grabbed the laptop resting on top of her luggage, went back to the bed, and inserted the USB flash drive into the port on the side of the laptop.

As before, she double-clicked on the icon and opened the folder, *A Week With Mr. Hopkins*. She opened the file, *The Email*, and skimmed through the email from Mr. Hopkins to Renny Jacobson. That name, *Freeze*, caught her attention the most. Anne minimized the email and then pulled up the Internet where, in the search bar, she googled Freeze. The results were scattered, mostly about the science of freezing—meaning liquid turning into ice or any other solid—but not an actual person. Anne scrolled down the site and finally came across a blacked out image of a man with a caption underneath which read, *"Number One on the FBI's Most Wanted List."* She found more images, all blacked out, some even deleted from the Internet.

Next, she clicked on the Video section. There were many videos on this elusive "Freeze" figure, most, if not all of them, had been removed from iTube due to legal or copyright issues. She managed to watch one video on iTube, which was a fifty-eight second clip on Freeze (well, more like a glimpse of what appeared to be Freeze). Anne read the date on the bottom. It was from thirty years ago, October, and the video was filmed with a super 8; the cameraman, possibly a civilian caught in the right place at the right time, was perched on the corner of the street while a robbery was taking place inside a convenient store. Anne leaned closely to the screen, cranked up the volume, mostly fuzz and heavy breathing, and watched this so-called "Freeze," dressed in a stylish silver suit, blonde hair like a frozen tidal wave, eyes like stars, sneak up behind the robber. The robber turned around, accidentally firing off a shot—the bullet struck the ceiling, *not* Freeze or pedestrians. Then, something happened! The robber froze in his tracks, literally. So too did the clerk, more so, however, in amazement. The robber stood as still as a statue while this debonair-looking man—dressed as if he was about to attend a Hollywood premiere—peered into the robber's eyes. Then, something else happened! Something strange! Both of his eyes glimmered faintly, which to Anne, appeared more like a lens flare from the old camera. The sound of a police siren from a distance quickly sent the cameraman scrambling.

Then, the video went black and staticky. . .

She closed the video and scrolled through the next page, mostly bogus websites made by fanatics and conspiracy theorists; however, there were a couple of interesting links. . .

www.blackwateruniversity.dot/About/Freeze

Then, another one. . .

www.theoffdistrict.co

. . . which seemed legit.

Every link Anne clicked on, including a couple of government websites, didn't function properly, which was *no* surprise. There was even a Wikipedia page on Freeze, not the science of freezing or Mr. Freeze, a villain in the *Batman* comic books, but *the* Freeze, this "Most Wanted" guy. As with all the other websites, she received the same response: PAGE NOT FOUND.

At first, Anne wondered if Jamie's Internet was down or if the servers were faulty, but the signal on her laptop was running strong. Anne decided to cancel the search on Freeze. She googled Marcus Hopkins, but, like before, she couldn't find a single thing on him, no MyCircle page, no Chatterz page, nothing substantial to link him to the email. Anne even went on White Pages, but there were so many people with the name Marcus Hopkins, from young to elderly, that she didn't know where to begin.

She closed the Internet and pulled up the Finder. There, she ran the cursor over the *Photos* folder inside the USB flash drive. She read the details across the columns of the Finder.

Name: Photos
Date Modified: October 20, 2014
Size: 1.41 GB
Kind: Folder

Next, Anne double-clicked on the *Photos* folder. There were at least fifty photographs in the folder, all of them being JPEG images, decent quality, all taken with Renny's snapshot camera, two blue folders at the bottom, one named *HEAD* and the other named *Study*. The first twenty photographs were taken from the 13th of October to the 16th. The remaining photos were all taken on the 19th of October. Anne started with the first JPEG, which was a photograph taken of the backside of a car. The photograph was blurry and hard to make out, mostly an ash gray sky with a ray of sun trying to break through. She scrolled to the next one, which was clear. The photograph was of a postcard-like shot of a small coastal town. Anne couldn't quite make out what coast. Strangely, she assumed the town was located somewhere up north, not only from memory (?) of the town, but also from the rocky shore, as well as the white northern pines etched across the coastline. More photos: two of them of a winding road with more of those white northern pines on either side. Then, she scrolled to the fifth photograph: an old mansion with a cast iron gate guarding a well-manicured lawn and a pristine garden. Alongside the long and narrow driveway was a row of maple trees, varying in different colors, browns and oranges and reds, from the change of seasons. In front of the mansion, the driveway circled around an old fountain made from limestone. Another photograph, a much closer shot: a statue of Apollo holding a phiale. Water was pouring from Apollo's phiale and into a fountain below. She scrolled through more photographs. She came across two photos in particular, one of rabbit statuettes huddled near the doorsteps and then two deer statues standing in the backyard. She didn't understand why Renny took the photographs of the stoned animals, but she didn't spend enough time thinking about it to even care. Other photos, three of them (each one the same), were taken inside the large mansion: bare wall hangers but no paintings. Another: a bronze bust of Marcus Aurelius perched next to a grand staircase, which curved around the massive living room.

Anne paused and turned away from the laptop.

The bust, Anne saw, was familiar, so much so that she had seen it before. She couldn't exactly remember how or when. But she had seen that bust before.

The man from my dreams, the model. . .

Next, Anne pulled her eyes back to the laptop and came across photographs taken on the 15th of October. The photos were mostly of the woods, more northern white pines as before. One shot in particular had not only caught the photographer's eye (whom she assumed was this Renny guy), but also Anne's eye. There were at least five or six photographs of two different headstones. Another photograph: a close up of a headstone. "R.I.P.," the headstone read. "William James Dorsey." Then, another: "Peter Dorsey."

Next, she opened the other photos from the *Study* folder, which were taken on the 17th through the 20th.

There were photos of a young girl, mostly old Polaroids, all of which were secured in a leather photo album. The Polaroids ranged from birth to childhood:
Polaroids of the girl—no older than three or four
years old—holding a baby boy in her arms; Polaroids
of the girl holding hands with a handsome man with
bleached blonde hair, presumably her father; Polaroids of an attractive woman with brunette hair, presumably her mother, with the same blonde haired
man and the young girl seated between the two (the
blonde haired man kissing the woman's cheek, the
young girl below smiling from ear to ear).

As a haunting feeling came over Anne—almost a
feeling of nausea—she scrolled to the next photograph, a photograph of herself!

She gawked at the photo. She remembered the
exact day she took *that* photo with her smartphone—
taken only three months ago, in the bathroom, in
front of the mirror, minutes before Michael picked
her up for their one-year anniversary. She was wearing a backless red dress, her hair tied around the
backside of her head. The feeling that Anne felt that
night, so intoxicating it was, so spectacular, felt as if
she was the most beautiful woman ever. Anne's face
went long and expressionless. Her eyes billowed in
awe. *What in the...* the photo was copied from her
MyCircle page and pasted into this folder. Then,
there were more of them, more photographs of Anne,
ones from her MyCircle page and even a couple from
her FindYourRomeo page, personal photos—mostly
selfies taken in front of the mirror—and then black
and white photos, which were much better quality,
taken from a distance, black and whites of Anne leaving USR, eating dinner with Michael, exiting Fitness
City, jogging in Josette Park—all of them taken without Anne's consent; in fact, Anne wasn't even aware

that she was being photographed during the time of these events. If this was really Renny Jacobson, Anne wondered, the same writer from *Flashback* magazine, why did he have these personal pictures stored in a flash drive. Was this man stalking me? Did he hire a private eye? Where. . . (most importantly) how did he get these?

The *squeak* of a door!

In the corner of her eye, the bedroom door cracked open.

"What are you reading?" Jamie asked from the doorway.

She pulled her red eyes from the screen and quickly closed the laptop.

"Ah. . . nothing. . . "

"You on MyCircle?"

"Nope," Anne said, shaking her head.

"I'm sorry," Jamie said. "Didn't mean to interrupt."

Anne gradually cracked open her mouth to speak, but the words never came.

"Do you need anything?"

"Ah. . . " Anne hesitated, ". . . I'm good."

"Well, just let me know if you need anything," Jamie said and then nodded to the living room behind her. "I'm gonna watch some TV. They're playing a whole marathon of Paradise Lost. So far, I've watched like two or three episodes and I'm hooked. . . "

Jamie noticed the disinterest in Anne's face.

"Wanna join?"

"Maybe," she said. "Yeah. Just going through the email." Anne suddenly corrected. "My email. "

A long pause filled the room.

"Well," Jamie said hesitantly, "I'll be in here if you need me."

Anne said abruptly, "Okay."

Jamie secretly eyed the laptop before closing the door.

Then, Anne reopened the laptop once Jamie was gone.

She closed the photographs from the Preview application and opened the first journal entry, *Thoughts*, from the Journal Notes folder.

Then, read to herself:

Note to self: Never get on Stew's bad side. It's scary how much the guy knows about computers. Like he's been inside one for so damn long that he actually thinks he's a part of one—his veins, the wires; his brain, a motherboard; his fingers, a mouse; etc. Regardless, if there's anybody you want in your corner, it's Stewart Badger. Till this day, I still don't know how he does it, how he works his magic. I swear Stew's like a wizard back there in that foxhole he calls an office with the keyboard, his wand; the computer, his cauldron. Stew's the guy who knows everything about you, even if he's never even met you in person. *That* type. Thank the World Wide Web for that one. He knows your favorite hobbies, sports team, books, who you voted for, or what websites you frequently visit. The good ole Internet: a vast wonderland of knowledge *or* a vast landfill of waste. Come on! Who doesn't get a kick out of watching two bulldogs hump each other until they puke their guts out? That's the world we now live in. Decency?!? Privacy?!? No such thing anymore. Trying to rid the filth from the Internet would be a fool's errand. As Mr. Cronkite once said: "And that's the way it is." You can either do two things: use the Internet to your advantage or let it take advantage of you. If you've gotten this far in life, then you're already damaged goods. So, welcome to the club, *The Damaged Goods Club*. After President Shaw passed the Full-Disclosure Act last year, it's like Big Brother all over again. NSA's keeping tabs on every digit you dial on your phone, recording every conversation.

The Feds watching every single stroke you make on your keyboard. No pun intended. I'm sure things have been going on this way for a long time, *long* as in long before the Tricky Dick days. You'd be living under a rock if you haven't heard of the government pulling a couple of shady tricks underneath its sleeve every now and then. Some people want transparency, yes, and others want to be left alone with their TVs and AK47s. And then there are others who want a little slice from both of the pies. That's probably where I fall, *the food taster*. I imagine George Orwell is rolling over in his grave right now. The guy was a visionary, even though the *real* world was thirty years late—at least things aren't nearly as bad as they were in Mr. Orwell's self-created world. Hard times await us. I'm sure people like my dad were saying that during the Reagan years, but look how we turned out. Somehow, the world keeps spinning and people keep fucking and spitting out kids. Natural selection. Right? Who knows? Who cares? On the contrary, Shaw has done a couple of good things: the economy is improving but it's still below expectations, especially after the shitstorm left behind from the recession, and the war on terror has become a thing of the past. But with all good things, there is always the bad: the infamous sex scandal with the Secretary of Defense, the tax fraud thing a couple of months ago, insider trading, and most importantly, the controversy surrounding the Arms Deal across the border. Nobody knows if Shaw was involved in selling automatic weapons to our good neighbors south of the border. Right now, it's only hearsay. In all odds, a bitter politician on the other side of the party started the rumor. You can point the finger all day, but it's not going to get us anywhere. Nonetheless, Shaw's campaign ran off transparency; however, a cloudy fucking mess is what we got. It wouldn't be the first. Stew put it nicely the other day. He called it "*politricks*." Despite how much I don't agree with Stew on certain topics, the guy sure does come in handy when you need him the most. He can sneak into anything that has a hard drive and an Internet connection. Stew managed to pull Hopkins' record from JeneCorp's "secure" website. A word like *se-cure* doesn't exist in Stew's vocabulary. Never asked him how he did it. "Piece of cake," was all he gave me and then he did that annoying thing where he leaned back in his chair and cracked his knuckles. Did I not mention that Stew is a conceited slippery fuck? His nickname should be the Salamander. Stew is well aware of his importance at *Flashback*, a bona fide extortionist Stew is. There weren't any images of Marcus Hopkins, none Stew could show me as to whom I was up against. The only one we found was blacked out. He served as an enforcer for Freeze's former employer, the monster energy company, JeneCorp, which he had called the Company. Then, five years after an explosion in '99 ("a training exercise gone wrong," which was what the report said), Marcus Hopkins retired due to health reasons. Last known whereabouts was somewhere in Tucson. Then, in 2006, he did an abra-cadabra, and like that, poof, he pulled the greatest trick of them all. Never to be heard from ever again. So, I gave it a shot and emailed him back. Within the hour, Marcus Hopkins replied to my email, and Whisperfront, Maine, is what he gave me. I got Stew to check out the address. The house was registered under a Brit, a wealthy industri-alist named Charles S. Leatherby. Could be a fake. But what did I have to lose at this point? Edie wasn't too pleased to hear the news. When I told her about the email, she flipped a lid and did that thing where she stands like Captain Morgan and looks down at me with a look of dis-gust. She gave me an ultimatum. Either I do the Stacey Dilworth story or I pack my shit. Ever since Edie and I hooked up, things have been tense between us. I was drunk and didn't remember a thing about that night. We were having a couple of late-night cocktails at Flynn's in Manhattan when something came over us. I never liked Edie in a sexual way, not because she wasn't attractive, which she was (she put the word *cougar* to good use), but because she was way out of my league. Don't know if it was the dim lighting or Sade, but we couldn't get out of there soon enough. Not a bragger. Never been. The world's filled with enough of them. Biggest mistake of my life was giving her the big O. Later, Gretel, from the art department, told me that was a big no-no on a one-night stand. "Us girls," Gretel told me, "we will marry any man who can give us the big O." Now, Edie looks at me differently. At times, I don't know if she wants to strangle me or fuck me or both. I spent all of Sunday night into Monday morning pleading with Edie. I mean, Freeze, really. When has there been a story on Freeze? And how much of it was actually the truth? Having grown up around Lansford, I knew how much it meant for me to do this story on Freeze. Edie, not so much. If Hopkins was *right*, then this was my chance. Maybe my only chance! Edie was skeptical (I didn't exactly use the word *goldmine*, but she knew where I was headed). When I mentioned how much attention this Hopkins story would bring to the magazine, she caved. Attention was money. And money was a happy Edie. Better than an angry Edie. Once she gave me the green light, I booked a flight to Bangor, Maine. From there, I was looking at about an hour and a half drive to Whisperfront. It almost seemed too good to be true. Week before the first deadline I get handed one of the most incredible opportunities of a lifetime, that is if Hopkins was right. If he was, then I had the story of the century on my plate! For about two weeks now, I've been working on this MISSING CASE story: a ten-year-old girl, Stacey Dilworth, who disappeared two years ago. Edie, who's been constantly breathing down my neck for the past three days, thought it would make a gripping story. Before Edie got demoted from Executive Editor, she wanted to bring an edge to the magazine and she thought I was the right guy for the job, which was flattering coming from a woman who eats senior writers for breakfast and then assistant editors for a late afternoon snack. Show readers that we're not only known for writing stories about entertainment icons or pop culture. Crime cases were the next hot item, hotter than any bullshit celebrity story. Edie Cohen was in the moneymaking business, and, besides institutions or teenyboppers, people weren't really buying magazines anymore—at least not in the stores or on the stands. Most of the money we made was from eMags. Digital was in, and paper was on the way out. But what can you do? It's like trying to put out a fire with gasoline. Sometimes, it's best if you just let it burn. A fight you'll never win. Like the Internet, a fool's errand. As much as you'd like to, the odds are against you. Either way, Edie wanted to expand our horizons and open up a broader audience. So far, I haven't really dug up enough information to tell a little more about Stacey, more than people already know. What separated us from the parasites and the vultures in the media circus was that our stuff was based off the hard facts, straight to the core, no bias, no opinions (I know it's hard coming from a guy like me; but when it comes down to a story, I put all the bullshit and personal nonsense aside as if I was a newborn soaking up everything like a sponge), no hidden agendas, no political influence, no one-sided hoopla that you get on both the left and the right. *Flashback* was the Walter Cronkite of the magazine world and we had a saying of our own: "It is what it is." We told it how it was, how "it is," no strings attached, no harping, no bullying. We're not in the kicking-a-man-when-he's-down business, although Edie's been known to do that from time to time. I've done about twenty interviews so far on the Stacey Dilworth story. Stew helped me with the background checks. The truth: Stacey Dilworth was about as plain as Jane, your ordinary girl from a small town. In my eyes, the story was losing its wings and tail spinning directly toward the recycling bin. Needed a story and needed one fast. Cue Marcus Hopkins. This is the story that either makes or breaks a writer or even worse, gets his ass fired. The deadline was closing in. Frantic Friday, fourth Friday into the month, was right around the corner. The one day of the month contributors and editors alike scrambled around the offices like ants fleeing from a trampled anthill, making sure every last word was in order, no grammar mistakes, that sort of thing. I had roughly a little over a week to start and finish a whole new story while the one I had been working on was soon facing its ultimate demise. Let's face it. Stacey Dilworth's story was old, and at this point, only a miracle could ignite a spark to this dying flame. That is if you believe in that kind of stuff.

She stopped reading for a moment, skimmed back over that one town in Maine, *Whisperfront*.
Intrigued, Anne said to herself, "Whisperfront?"
Her head slightly tilted to the side.
Whisperfront, she thought.
Anne moved her eyes back to the screen.

Prior to Freeze's disappearance, every kid my age enjoyed reading the newspaper articles on him, the books, most of them fictional, the comic books, or playing with the Freeze toys (and yes, I'm not afraid to admit that I used to own the Freeze action figure, the limited edition sunglasses trademarked by Freeze, and even those eye contacts that glow in the dark). Despite all of that, Freeze still hasn't received the proper treatment for his story. If Mr. Hopkins is telling the truth and Freeze's real name is Leon Dorsey, I assumed JeneCorp played a key role in keeping Freeze's identity from the public. It's hard enough trying to find information on the Internet. Tried numerous times. Dead end. Seen a couple of videos posted by Freeze enthusiasts. With today's technology and affordable video editing software, it's hard to tell what's real or not. I figured the old fashion way was the best way to write the story—not the easiest way by any means—but the best way. Besides, it puts the excitement back into writing a story. I remember hearing stories about the great Freeze when I was a kid, the myths, the legends, seeing rare glimpses of him on television. Over time, he became a cartoon character. With the exception of Freeze and the publicity he received throughout the years, JeneCorp was one of those companies that stayed under the radar despite having been worth billions of dollars. Their employees were like these men in black, not from the movie, but from

the UFO stuff back in the late forties and well into the fifties. They were always with Freeze—at least that was
what rumors said—but one could never actually recognize
their faces or spot them in a lineup. In a way, they were
like shadows of the night. I took a late departure, a two
o'clock flight to Bangor, Maine and had a bite to eat on the
plane. Haven't been so nervous about a story since I
joined the *Flashback* staff. No question. During the entire
flight, I did a little research on Whisperfront. . .

Unsure whether or not I was going to get Internet access
on the airplane, I printed a couple of tidbits from the Internet, mostly from Wikipedia, which, the way I looked at it,
was better than arriving in Whisperfront with my dick in
my hand even if the information probably came from a
pimple-popper sitting behind a computer all day. Whisperfront is a town in Beaux County with a population—
according to the 2010 census—of 4,650, but I suppose the
population has grown, possibly even doubled *or* lessened
since then, especially after the legalization of marijuana.
According to Wikipedia, Whisperfront, known as being a
summer colony for its boom during tourist season, gener-
ates most of its income during the summer months. There
wasn't much history I could dig up on the Internet, other
than the town was settled in 1769 after the French and Indian War, and that a British colonist, Sir George Ketchum,
came up with the name, Whisperfront, from its whispering
winds during the brutal winters. Except for a rough patch
of turbulence toward the end of the flight and me about
losing my lunch, the trip wasn't that bad. Smoother than
most I've been on. Never in my ten years of flying have I
ever gotten used to flying. The alcohol helps. After I
grabbed my luggage from the conveyer belt, there was a
mysterious man with a pencil-line mustache, bald, black
suit, coattails, black shades, face like a wall, holding up a
sign with yours truly. The man was direct, stern in manner, and had a Spanish accent, but he spoke perfect English. He guided me to a black Rolls Royce, a sweet ride.
Hopkins has a butler and he's loaded. The story was get-

ting better by the minute. But what's the catch? I admit I was excited, nervous, and to be honest, a little terrified as to what exactly I was getting myself into. During the drive, which lasted a little over an hour, as forecast, I skimmed through a couple of stories that I had in my library. One was called *Larger Than Life*, a nonfiction book about Freeze's track record, which, for any man of the law, was quite impressive. Most of the book was about the criminals Freeze had brought down throughout his brief success and how he slashed Lansford's crime rate to nearly zero percent. That's right. Zero! During that span from '84 to '89 (hard to believe it was only five years), any flavor of criminal was put to the test. Most of them wised up and picked another hobby; but for those who decided to test the waters, there was always that one icy name in the back of their minds. Another one was a graphic novel called *Gaze,* which was about the legendary string of hostage standoffs in 1984 known as Red Strike.

She closed the document and opened another one, *Journal Entry 10.13.2014.*
Then read.

Day one in Whisperfront. Diego didn't say one word throughout the entire drive. When I asked him where we were going, he didn't respond or change the expression on his face, his sharp, beady eyes occasionally crossing the rear view mirror. We drove along the rugged coast of Maine. A pleasant view, although it was much colder outside and overcast. I was wearing my favorite wool coat that I splurged on last year. We drove up a steep hill, which was heavily surrounded by fir and spruce and pine trees, up a narrow two-lane road, as windy as a snake's tail; and the potholes, it was like a Detroit expressway, bending each way as Diego and I ascended to our inevitable doom. The trees, reaching peak season, brightened up the scenery and made a nice view. When we reached the top of the hill, we drove down another winding road to get to the mansion. On the way, I didn't see a house in sight, but, still, I wasn't the least worried. Still nervous but not worried. I was more nervous about not having any bars on my phone. Not even one. At one point, I started to question why exactly I came all the way out here, to the dead zone. Of course, I had doubts. Who wouldn't? For years, Mr. Hopkins had been off the grid. Why now? Most importantly, why me? We finally made it to Mr. Hopkins' place. Welcome to Leatherby Manor. From the outside, it looked like any other mansion built in the 1800s, during the Neo-Renaissance Age. The structure had significant wear to it, as if it had seen its share of bad storms. There was a fountain in the front. Not sure what the statue was, but it looked Greek. There were formal gardens. Inside, I was completely overwhelmed by the size. The walls appeared bare, as if they were once covered with paintings. We were losing light. Diego, who still hadn't said a word to me ever since he picked me up at the airport, didn't waste any time taking me to Mr. Hopkins. Somehow, I got the feeling that I was being rushed as if time was running out. But for whom? Me or Mr. Hopkins? Soon, I found out in our first interview what the rush was about. Diego walked me to a courtyard with a sunroof in the center of Leatherby Manor. A beam of sun barely poked from the thick gray above and cast a light on an old, arthritic man who was slouched in a wheelchair. Diego pointed to the man in the chair and then left the courtyard. "You must be Mr. Jacobson," the old man said with his back facing me. "I've been following your work for some time now." His voice was booming and yet raspy, like an actor who did voiceovers for movie trailers. A lot of pain in his voice and yet, strangely, a lot of comfort. "Thank you," I finally told him. "Marcus Hopkins?" He hesitated and then said, "In the flesh. Call me Mr. Hopkins." I approached Mr. Hopkins and got a better look at his face. Surprisingly enough, he looked way too old to be this Hopkins fellow. I assumed he was in his late forties, early fifties, but he looked like a man who was pushing 80. I was frank with Mr. Hopkins, despite my guest status. I told him about his elderly appearance, how I thought Marcus Hopkins was much younger—as if I knew a thing or two about him, more than I let on. He laughed quietly to himself and told me that the line of work he was in—the *"disposal business,"* he said—put a lot of age on a man, especially from all the stress and workload of the job. I asked him to give me proof that he was, in fact, Marcus Hopkins, Freeze's old partner. But why would this guy fly me all the way out here if he wasn't the real deal? I had to make sure. Apparently, he already knew the question would come up. He told me to look over my shoulder. So, I did. On a small round table, next to a vase of blue roses, I found a picture frame of Freeze and another woman—I believe his wife—standing together on a beach, which Mr. Hopkins said they used to frequent on the weekends. I didn't ask him who the woman was, at least not yet. The picture frame wasn't enough. I needed more proof. How do I know he didn't steal the picture? Then, he told me to turn it over and pull out the picture. There was a personal note on the back of the picture addressed to Marcus. He told me to read it to myself. So, I did. The note read, "To my friend, Marcus. My brother for life." The note was signed *Leon.* I still needed a little more proof. I asked him if he had any identification. Diego came up from behind me and showed me a driver's license, which was taken many years ago. Obviously, if this was Mr. Hopkins, he was in no condition to drive. The man in the photograph looked similar to the old man before me, at least his profile; however, the photograph was taken many years ago, over ten years, and he says time hasn't been good to him. I asked if he had any other pictures of himself, mainly him or Freeze, but his first response was that he wasn't too fond of taking pictures, especially of himself. Then, with a shade of reflection on his face, he said, "If Leon was here today, he would tell you the same thing. Hard to believe coming from a man who used to pose half-naked for magazines." He let out a sigh, long and heavy as if it had been contained somewhere dark inside him, and now, a fraction of it was being released. "I hated the camera. Call me, 'camera shy.'" Hence the man behind the curtains, I suppose, the silent partner. That was all the proof I needed, not the response, not that he called Freeze by his first name, but the expression on his face. That look of *reflection*. I asked him if he didn't mind me filming the interview. He agreed. About five minutes into the interview, he asked me to stop filming. He said he'd rather not show his face to whomever I was going to show it to, even though I told him it was for my own amusement. Out of respect, I turned off the camera. I pulled out my phone and placed it on the table next to him. That was when I caught a closer look at his face. His skin was severely wrinkled, blemished and darkened around the eyes. He was wearing thick black shades that covered his entire eye. His hair was gray and thin, balding. I sat down across from Mr. Hopkins and pressed the record button on the Recorder App. Let the madness begin. . .

Anne stopped reading the journal entry and recalled skimming through a folder called *Tape Recordings* before Journal Notes. She minimized the document and opened the folder, *Tape Recordings*. There were many recordings, Anne discovered, all wave files. Each one was labeled INTERVIEW with a number sign, as well as a number beside it.

She opened the first wave file, *Interview #1*.

The QuickTime application launched.

Then, the first interview:

RENNY [COUGHING]: Excuse me.

(*He removes a water bottle from his bag next to his feet, takes a small sip, and there adjusts himself in the chair.*)

MR. HOPKINS: Ah ha! Smoker's cough.

(RENNY *chuckles to himself.*)

RENNY: Afraid so.

(*He pats his breast pocket, which holds a pack of cigarettes.*)

Bad habit. I guess.
MR. HOPKINS: Would you like Diego to bring you some tea? He's good at making a cup. One of his many specialties.
RENNY: No thanks. Maybe later. By the way, who's Diego?
MR. HOPKINS: Diego is my butler.

(*He tilts his head to the side.*)

He didn't introduce himself on the way over here?
RENNY [SOFTLY]: So, that's his name.

(*He clears his throat, quietly.*)

No. He didn't.
MR.HOPKINS: I apologize for that.
RENNY: No. You shouldn't have to. So ahhh, how long have you known Diego?
MR. HOPKINS: I didn't bring you all the way out here to talk about my butler, Mr. Jacobson. I brought you here to talk about Leon Dorsey.
RENNY [SOLEMNLY]: Right. Then, I guess we'll go ahead and get started. The video camera is off and now we are rolling on the recorder.
MR. HOPKINS [GRAVELY]: Splendid.
RENNY: But first, may I ask?
MR. HOPKINS: Fire away, Mr. Jacobson.
RENNY: Why come out with Mr. Dorsey's story now? Aren't you afraid of what this Company will do to you?

(MR. HOPKINS *lets out a lengthy sigh.*)

MR. HOPKINS: They can't do anything to me that they already haven't done, Mr. Jacobson. I presume you've done a background check on me, and I with you.

RENNY [UNCOMFORTABLY]: Well—

MR. HOPKINS: And now you're probably wondering about the name of the house. Aren't you?

RENNY: Charles S. Leatherby. You beat me to the punch, I suppose.

MR. HOPKINS: Unfortunately, Mr. Leatherby only exists on paper.

RENNY: And why is that?

MR. HOPKINS: Mr. Dorsey was a private person, as I was told. He owned one of the largest retail stores on the West Coast called Dorsey's. He had several houses across the country. When he passed, his son and grandson, Leon, were *not* left empty- handed. Let's just say Leon didn't have to worry about going to college. Anyway, Mr. Dorsey gave his son this very place, Leatherby Manor.

(RENNY *slightly drops his jaw in awe.*)

RENNY: Wait a second. What do you mean *this* place? Are you telling me this is the same house Freeze grew up in?

MR. HOPKINS: Leon. Please. Or Mr. Dorsey.

RENNY: Okay. So, Leon Dorsey grew up in this house?

MR. HOPKINS: That's correct. But the twenty-five thousand dollar question: What am I doing here?

RENNY: What are you doing here?

MR. HOPKINS [ECSTATICALLY]: Ah ha! I retreated here many *years* after Leon's disappearance. This place was my only safe refuge. But we'll get into that later.

RENNY: Okay. So, Leatherby Manor. Why exactly did Mr. Dorsey use that name?

MR. HOPKINS [PROUDLY]: Quite persistent you are, Mr. Jacobson.

(*He points his gnarled finger in* RENNY'S *direction.*)

Besides the privacy, it was to protect his identity. The Company would never find me here.

RENNY: You never answered my question, Mr. Hopkins. Why tell Mr. Dorsey's story now?

MR. HOPKINS: Ah! The million-dollar question!

RENNY: Sooner or later, people are going to wonder where I obtained all of my resources. Surely, I can't lie.

MR. HOPKINS: Of course you can't, Mr. Jacobson. But the truth must be revealed. Leon was the closest thing I had to a brother. It's time for people to know who Leon really was. And by the time your story is published, I won't have to worry about my well-being.

(*He coughs, wet and phlegmy trembling while doing so, as if he's hacking up part of his lung. After the episode, he reaches into his breast pocket and pulls out a handkerchief and wipes away the saliva from the corner of his mouth.*)

RENNY: Smoker's cough?

MR. HOPKINS: I wish. As you may not already know, Mr. Jacobson, I am a sick man. I have a cancer inside me that I'm afraid is now out of my hands. Soon, it will continue to spread throughout my entire body. And *soon*, I will be dead.

RENNY: How far?

MR. HOPKINS: Stage four. Pancreatic cancer.

RENNY [SERIOUSLY]: I'm sorry to hear.

MR. HOPKINS [ANGRILY]: Don't be. I've accepted the fact that I'm going to die.

RENNY: Well. Then, let's begin.

(MR. HOPKINS *cracks a faint smile as he points at* RENNY.)

MR. HOPKINS: I like your attitude. All work. No play. Leon, he shared a similar attitude, although he sure did love to play.

RENNY: So, he was a work-hard-play-hard kind of a guy?

MR. HOPKINS: Absolutely. Leon loved to play. He used to have the ladies lining up to be his wife.

(*He giggles, childishly.*)

He always told them to take a number and get in line. That was Leon for you, a stand-up kind of guy. Confident too.
RENNY: I'd say.

(MR. HOPKINS' *manner changes from excited to grim.*)

MR. HOPKINS: When I arrived at Leatherby Manor, Leon left behind all of his stuff, fancy automobiles, even a helicopter. The way I look at it, they're just toys. They possess no meaning in a man's life. I ended up selling most of Leon's collection a long time ago. Anonymously gave the money to local charities and homeless shelters.
RENNY: And that's what Mr. Dorsey would've wanted?
MR. HOPKINS: *Absolutely.* That's the kind of man Leon was. He'd give you the shirt off his own back, if he had to. Diego kept a couple of things, like the helicopter. Diego said it might come in handy if anything was to happen to me. They don't mean a thing to me, though.
RENNY: So, tell me about yourself, Mr. Hopkins.
MR. HOPKINS: What do you want to know?
RENNY: Start with where you grew up.
MR. HOPKINS: A little place called Montgomery Hills, a few miles outside Nashville, Tennessee.
RENNY: Nashville? Really?
MR. HOPKINS: You sound surprised.
RENNY: Well, you don't have an accent.
MR. HOPKINS: Well, after you travel the world for many years, the accent tends to wear off.

(*He points his finger in* RENNY'S *general direction.*)

You can tell a lot about a man just from the sound of his voice, the miles he's traveled, the different dialects he's picked up along the way. I wasn't in Montgomery Hills for too long, though. We moved to Baltimore when I was a teenager.

RENNY: Baltimore. I'm sure it was a lot different than Montgomery Hills.

MR. HOPKINS: We got used to it. We had to. I miss it, though, the mountains, the music. . . the southern gals.

(*He cracks a smile.* RENNY *smiles as well.*)

RENNY: Any brothers or sisters?

(MR. HOPKINS *clears the wet phlegm from his throat.*)

MR. HOPKINS: Ah, two sisters, both older than me.

RENNY: Do you ever see them?

MR. HOPKINS: Patricia, my oldest sister, she passed away March 20th, 1987. She had a blood clot in her leg, which, later, spread to her heart. Then, Destiny, December 2nd, 1994. Car accident.

RENNY: I'm sorry to hear about that, Mr. Hopkins.

MR. HOPKINS: Thank you. I may have been the youngest, but, in a way, I was like a father to them, at least when I got a little bit older. For so many years, Patricia and Destiny were like my guardian angels. Protected me from bullies. But when I hit that growth spurt, boy, did the tables turn. Then, I was the one protecting them. When they passed, Leon was the only family I had left.

RENNY: What did your father do?

MR. HOPKINS: My mother said he was a car builder or something like that. Lived in Detroit. Don't remember much about him.

RENNY: No relationship?

MR. HOPKINS: None.

RENNY: When was the last time you saw him, your father?

(MR. HOPKINS *sighs loudly while letting out a loud "Oh."*)

MR. HOPKINS: When I was around five years old. That was when he struck my mother in front of me and my sisters. My mother, now, she didn't put up with my father's shit. You see, back then, the woman usually—mostly—stayed at home while the man worked. My mother was a trailblazer for her time, working two jobs to support us, mostly jobs which were considered a man's job. . .

Anne fast-forwarded through parts of the interview.

. . . Had many friends. At that time, we weren't as segregated as the South, but you get the point. . .

She fast-forwarded some more, two minutes ahead.

. . . Eleven, no, twelve years old when JFK was assassinated. I remember the principal announcing it over the intercom. My teacher, Mr. Clarkson, broke down and cried in front of the entire classroom. Sad day. . .

Anne fast-forwarded some more, now three to four minutes ahead.

. . . I was recruited three years after I finished at Jefferson. They didn't have a name for their organization at that time—we just called it the Company. I *wanted* a change. I needed the change. . .
RENNY: What was your title at JeneCorp?
MR. HOPKINS: I was an enforcer for the Company—Senior Officer, as I explained in the email I sent you.

Lastly, Anne fast-forwarded the recording until she heard that one name, *Dorsey*, and then she rewound the interview a couple of seconds back.

RENNY: How long did you know Mr. Dorsey?

MR. HOPKINS: Twenty-two years, maybe more. I was working an undercover job in Kandy, located in the Central Province of Sri Lanka, a beautiful city with beautiful people. Have you ever been, Mr. Jacobson?

RENNY: I'm afraid I haven't.

MR. HOPKINS: You *should* go sometime.

RENNY: It's hard to find time right now.

MR. HOPKINS: Have you ever left the country?

RENNY: . . . No. Afraid not.

MR. HOPKINS [CLEARLY]: Really? And why is that, Mr. Jacobson?

RENNY: Again. Don't have the time. I would like to—I mean—I plan to whenever I can find the—

MR. HOPKINS: —You should make time, Mr. Jacobson. You're a good writer, but you could be a better one with the knowledge you gather from traveling and exploring and ex-periencing different cultures, other walks or ways of life.

RENNY: Well, I get all of that just by living in New York City.

MR. HOPKINS: True. Traveling is good for you, though, good for the body. It opens up this special place inside you. Makes you appreciate the little things in life.

RENNY [AWKWARDLY]: I will someday.

MR. HOPKINS: *Someday.* What are you so afraid of, Mr. Jacobson?

RENNY: I'm sorry.

MR. HOPKINS: What are you afraid of?

RENNY [STUTTERING]: I'm not afraid.

(MR. HOPKINS *wears a grin on his face.*)

MR. HOPKINS: Sure.

RENNY: Right now, time is money. When you live in a big city like New York every penny counts.

MR. HOPKINS: Not necessarily. Money is not the answer to life.

RENNY: Well, it puts a roof over my head.

(*He smiles, wide and awkwardly.*)

MR. HOPKINS: Sometimes a simple thing *like* a roof can be the root of a man's fears.
RENNY: I'm not here to talk about myself, Mr. Hopkins.
MR. HOPKINS: Of course, but we'll see.
RENNY: I'm a hard man to break, as you can tell.
MR. HOPKINS [SOLEMNLY]: Any man can break, including you, Mr. Jacobson.
RENNY [CHEERFULLY]: So, you were talking about Sri Lanka. . .
MR. HOPKINS: Yes. . . Sri Lanka. I was on a routine scouting mission for the Company, to gather vital intelligence from a senior officer stationed outside Kandy and then report it back to the Company. You'd think finding a six foot, three inch tall white man with blue eyes and bleached blonde highlights in his hair walking around Kandy would be a walk in the park. That wasn't Leon's style, though. He was careful. He knew people. He had many, many friends, friends in high and low places. Leon was extremely good at that, blending in like a chameleon, which made it even harder tracking him. At times, I swear it was like chasing a ghost. Just a week into my mission, I was approached from behind at this hole-in-the-wall café shop. Sure enough, it was Leon. He noticed the shades I was wearing, a special pair of mirror-tints. Sort of a dead giveaway. But it was better than being dead.
RENNY: The shades? Because of his eyes. Correct?

(MR. HOPKINS *slowly bobs his head, sensing another coughing spell.*)

MR. HOPKINS: The shades, they helped keep Leon's powers at bay.

RENNY: I remember the cops used to wear them whenever they worked with Freeze. . .

(*He corrects himself.*)

. . . Mr. Dorsey. They never explained why, only that they used them for their *own* protection.
MR. HOPKINS: Yes. That's right. They called them visors. I was wearing Aviators, *not* visors. I preferred not to walk around wearing those silly things. One: it would've easily given away my cover. And two: well, I didn't want to look like a complete fool.
RENNY: Better than being dead.
MR. HOPKINS: You got that right. It was too late, though. The very first thing that came out of Leon's mouth [DEEPLY]: *Hey. Nice shirt, Pretty Boy.*

(*A snicker from* RENNY.)

One of the many nicknames he had for me. One in particular was Stripes. After a while, everybody in the Company was calling me Stripes, all thanks to Leon.
RENNY: Stripes? Why Stripes?

(MR. HOPKINS *shrugs his shoulders.*)

MR. HOPKINS: I don't know. I never really asked Leon. I assumed it was because the way I wore my hair.
RENNY: And how did you wear your hair?
MR. HOPKINS: Well, back then we used to call it a *part*. Not sure what the kids are calling it these days, or if they're still wearing it. If there's anyone who knows anything about pop culture, it's you. Right? I'm sure you know how trends change all the time.
RENNY: Now, that whole 1950's look is starting to come back. Short on the sides, long on the top. Like James Dean.

(MR. HOPKINS *reaches his weak, bruised hand to his forehead and points along the side of his scalp.*)

MR. HOPKINS: I had these two razor thin parts on the side of my head. I didn't have much taste in fashion, not like Leon. Later on, I stuck with the name. One day, it was two parts. Another, three parts. There was one time I colored two white stripes, like racing stripes, down the side of my head. Thinking back now, I did stick out like a sore thumb, even though that wasn't my intention at all. That shirt was what really did it. What a fool. . .

RENNY: What kind of shirt were you wearing?

MR. HOPKINS: A pink Hawaiian shirt, a bright and ugly thing. I bought it from some pushover at the market for a hundred rupees. Leon, on the other hand [HISSING], the man sure did know how to dress even if it was a hundred degrees outside. Anyway, I bought Leon a cup of coffee and then did my little pitch. I told him how, despite what happened in the past, the Company was interested in a man such as himself, how, we would train him to control the power and use it for the greater good. Next, Leon told me to remove the shades.

RENNY: What did you do?

MR. HOPKINS: The only thing I could do. I removed my Aviators, and I looked him directly in the eyes and told him that there was still a chance to redeem himself.

RENNY: Redeem himself from what?

(*A long pause swells over the two—a click!*)

MR. HOPKINS [COLDLY]: From murder.

(SOPHIA *opens the glass door from behind.*)

SOPHIA [PATIENTLY]: Mr. Hopkins?

MR. HOPKINS: Ah, Sophia.

SOPHIA: It's time for your bath.

MR. HOPKINS: Yes. Right. Sophia, I'd like you to meet Mr. Renny Jacobson, journalist from *Flashback* magazine.

(SOPHIA *greets* RENNY.)

RENNY: Well, contributing editor.
SOPHIA: Very nice. I've heard lots about you.
MR. HOPKINS: I wouldn't be here if it wasn't for Sophia.

(SOPHIA *blushes from the comment.*)

RENNY: I see. Nice to meet you.

(*He stands up and firmly shakes* SOPHIA'S *hand. They both exchange smiles.*)

SOPHIA: It's a pleasure to meet you, Mr. Jacobson.
RENNY: *Renny.* Call me Renny.
MR. HOPKINS: Mr. Jacobson here will be staying with us for a while.
SOPHIA: Is that so?
RENNY [HESITANTLY]: Well, we'll see. . .
MR. HOPKINS: Now, if you would, Sophia, my dear, please have Diego show Mr. Jacobson to his room.
RENNY: I'm sorry. My room? I was planning on staying in a hotel in town.
MR. HOPKINS: Nonsense. We have more than enough room here.

(SOPHIA *walks behind the wheelchair and unlocks the wheels.*)

RENNY: I appreciate the offer, but. . .
MR. HOPKINS: No buts. You have a deadline you must reach by next Friday, and as you can tell, Mr. Jacobson, I'm not getting any younger. Trust me. We haven't even begun to scratch the surface.
RENNY: What about an Internet connection?

MR. HOPKINS: What about it?

RENNY: Well, I need to have a connection in order to do my work properly. Plus, if I need to contact my editor, there's no reception up here.

MR. HOPKINS: Guess you'll have to do it the old way, Mr. Jacobson.

RENNY: And how's that?

(MR. HOPKINS *points to the hallway, signaling for* SOPHIA *to push him from the courtyard.*)

MR. HOPKINS: I believe you already know the answer to that question, Mr. Jacobson.

(RENNY *nudges his head to the side.*)

For a second, a fuzzy silence played over the audio recording, which pulled Anne even closer to the laptop's speaker.

Enjoy your tea, Mr. Jacobson.

(DIEGO *opens the door for both* MR. HOPKINS *and his nurse. In his white-gloved hands, he carries a metal tray holding a pot of tea, as well as an empty mug and a stirring spoon.*)

The interview cut off.

Anne minimized the wave file from the Quick-Time Player and opened yet another interview, *Interview #2*, from the folder, Tape Recordings.

RENNY [CURIOUSLY]: I've noticed you removed the sculpture from the living room. Marcus Aurelius.

MR. HOPKINS [AMUSINGLY]: Impressive, Mr. Jacobson. You know your history. Diego, he does that from time to time.

RENNY: Does what?

MR. HOPKINS: Ah, moves things around.
RENNY: Any particular reason?
MR. HOPKINS: Redecorating.
RENNY: I see.

(*He pulls out a notepad and places it on the table.*)

Well, why don't we start by talking more about Mr. Dorsey? When did he first realize he was special?
MR. HOPKINS: Leon never thought he was special. He was an outcast throughout most of his childhood. Like any outcast who spends most of his day inside his own thoughts, he knows there's something out there for him. . . a *purpose*.
RENNY: What kind of purpose?
MR. HOPKINS: Any kind of purpose.

(*He lifts his hand from the armrest and holds up two fingers.*)

You see there are only two kinds of outcasts: the one who chooses to be an outcast for the attention and then the other who doesn't choose to be an outcast, yet society makes him or her an outcast.
RENNY: And which one was Mr. Dorsey?
MR. HOPKINS: You'd think kids would want to hang out with Leon since he grew up into money. That wasn't the case at all. He had a target on his back. The first time he came home with a black eye, he covered it up with makeup and hid it from his father. His father never suspected a thing. Leon would even wear long sleeves during the summers to cover up the bruises on his arms. For a couple of years, that was his routine—learning how to hide. And if Leon never found Tammy, then those bullies might've gotten the very best of him.
RENNY: Why did he hide the bruises from his father?

MR. HOPKINS: He was embarrassed. But all of that changed at the age of fifteen. That was when he first discovered his powers.

The volume was low, noisy, and hard to make out; consequently, Anne turned up the volume on the laptop and listened closely.

Tammy Chessman was his first victim?
RENNY: What was the relationship like between Mr. Dorsey and Tammy Chessman?
MR. HOPKINS: She was his girlfriend.
RENNY: Girlfriend?
MR. HOPKINS: He absolutely adored her. Almost everyday during Third Period, Leon would write Tammy a letter and give it to her during lunchtime. Then, Tammy, she would write Leon letters. They did this, oh, for about a month or so, writing each other letters until Leon finally got the nerve to ask her out. He was so damn nervous that he couldn't even carry a single thought in his head. The night before, he rehearsed lines of what he was going to say to Tammy. When it came time, he couldn't remember one line that he rehearsed the night before.
RENNY: Did he ask her out?
MR. HOPKINS: He did, eventually [FLUIDLY], but he couldn't recall a single word he said to Tammy.
RENNY: If he adored Tammy so much, then why did he kill her?
MR. HOPKINS: Leon didn't kill Tammy. It was the powers that killed her. At the time, he was going through a change in his body, mentally and physically, as most fifteen year olds do. Change was out of his hands. The *power* that was given to Leon was out of his hands. Leon had no control over it.

(*A ruffling sound coming from* MR. HOPKINS.)

RENNY: How exactly did Tammy die, Mr. Hopkins?

MR. HOPKINS: It happened while. . . while the two were [ANOTHER PAUSE], you know, being intimate with one another. Since it was the first time for both of them, they were equally nervous.

RENNY: You mean it happened while they were having sexual intercourse.

MR. HOPKINS [PLAINLY]: I never cared for using that one particular word.

RENNY: What? Sex?

MR. HOPKINS: I prefer making love.

RENNY: What's the difference?

MR. HOPKINS: There's a big difference, young man. Tell me, Mr. Jacobson. Are you married?

RENNY: That's personal.

MR. HOPKINS: Are you married? It's a simple *yes* or *no* question.

(RENNY *sighs, a sharp click follows.*)

RENNY: No.

MR. HOPKINS: Girlfriend?

Anne listened even closer.

There was a heavy silence over the player.

She fast-forwarded the interview until a voice came back on—a *rough patch.*

RENNY: *We're going through* a rough patch.

MR. HOPKINS: What's her name?

RENNY: Heather.

MR. HOPKINS: And do you love Heather?

RENNY [HESITANTLY]: Yes. I do.

MR. HOPKINS: You don't sound too confident with your answer, Mr. Jacobson. I have shared a lot with you so far and plan on sharing more, if that is all right with you. Of course, this will be off the record. Since we're going to be spending time together, you might as well be honest with me. Besides, I don't know how much time I have left. The very least you can do is indulge an old man before he dies.

RENNY [BLUNTLY]: She's cheating on me.

(MR. HOPKINS' *face grows long and slack*—"Oh.")

MR. HOPKINS: Sorry to hear.

RENNY: Don't be. It's not like I caught her in the act with another guy.

MR. HOPKINS: Then, how do you know she's cheating on you?

RENNY: I know.

MR. HOPKINS: How? Do you have any proof?

RENNY: About a month before I started working on the Stacey Dilworth story—I'm sure you've heard about it.

MR. HOPKINS: The missing girl?

RENNY: Yes.

MR. HOPKINS [DESPONDENTLY]: Diego read me an article about her.

RENNY: Anyway, Heather came over late and spent the night at my place. All day, she was ignoring me, my texts.

MR. HOPKINS: Maybe she was busy. Does Heather work?

RENNY: Dancing instructor. Does competitions as well. Travels a lot.

MR. HOPKINS: Woman of the arts. She sounds like a good catch.

RENNY: Well, I guess it was too good to be true. I met her at a local restaurant that we frequented and we had a drink. After that, we came back to my place. Before that night, I hadn't seen her in four or five days. We were talking on the phone, briefly, between those days. Both of our schedules conflicted. Anyway, you know, I was feeling in the mood. Had some candles going. Very romantic.

MR. HOPKINS: Ah. Nice.

RENNY: But she wanted to go to bed. I knew it right then and there. The truth was in her eyes, the guilt. When she was asleep, I checked her phone and found this text from a guy I've never even heard of, some guy named Jerold. *I had a wonderful night. Can wait to see u again*, with a smiley face at the end. I just knew. Didn't sleep that night.

Anne paused the interview and rewound it back a couple of seconds until she heard the word *guilt*.

. . . checked her phone and found this text from a guy I've never even heard of, some guy named Jerold. *I had a wonderful night. Can wait to see u again*, with a smiley face at the end. I just knew. Didn't sleep that night.

MR. HOPKINS: Did you confront her about this particular text?

RENNY: If I did, she would know I was snooping around her phone. I can't be that guy. I know a lot of guys like that, the possessive type. I will *not* be that guy.

MR. HOPKINS: You're still young, Mr. Jacobson. You *still* have time to find somebody.

(He braces himself against the armrests of the wheelchair and leans forward.)

Remember, Mr. Jacobson: Don't settle for less. Don't ever settle for less, even if society or a *girl* tells you to be a certain way. Find a woman who loves you for who you are, *not* for what you do. I know you don't write for money or fame, except for buying a roof over your head. Writers—like you, Mr. Jacobson—you're the ones who aren't afraid to speak their voice; and it's *that* voice, an indomitable voice, that will either lift a society to its fullest potential or bring it to its knees. You, Mr. Jacobson, *you* are the lone wolf searching for clues in a room which holds no light, only darkness. In this room, you, the wolf, shine your flashlight on the things that most of us do *not* want to see or choose *not* to see.

RENNY [MINDFULLY]: Clever, wolf in a dark room. You sound like a writer.

(MR. HOPKINS *frowns and waves off the comment.*)

Heather was one of the few who accepted me as a writer. She said she admired me for being a writer during a time of illiteracy.

MR. HOPKINS: Illiteracy? Huh?

RENNY: She also said I'd be better off writing smut novels.

MR. HOPKINS: Why is that?

RENNY: Because a person who writes smut novels makes a better living than most literary authors.

MR. HOPKINS: And you don't consider a smut novelist to be an author?

RENNY: No. I don't. Anybody can write smut.

MR. HOPKINS [PROFOUNDLY]: Writers like you, Mr. Jacobson, journalists, authors, smut novelists, or whatever, they write because they have to, *not* because they want to. I'm sure you can agree.

RENNY: You mean they didn't choose writing. Writing chose them.

MR. HOPKINS: Yes. You will *always* have a choice in life. But to go against your gut—

(*He points to his chest, his heart.*)

—your heart—that would be the ultimate crime. As I was saying earlier—about money—writers don't write for financial gain; and if they do, it wouldn't be genuine. They do it because they *have* to. They do it, Mr. Jacobson, to promote and sustain life. And then money and everything else that comes in between is like a bonus.

RENNY: I agree. I really do to some degree. But you gotta give the public what it wants. Am I right? I mean, people are perverts.

(MR. HOPKINS *quietly chortles.*)

MR. HOPKINS: Is that so?
RENNY: Yeah. They are.
MR. HOPKINS: People are curious, Mr. Jacobson. That's all.

(*He wipes away the saliva from the edge of his lip with a tissue. Then, he sticks the tissue into his pocket.*)

Please, Mr. Jacobson, tell me more about Heather. Was she the only serious relationship? Or were there others?
RENNY: There have been others. Three or four that had potential.
MR. HOPKINS: What happened?
RENNY [CANDIDLY]: *Money.* That's what happened. I think every relationship I've been in ended because I didn't make enough money or because of my job or lack of friends.
MR. HOPKINS: Maybe you don't give them enough attention. Women like that, Mr. Jacobson. They want to be loved, to be taken care of. It's comforting for a lady to find stability in a man. Same goes for a man.
RENNY: I *did* take care of Heather. I *gave* her the attention. Took her out whenever we had the time. Texted her a lot. [SHRUGGING] Maybe a little *too* much. . . I know, at times, I put the job ahead of Heather. But, you know, whenever we saw each over, I treated her as if she was a queen, as if she was the only woman left on this planet, yet I hardly received anything in return. At times, I felt like this. . . this stray dog waiting outside in the pouring rain.
MR. HOPKINS: I never got into the whole texting thing. Diego tried to explain it to me once.

(RENNY *shrugs his shoulders yet again.*)

RENNY: It's more convenien—

MR. HOPKINS [INTERRUPTING]: —It's lazy.

RENNY: That's one way of putting it, I guess.

MR. HOPKINS: Technology will always have its many *strengths* and its many *weaknesses*, but do the strengths outweigh the weaknesses and, essentially, will the weaknesses lead to the downfall of humanity?

RENNY: You seem to know a lot for a man who doesn't get out that much.

MR. HOPKINS: I used to get out a lot. Doctor's orders. Diego would drive me into town. I've always enjoyed the company of others.

RENNY: This was before you became ill?

MR. HOPKINS: Yes. Before I became ill and after.

RENNY: What do you think about social networking?

MR. HOPKINS: Social *what*?

RENNY: Social networking.

MR. HOPKINS: You mean the Internet?

RENNY: Yeah.

MR. HOPKINS: Well, I think it's a good tool for any entrepreneur who is trying to start up his or her own business. Other than that, I don't see the need in it. If you want to socialize with another person, then it's only natural to do it face-to-face, eye-to-eye. Like Leon, I too was an outcast. The one thing I learned: put yourself into the fold, despite what other people think. There will *always* be bad people out there. You can't let the bad inside. Negativity can be like a germ. It only gets stronger the more it lingers around. So, let yourself be known, physically, emotionally. Appearance builds character.

(*He clears his throat, gradually.*)

But, as I was saying earlier, do the strengths outweigh the weaknesses, these weaknesses being the loss of human connection?

RENNY: That's a good question. In my view, the ultimate question.

(MR. HOPKINS *drifts into thought.*)

Have you ever tried it?
MR. HOPKINS: Tried?
RENNY: MyCircle, FriendZone, Chatterz?
MR. HOPKINS: And these are all social networking web-sites?
RENNY: Yes.
MR. HOPKINS: Then, no. I haven't.
RENNY: They do have certain advantages.
MR. HOPKINS: Like?
RENNY: Say you want to rekindle a relationship with an old friend or you're looking for someone in particular, you can find anyone on MyCircle.

(MR. HOPKINS *hangs his head for a moment.*)

MR. HOPKINS [GRIMLY]: Not anyone.
RENNY: I think the only way we can secure a positive future: *moderation.* Sure. As with any brand new device or any operating system or social networking site that improves or makes our way of life more convenient, there will always be drawbacks. Always.
MR. HOPKINS: Love is *not* convenient, Renny. If you fall in love, you must work hard to keep that love alive. For instance: your texting. Right. It's impersonal, as cold as the machine itself, but you already know this. When you listen to someone speak, Renny, you hear the emotion in his or her voice. There's nothing better than listening to a person's voice, especially the voice coming from the one you love. That voice, it stays with you, Renny, *forever.*
RENNY: Of course. Although, now that I think about it, there is a new smartphone app called i2i. Spelled with the letter i. Similar to Facetalk.
MR. HOPKINS: An app?
RENNY: i2i. It's like a program that allows you to talk to another person face-to-face on the phone.

MR. HOPKINS [SOLEMNLY]: You're right. I don't get out that much.

(*He shakes his head in disgust.*)

Let me say this and then we'll get back to Leon. Most importantly, this is for young people like you, Renny. Finding love or stumbling into love, it's all a game. Like golf.
RENNY: Never really been a fan.
MR. HOPKINS: But you are aware of the concept?
RENNY: Yes. My brother tried to get me into the sport. Played once. Epic fail.
MR. HOPKINS: Excuse me?
RENNY: Sorry. What I meant to say is that I wasn't that good at it.
MR. HOPKINS: Well, of course. You can't just pick up a golf club for the first time and shoot a low score. It takes practice, lots and lots of practice. There's nothing wrong with failure, Renny.

(*He leans closer to RENNY.*)

In order for one to be successful, one *must* fail. If you don't fail, then how do expect to learn?
RENNY: Well, it was probably one of the worst experiences ever. Literally took us all morning to finish nine holes. People kept playing around us. We ended up calling it quits on the fifteenth hole because it was getting dark outside and you could hardly see the ball in front of you. It was a mess.
MR. HOPKINS: Golf is a game of great patience. It can get messy at times. . . like love, Renny. You can't just jump into love and expect everything to go smoothly or by the numbers. That's *not* how it works. There will be many hazards on the course, many women on the playing field. Occasionally, you hit the ball into the hazard, sand traps, a bunker, the rough, water, then you know, you learn how to

avoid the many hazards, the women who will get you in trouble. But that is all a part of the game, Renny. It takes incredible patience, hard work, determination, and focus, and persistence—which you don't have to worry about—and practice, most importantly, *compromise*. The wind may play a factor at times—manipulating which direction the ball will carry. At times, you may enjoy the thrill, the chase. . . the danger. It makes you stronger. Love forces us to become stronger men, better men. But that is *not* why we play. Is it, Renny?

RENNY [QUIETLY]: Why do we play?

MR. HOPKINS: We play, Renny, for that one shot, the shot we've all longed for, the hole in one. Sometimes we come *that* close. . .

(*He uses his fingers, both thumb and index finger inches apart, and raises them up for* RENNY *to see.*)

. . . to making it into the cup, so close we can even taste it on our lips. But we try again and then again. Then, once you've finally hit that one shot, once you've found that right woman in your life, then there's no reason to play the game ever again. No shot will ever beat the hole in one. In that moment, as a man, you choose whether or not the game is over. Do you play the game over again or do you settle? Provide? Do you nourish? Do you bring new life into the world? If we do hit a hole in one, then why do we try to hit another? That, Renny, is the ultimate question.

She stopped the interview for the time being, switched screens, and opened the next entry, *Journal Entry 10.14.2014*, from the Journal Notes folder.

Then, read:

Didn't get much sleep last night. The first interview went well, despite having been cut short. My stomach is a little upset from the squash soup Diego fixed. I feel like there's something special going on here, especially last night when I was roaming through the entrails of Leatherby Manor. I came across a library in the North Wing, which was twice the size as my apartment in New York City. Mr. Hopkins owns about every hardback known to man, especially the classics—most of the fabulous authors I grew up reading in school: Dickens, Steinbeck, Poe, etc. When I asked him about his extensive collection, he said most of the books belonged to Mr. Dorsey. He also said Diego is quite the bookworm. At night, he reads him bedtime stories. Still can't believe I'm in the same house Freeze grew up in. Mr. Hopkins isn't much of a sleeper. Neither am I. Not used to sleeping in such silence, not a natural silence, but the kind of silence that creeps up on you, an old house speaking in many tongues throughout the night. Mr. Hopkins was one of those many tongues, a sweet old man struggling to sleep despite the demons that haunt his nightmares. He is definitely in pain, both from the cancer as well as something else. Whatever is haunting Mr. Hopkins, I will soon find out.

Anne scrolled farther down the page and came across more writing in the journal entry.

(Cont.)
I am still left baffled after the second interview with Mr. Hopkins this morning. Since he said he wasn't feeling too well, we decided to resume the interview in the afternoon. Despite his sickness, Mr. Hopkins seems pretty sharp and in tuned to what's going on. He is a gentle man with a tender heart who is living with a burden, one I haven't extracted yet, and not the cancer. He said the cancer was nothing—an "inconvenience," he told me. At times, it appears as if he has lost someone he loved, although he ignored the question when I asked him after he ended the interview. He is not bitter by any means. Mr. Hopkins is—more or less—a man who believes in other people and/or is trying to believe. He called the fascination with MyCircle a fad like "bellbottoms in the Sixties." Surpris-

ingly enough for a man who hardly leaves the house, he knows the identity crisis that our country is facing. I can't lie. I'm guilty as charged when it comes to chattering (if there was such a word called *hypercrite*, I would definitely fit the bill) or texting, which, by the way, Mr. Hopkins disapproves, as I'm sure any elder does. No surprise there. He is right about one thing: if we do continue along this sketchy path of detachment, the world will, indeed, become as cold as the machine. He told me a good quote: *"Only when we unplug ourselves from the Machine can we be free."* A few years from now marrying oneself will be like the new legalization of pot. Bob Dylan once sang, "Don't criticize what you can't understand." I totally understand the issues at hand, but there comes a point when you can't debate with *Crazy*. What exactly are we evolving into? And who is to blame? We have turned into a bunch of fucking narcissists and deep down inside we're waiting for a *big* event to happen like the zombie apocalypse or something extreme to wake us up from our digital comatose state. Is it technology's fault? How about our arrogance? Or has the Internet turned us into a society entitled to everything? You can glamorize technology all you want in million-dollar commercials, inspire hope and innovated ideas to the everyday viewer, but it doesn't help our current state. Technology has its perks. No doubt. I'm still waiting for an option where you can freeze your own body and set a time when you want to be unfrozen like *Demolition Man*. I'm more curious to see if the future is as intriguing as it is in the Philip K. Dick's or Isaac Asimov's novels. Flying cars, augmentation, holograms, time travel. The rate we're going I don't see that happening in my lifetime. So save us the trouble and let it rest in the realm of fantasy. Deep down inside, *way* deep, another part of me wants to believe Mr. Hopkins, that there can be hope for this great country without *tech*nology, but I know it's not going to happen. He is a very private person with an old school way about him. Reminds me of Freeze. Those types don't seem to exist anymore. The stoic man who dresses nicely the minute he rolls out of bed. Makes sense why they were so close. Also noticed one thing in particular about Mr. Hopkins, but I haven't found the right way to ask him yet. Perhaps I may slip it into the next interview. . . his shades. The man is always wearing shades. Since I've been here, not once have I actually looked the man in the eyes, which makes me wonder what's really going on with him; and if there is something, why is he not telling me? Depending on how the next interview goes, more than likely I'll stay in a hotel tonight. I'm sure Mr. Hopkins won't be too pleased to hear about the news—that is if I leave—but I must get a hold of Edie and tell her about the story. I assume Edie is worried sick about me right now, wondering whether or not I got a gripping story for her. So far, there *is* a story, not as gripping as I hoped for, but since Mr. Hopkins is sick, it's going to take much longer than planned. Only two things keeping him alive, Mr. Hopkins said, the pills (he takes so many that he can't even keep up with them) and the other thing he never got around to telling me this morning. He will, though. Whenever he's ready. If I plan on spending a week with Mr. Hopkins—if all goes according to plan—then I expect to have a great story before Frantic Friday. That is if Mr. Hopkins is healthy enough to carry on. The interview that Mr. Hopkins and I had was pretty intense and made me think about my life, as if, in a way, he already knows everything about me, especially what he said about Heather. It makes sense, not perfect sense, but some kind of sense.

Anne picked up the pair of ear buds, inserted the jack into the headphone port on the side of the laptop, and then stuck the ear buds into her ears. She played the recording from the next interview, *Interview #3*.

RENNY: If you don't mind, please tell me a little bit more about Tammy Chessman's death—from what Mr. Dorsey told you.
MR. HOPKINS: He never liked talking too much about it. They were in bed together, Tammy and Leon.

RENNY: Making love?
MR. HOPKINS: Yes. That's right.

(*He sighs, provoking another cough.*)

Leon was on top of her. Then, all of a sudden, Tammy's eyes switched over almost like a shark's eyes seconds before it's about to attack its prey. She was choking. Her limbs fell to her side as if the nerves had been completely severed. The veins in her face became dark. Leon didn't know what was happening to this girl he loved. Then, he pulled away from her. It was already too late. Leon was horrified, confused. His father heard screaming coming from downstairs and rushed into his son's bedroom. Once he witnessed Tammy, stiff as a board, he knew who his son was and [EMPHASIZING] *what* he had become.
RENNY: What had he become?

(MR. HOPKINS *gets up from the wheelchair on his own, grabs the cane from behind the wheelchair, and walks to the study's window. Next,* RENNY *gets up from his chair and then reaches out to* MR. HOPKINS.)

MR. HOPKINS: I'll manage.

(*He waves off* RENNY.)

RENNY: You sure?
MR. HOPKINS: Yes. I'm fine.

(RENNY *stands behind* MR. HOPKINS, *just several feet away.*)

RENNY: Mr. Hopkins, what did Leon become?
MR. HOPKINS [SOMBERLY]: Something that he *never* ever wanted to be. In a way. . . it found him when he was most vulnerable.
RENNY: What found him?

(MR. HOPKINS *turns his shoulder.*)

MR. HOPKINS: The ability to do remarkable things—a power, which, at the time, he had no control over. But soon, he would.
RENNY: So that's why Mr. Dorsey fled to Sri Lanka? It was because he accidentally killed Tammy?
MR. HOPKINS [QUIETLY]: Yes. You'd be surprised how many people Leon's father knew. But he had no other option for his son. He knew other people would be after Leon, not the authorities, but *bad* people, dangerous and corrupted people who wanted what his son had inside him, *this power.* If Leon's new power had somehow gotten into the wrong hands, then the world you know, Renny, would cease to exist. So, he did the only thing any loving father could do. He said goodbye to his son. And that was the last time Leon saw his father.

(*He ambles back to the wheelchair.* RENNY *helps him to the seat.*)

MR. HOPKINS: Thank you, Renny.
RENNY: You're welcome.

(*He walks back to his chair. Sits down.*)

Did you ever ask Mr. Dorsey where he got his power? I heard the rumors. Some say he was involved in an accident. Others say it's from radioactivity.

(MR. HOPKINS *laughs, then coughs.*)

MR. HOPKINS: I asked him numerous times about his. . .

(*He clears his throat.*)

. . . his gift.

RENNY: And is that what you thought it was, a gift?

MR. HOPKINS [STERNLY]: If it wasn't a gift, Renny, then what was it?

RENNY: A freak of nature?

MR. HOPKINS: That's one way of looking at it. Some people wondered if what Leon did was the work of God. Then, there were other people who thought he was doing the Devil's work. Me. . .

(*He points to his chest.*)

. . . personally, I didn't see Leon work his magic until that first day in the training labs in Death Valley, one of the main headquarters of the Company, where I observed this. . . *wrath* being channeled through the eyes of a man. A part of me took it as a miracle, a gift, taking away the *im* from impossible and making it *possible.* Another part of me knew exactly what it was, but I was too afraid to admit it.

RENNY: Which was?

MR. HOPKINS: A curse. Nobody really knew where Leon acquired the power, the ability to turn a living. . . breathing thing into stone. Every time I asked Leon, he always avoided the question. But I assure you the rumors you've heard are all false. Leon *wasn't* involved in an accident. He *wasn't* exposed to radiation. He was like you and me, Renny, only with one exception.

RENNY [GLEEFULLY]: Yeah! One big exception!

MR. HOPKINS: I believe Leon was born with the power. That's my personal opinion.

RENNY: Like a freak of nature?

The interview went silent for a few seconds, prompting her to listen even closer.

RENNY: When was the first time you saw Mr. Dorsey use *the gaze?*

MR. HOPKINS: The gaze.

(*He laughs merrily.*)

I haven't heard anybody call it that in years. Let me think for a second.

(*He pauses for a moment to gather himself from the excitement.*)

I was still showing Leon the ropes. The man had the attention span of a four year old.
RENNY: Really? When I think of Freeze, I always think of this stern, debonair, *always*-focused man.
MR. HOPKINS: He was. Well that came later, I suppose. Leon, he certainly knew how to put on a game face in front of the camera.
RENNY: Of course. [TENTATIVELY] I have this article here you may like. Practically grew up with this guy. His name is Arthur Mitchell.

(*He reaches into his satchel and pulls out a newspaper. He flips to the second page of the newspaper and shows* MR. HOPKINS *the article entitled "Tailored for Greatness."*)

MR. HOPKINS [EXCITEDLY]: Is that right?
RENNY: Read his stuff like everyday.
MR. HOPKINS: Did you know Leon and Arty were very close friends?
RENNY: No. I did not.

Anne paused the interview for a moment and minimized the player. She opened that one article she came across while skimming through the files on the USB flash drive. She double-clicked on the folder, *Miscellaneous*.

After that, she opened another folder, which read TAILORED FOR GREATNESS.

Inside the folder, there were two other items, one a JPEG image called *Article* and another a folder called *Open*.

Anne double-clicked on the JPEG, launched the article, and read to herself:

TAILORED FOR GREATNESS
By Arthur Mitchell
Columnist *The Lansford Tribune*

"TO ALL YOU criminals out there, there's a new sheriff in town and his name is Freeze," said our newly elected mayor, Mayor Pratt, to the overly eager people attending the rally two nights ago on a packed Third and Harper Street.

Despite the frigid weather, the people who came out for the festivities didn't let the extreme conditions ruin all the fun. Thomas S. Fink, an English teacher from Roseberry Academy, both of his feet numb from standing in the cold for four hours, called the event, "New Year's Eve celebrated all over again, but without a pulse." Unsure of the turnout, there were dozens of volunteers dressed in pale blue tee shirts, handing out free cups of hot chocolate on every street corner while nearby bars were overflowing with thirsty patrons, standing shoulder-to-shoulder, their bodies furrowed in close attention, bundled up like a religious tribe with their eyes glued to Mayor Pratt speaking from the television screens above. Every now and then, a patron would whisper in another's ear, "Can you actually believe this?" Like many, the frequent questions never obtained sure answers, only mere speculation. For most, it was hard to swallow knowing that a person who possessed such unimaginable powers lived right here in the city of Lansford and not in a city like Metropolis or any other fictional city because, to the many people who grew up around the Triad area, that was exactly what it felt like: a movie or a thing only read about in comic books.

Three days have passed since the Hostage Situation at Central Reserve, and the buzz is still spreading around Lansford like a wild fire. One couldn't walk a block without hearing about Freeze, a name talked about in high spirits around town and at the same time, whispered with a tremor of trepidation in the darkest of alleyways. Soon, I would learn firsthand from the horse's mouth of that one name.

Four of us, three journalists—myself included— all from the Triad, and an intern from the Morning Blues, are standing outside the quiet Precinct 32 and freezing our tails off in ten-degree weather. As the snow comes down sideways, I remind myself that he will be out any minute now and that my patience will soon pay off. The atmosphere is eerie, a calm before the storm. However, each and every one of us has the same purpose: to see a glimpse of this new sheriff in town and, hopefully, if all goes according to plan, to sneak in a question or two for the newspaper. How ironic it is to feel like a human icicle, a shivering body waiting for an elusive man who is remarkably gifted with the power to "freeze" a criminal in his or her boots. Was Freeze looking at us as this very moment, possibly somewhere behind a tinted window? I remind myself that it's only the cold weather. When I first saw the hostage situation unfold on television and then later witnessed cops lugging out the two perpetrators involved, one of their bodies partially turned to stone, I couldn't help but rush to judgment and wonder if this man, Freeze, was real or not without knowing the cold hard facts. Was it possible for a human being to hold such a talent or was the act smoke and mirrors, an illusion, Bigfoot? If the latter was true, then Freeze would've given Harry Houdini a run for his money. Having worked in the media for seven years now, I've learned the most important lesson: to keep such personal views to myself in order to report a story with the utmost humility and, no matter what, with ethics and dignity. Not a single person, scientists included, was aware of how Freeze was capable of committing the very act that defied nature. They were equally as flabbergasted as I and many others were. During an interview last night, Commissioner Quinn called the act, the "turning point for mankind." Over numerous times, I've tried to reach out to Lansford Police Department and talk to them, but they wouldn't comment on the matter.

Two excruciating hours passed until an entourage of police officers, lawyers, and what appears to be government officials, finally step out the front doors. In the middle of the entourage walks a twenty-five year old, six foot, three inch tall man with blonde highlights and a face shaped like a marbled sculpture and the sturdy physique of a power forward. From first glance, he looks much older than his age. They call him Freeze, and from the way he moves, he appears to have no intention of stopping to talk to us. Before he makes a left to the parking lot, he slips from the entourage and strolls directly our way as we stand shivering in the cold, while tiny clouds rise from our clinking teeth. He's wearing a black suit—collar raised around his neck—with a red shirt underneath, black silk tie, black shades, despite the darkness of night and the only source of light coming from a flickering street light above. From the way he moves, calm and smooth like a tide rolling into shore, he doesn't appear to be bothered by the bone-chilling weather. The man carries himself with great confidence, a man who is well aware of his own self-importance and responsibility. Before I know it, Freeze is only feet away from us. Prior to his grand exit, I re-hearsed six or seven questions in my head but only one remained intact by the time Freeze arrived at the curb. The three others I'm standing with are left at a complete loss for words, which makes me wonder if he used this so-called "gaze" on them and, for some reason, singled me out. Certainly, not from my good looks. I am first to speak, but the words stumble from my lips, which are about as chapped as old car seat leather (It was a good thing I brought my tape recorder because I didn't remember a word that came from my mouth). "So, how does it feel to be the new face of justice, Mister?" I asked him. He slowly removes the shades from his face. Two of us flinch, but I stand my ground. Both his face and body are still lost in the shadows—only a strip of light is highlighting his eyes like in the mov-ies. From a closer inspection, I can tell that he is an attractive man, toned, and healthy. His eyes are gleaming, blue, and penetrating. Freeze responds, calmly and smoothly, with a question of his own, "Is this going to be in your newspaper?" I quickly fol-low, "Yes." I remove the glove and extend my hand. "Mr. Mitchell, Arthur Mitchell," I say, my jaw shaking, "Lansford Tribune." He reaches out and shakes my icy hand. His grip is firm and yet his skin is incredibly warm to the touch. "Nice to meet you, Mr. Mitchell," he says in his booming, reso-nant voice, which is unusually calming. "You can call me Freeze from now on." I repeat, "Freeze?" I crack a smile, which soon draws a smile onto Freeze's face. "I like that. Very catchy name. Good for the papers." I can't help but smile like I'm a giddy child meeting his favorite idol for the first time. Another journalist sneaks in the same ques-tion and interrupts halfway through my sentence.

"How does it feel to be the new face of justice?" He doesn't respond to the journalist. His smile dissolves from his face. His eyes move away from me and toward the other journalist, Craig Basse from the Madison Observer, a good friend of mine. Craig doesn't know what to say from the icy expression. Eventually, after a few tense seconds, Freeze turns my way and stares at me with those same penetrating eyes. I finally ask, "How does it feel to be the new face of justice, Freeze?" I make sure to include that one name, *Freeze*. He replies with a mischievous grin breaking through his icy glare, "It feels," he thinks for a moment and then says directly, "cool." I immediately follow up, "If you don't mind, can you elaborate more for the people of Lansford?" He puts his shades back on his face (a strange glimmer dampening from his darkening face), pats me on the arm, and responds, "You're the writer, Mr. Mitchell." I soon remind myself that this man, as debonair as he may be, is only twenty-five years old, and all of the overnight success is possibly new to him. He walks away and says over his shoulder, "Be seeing you 'round, boys," and then, in the blink of an eye, he vanishes into the night. From a distance, two bright headlights open like a pair of eyes from the hood of a car and light up behind a wall of snow. Freeze drives away in a silver Lamborghini Japla while I'm still left going through the recent exchange in my head. He was a man of few words. A walker. I had a good feeling, as did a lot of people who I talked to, that this wasn't the last time we would see Freeze. I just hope that next time he'll give me a little more material to work with.

Anne closed the JPEG, pulled up the player, and hit the space bar, which played the interview.

MR. HOPKINS: Which one?

(*He doesn't grab the article.* RENNY *places it on the table.*)

RENNY [STRANGELY]: *Tailored For Greatness.*
MR. HOPKINS: Yes. I remember that write-up. Actually, I still have it somewhere around here. He kept all of Arty's articles.
RENNY: Mr. Mitchell was one of the reasons why I went into journalism.
MR. HOPKINS: Is that so?
RENNY: When I was a kid, I saved all of his articles and kept them in a scrapbook. When my father got a new job, we moved to the South. I lost the scrapbook during the move. Nearly killed me.

(*He shakes his head in disappointment.*)

Anyway, so, you knew Arthur Mitchell as well?
MR. HOPKINS: Leon did mostly. He and Arty were like this.

(*He twists both his index and middle finger together like a pretzel.* RENNY *stares at* MR. HOPKINS, *the smile creeping on his face.*)

Leon was never bashful when it came to publicity or the media. Unlike some people in the spotlight, Leon loved the attention. His kryptonite, though, was women. I tell you if you cut open Leon's chest, you'd probably find a giant marshmallow instead of a heart.
RENNY: So, he was a softy?
MR. HOPKINS: Not a softy. Not by any means. He was tough when he wanted to be, when he *had* to be. He just had a soft spot for the ladies.

(*He raises his hand to his chin—thinks.*)

We were doing a gig in New York City. Leon couldn't keep his eyes off the ladies. Good thing I was there to keep his sorry butt in line. The Company wanted Leon to [QUOTES] convince an investor/shareholder, Bob Schubert, to keep throwing money at JeneCorp's stock. [END QUOTES] Since Mr. Schubert was one of the wealthiest fools on the planet, the Company would more than likely go under if it wasn't for Mr. Schubert. Mr. Schubert wanted to pull out— personal reasons. I was pretty nervous going in, Leon not so much. At the time, I didn't know how well Leon had mastered his gaze. [MORE EXCITEDLY] Was I wrong! We arrived at Mr. Schubert's million-dollar penthouse. He was upset with the Company's threats and so forth, told us he wanted out, that he was sick and tired of looking over his shoulder, wondering when the Company would sic the dogs on him. You should've seen what happened next. Leon removed his VBans from his face and looked Mr. Schubert directly in the eyes, gave him the gaze. Watching Leon give Schubert the gaze was like watching a master puppeteer control a puppet, controlling every thought, removing thoughts and *freezing* thoughts. Not only could he use his powers to stop criminals dead in their tracks, but he could also use his powers to persuade. That was actually his first name, *The Persuader*. Leon could control the gaze just by looking into a person's eyes, penetrate the mind, the thoughts, turn certain thoughts to stone. It was as if he used his eyes as a scalpel and mentally cut through a person's mind without that person even knowing it. I tell you, Renny. It was something else. And now, you see why the Company wanted him so badly, to train him for their own personal gain.

RENNY: He was a human weapon.

MR. HOPKINS: He was.

(*His manner turned dourer, dark in tone.*)

But like all things, Renny, there was a drawback to Leon's gift. A couple of months later doctors found a tumor in Mr. Schubert's brain. He died about a year later. They never suspected Leon. I knew, though. I knew it had to do with what happened in New York.

RENNY: After Mr. Schubert's death, did the Company go under? What happened to their stock?

MR. HOPKINS: Surprisingly, it shot up like a beanstalk. Believe that? Eventually, they found more investors. More investors meant more shareholders. And more shareholders meant more money, which could keep the Company around a little longer. The Company had many hands in many wealthy pockets. And of course, Leon, he was a good pet to have.

RENNY: Did you ever work with Leon when he partnered up with the LPD in 1984?

MR. HOPKINS: Briefly. I was more like. . . like a supervisor.

RENNY: Did you ever have to wear a visor?

MR. HOPKINS [SUDDENLY]: Hell no!

(*He chortles, which suddenly causes him to cough violently.* SOPHIA *rushes into the room.*)

SOPHIA: Is everything okay?

(MR. HOPKINS *waves away* SOPHIA.)

MR. HOPKINS: We're fine.

(SOPHIA *discreetly lifts up the blanket from* MR. HOPKINS' *lap. First,* SOPHIA *checks the suprapubic, making sure its properly attached and then, secondly,* SOPHIA *lifts up* MR. HOPKINS' *right pant leg, and checks the urine bag strapped to his leg.*)

Please, Sophia. Not in front of our guest.

SOPHIA: This will only take a minute. I promise.

(She walks over to a cabinet, pulls out a urinal, and empties the dark urine from MR. HOPKINS' bag into the bottle.)

There. All done.

(MR. HOPKINS hangs his head in despair.)

(She takes a mental note of the amount of urine in the urinal, as well as the dark color, dumps the urine into the toilet, flushes the toilet, and then exits the room.)

RENNY: We can continue tomorrow if you like?

(MR. HOPKINS shakes his head.)

MR. HOPKINS: No.
RENNY: Okay. So, where was I? Right. The visor. Why didn't you have to wear one when you were around Leon?
MR. HOPKINS [BITTERLY]: I never needed it. Even if they told me to, I would never wear that ridiculous thing. Everyone else did, except me. One time, I remember, they told me if you work with Freeze, then you had to wear a visor. I never did, though.
RENNY: What was the *real* reason?
MR. HOPKINS [CONFUSEDLY]: Reason?
RENNY: Why officers had to wear a visor?
MR. HOPKINS: The visors made sure Leon didn't do anything stupid like accidentally gaze a cop.
RENNY: Why would he do that?
MR. HOPKINS: Well, let's just say, Leon quickly developed a lot of enemies when he joined forces with the LPD. Cops didn't like knowing that they were incapable of carrying out a job. Leon was their go-to guy for the big jobs, the bank robberies, kidnappings, and hostage situations. None of that petty shit. Leon always looked after the little man despite his flaws. Speaking of which, the Go-To Guy was one of the many nicknames he earned while helping out the

LPD. Leon liked that name especially, *Go-To Guy*. He liked knowing that people could depend on him no matter what the situation. It gave him even confidence [THROUGH THE CORNER OF HIS MOUTH]—as if he didn't have enough confidence already. There was Freeze, of course, which stuck the most. Freezer, the Freeze Man, Freeze Machine, the Persuader, the Closer, Pretty Eyes.

(*He flashes a smile on one side of his face.*)

Leon couldn't stand that one, *Pretty Eyes*.
RENNY: And who came up with that name?
MR. HOPKINS: Who do you think?

(*The smile spreads across his entire face—like a bashful child.*)

Leon didn't like being called Pretty Eyes as much as I didn't like being called Pretty Boy. Then, there was the Stone Cutter, Gazer. . .
RENNY: Why Freeze? Why did that name stick the most?

(MR. HOPKINS *tilts his head slightly as he furrows his brows and thinks for a moment.*)

MR. HOPKINS: I'm not sure. Arty was actually one of the first ones to bring that name to light, not Pratt. However, the mayor took all of the credit for the name. I think, though, Leon picked up the name from the cops and that one saying they used all time, [QUOTES] Freeze! [END QUOTES] Instead of saying Freeze, well, you get the picture. They had Leon. But he didn't actually turn people to ice. One thing was for sure: he would stop them dead in their tracks. [SMOOTHLY] *Oh yeah.* Leon spoke fondly about catching criminals in the act and seeing the looks on their faces. He compared it to. . . to watching a movie and pushing the pause button in the middle of an action scene. I

believe, in the film industry, they call it a freeze frame or
ah. . . a still. . .

RENNY: Correct.

MR. HOPKINS: Anyway, they would make the silliest
faces—Leon would tell me. For most, that facial expression
was permanent and ended up staying with them throughout
their entire jail sentence—like Freeze's personal stamp. The
ones who were less fortunate are now either courtyard statues or doing time in Mercy Mental Institution. And believe
it or not, Leon was quite the negotiator too. Had a zero
percent casualty record. Nobody died on his watch.

RENNY [SERIOUSLY]: Except for Bob Schubert and Tammy
Chessman.

(MR. HOPKINS *doesn't respond. He remains stern, quiet.*)

I remember watching the Red Strike on television when I
was kid. I wanted to be just like Freeze after that day. I
even had a poster of him hanging on my bedroom wall.
Think every kid my age did.

(MR. HOPKINS *cracks a smile, fully.*)

MR. HOPKINS: What was there not to like? Despite everything that happened to Leon, he always was an ambassador
to Lansford. Probably the most beloved and yet hated person in America—despite being as elusive as he was. Adored
by ordinary citizens. Feared by criminals. In a way, he
needed his enemies as much as they needed him.

RENNY: How so?

MR. HOPKINS: They kept him sharp, always on his toes.

RENNY: Keep your friends close and your enemies closer.

MR. HOPKINS: Most definitely. But where there is fame,
there is always envy. For Leon, it became a problem. Inside
a dark alley, behind every blind corner, there was a has-been
gunning for Leon, a *nobody* trying to be a *somebody*. Some
tried. *Some.* But all of them failed. After Red Strike,

Mayor Pratt gave Leon the key to the city. As usual, he was fashionably late. The man always knew how to make an entrance. I was jealous, of course, but at the same time, I was happy for Leon. Then, after all the hype, the fame, those all-or-nothing days, the *glory* days, Leon turned into a legend, a myth, nothing more than a strange name whispered on the streets, Big Foot—Arty would say. Sure. There were impostors. But none of them were the *Freeze*.

(RENNY *flips through his notes.*)

RENNY: How about Leon's father? What did he do for a living?
MR. HOPKINS: That's enough for today, Renny. I believe Diego has prepared a dinner for you. Do you like beets?
RENNY [TENTATIVELY]: Beets. Uh. Yeah. Sure. I don't mind beets.
MR. HOPKINS: Good. You'll love his famous beet salad. All fresh from the garden. To die for.

(*He grabs a bell from the table and rings it two times. Seconds later,* SOPHIA, *without saying a word, slips into the study and pushes* MR. HOPKINS *from the room.*)

Have a good night, Renny.
RENNY: Mr. Hopkins?

(SOPHIA *stops and turns the wheelchair around.*)

MR. HOPKINS: Yes, Renny.
RENNY [SOFTLY]: I was meaning to ask you earlier. Is there anything I can do to help?
MR. HOPKINS: No, Renny.

(*He carefully searches for* SOPHIA'S *hand near the back of the wheelchair. He finds her left hand and then taps the top of it.*)

My Sophia here has spoiled me enough. Normally, I wouldn't mind taking advantage of your generosity, but then if I did, Sophia would be out of a job.

(SOPHIA *smiles, sincerely*.)

RENNY: Well, if there's anything you need. . .
MR. HOPKINS: Thank you, Renny.

The interview stopped.

Anne closed the file and opened the *Journal Notes* folder.

As she removed the buds from her ears and double-clicked on the entry, *Journal Entry 10.15.2014*, she heard an explosion and then the rattle of a speaker coming from the television in the living room. Following the explosion, there was gunfire and then more rattling.

Jamie grabbed the remote and turned down the volume from the television, as she did throughout the entire show, up and down, *up* during the character's dialogue, and then *down* during the action scenes, which, to Jamie, was more annoying than entertaining.

Anne placed the buds back into her ears, opened the eHits application from the dock, and then scrolled through her vast library of songs until she came across a Mona's Arch song, a gem called "Last Ride Home," from their sophomore album, *Machine Mistress*.

As the song played, Anne read from the journal entry:

A couple of minutes after midnight. Can't sleep again. What else is new? Down to three smokes. But I don't feel like making a run. It's not my nature to sleep during a story, especially a story this good. Learning more and more about Leon Dorsey. It's a slow process. But the ball is rolling. Working my way through my second bag of Doritos and Coke. The orange, greasy fingerprints on the keys and the bloodshot eyes: a clear sign of how enthralled I've become with Freeze's story. Spoke to Edie over the phone, sent her a text as well, but she sounded as if she was in a hurry. Told her about the story, gave her the address to the mansion in case she doesn't hear from me in a week. Ended the conversation with, "Get *her* done," her, as in the story—a line I've only heard Edie say when the shit has hit the fan. The pressure is on, that looming deadline slithering around the corner. For some reason, I can't stop thinking about the recent altercation with Mr. Hopkins before I slipped from Leatherby Manor. The story is about Freeze, and yet, it has a lot to do with me. Like I was meant to tell his story to the world. I couldn't think of any other way to tell Mr. Hopkins. So, I just did. I told him that it was crucial for me to make a couple of calls, one being to my editor to tell her that I have a story, and that, if all goes according to plan, it will be ready by the end of next week. Mr. Hopkins didn't seem too thrilled. He wasn't wearing his shades, which was a first. I couldn't make out his eyes, though. It was dark, only one light was burning, and he stayed very close to the shadows. Mr. Hopkins told me that Diego could drop me off at the nearest hotel, which was about eight miles away, and then he could pick me up first thing in the morning. As I was leaving, Mr. Hopkins brought up Heather's name and asked if she was one of the persons I needed to call. I hesitated at first. Then, I told him yes. I don't know why I told him that. I was never going to call Heather. To make matters worse, Mr. Hopkins went along with the lie. Finally, he told me that when Diego did the background check on me, there was one particular subject that I failed to mention. The second Mr. Hopkins brought up her name, I knew exactly where he was going with the conversation. I didn't think Mr. Hopkins was *that* thorough, especially Diego, a man who looked as if he's never used a phone in his life. I was wrong about Mr. Hopkins, about

Diego, about everything, as if I was walking straight into a trap. My immediate reaction was why. They knew everything about me, the restraining order, and yet when I spoke of Heather as if she was my own, your average couple going through a small hiccup in their relationship, he went along with the lie, as if he didn't have a clue about our history. His response was that he knew everything. "Not everything," I said to him.

Anne paused the song, "Last Ride Home," removed the buds from her ears, and read closer. . .

Mr. Hopkins may or may not know what it's like to want someone so badly even though it's physically impossible, how the thought of her brings so much joy and yet so much pain. Heather was, and forever will be, that ache in my chest. Life will never be the same without her. Then, I think about the way she treated me, how she ignored me, how badly she *burned* me. Mr. Hopkins questioned me, mainly why I lied to him. "The truth," I told him, "Heather was my girlfriend, *was*, but not anymore." We weren't seeing each other anymore. I was mildly obsessed with her. "Mildly?" Mr. Hopkins said. "I think 'mildly' might be an understatement." Mr. Hopkins was right. I may have been obsessed with Heather. But was I wrong? Am I lesser of a man because I cared so deeply about another person? Does it make me weak? Heather was *my* everything, and even till this day, I'm in love with her despite what she did to me. The real question Mr. Hopkins should have been asking: Is love and obsession the same thing? If you love someone so deeply that you would sacrifice everything for him or her, what does that make you? A sucker? A fool? Maybe I was living in denial. Maybe the idea of love is so wonderful and yet so out of reach that it's what keeps me bound to a life of loneliness. Exactly a year into our relationship, I told Mr. Hopkins, I knew I was losing Heather, but there was nothing I could do to get her back. She had a nice job, she traveled, and none of those things included me. In the prior weeks before we broke

up, she was traveling more, which meant I was seeing her
less often. She would only come home for a couple of
days, and in those days, she was busy training for her next
competition or instructing her students. And I was only at
her beck and call. I told her that one day I wanted children
and that I wanted her to be the mother of my children. She
was thirty-seven, and I knew she was pushing the bar
when it came to having kids. She called her own students
her children. The fact: she was growing apart from me,
and yet, I didn't want to believe it. I was only lying to myself, telling myself that it would work in the long run.
Eventually, she *would* settle down. We would live a life
together. I would not be alone anymore. . .
We would have each other forever. Heather always carried around this stern composure, which made me love her
that much more. She appeared unbreakable; and yet, when
she danced, all of that emotion she kept inside poured out
from her body—"*poetry in motion*," that's what she called
it. The first time I met Heather she was waiting in the
checkout line of a bookstore down the street from my
apartment. She was holding a book by Hemingway in her
hand. I tapped her on the shoulder and carefully whispered in her ear, "The main character dies at the end." Her
head jarred back as if my breath smelled of something
nasty. Within that stern demeanor, a smile broke through
and stretched across her face, revealing a narrow gap between her two front teeth. Her eyes twinkled like stars,
and the world around me had fallen into oblivion, as if we
were the only two people on earth. From that day forward,
all that mattered in my life was Heather. I'm not a rich
man. I don't drive a BMW. I don't have season tickets to
the Knicks. I don't own a boat off Lake Ernest Point. I
might not be able to buy Heather fancy things in a snap of
a finger; but, in that bookstore, I swore to myself that everything I did from that point forward would be for her, and
only her. Then, the world around me started to come to
light; the pieces were being put back into their proper
place, a world once left in ruins, now rebuilt. Then, a year
later, that world began to crumble. My dreams of spend-

ing a life with her were shattering, the ground beneath my feet cracking. She told me she found a new job in Taiwan, an instructing gig where she was going to teach Taiwanese Argentine Tango, which she had learned at a young age from her homeland. Before I had a chance to say goodbye, Heather was gone and I was left heartbroken for days, weeks. She was never good at saying goodbyes. Neither was I. She was all I thought about. I kept calling her, texting her. Many nights were spent wondering what she was doing, where she was, or if she was with another man. The thought alone of her being with another person sickened me to the core. The calls were brief, the texts shorter. Then, she stopped returning my calls, my texts. That's when I received a letter from a judge. The hardest part was *not* knowing if I had done something to make her shut me out for good. There was a connection. I wasn't afraid to run from it. I could feel it inside me, in my bones, a feeling that I haven't felt in a long time, and like that, she vanished from my life as if she never existed. She was, in essence, a ghost. All I have now is a memory of her, the images in my mind of us making love, her dancing Vietnamese Waltz in the pale moonlight, her smile, which, everyday, fades like an old ink spot. At times, I find myself thinking about Heather when I look to the sky and watch an airplane fly above, wondering whether or not she's on that flight, and if she is, what is she thinking about. Is she thinking about me? Or has she completely erased me from her life? At times, I wonder if she thinks about me at all, the times we shared together. Did they mean *anything* to her? You live and you learn. Right? Don't Cry For Me, Argentina. In these past couple of weeks, I've waited for that one special girl to come along and completely destroy all memories I had of Heather, of Argentina, so I can be spared the pain. I still haven't found that woman yet. The one question that haunts me everyday: *What if* she never comes along?

—

Anne stared at the journal entry on the screen. She finally blinked, releasing the tears from her eyes. One by one, the tears flowed from her eyes; however, Anne never sobbed or sniveled. She just sat there, letting the tears crawl down her face, as she stared at the laptop's screen, not thinking much at all of Renny, only herself, and how that question, which, like Renny, had haunted her everyday, the one question that always went without an answer. And that was what it was: a *what-if* question. There was more to read, but she decided to close the journal entry and open the next interview, *Interview #4*.

MR. HOPKINS: How did you sleep, Renny?
RENNY [TENTATIVELY]: So-so.
MR. HOPKINS: I reckon you will sleep well tonight. We have a lot of ground to cover.
RENNY [SERIOUSLY]: Let's hope so.
MR. HOPKINS: I will tell you this, though. You can't just come and go as you please, Renny. Do you understand?
RENNY: Yes, of course.

(*He finds a framed photograph of a young girl perched on the dresser.*)

This must be Mr. Dorsey's daughter.
MR. HOPKINS [SUDDENLY]: Excuse me.
RENNY: The girl in the picture.

(*He holds up the picture frame for* MR. HOPKINS.)

MR. HOPKINS: Yes. That's right.
RENNY [SUSPICIOUSLY]: You must've been close to her.
MR. HOPKINS: We were.
RENNY: So, *you* don't—

MR. HOPKINS: —I also want to apologize for what I said to you last night before you left. I was out of line.
RENNY: No. Don't be. I'm glad you called me out.
MR. HOPKINS: Did you contact your editor?

(RENNY *sighs and sits down in the chair across from* MR. HOPKINS.)

RENNY: I did. The heat is on.
MR. HOPKINS: Well, that's good to hear.
RENNY [EXUBERANTLY]: So, where do we begin?
MR. HOPKINS: Coffee?
RENNY: Sure. I could use another cup. I'm sure Diego can make a better cup than that watered down crap they were serving at the motel.

(MR. HOPKINS *rings the bell.*)

Five seconds later:

(DIEGO *enters the master bedroom.*)

DIEGO: Sir.
MR. HOPKINS: Can you bring Renny here a cup of coffee?
DIEGO: Yes, Master Hopkins.
MR. HOPKINS: Thank you, Diego.

(DIEGO *leans his upper body forward in a bow.*)

DIEGO: You're welcome, sir.

Anne clicked on the fast-forward button on the player and skipped about a minute or two through the interview.

RENNY: Smells delicious.

(*He blows the steam from the mug before taking a sip. After the first sip, he frowns and tilts his head with amusement.*)

MR. HOPKINS: Not bad, huh?
RENNY: Very good.

(*He gently places the mug onto the plate and then places the plate back onto the table.*)

May I ask you a personal question, Mr. Hopkins? But strictly off the record, of course.
MR. HOPKINS: Sure.
RENNY: Do you ever get scared?
MR. HOPKINS: Well, I wouldn't be human if I didn't.
RENNY: What I mean is. . . do you ever get afraid of dying alone?
MR. HOPKINS: I have Diego. He's all the family I need.
RENNY: I mean having your loved ones next to you, like your sisters. Do you ever get upset that they won't be around when you pass?

(MR. HOPKINS *thinks carefully about his next answer.*)

MR. HOPKINS: All the time. But I know they will be there with me in spirit. You know, I used to think a lot about that saying [QUOTES] You are born in this world alone and you will die alone. [END QUOTES] As I grow much closer to death, I realize how—excuse me—how bullshit that saying is. The second you enter this world, you are welcomed by two open arms, ready to catch you from the darkness of your mother's womb; you are embraced and you are loved; you are celebrated and raised high as if you were a trophy—a mark of achievement *and* optimism; you learn about the world that you have been brought into and you experience its natural wonders; you develop, mature, and while you mature, you surround yourself with people. . . people *you love*, Renny, and in return, people who love you. . .

(He catches his breath from the long-winded comment.)

. . . People who go out on a limb and put themselves into the equation—even in your most desperate hours—people who stand by you, through thick and thin, people who support you, most importantly, people who would die for you. No matter how different we may be, the human race, we are all the same in that we all owe a death, some of us choose to die alone while others chose to die the way they were born: *embraced, loved, celebrated.*
RENNY: And how do you want to go out, Mr. Hopkins?
MR. HOPKINS: The way I was born.

(He holds his head down.)

But. . . but sometimes, Renny, you don't always get what you want in life.

(He raises his head, proudly.)

If you want something or someone bad enough, Renny, you have to work at it.

(He points at RENNY.)

Persistence, Renny.
RENNY: I see.
MR. HOPKINS: Everyday, we surround ourselves with people. Are these people our friends or loved ones? What makes them special? Ask yourself, Renny: What would these people do for you? How far would they go out of their way to please you? Would they risk their lives for you?
RENNY: I don't know too many people like that. Most of them only care about themselves. Serious. But I'd like to think that there are decent people out there who would prove me wrong. Expect the worse and hope for the best, right?

MR. HOPKINS: I'm sure there's at least one person out there who would risk his/her life for you.

RENNY [DULLY]: Doubt it.

MR. HOPKINS: Sure there is, Renny!

RENNY: Well, agree to disagree.

MR. HOPKINS: Why are you so hard on yourself?

RENNY: I'd rather not talk about myself. Last time I checked, I was the one interviewing you. Remember?

MR. HOPKINS: Of course.

(RENNY *flips through his notepad, searching for the right questions to ask* MR. HOPKINS.)

I'd like to think that there's *still* good in this world and one day it will overcome all the bad. Hell! If all you want to hear about is the bad in the world, all you have to do is turn on the news. No offense.

RENNY: None taken. My father used to watch the news, like it was religion. I remember I'd walk in on him yelling at the TV as if the TV was talking back to him.

MR. HOPKINS: Diego. He gets that same way.

RENNY: Really? He doesn't strike me as the type.

MR. HOPKINS: He doesn't show it, but I can sense it.

RENNY: Some of us are good at hiding, more so than others.

(He gives MR. HOPKINS *a chance to respond to the remark. He receives nothing.*)

At the time, I just thought my father was another grumpy old man who, like other grumpy old men, couldn't accept the constant changes of the world. If there's one thing *I've* learned: the world keeps spinning round and round. Later on, my mother became aware of how one-sided the news channels had become. She stopped watching. *Consider the source*, that's what she used to tell me.

MR. HOPKINS: And your father, does he still watch the news?

RENNY: Eventually, he stopped watching as well. Doctors said it wasn't good for his blood pressure. He still read the newspaper all right, every morning too, like a ritual. Don't take the man away from his rag.

MR. HOPKINS: Do you ever read the newspaper?

RENNY: Now you read through a whole bunch of filler before getting to the actual news.

MR. HOPKINS: So, no?

RENNY: Sometimes. It's hard to know what the truth is anymore. It's like when we were kids. In school, our teacher would have us sit in a circle around the classroom. She would start at the beginning of the circle and whisper a word into one student's ear and then *that* student would then whisper the word into another student's ear; and by the time it reached the end of the circle, the word was completely different from the original word.

MR. HOPKINS: What was the lesson?

RENNY: Our teacher wanted to demonstrate a rumor.

MR. HOPKINS: That's right. A rumor will always be a rumor. *Not* truth. Rumors can even be created simply out of spite.

RENNY: Or jealously.

MR. HOPKINS: Jealously. Yes. Or even someone having a little too much fun. I've dealt with my share of them.

(*An awkward pause in the conversation.*)

RENNY [CARELESSLY]: Well, you probably should've gone into journalism.

MR. HOPKINS: Me? Nah. I like the action too much.

RENNY: A thrill seeker, huh?

MR. HOPKINS [SMOOTHLY]: Oh yeah.

Anne heard a sudden *click*!

The interview stopped without her touching a single key on the laptop.

Then, it resumed play.

RENNY: We live in a selfish world, Mr. Hopkins. I mean, when exactly did taking pictures of yourself become the norm?

(*He shakes his head in shame.*)

MR. HOPKINS: You don't have any room to talk, Renny.

RENNY: I know. I'm guilty as charged when it comes to taking selfies.

MR. HOPKINS: Diego told me all about this phenomenon, these selfies.

RENNY: I wouldn't exactly call it a *phenomenon*. The fact is pretty clear. We're slowly turning into a bunch of self-absorbed assholes.

MR. HOPKINS: I heard they even made it a new word in the dictionary. Is that true?

(*He leans forward in the wheelchair.*)

RENNY: It's true. Diego tells you a lot of things. Doesn't he?

MR. HOPKINS: He does. I'm sure you're aware that Leon was a model at one point in his career.

RENNY: How could I forget? I remember that one where he was topless and advertising blue jeans.

(MR. HOPKINS *laughs from the response, which turns into a phlegmy cough.*)

MR. HOPKINS: No question about it. He did have that *look* of a model, especially when he was all dolled up for a night out. He wore suits that costs thousands of dollars. Wore them as if they were costumes. And whenever he would strut into a room, a spotlight would shine down on him. Dimming out everything around him.

RENNY: During that time, suits were pretty popular.

MR. HOPKINS: Fashion is like the moon. It comes in cycles.

RENNY: True.

MR. HOPKINS: You talk about rumors. There was even one that I was with Leon. You know, like, *with him*. They call them uh, you know—what is it?

(*He snaps his fingers together.*)

Partners.

RENNY [SURPRISINGLY]: Get out of here!

MR. HOPKINS: The rumors weren't true, of course, but Leon sure did get quite a kick out of 'em. Only a man who feels resentful of another man's sexuality must first question his own. Leon, he wasn't the least bothered by these rumors. He was extremely confident in the way he carried himself. Except for the whole modeling thing—which Leon didn't care much for—Leon *never* flaunted himself or his money.

RENNY: So, would driving around in a Lamborghini Japla be considered flaunting your money?

MR. HOPKINS: They were just toys, Renny. Sometimes, Leon would drive around the city and let people ride around in whatever fancy car he was driving that day. He had great respect for people, *except* for the authorities. At times, he had a reputation of being hardheaded. *But* he had great respect for people. And that's the key, Renny. You have to respect yourself before you can respect others. Back then, as you said, in the Eighties, we had our antics and whatnot. We acted like fools, but at the end of the day, we had *respect* for one another despite our differences. We showed class whenever we needed to. We *respected* our elders, even if they were full of shit?

(*The comment provokes laughter from* RENNY.)

RENNY: Whatever happened to those days?
MR. HOPKINS: Don't know, Renny.
RENNY: Bad parenting?
MR. HOPKINS: Or no parenting at all. . .

(*He pauses after the response and then hangs his head for a moment.*)

RENNY: There are a lot of parents out there who shouldn't be parents.
MR. HOPKINS [CLEARLY]: I can tell you were raised by good parents.
RENNY: I guess. I had a roof over my head and a hot meal on the table at the end of the day. My parents weren't big spenders or socialites by any means. They were humble, hard-working folks who always wanted the best for me, even if it wasn't what I wanted to do.
MR. HOPKINS: And what did *you* want to do, Renny?
RENNY: *This.* Writing. Telling people's stories.
MR. HOPKINS: Would you ever write your own story?
RENNY [TEASINGLY]: I don't know. Thought about it a couple of times. It might bore you to death.
MR. HOPKINS: Nobody is boring, Renny. Remember that. There is something special in all of us. So, when did you move to New York?
RENNY: I was born in Lansford and then we moved to Sharlot, North Carolina. About three years after college, I moved to the Big Apple.
MR. HOPKINS: How did you like Sharlot?
RENNY: Nice place with nice people—at least when I first moved there. It always had potential to be a big city. It became one, eventually. Once a small city. Now a bigger one.
MR. HOPKINS: Well, sometimes, things change like the seasons. It's part of life. Other times, things just become what they're supposed to be.

RENNY: Last time I was in Sharlot, I couldn't even recognize it. Nothing like that relaxed, easy-going environment I knew years ago. Now, it's like everybody's in a damn hurry or trying to be someone who they're not.

(*He shakes his head. Sighs.*)

A rat race. Feel bad for the next generation. Talk about pressure.
MR. HOPKINS: I'm sure your parents said the same about your generation.
RENNY: I don't know. No. It's getting worse.
MR. HOPKINS: How bad can it be? I'm here.

(*He nods at RENNY.*)

You're here.

(*He points at the ceiling above. . .*)

The sky is still above us.

(*. . . then at the floor below.*)

The ground is still below us.
RENNY [ANXIOUSLY]: Yes.
MR. HOPKINS: It's relatively easy why people are in a hurry nowadays, *not* only in Sharlot, but in any big city.
RENNY: And why is that? People have jobs. People have places to be, families and things to take care of.
MR. HOPKINS: No, Renny. They're always in a hurry because they haven't found any meaning in their lives. They think that these *materials* or *possessions* will make their lives better. That's why they're always in a hurry, because they're always looking for something better, something bigger, something that will give them *meaning*, whether it be a new car or new lady. Whatever.

(*He suddenly pauses and clears his throat.*)

Leon was *always* in a hurry. But [QUOTES] to each his own. [END QUOTES] As I was saying earlier, Leon sure did have a way of lighting up a room, *not* only from his looks or what he wore, but also from the way he carried himself. However, deep inside, he had many flaws like you and me. And over time, he became the ideal candidate for *hate*. However, not once did Leon ever show them, his flaws—at least never in public. One day, I asked him about the modeling and why exactly he did it. At the time, he was doing modeling for these sunglasses.
RENNY: VBans.
MR. HOPKINS: That's it.
RENNY: I remember. Had a pair of my own.
MR. HOPKINS: I'm sure you did.
RENNY: Hey. [INNOCENTLY] They were in style, in cycle.
MR. HOPKINS: That's right, Renny. Leon told me he was pressured into doing the modeling. He never felt comfortable about it, even if they were paying him boatloads of money. Leon told me he was sick and tired of people staring at him. He knew he was sending the wrong message to people. He asked me what am I [LEON] doing? Am I [LEON] really helping out people?
RENNY: What did you say?
MR. HOPKINS: I told him to do what he felt was right in his heart. He knew that people, individuals, were all different, and models, they have this way about them, saying that we should all look like them, or wear our hair like them. . .

(*He points in* RENNY'S *general direction.*)

. . . People shouldn't have to dress a certain way. It has, and always will be, about being *unique*, Renny. So, about the whole selfly thing. . .
RENNY: Selfie.

MR. HOPKINS: Selfie. Whatever. I think there are more important things to do besides taking pictures of yourself. But if it makes you feel better about yourself or if it makes you *respect* yourself and others, then go ahead. Who's stopping you?
RENNY: I got suckered into doing it.
MR. HOPKINS: By whom?
RENNY: Nobody in particular. It's the thing to do, I guess.
MR. HOPKINS: Why be like everybody else, Renny? Are you the wolf or the shepherd *or* are you another sheep?

(RENNY *smirks and then bobs his head.*)

RENNY: Wolf sounds straight to me.
MR. HOPKINS: That's what I thought.

(RENNY *flips through his notes.*)

It's up to you to decide whether or not you choose to roll with the times or stay true to who you are and not let the things around you persuade you into becoming someone you are not.

(RENNY *raises his shoulders and holds them there until the response comes to him.*)

RENNY: I know who I am.
MR. HOPKINS: Are you sure, Renny?

Anne heard another *click*, but this time it sounded soft and distorted.
There were a couple of seconds of dead air.
Then, the interview came back on.

MR. HOPKINS: Diego tries to keep me up to date with everything that's going on in the world. He's good at doing that.

RENNY: Sounds like he's good at a lot of things.

MR. HOPKINS [EMOTIONLESSLY]: Yes. He is. He told me about a program where you can download anything you want at any time onto your computer and that you don't even have to go to a store to purchase it. Where's the fun in that?

RENNY: It's the world we now live in. Everything is shared for free on the Internet. Everybody is in a—

MR. HOPKINS: —A hurry?

(RENNY *barely smiles.*)

RENNY: Right.

MR. HOPKINS: When Leon and I were starting out, we didn't have time to go out in the public and act normal. But whenever we did have the time, we would always hit up the record store and pick out whatever was hot during that time. Leon was a big fan of music. Told me that [QUOTES] music holds the key to our hearts. [END QUOTES] Leon could go on for days talking about the genres or history of music.

(*A smile creeps onto his face.*)

Leon would have to disguise himself, of course, whenever he went out in public.

RENNY: And you?

MR. HOPKINS: No. There was no need.

RENNY: So, Leon didn't like interacting with people?

MR. HOPKINS: No. He loved people. He wanted to be known as Leon, not *Freeze*, or Leo—he also went by that name. Don't get me wrong. At first, Leon loved the attention, the cameras, the spotlight. Then, over time, I guess he wanted something more in life.

RENNY: He wanted meaning?

MR. HOPKINS: Oh yes. It happened sometime in the late Eighties—Eighty-nine, I believe—he wanted to live a normal life, especially after everything he'd been through. I remember Leon always enjoyed the process of buying a CD: driving to the store, being greeted at the door by some friendly hippie fellow, shuffling through CD's, picking out a CD, buying it with his own money, starting a conversation with the checkout clerk. For Leon, it was an experience, an *interaction*.

RENNY: How about you?

MR. HOPKINS: I didn't care about the music. I was just glad to be hanging out with my friend.

(*A long pause, comfortable.*)

RENNY: So, Mr. Hopkins, since we're now on the subject of friendship, I have one more question. *Yes* or *no*, if you like.

MR. HOPKINS: Sure.

RENNY: Would Leon ever die for you?

(MR. HOPKINS *turns away.*)

Mr. Hopkins?

MR. HOPKINS [SULLENLY]: I heard you.

RENNY: Well, would he?

MR. HOPKINS: *Yes.* He would.

(*A tense silence momentarily swallows the interview.*)

Another *click*.
Then:

RENNY: So, Mr. Dorsey's father, Peter?

MR. HOPKINS: Correct.

RENNY: Can you tell me more about Peter?

Anne paused the interview and stretched her legs by walking several laps around the bed.

Before Anne resumed the interview, a phone rang outside the bedroom. She sauntered across the bedroom until she reached the door. There, she pressed the right side of her face against the door and listened closely to Jamie talking on the phone; however, she wasn't speaking English, Anne gathered.

Anne quietly opened the door and witnessed Jamie standing in front of the living room window.

"*No puedo*," Jamie said quietly on the phone.

Anne couldn't make out what Jamie was saying. She tiptoed closer.

Now, Jamie was begging, "Por favor, *Diego*."

Anne listened carefully as she tiptoed even closer.

"*Sí*," Jamie said, unaware of Anne approaching from behind.

The floor beneath Anne suddenly *squeaked*, which caused Jamie to freeze!

She turned her shoulder, only to find Anne standing in the hallway.

"Listen, Mom," she said quickly on the phone, "I have to run." Jamie nodded several times. "Okay. I love you too. Bye."

Jamie ended the call and then held the phone in the air.

Anne asked, "Who was that?"

"My mother," Jamie answered hesitantly.

"I didn't know you spoke Spanish."

"Well," Jamie said, again, with hesitation, "I'm a little rusty."

"You didn't sound rusty."

"I struggle with it sometimes," Jamie said. "It's like playing an instrument. If you don't practice all the time, the skill wears off. My mother doesn't speak English too well."

"Does she live here?" Anne asked.

"Yeah," Jamie said, bobbing her head. "She lives in Queens Dive."

Anne pointed to the kitchen.

"I was going to grab a glass of water."

"Sure," Jamie said. "Be my guest. Glasses are in the top cabinet."

Anne walked into the kitchen and opened the top cabinet.

"No," Jamie said as she redirected Anne. "The one to your left." She walked to the edge of the kitchen and leaned over the counter. She asked, "Are you hungry?"

As Anne opened the correct cabinet—the one on the left, as Jamie had told her—and grabbed a clean glass from the shelf, she shook her head and answered, "Not really. How about a snack?"

"Sure," Jamie said as she pointed to Anne's left, "there's some stuff in the pantry. If you get hungry, let me know."

"I will," she replied as she poured herself a glass of water from the dispenser in the refrigerator. She checked out what Jamie had to offer in the pantry, mostly granola bars and bags of rice and canned vegetables. She found a protein bar on the bottom shelf. She grabbed the bar, turned to Jamie, and said, "Thanks."

As Anne walked back to the guest room, Jamie said from behind, "Anne?"

Anne turned around and faced Jamie.

"Yes."

"Everything's going to be okay," she said.

"Thanks," Anne said and then made her way back into the guest bedroom.

8:25 PM

WHILE snacking on the protein bar, Anne picked up the laptop and resumed the interview, *Interview #4*.

MR. HOPKINS: He was an explorer, an archeologist, a passionate man, Leon told me. He devoted his life trying to discover the answers to our origins. As a young child, Leon hardly saw his father. Peter was too busy traveling around the world.

RENNY: And how about Leon's mother?

MR. HOPKINS: Her name was Daniella.

RENNY: How did Peter meet Daniella?

MR. HOPKINS: Leon's father was doing some work in the City of David in Jerusalem. At the time, Leon's father was living abroad. One weekend, Peter decided to take some time off in Tel Aviv. That was where he met Leon's mother, Daniella. The two ended up spending the entire weekend together before Peter went back to Jerusalem. Peter went back to Tel Aviv the following weekend to visit Daniella. From there, the relationship took off. Peter fell in love. He moved in with Daniella a few months later. Then, they had Leon a year later. There were some complications during the pregnancy. Daniella died during childbirth. Leon hardly talked about *her*, though, about Daniella. The most he knew about her was from what his father had told him and from the pictures he had.

RENNY: Was their any resentment there, between Leon and his father?

MR. HOPKINS: At first, yes. After Leon was born, Peter traveled a lot. He wanted nothing to do with Leon. In a way, I believe Peter was looking for her, for another Daniella, a woman to fill the empty shoes Daniella left behind.

RENNY: Did he ever find her?

MR. HOPKINS: Not *her*, Renny. Him.

RENNY: Him? Him who?

MR. HOPKINS: Peter's travels brought him to Venezuela, South America.

(*He lowers his head and remains quiet.*)

RENNY [STRICTLY]: Mr. Hopkins? Is there something wrong? Something you're not telling me?
MR. HOPKINS: I'm afraid, Renny, this is as far as the story goes.
RENNY: But Mr. Hopkins, if I'm going to write a story on Freeze, I need to know everything about him. *Everything.*

(MR. HOPKINS *looks toward* RENNY'S *vicinity.*)

MR. HOPKINS: Is he close by?
RENNY: Is who close by?
MR. HOPKINS: Diego. Is he close by?

(RENNY *glances around the room, the hallway outside.*)

RENNY: No. I don't see him. Does this have to do with what happened this morning?
MR. HOPKINS [ABRUPTLY]: What happened this morning?
RENNY: Ah, when he picked me up from the motel [FLATLY] I'm sure it's nothing.
MR. HOPKINS: What is it, Renny?
RENNY: He didn't look too well. Me being a writer, I know that look when someone pulls, you know, an all-nighter.
MR. HOPKINS: All *what?* I don't understand.

(*He leans forward and listens closely to* RENNY.)

RENNY: He looked, I don't know, tired. That's all.
MR. HOPKINS: Oh. Gotcha. It's probably nothing. He does a lot around here.

(*He releases the brake from the wheelchair.*)

I want you to make me a promise, Renny. Can you do that?
RENNY: First, I got to know what I'm making a promise to.

Anne turned up the volume and listened closer to the interview. That one name, *Diego*, was still fresh on her mind. And when Anne heard it through the speaker of the laptop, it sounded like a distant echo in her mind. The voice saying the name wasn't Renny or Mr. Hopkins for that matter. . .

MR. HOPKINS: You have to trust me. Can you trust me, Renny?
RENNY: Sure.
MR. HOPKINS: Can you?
RENNY: *Yes.*
MR. HOPKINS: What I'm about to tell you is delicate information and if you *or* anybody else were to expose this kind of delicate information to the public, then not only will you put Diego's life in jeopardy, but also your own life as well. Do you understand?
RENNY: Sure.
MR. HOPKINS: Do you understand, Renny?
RENNY: *Yes.* I understand.

(MR. HOPKINS *waves at* RENNY.)

MR. HOPKINS: Why don't we grab a breath of fresh air?
RENNY: What do I have to do?
MR. HOPKINS: All you have to do is push.
RENNY: I can do that.

The interview came to an end.
Anne closed the wave file and opened the next one, *Interview #5.*

MR. HOPKINS: I love that sound.

RENNY: What sound is that?

MR. HOPKINS: The sound of the rain, the way it beats against the copper rooftop. For years, I didn't pay too much attention to the sound. Now, the sound is every-thing. Every living thing makes a sound, its own music.

Extremely curious to know more about this *Diego* character and his background, Anne stopped the interview and searched through the files on the flash drive. She couldn't find any file with Diego's name, not in the Journal Notes or in the *Miscellaneous* files. In the search bar of the Finder, she typed in the name *Diego*.

The results varied; however, the third file, she saw, was from the entry, *Journal Entry 10.15.2014.*

Anne opened the file and scrolled down until she found the name, Diego, on the screen.

(Cont.)

We cut the interview short today. I wheeled Mr. Hopkins back to his room where Sophia was already waiting for us. While Mr. Hopkins was getting cleaned up for dinner, I decided to take a walk around the property. I came across a couple of old headstones in the woods, one belonging to Leon's grandfather and another belonging to Leon's father, Peter. I was still a little jumpy, not from the headstones, but from the previous conversation I had with Mr. Hopkins. I checked my phone to see if there was a signal. Surprisingly enough, I had one bar, pulsing like a faint heartbeat. I googled Diego's name but found absolutely nothing on the man, which, after having recently learned his history, wasn't a surprise. I made a promise to Mr. Hopkins not to mention Diego in the story, even though Diego played a pivotal role in Leon's upbringing. His full name is Diego Tovar, the son of a farmer, formerly Mr. Dorsey's butler. Looks as if he doesn't age. Frankly, I don't know exactly how old he is. Mr. Hopkins said he ate a lot of avocados. A long time ago, Diego was connected to a cartel, one of the bandidos malvados. The cartel had another name for Diego: the jungle spider, or "*la araña de la selva*." Mr. Hopkins said he had the ability to sneak up on an enemy, his fingers like a spider's legs. Leon's father, Peter, discovered Diego when he was fifteen, curdled up like a newborn in the back of an ancient Inca temple deep in the amazons of Peru. This mysterious cartel (Mr. Hopkins didn't tell me exactly which one because, at the time, there were so many) recruited Diego when he was young, still a kid, nine years old. As a part of his initiation, they made Diego prove his loyalty to the cartel by murdering his own family. Mr. Hopkins said he and Diego had become close over the years. They spoke frequently about their pasts. However, they never spoke much about Diego's childhood before Peter found him, at least not until lately. Mr. Hopkins had heard accounts from Leon, about Diego and his troubled past, but he never went into much detail. When Mr. Hopkins asked Diego about his childhood, Diego went to his bedroom, pulled out a copy of Charles Dickens' *David Copperfield* from the drawer, and showed it to Mr. Hopkins. Part of the book was wrinkled and stained with old blood. Diego found the book in the jungle when he was around eleven years old. At the time, Diego didn't know how to read. One of the cartel members, a young vibrant man named Emilio, who was a couple of years older than Diego and grew up not too far from the farm, taught him how to read, but all done in secret. If the cartel found out, then they would cut off their tongues, both Diego and Emilio. Every night, Emilio sat with Diego in front of a campfire and taught Diego how to read. Over time, Diego befriended Emilio. They talked about leaving the cartel, running away to America. These, of course, were all pipe dreams to them, fantasies. One day, Diego ventured away from the camp. One of the head members of the cartel found Diego's friend with the book, that same book, *David Copperfield*. Diego heard screaming and rushed back to camp. When he got back, his friend was on his knees, bleeding

from the mouth. That was the last time he spoke to
Emilio. Diego was stricken with rage. The one person he
had grown to love could no longer speak to him. For
years, Diego waited for that right moment to catch the cartel with their pants down and take them out. Then, at the
age of fourteen, Diego got that opportunity when he witnessed three of cartel members murdering a group of tourists. Diego stumbled upon them, the tourists, four Ameri-
cas, two Europeans, one Asian, hanging upside down from
the trees, the intestines hanging from their bodies. For
Diego, it didn't matter who they were, these tourists. For
all Diego knew, it could've been members of a rival cartel.
Diego saw it as an opportunity. Like the jungle spider he
was, he snuck up on the cartel members and took them out,
one by one, with his blade. Somehow, the rest of the cartel
found out about Diego and what he had done. From there,
Mr. Hopkins said, it turned into a flat out gunfight. Diego's friend, Emilio, got shot during the gunfight, fueling
Diego's reign of vengeance. However, Mr. Hopkins
wasn't clear if Emilio had died. A couple of the cartel
members managed to escape. Diego only suffered minor
injuries, but that thirst for vengeance was never quenched.
For about a year, Diego lived on the run, no family, no
friends, no *Emilio*. Diego survived solely off the jungle.
Then, the cartel resurfaced, but this time stronger than before, a power greater in numbers. As Diego planned his
retaliation for what the cartel had done to Emilio, as well
as the hundreds and thousands of innocent bodies they had
left behind in their wake, so too did the cartel. They
hunted down Diego like a hound sniffing out a trail. They
closed in on Diego outside the border of Colombia where
Diego barely escaped with his life. For months, they
gained ground on him, following his every move. Then,
one day, Leon's father, Peter, came across a trembling
young man hidden inside an Inca temple with that one
book, *David Copperfield*, tightly curled in his bloody
hands. The cartel never found Diego nor Leon's father
and his crew. After about a year of hanging around,
Leon's father finally took Diego under his wing. He and

Peter became friends, not so much like a father and a son, but like a mentor and a student. Eventually, Peter adopted Diego and brought him home to America, to this home where Peter introduced him to Leon and his caretakers, one of them by the name of Calvin Diggs, who had been with Peter's father, William. Over time, he and Leon become close. Before Leon's father passed, he made Diego promise, that no matter what, to look after Leon. So, Diego did. Then, a couple of years later after Peter's passing, Calvin, who had been with the Dorsey family for many years, passed away from pneumonia. Calvin and Diego didn't get along at all. Mr. Hopkins said Diego couldn't stand the grumpy old man at first. They could hardly be in the same room with one another. Even though he was afraid to admit it, Diego admired Calvin the same way a son admires a father figure, even more so than Peter. Before Calvin passed, Diego vowed to fill his shoes, to put on the "suit," as Mr. Hopkins said. And that was what he did.

Anne closed the journal entry and opened the interview, the one from before, *Interview #5.*

MR. HOPKINS: I love that sound.
RENNY: What sound is that?
MR. HOPKINS: The sound of the rain, the way it beats against the copper rooftop. For years, I didn't pay too much attention to the sound. Now, the sound is everything. Every living thing makes a sound, its own music.
RENNY: Are you ready to begin?

(MR. HOPKINS *flinches from* RENNY'S *voice.*)

MR. HOPKINS [UPSETTINGLY]: Yes. I'm ready.
RENNY: So, how many kids did Mr. Dorsey have? Leon, I mean.

(*A long pause from* MR. HOPKINS—*a heavy silence.*)

Mr. Hopkins?
MR. HOPKINS [DEPRESSINGLY]: He had two children, a
boy and a girl.

(RENNY *glances at the picture frame, same one of the girl,*
LEON'S *daughter.*)

RENNY [CURIOUSLY]: Have you ever met them before?

(*Another tense pause from* MR. HOPKINS, *but this time much*
shorter.)

MR. HOPKINS [UNSTEADILY]: I have.

(RENNY *frowns from the strange response.*)

RENNY: What were their names?
MR. HOPKINS: Chloe and Dom, which was short for
Dominic.
RENNY: What are they doing now?
MR. HOPKINS: Dom passed away fifteen years ago. . . And
then Chloe. . .

(*Yet another pause. His face goes still and blank.*)

RENNY: Mr. Hopkins?
MR. HOPKINS: I couldn't tell you what she's doing now.
RENNY: How did Leon's son pass, Mr. Hopkins?
MR. HOPKINS [STERNLY]: He was murdered.
RENNY: I'm sorry to hear. What happened?
MR. HOPKINS [VACANTLY]: Leon, he killed him.
RENNY: What do you mean?

(MR. HOPKINS *sighs and then grimaces.*)

MR. HOPKINS: For years, Leon thought about leaving the
Company. It got to a point where he was so aggravated by

the way he was treated. The last mission before Leon left the Company was in Rural, Texas. The task seemed simple enough: convince a landowner [SIGHING], Isabel Cox, to sell her land to the Company. What Ms. Cox didn't realize was that she was sitting on top of a goldmine, one of the richest deposits in the south—*The Blood of the Earth*. And the Company wanted it all, every last drop of it. Greedy fuc'n bastards. [ANGRILY] If they only would've left it alone. . .

(*He pauses once more to catch his breath.*)

The Company sent Leon to take care of Isabel Cox. Turned out being one of the worst mistakes they ever made. He didn't even like her at first. She liked to play hard to get. *That* type. Didn't play games, though. Just plain stubborn. That's what Leon told me.

RENNY: Did you go to Texas with Leon?

(*Another long pause from* MR. HOPKINS, *which causes* RENNY'S *face to wash over with bafflement.*)

MR. HOPKINS: No. I sat this one out.

RENNY: Why?

MR. HOPKINS: The Company thought Leon could handle it all on his own. Easy job. Right? *Wrong.* Leon came back from Rural and said he was going away for a long time. There was a chance Leon might never come back. Before he left, I saw a change in him. He looked like a man who was madly in love. You could see it there in his eyes, hear it in his talk. I've known Leon for quite some time, and I know he's been with lots of women, if it was through a fling or a girlfriend; nonetheless, he would never leave on bad terms with them. But Isabel, she did something to him, something that no woman has ever done to him.

RENNY: Which is?

MR. HOPKINS: She made him a better man, Renny, through and through. There were many times when Leon said he was in love or at least thought he was in love. He didn't find true love until he met Isabel. She showed him what love was really like. I'm not talking about making love. For Leon, that was the easy part, the easiest part, he told me—physical part that is. If the equipment doesn't work anymore, then they have drugs that can fix that, like they have a drug for everything nowadays. But love, Renny, love is a drug you *can't* buy. Love is the *fix-it-all* drug. And once you have found it, found love, you can do anything you set your mind to. They were in love, Leon and Isabel, like two high school sweethearts. She showed Leon how to nurture, how to be a provider, Renny, how to be a better man.

RENNY [STRANGELY]: And that's what Leon told you?

MR. HOPKINS: Yes. When Leon met Isabel, he said he could see it in her eyes.

RENNY: See what?

MR. HOPKINS: Heaven, Renny, wrapped in her eyes like a blanket of light.

RENNY: Have you ever been in love, Mr. Hopkins?

(*He looks closer at* MR. HOPKINS.)

MR. HOPKINS: Once. But it didn't work out.

(*A calm silence settles over the two.*)

RENNY: Mr. Hopkins, what happened to Isabel?

MR. HOPKINS: She died the same way Dom died.

(RENNY *readjusts himself in the chair as he runs his hand across the bottom of his chin.*)

RENNY: Something's not quite adding up, Mr. Hopkins. If Leon loved his wife and son, Dom, so much, then why did he kill them?

MR. HOPKINS [VACANTLY]: As much as he wanted out, the Company wouldn't let him. After they married, Leon and Isabel had no other option. The two of them ran away. Everywhere they went the Company was right there on their tails. In the spring of Eighty-nine, they spent their honeymoon bouncing from one country to another, fighting off whatever scumbags the Company threw at them. Later that spring, Leon and Isabel finally settled on a farm south of Paris. Then word got out. Spring came, went. When we showed up in France, we found a note saying, [QUOTES] Nice try, Assholes. [END QUOTES]

RENNY: We? What do you mean *we*?

MR. HOPKINS: I was a part of a special cleanup crew. The people in charge of the Company knew if *I* was there, then Leon would surrender without a fight. I didn't want to do it.

RENNY: Then, why did you?

MR. HOPKINS: Because I didn't want anything bad to happen to Leon. I fought tooth and nail trying to convince them to leave him alone. They told me to choose a side. I had no other choice. They were going to kill me. Next thing we know, he's living somewhere in Germany and then Portugal and then Hong Kong, New Zealand, Moscow, zig-zagging his way across the entire globe. Isabel gave birth to their first child in Tokyo. A girl. Chloe. Then, not too long after, Dom was born in Trinidad. Two more years went by after Dom's birth. Isabel was fed up with living on the run. So, they moved back to Texas, not too far from where she grew up. They figured the Company would never look for them there. Isabel wanted to be close to her parents as well. They were buried in a cemetery outside Rural. Chloe had just turned nine years old.

RENNY: You said you were close to the daughter, Chloe. Correct?

MR. HOPKINS [HESITANTLY]: Uh. Yes.

RENNY [CLOSELY]: And when did you see her last?

MR. HOPKINS: I saw Chloe briefly before the massacre.

RENNY: Massacre?

(*He looks at* MR. HOPKINS *with a strange look on his face—his face fills with certainty, not confusion.*)

What *massacre?*
MR. HOPKINS: It all happened on August 20, 1999. Two days prior, I received a call from the Ghost of Christmas past.

(*A fraction of a smile flashes across one side of his face. Then, it fades back into his face before it can be fully recognized.*)

It was good to hear his voice. For the longest time, I thought he was dead, that the Company had killed him and hid it from me. Leon told me he wanted to bury the hatchet—all the ties had to be cut free. He pleaded with me, told me he had a family now and wanted to squash any debt he owed to the Company or else more people would die. Those fools had too much pride to let one of their most valuable assets walk all over them and let him get by with these demands. So the Company sicced the dogs on Leon. Bad mistake.
RENNY: Where were you when all of this was going down? Surely, you had some kind of say-so in the matter. You were friends with Leon. *Brothers.*
MR. HOPKINS [DOURLY]: No, Renny. There was nothing I could do. I told you. It was either him or me. I chose to live.

(*He looks away from* RENNY *and then listens to the beating rain outside the window.*)

I loathed Texas in the summer—the hot weather. When we arrived late afternoon in Rural, a small town along the border, Leon was kicking the ball around with his kids. The temperature was in the hundreds and it was humid too. I was told to double my intake of fluids. What did they know? There's no such thing as dry heat during a Texas summer.

RENNY: How *many* of you were there?

MR. HOPKINS: One team. Twelve men. Three drivers. Nine hired guns, including myself. Bryant, a mean SOB, was in charge of the whole operation. We weren't there to kill Leon.

RENNY: Then, why were you there?

MR. HOPKINS: We were there to send a message.

RENNY: What message was that?

MR. HOPKINS: Sort of. . . you break something that is ours. We break something that is yours. Eye for an eye. That sort of thing. . . You would think ten years would be long enough to forget about what had happened back in Rural. You'd think they would've gathered their losses and moved on with their lives to worry about other things, like learning from their previous mistakes. There's one thing you should know about this company, JeneCorp: they *never* forget. [SCOWLING] They get even. Before our team arrived, Leon and I spoke, though, only briefly. We never really got a chance to catch up on old times. Most of the conversation was me warning him about the Company and how someone close to him found out where they were staying and how the Company was coming for him and his family and if they didn't pack their things and get the hell out of dodge, then there was going to be hell to pay. He told me he was tired of running, tired of being afraid, tired of constantly looking over his shoulder.

RENNY: Why did he call you on that specific day? Did he know he was being followed?

MR. HOPKINS: Yes. Obviously. I managed to slip away for a moment before we came after them. When I met up with him, I saw a man who was bursting from the seams with contentment, a man who actually looked happy. In all the years I've known Leon, I have never seen such a look on his face. He had the eyes of a man who finally found peace in the world. Forget about all the fame or the glory he received. To Leon, he finally *made it* in life, wife, children. After those years of living abroad with his family, Leon finally found a place he could rightfully call his home. So, I knew this wasn't going to go down the way I wanted it to. I knew it was gonna be a goddamn bloodbath.

RENNY: I don't understand, Mr. Hopkins. If you were so close to Leon, why didn't you call off this witch-hunt?

MR. HOPKINS [BITTERLY]: I told you. It was already too late. And even if I got in the way, then. . . you get the point. I wasn't as strong as Leon, Renny. Me, I was just an ordinary person. You have to understand. I was only doing my job, Renny.

RENNY [INTENSELY]: What happened?

(MR. HOPKINS' *left hand trembles in his lap. He uses his right hand to ease away the tremble.*)

MR. HOPKINS [GRAVELY]: Before Isabel could make sense of what was happening, Leon was rushing toward her with Dom and Chloe. We knew this would happen and that Leon wasn't going down without a fight. So, we came prepared as well. It didn't matter, though. Leon would find a way to kill us, even myself if I was to get in the way. Friend or no friend. If I was with them, the Company, then I was as dead as any man who got in his way. A little piece of plastic covering our eyes wasn't going to make any difference. I stayed back while Trent and the rest of the guns flanked the house. That's when the massacre took place. . .

(*He sniffles the phlegm from his nose.*)

. . . the horror. He had no control. Later, he told me he took an extra dose that day.

RENNY: Dose? What kind of *dose?*

MR. HOPKINS: It doesn't matter.

(RENNY *puts aside his notes and listens closely.*)

Anne listened, as well.

MR. HOPKINS: All I could hear were gunshots ringing out and then the silence and the smell of gunpowder in the air. Most of the hired guns were so badly mutilated that their faces were beyond recognition. The thing about a visor is that, sure, it can stop a gaze but not a slug. But I warned them about Leon. Before we left for Rural, I *warned* those fools. But did they listen? No. They expected Leon to waltz outside and give them the gaze. They didn't know Leon like I did. He was the complete package. Best damn partner an associate could ask for.
RENNY: If Leon was in your shoes, would he have done the same thing?

(MR. HOPKINS *ignores the question.*)

MR. HOPKINS: It was actually Kin who nabbed him.

(*He shakes his head in disgust.*)

That shrimp, that tiny Asian bastard snuck up on Leon like a common cold and told him to drop the shotgun or else he was going to put one in his ear. He had no other choice. They dragged him to the front lawn. Put a bag over his head like a prisoner of war. By the time he came to, Kin and the remaining guns found Isabel, as well as Dom and Chloe hiding in the basement underneath the kitchen. Bryant insisted. . . that the children watch. I didn't know how much longer I. . . I could watch. . .
RENNY: Then, why did you, Marcus? Why did you watch?
MR. HOPKINS [SHARPLY]: I *had* to watch. I *wanted* to watch.

(The tremble runs like a skittish little creature through his hand, the same one—the left one. He clutches the armrest of the wheelchair.)

After they removed the bag from Leon's face, I remember him turning to me.

(He sighs deeply.)

The look. I will never forget that look.

(His breath becomes labored, heavy.)

Leon. . .

(Heavier now.)

His eyes were as blue as sapphires, glowing, convulsing; these dark rings circling around them. In all. . . in all my years of working with Leon, I've never seen the gaze like this. It was like there was a demon eating away at whatever good was left inside him. Everything that Leon had worked so hard for over the years was now being taken away from him and he couldn't let that stand. The skin on his face began to crack like broken glass. Had skin like ah, ah, a snake. Somehow, I knew that if I wasn't wearing a visor like the others, then I would still be on that ranch, still standing there like a statue. Till this day, I can see Leon's expression in my mind, that *look* of betrayal. Leon was doing all he could to fight off the two guns. Bryant was giving his little speech about messing with the Company. He said he was [QUOTES] dying to see the great Freeze work his magic. [END QUOTES] In a way, so was I. But NOT on Isabel. *Anybody* but Isabel. Leon was shouting at Isabel, telling her not to look into his eyes. Hard to do when you have speculums attached to your face.

(*His skin turns pale. Breath now faint.*)

As the—
RENNY: Mr. Hopkins? Are you feeling okay?
MR. HOPKINS [STUTTERING]: Fa. . . fa. . . fine. As the gah. . . as the gun was using the cattle prod on Leon—
RENNY: Cattle prod? Why cattle prod?

(MR. HOPKINS *clears the sweat from his forehead.*)

MR. HOPKINS: To. . . bring out the gaze. Another gun placed speculums across his eyes. [QUOTES] Say goodbye to your wife, Freeze. [END QUOTES] That was the last thing Bryant said to Leon before the impossible happened. Dom and Chloe, they warr. . . they were forced to watch what their father was capable of doing to another human being. Then. . .
RENNY: Mr. Hopkins? We can stop, if you like.

(MR. HOPKINS *grabs his chest. Then, he shakes his head.*)

MR. HOPKINS: Then, Dom freed himself and ran to his mother. He got [COUGHING]. . . got caught in the crossfire of Leon's gaze. I. . . I had no other choice. They were going to kill—

(*He suddenly flops forward, slides from his wheelchair, and crashes to the floor. The shades slip from his face and skip around the floor before coming to a halt next to the bedpost.*)

(RENNY *springs from his chair and then darts toward* MR. HOPKINS.)

RENNY [FRIGHTENINGLY]: Marcus!

(*He turns to the hallway.*)

Sophia! Help!

(*He cradles a pale and clammy* MR. HOPKINS *in both of his arms. While doing so, he makes sure* MR. HOPKINS' *head is upright.*)

Diego! I need some help in here!

(*He holds* MR. HOPKINS, *gasping now, closer to his body and whispers in his ear.*)

Stay with me Marcus. Just breathe now. Damn it.

(*He studies* MR. HOPKINS' *face, especially his eyes, but there are none. He studies the two empty sockets where* MR. HOPKINS' *eyes used to be; now, all that remain are the scar tissue and everything else, which, over time, has been callused over. He tries to focus on* MR. HOPKINS, *his chest, his shallow breathing. He turns his head over his shoulder.*)

Get in here! Now!

Anne heard lots of commotion on the recording: a group of muffled footsteps and then, a couple of seconds later, objects being moved around the hardwood floor.

A sudden *thud*. . .

Renny's voice was more faint now, so too were Sophia's and Diego's.

As the commotion grew farther away, Anne turned up the volume as high as it could go. The most she could make was a couple of words from Renny's hurried explanation—about Mr. Hopkins' and his "labored breathing," and how he was "sweating a lot and grabbing his chest," before he collapsed.

Throughout the dwindling commotion, he voiced that maybe Mr. Hopkins could've been having a heart attack. He was showing the classic symptoms. There was more commotion throughout the room, objects shifting and then *squeaking* across the hard-wood, and then a fuzzy silence. The tape ran on for about another ten minutes until it finally flatlined.

Then, after about five seconds of nothing, a sudden spike in volume: *I can hear* her voice, Ren—*her voice*, talking to me in the darkness.

RENNY: Who's voice, Marcus?
MR. HOPKINS: Isabel.
RENNY: What does she say?

Anne turned down the volume a little.

MR. HOPKINS [WEAKLY]: She tells me that she forgives me. And Dom. I can hear him too.
RENNY: What does he say?
MR. HOPKINS: He says when can we play. He loved to play. And Chloe. . .
RENNY: What does Chloe say?
MR. HOPKINS: She tells me. . .

There was more dead air on the recording.
Once more, Anne turned up the volume—like be-fore—to the max.

RENNY: What does she tell you?
MR. HOPKINS: To *stay* strong. To *hold on*.

Anne noticed the time on the bottom of the wave file and how it ran on for an extra twenty minutes.
She fast-forwarded through the dead air until she heard a sudden disturbance.
The tape suddenly stopped!

Nothing but loud silence. As before, another flat-line. . .

Then, a voice, shaky at first, came back on.

That voice was Renny's:

Quarter till nine.

(*He paces around the room.*)

Just arrived at my room. Went to check on Mr. Hopkins. He was uh, saying things, uh, strange things about Leon's children, about Isabel. Not sure if he's going to be okay.

(*He stops in his tracks and then hits the* STOP *button on the recorder.*)

Click!

Three seconds of silence.

Anne listened closer.

Then, a *pop*. . . another *click*. . .

Oh yeah. The eyes. That's right. My suspicions are true. Mr. Hopkins is, in fact. . . blind. Not only that, but they appear as if they have been surgically removed. A piss-poor job if you ask me. Can't help but wonder if Leon had something to do with it. Possibly for what Mr. Hopkins did, or better yet, didn't do. Eye for an eye.

(*His pace quickens around the guest room.*)

Sophia believes that Mr. Hopkins suffered a mild heart attack while he was explaining to me what happened in Rural. He is now resting in the upper West Wing. Obviously, there's a great deal of grief and pain resulting from that one day. I'm starting to wonder about the Company, what their motivations were, if they're a part of the government and if so, exactly how much power do they have? Let's face it. If

this thing makes it to print, this *will* be the story of the year.
I can just see it now. . .

(*He extends his arm and pans his hand in the air from left to right
as if he's tilting a headline.*)

. . . *The Untold Story of Freeze, the Legend, the Myth, the Face of
Lansford.* What a groundbreaking story it will be! Hopefully, if all goes well tomorrow and Mr. Hopkins is feeling
better, I will—

(*He hears a sudden crash coming from the West Wing. He stops
pacing and listens closely.*)

What the hell was that?

(*He decides to check out the noise. He creeps down a long and
narrow hallway until he reaches the West Wing.*)

MR. HOPKINS: . . . et plan B, Diego.
DIEGO: I don't trust him.
MR. HOPKINS: . . . work goddamn it!
DIEGO [SEETHING]: We're running out of time. The story
must be finished by Sunday, otherwise this will all be for
nothing. . .

(RENNY *tiptoes toward* MR. HOPKINS' *bedroom. He notices
the door is cracked open.*)

MR. HOPKINS: Please, Diego. Just give him a few more
days.
DIEGO: He's not asking the right questions, sir.
MR. HOPKINS [BEGGING]: But he will!
DIEGO: I told you *not* to get close. Didn't I? I told you
this would happen.
MR. HOPKINS: It will work.
DIEGO: What makes you so sure?

MR. HOPKINS: I have faith in him, Diego.

DIEGO: When this is all over, and when they come looking for him, what excuse will we giv—

MR. HOPKINS: No, Diego! There will be another way! There must!

(An explosion from his chest. The cough sputters like a dying engine.)

Just remember, Diego. It's all about the story. Do you hear me? That's what matters the most, the story. We can't give up now. We've come too far. . .

(The hardwood floor beneath RENNY'S feet creaks!)

RENNY: Shit. . .

(On the way back to his room, he comes across another hallway.)

Never been down here before.

(He comes across a secret room. He searches the wall for a light switch, but cannot find one. Finally, his eyes adjust to the darkness and he sees the dark figures scattered around the room: manikins dressed in various garments, cloaks, gear, armor, and equipment from ancient times, medieval, Samurai, Native American. Old paintings and sculptures are stacked and cluttered and mounted on each side of the walls. He pulls out a camera from his pocket, flips on the flash, and takes a few pictures. Something catches his eye in the back of the room! His eyes flicker toward the main aisle. Ahead, he spots a wooden post with a glass dome. Inside the dome perches a shriveled up head, almost corpse-like—gray in color. Streaks of pale moonlight shine over the glass dome and bring out each dark contour of the cryptic face.)

It seems to be like some kind of preserved head.

"Preserved head," Anne said as she eased against the iron headboard.

The thought alone of that one word *head* suddenly came to her for some reason. She remembered skimming through the files on the flash drive, mostly JPEGs and folders—one in particular, a folder named *HEAD*. At the time, Anne was so intrigued from the other photographs, the JPEGs, mainly the ones of herself in the *Study* folder, that she completely ignored the other folder, *HEAD*.

She paused the recording, opened the Finder window, and double-clicked on *Photos*. In the folder, she scrolled down to the bottom where she came across yet another folder, *HEAD*. She double-clicked on the folder, and did so warily. A whole new set of JPEGs was revealed—most of them taken in a dark narrow room. Anne started with the first JPEG, a close up photograph of an amphora from 530 BCE. The composition on the amphora was identical on each side of the vase; on one side Achilles and Ajax, both playing a game of dice, were painted as black figures. On the other side Achilles and Ajax were painted, not as black figures, but as red figures—this technique known as a *bilingual vase*. This, Anne observed, wasn't the only artifact inside the room. She clicked on other JPEGs. There were other significant artifacts: ancient vases like the amphora in the first photograph; ancient bowls from Sumer; other Sumerian art such as these alien-like statuettes of two worshippers carved from soft gypsum; other paintings, including the *Lion Hunt* by a Flemish painter, Peter Paul Rubens; many busts, including the same one Renny had come across in the great room, the bust of Marcus Aurelius, which rested on top of an oak chest; and then several sculptures—one of them, Anne saw, of Hero and Centaur (Hero believed to be Herakles and Centaur, Nesso, a

half man/half horse) of 720 BCE, approximately four
and a half inches tall, made from bronze. There were
dozens of human-sized statues as well, all of them
made from what appeared to be stone, not marble.
Most of the statues were posed with tormented expressions, contorted and curled in incredible agony.
Then, four photographs of this strange head, which,
Anne could only assume, came from the title of the
folder. In the first photograph of the four, Anne
couldn't make out the head in its entirety. The photograph was taken from a distance; and from the way
the moonlight cast from behind, the head appeared as
dark as a silhouette. The second photograph was
blurry, completely unrecognizable. The third one
wasn't too far off from the second one; but unlike the
second one, she could partially distinguish the profile
of the head. Finally, the fourth one was taken a couple of feet away. Part of the photo was cut off, only
revealing one half of the gaunt face. The light from
the camera's flash brought out more detail: scaly skin,
which appeared mummified; a sunken eye socket, as
dark and hollow as a burrow; a cheekbone, as jagged
as a blade; and a couple of teeth, which didn't look
like teeth at all but the fangs of a reptile, gnarled too
from an unbounded time of decay. What really
piqued Anne's curiosity was the skin—the scales, she
noticed—and how some of them were missing, as if
someone had plucked them from this strange face.

Lastly, there was one more photograph—a mysterious *fifth* one.

She scrolled to the last photo, a dark silhouette of a
man standing at the lit doorway. The man—from
what Anne could see—was dressed in black, short
(about five feet, six or seven inches), with a head as
smooth and waxy as a bowling ball.

She closed the folder and played the rest of the recording.

(A throaty *creak* from afar!)

DIEGO: Are you lost, Mr. Jacobson?

(*He steps forward into the moonlit room.*)

RENNY: No. I was just. . .
DIEGO [COLDLY]: Just leaving.
RENNY: Right. I was just leaving.

(*He clears his throat.*)

DIEGO [CURTLY]: You know you're not allowed in here.
RENNY: Sorry.

There was a ruffling sound before the recording suddenly shut off.

Anne closed the wave file, *Interview #5.*

Without wasting a moment of her time reflecting over the recent chain of events, Anne opened the next journal entry, *Journal Entry 10.16.2014.*

11 PM. I've tried to shut my eyes for a couple of minutes, but I can't sleep as usual. I keep having this reoccurring nightmare. It starts out the same as the others: me wandering through a dark hallway that never ends. It's like something out of a Freddy Krueger movie—an endless hallway or just an illusion made to look as if it never ends. Eventually, I find a door that is cracked open. I step inside the moonlit room. It's extremely cold. I can see my own breath in the air. The room looks like the inside of a ramshackle warehouse where manikins go to die. There are hundreds of manikins, mostly covered with worn plastic, all staring at me with dead black eyes. The ceiling above

me is black as well, but not like the manikins' eyes. This is a whole new level of black, as deep and cavernous as an abyss. I look up at this strange ceiling—as I always do in the nightmare—at all the black, and I stare at these sea creatures swimming above me. Their bodies are as weightless as phantoms, and they appear as if they're flying throughout this abyss. I can't make out *who* or *what* they are. A glitch or a flicker of pale light brings out a creature or two. Like the manikins, they appear as if they have been trapped in this realm for many years, centuries perhaps. As I look closer, one of the manikins suddenly grabs me by the arm. I turn around and the manikin is wearing the same clothes as me. I look at its face and then into its black eyes. I realize that the manikin *is me*. Then, I wake up. That's the nightmare: a long hallway and a strange room filled with manikins and a moving ceiling. A minute into this nightmare feels like an eternity. Never been much of a dreamer. Never really looked into the symbolism of dreams as most people I know do. But I can't help but wonder what it means. Why do I keep having the same nightmare? Haven't been able to eat much either. My stomach feels like it's twisted in knots. I've been making sure to drink plenty of fluids. Now is not the time to come down with anything, especially at such a critical stage in the story. I can't stop thinking about the recent confrontation with Diego. I don't know what he's going to do to me. Not only that, *the recording*. I've listened to it about a million times, and still, can't understand what Diego means. Does he mean *him*, as in me? And if so, what is his plan with me? Most importantly, Sophia claims Mr. Hopkins had a mild heart attack, but he doesn't sound like a man who recently blew a gasket in his ticker. What the hell is going on here? I must find out, but now the story is getting too thick for me to pull out. And that room, what the hell? Must've been artifacts Peter had collected over the years. Mr. Hopkins claims they are redecorating. But redecorating for what? Is it a lie? By all accounts, Mr. Hopkins may be right. Many people redecorate. Nothing out of the ordinary. But why keep the arti-

facts in that room a secret? There are things in there that
I've seen in the Louvre—from pictures that is. But what is
Mr. Hopkins doing with them? Are they replicas? Or are
they the real thing? Are they stolen? Perhaps that's why
Diego is so protective. Other stuff that I've never seen
before, stuff from the neoclassical period. Not sure as to
why these paintings and sculptures would be hidden from
me. What intrigues me the most is that head. The head is
mounted on a post and covered by a glass frame of some
kind. From what I can tell, the head is mummified, definitely not a sculpture or bust like the others in the room.
To be continued. . .

Anne closed the journal entry on the screen and, as
before, without wasting any time, opened the next
entry, *Journal Entry 10.17.2014.*

Early Friday morning. Somewhere near the crack of
dawn, around 4 or 5 AM. Had all the right reasons *not* to
sleep. I'm still amped from my recent discovery. Too
much racing through my mind, mainly Mr. Hopkins' own
personal Hangar 51 in the South Wing. I have to find out a
little more about that room in particular, especially *that*
head. As one already knows from the countless retellings
of stories, mostly films with its remakes or its revamps or
redoes or *re*-fucking-whatever—which, brings another
thought to my mind, as a longtime moviegoer, I feel
strongly about passing a law against remaking the classics,
slap a label on them, R.I.P., *Rest in Peace*, meaning leave
me the fuck alone and let me sleep with all my other dead
classics (I mean, seriously, Holly-fucking-Wood, come up
with something new for once)—anyway, where am I?
Right. This is the part of the story where the writer, *me*,
starts sticking his thirsty snout into a place where it
shouldn't be; and that's when the shit hits the fan—
Climax, resolution, credits, *the* fucking end! In traditional
storytelling, we call this part a "red herring," a literary device used to mislead the reader. But I'm not in the fic-

tional business, and this isn't a story about wizards or dragons or hobbits. This is a story about a man who had the ability to turn a human being into stone. Did I say I'm *not* in the fictional business? Though, I can't help but wonder if that room is exactly that, a red herring point used to draw me away from the truth. But, like the curious cat I am, I had to find out. Around three o'clock, I snuck out of my room. The entire house was dead quiet; however, I could feel Diego's presence skulking in the shadows—the *la araña de la selva*. I went directly to that same mysterious room as before. The door was locked. Go figure. I recalled a window from earlier, the moonlight casting over the head. Where there was a window, there was a way. I snuck outside via the backdoor. The temperature must've been in the twenties, but the adrenaline was running warm through my veins. Luckily, I found a trellis, which ran up the side of the South Wing, but I had to make at least a ten-foot cross to the room's window. I climbed up the trellis, which wasn't a problem. When I arrived at the second story, I ran into a hitch. Except for the spacing between each brick, there was hardly anything to grab onto. Thinking about it now boggles my mind: how I shuffled my way across the side of the house, only using the tiny crevasses between the bricks. I might have the cold to thank for that. After all, I couldn't feel my fingers or my toes. If it was any other day, I would've still been clinging to that trellis like a house fly to Diego's spider web. I made it to the windowsill without breaking my neck. The head appeared to be mummified as I gathered from the photograph. From a close inspection, I couldn't tell if the head was human or a creature. The head by itself shared the same profile as a human, but the features were animalistic. The teeth were nothing compared to a human, long and sharp as if they had been honed; the skin wasn't like any skin on a human either, more scaly like a snake; and each strand of hair was thick and, like the skin, scaly too. I couldn't help but wonder if the head was a prop or, like I stated earlier, a *red herring*.

Anne stopped reading and noticed a break between the pages. She scrolled farther down and came across more writing. On a whim, she decided to continue reading.

So, it's true about Freeze. In the back of my mind, I knew it was him all along. The moment I laid eyes on him

Once more Anne stopped reading and closed the journal entry before Renny spoiled the big surprise. As with Renny, Anne too felt as if she knew who Mr. Hopkins was. But, like Renny, Anne had to find out from the horse's mouth.

She opened the next interview, *Interview #6*.

RENNY: How you feeling?
MR. HOPKINS: Much better, Renny. Thank you.
RENNY: You get any rest?
MR. HOPKINS: Slept like a baby.
RENNY: It's good to see you're doing better.
MR. HOPKINS: Second one this month.
RENNY: Have you seen a doctor?
MR. HOPKINS [NONCHALANTLY]: It's been a while. Doctors can't save me now. Diego and Sophia have always taken care of me, mainly Diego. He's been here since the very beginning. If you don't mind, hand me the glass of water behind you.

(RENNY *furrows his brows, not from the comment, but from* MR. HOPKINS' *keen awareness of his surroundings.* RENNY *grabs the glass, walks to the bed, and hands* MR. HOPKINS *the glass.* MR. HOPKINS *takes a sip from the glass and then hands the glass back to* RENNY.)

Thank you.
RENNY: You're welcome.

(He places the glass on the table.)

Are you going to be able to continue the interview?
MR. HOPKINS: Yes. Sophia said I was a lucky man. She said if it wasn't for you, Renny, my condition would've been much worse.

(RENNY bobs his head, respectfully, and then cordially smiles.)

RENNY: Do you still want me to write the story?
MR. HOPKINS: Of course.
RENNY: So, I guess I should clear the air before I start.

(MR. HOPKINS innocently smiles.)

MR. HOPKINS: I'm sure I have a lot of explaining to do.
RENNY: Why didn't you tell me, Marcus?
MR. HOPKINS: Tell you?
RENNY: You're blind. [FRANTICALLY] You don't have any eyes!
MR. HOPKINS [CRABBILY]: I know I don't have any eyes, Renny. Not like I was being discreet about it. I assumed you already knew. . .
RENNY: Did Leon do that to you?
MR. HOPKINS [MOURNFULLY]: Yes. He did.
RENNY: For what happened in Rural?

(MR. HOPKINS turns away from Renny and looks toward the window.)

MR. HOPKINS [FINALLY]: Yes.
RENNY: How does it feel?
MR. HOPKINS: How does *what* feel?
RENNY: You know. *To live in darkness. . .*
MR. HOPKINS: Before we start, Renny, I want to know more about the person who is going to be writing Leon's story. Why don't you tell me about your family?

RENNY: But you already know all about my family.

MR. HOPKINS: I do, but I want to hear it from you.

RENNY: What is there to tell? I never was that close to them.

MR. HOPKINS: How many brothers did you say you have?

RENNY: One brother. Four years older.

MR. HOPKINS: You're not close to your brother?

(RENNY *shakes his head no.*)

RENNY [SOMBERLY]: We don't have much of a relation-ship. We're practically strangers. Last time I saw him, he could hardly look me in the eye.

MR. HOPKINS: Why is that?

RENNY [DISMALLY]: I don't know. Resentment.

MR. HOPKINS: Resentment? Resentment for what? He's your brother.

RENNY: I know he is. I mean, now, the closest we ever get to each other is through a Christmas card in the mail every year. I might get a telephone call if I'm lucky.

MR. HOPKINS: Do you ever reach out to him?

RENNY: I used to. Stopped about two years ago after my mother died. Unfortunately, my parents were really the only two things keeping my brother and me together. And when they died. . .

(*He pushes out a sigh, which lasts a couple of seconds before it alters into a sharp inhale through his nose.*)

. . . Well, you understand.

MR. HOPKINS: I don't understand. I want you to *make* me understand.

RENNY: We just never got along, even when we were kids.

MR. HOPKINS: If they were alive, Renny, your parents, what would they think about this rift?

RENNY: They understood our differences—the both of them. They never got in the way. They were getting old too. For years, I prepared myself for their deaths, but nothing can really prepare you for death. You know losing a loved one is perhaps the hardest thing a person has to deal with.

MR. HOPKINS: Of course. How old were they?

RENNY: Father in his late seventies. Believe he was around seventy-six when he passed. Then, about a year later, my mother passed. She was only sixty-eight.

MR. HOPKINS: How did your father pass?

RENNY: Heart attack. He wasn't a thin man by any means. He had what I like to call a sweet tooth.

(MR. HOPKINS *chuckles but carefully.*)

MR. HOPKINS: Don't we all, Renny. And your mother? How did she pass?

(RENNY *hangs his head.*)

RENNY: A broken heart.

MR. HOPKINS: They must've been close.

RENNY [FAINTLY]: Yeah. They were.

(*His eyes glaze over for a moment, but he never sheds a single tear.*)

I will never forget that one day. It was Mother's Day. My mother was still recovering from a stroke she had a couple of months after my father died. I remember the doctors said that she would make a full recovery. I knew she would. She was a fighter. Always was. When I was a kid, I thought she was the toughest person in the world—even tougher than my father. I decided to give her a call and wish her happy Mother's Day. I hadn't talked to her in, geez, um [THINKING]. . . a couple of months. I was so busy with work. When she answered the phone, she didn't know who it was at first. She couldn't even recognize my voice. I told her, [QUOTES] It's me, your son. . . Renny. [END QUOTES]

She had forgotten all about me, my own mother. Eventually, it came to her [IMITATING HIS MOTHER'S VOICE]... *Renny*, she said. In my mind, I could see the smile stretching across her face. I wanted to...

(*He smiles as well—briefly. The smile slowly vanishes from his face as if it's never meant to be worn this way.*)

I asked her how she was doing. She told me she was doing okay, but my gut told me something different. I told her I was sorry I couldn't visit her and that I would visit her the first chance I got. She forgot that I was living in New York. [SHAKING HIS HEAD] It was like we had to redo every conversation we had in the past. She told me... she understood why I couldn't visit her. She wasn't the least upset. She said she was happy for me. Then, she said she would see me later and then I hung up the phone.

(*The tear builds in his eyes.*)

I wanted... I needed her to remember...
MR. HOPKINS [SOFTLY]: Of course.
RENNY: It was like a *hacker* had hacked into her mind and stole her memories... even the important ones. Those memories were hers. They... they were ours. And they were taken away by [GRIMACING] by some *thief*. I thought maybe they were *still* there, the memories... somewhere inside. They had to be. Right?

(*Once more, he shakes his head in great disgust. Then, he clears the tear from his eye. Face, now stern.*)

The fact: they were gone and they were never coming back.
MR. HOPKINS: Did you ever get a chance to visit your mother?
RENNY [DOLEFULLY]: No. She died later that day.
MR. HOPKINS: I'm sorry, Renny.

(RENNY *doesn't respond. Instead, he directs his attention toward the window—the trees outside.*)

Tell me, Renny. Why exactly did you stop reaching out to your brother?

RENNY: Every time I called Cliff, he would always talk about himself, talk about how successful he was, how much money he had. I was proud of him. Then, I guess I got tired of hearing about it all the time.

MR. HOPKINS: What line of work was Cliff in?

RENNY: Insurance. A few years ago, he accepted the *big job*. Six figures.

MR. HOPKINS: Where does he live now?

RENNY: Sharlot, actually. He lived in Connecticut for a while. That's where their headquarters is located. Then, they transferred him to Sharlot.

MR. HOPKINS: And your brother, Cliff, is he in a hurry too?

RENNY: He's on a different level of hurry.

MR. HOPKINS: Is that right?

RENNY: Every time we talked, he always talked down to me. Not once did he ever ask how I was doing. And every time I tried to talk to him or carry on a meaningful conversation with him, he would say he had to go or that he was busy or act like he didn't want to *hear* what I had to say. It was always about him. *Always*. . . even when we were kids. He always got the attention. Can't tell you how many times my parents told me to be more like Cliff, to dress more like Cliff, to *behave* more like Cliff. At times, I was. . . I was stranger in that house. Cliff and I always fought too. He used to give me a bloody nose, but I would always kick the shit out of his skinny ass. Even when I was born, the doctor told my mother that I was going to be the toughest one, *the fighter*—you know, being the youngest.

MR. HOPKINS: And were you?

RENNY: When I reached sixth grade, Cliff wouldn't dare mess with me. I used to get into this. . . this mode. I called it my [QUOTES] tiger mode [END QUOTES].

(*He suddenly smiles, eyes glistening.*)

MR. HOPKINS: Tiger mode?
RENNY: When I was in tiger mode, you'd better watch out.
MR. HOPKINS: Is that so?
RENNY: I swear we were polar opposite.
MR. HOPKINS: My opinion: the youngest are the toughest, Renny, *or* the weakest. They either learn from their older siblings' mistakes *or* they let their siblings' mistakes get the better of them.
RENNY: Cliff made a few mistakes when we were younger. I remember he came home drunk once. He was around fifteen or sixteen years old. My father found out. Did a number on him. When we were little, he would get out the belt when we acted out of line. But that one night, I re-member—as if it was yesterday—I was standing at the very top of the landing, leaning over the banister, and listening to my father. I've never seen my father that upset. His fa-ther—my grandfather—a firefighter—he passed when I was just a child. My mother said he used to be an alcoholic. That's probably why my father never touched a drink in his life.
MR. HOPKINS: What did your father do to your brother?
RENNY: All I remember: he was on top of him, strangling him, yelling at him.

(*He awkwardly chortles and then shakes his head.*)

Think he scared my brother shitless.
MR. HOPKINS: How about you? Did you ever get caught drinking?
RENNY: Oh!

(*He furrows his brows—head now bobbing.*)

All the time!
MR. HOPKINS: Did your father ever get upset?
RENNY [SERIOUSLY]: Never.
MR. HOPKINS: Why not?
RENNY: Maybe he saw too much of himself in me.

(*He sighs once more, loud enough for* MR. HOPKINS *to hear.*)

Anyway, I was the writer. Cliff was the athlete. Sports never took him anywhere. Besides, Cliff wasn't even that good at it. Believe it or not, I was actually better than him in sports.
MR. HOPKINS: Why did you stop?
RENNY: My heart just wasn't in it.
MR. HOPKINS: And what sport did you play?
RENNY [SARCASTICALLY]: Baseball.
MR. HOPKINS: Ah! The all-American family.
RENNY: You got that right. My father played as well.
MR. HOPKINS: Did he now? What position?
RENNY: Center field.
MR. HOPKINS: The backbone of the diamond.
RENNY: In fact, he played all of his life, even before I was born. Baseball was pretty much all he knew. *That* was his escape. He had scouts hounding him throughout high school. Went pro straight out of college and then threw out his arm.
MR. HOPKINS: That must've been hard on him.
RENNY: It was. . . I think. When I was a kid, we used to play catch all the time. Then, the curious writer now comes into the picture, starts poking around, wanting to know why his old man really quit playing. Was it the pressure? Was he scared? Was it because of my mother? My father met her around the time he went pro. Had his first baseball card, which was sort of a big thing back then. A mark that

you finally made it. It's just one of those things I'll never know.

MR. HOPKINS: You don't believe your father?

RENNY: I do. I just. . .

MR. HOPKINS: Whatever happened, Renny, it happened for a reason.

RENNY [QUIETLY]: Right.

MR. HOPKINS: It sounds like your father wanted to live out his dream through his children.

RENNY: I don't think so. I think all he wanted was for us to fit in. He was kind of a loner like Leon. So, I guess he didn't want us to be like him. But I don't know. Maybe you're right.

MR. HOPKINS: And how far did Cliff go in baseball?

RENNY: He stopped playing after college and ended up getting a job like my father because that was the logical thing to do. Right?

MR. HOPKINS: Cliff sounds like a provider. How about your parents? Were you close to them?

RENNY: Not really. Well, my mother. Whenever my father showed the least amount of interest in my writing, I would do other things.

MR. HOPKINS: Why did you stop writing?

RENNY: I never did *stop* writing.

(*He taps the side of his temple with his finger.*)

Every now and then, I get a really good story swirling around in here—a good whodunit.

MR. HOPKINS: You a mystery buff?

RENNY: Oh yeah.

MR. HOPKINS: You and Diego will get along.

RENNY: Well, I don't know about that. . .

(*A tense silence suddenly cuts through the air.*)

(*Then. . .*)

You know for so long I didn't want to be anything like them, my parents. And if they saw interest in something that I enjoyed or offered suggestions, then, I don't know, I guess it was a turnoff. . . I swear they were like June and Ward Cleaver from *Leave it to Beaver*. . .

(*He smiles, reflective.*)

. . . But I loved them.

(*He hangs his head for a moment.*)

I just wish. . .
MR. HOPKINS: You wish what?
RENNY: I wish they knew how much I loved them.
MR. HOPKINS: They did, Renny. They did.
RENNY [UNCERTAINLY]: Yeah.
MR. HOPKINS: They sound like nice people.
RENNY: Yeah, well. . . After I moved out, I eventually got back into writing. From there, I haven't looked back. I guess I was the only one in my family who actually followed his heart and pursued something that he loved. And for that, I got scrutinized for it, for following my heart, for following my passion.
MR. HOPKINS: I admire that, Renny. I really do.
RENNY: And I stuck with it. I never gave up, even when my family didn't support me.
MR. HOPKINS: But your mother showed interest in your writing. Correct?
RENNY: She did. . . A little. It didn't matter that much anymore. By then, it didn't bother me. I knew who I was. I was nothing like them.
MR. HOPKINS: No matter how big or small, there will *always* be a piece of your parents engrained in you and the way you live your life.

(RENNY *pauses for a moment, clears his throat, and falls into a state of reflection.*)

RENNY: I remember the first story I wrote for *Flashback*.

MR. HOPKINS: The one on the famous photographer?

RENNY: Archie Nightingale. That's the one.

MR. HOPKINS: Diego read it to me. It was, to say the least, an interesting story.

RENNY: I remember I was so excited when that story got published. I made probably two hundred bucks from the write-up. But I didn't care. I remember calling up everybody I knew, including Cliff, and telling them the good news.

MR. HOPKINS: What did your brother say?

RENNY [ANGRILY]: He tol' me [QUOTES] So Renny, when you gonna get a real job? [END QUOTES] No [QUOTES] Congratulations on the published story, Little Bro. [END QUOTES] No [QUOTES] Let me take you out to dinner, [END QUOTES] or buy you a drink. No. I got none of that. I finally found something that I loved doing and for that I got shot down by my own flesh and blood. Consider the source. *Right.* Cliff never had anything good to say about anything. Always *negative*, always a joke to compliment his negativity, always said his joke in a weird voice to mask the truth. I did my part, and I accepted Cliff, but I want to know why Cliff *can't* accept me.

MR. HOPKINS [CASUALLY]: Have you thought about asking him?

RENNY: It's not that easy.

MR. HOPKINS: Whoever said it was?

(RENNY *doesn't respond.*)

Listen, Renny. Your brother, Cliff, doesn't know any better. A brother, especially an older brother, he should be there to offer support *not* judgment. Cliff doesn't understand that writers, artists, musicians, these gifted individuals who open up their hearts to the world, who share their stories, same ones your brother probably reads or watches in a movie, these individuals have a rare power to save lives, to inspire good. These people should *never* be criticized. Yet, they should be hoisted upon the shoulders of giants and celebrated like gladiators. People like you, Renny, you will give others hope. Just remember, family is *important* despite their ignorance or their lack of understanding.

RENNY [DISGUSTEDLY]: Enough about me.

There was that same strange *click* that Anne had heard frequently while listening to the interviews. Then, after three seconds of an uninterrupted silence, the interview continued.

RENNY: Shall we get back to business now?
MR. HOPKINS: Ready when you are, Renny.

(RENNY *briefly skims over his notes.*)

RENNY: I want to talk a little more about what happened in Rural. If it makes you feel uncomfortable talking about it, then that's perfectly normal. We can move onto another topic.
MR. HOPKINS: What else do you want to know, Renny?
RENNY: What happened to Leon after the massacre?
MR. HOPKINS [SIGHING]: They didn't kill Leon, but soon after, they wished they had. Leon buried Isabel and Dom next to Isabel's parents just like Isabel wanted.

(He rolls out of bed. RENNY *springs to his feet and tries to help him up.*)

RENNY: Easy.
MR. HOPKINS: I'm all right.
RENNY: Are you sure?

(MR. HOPKINS *carefully waddles to the window and stares outside, the sun shining over his old face.*)

RENNY: How about Leon's daughter, Chloe?
MR. HOPKINS: What about her?
RENNY: How did she react to everything?
MR. HOPKINS: Like Leon, Chloe was still in a state of shock. Then, eventually, that shock wore off and all that remained was a bottomless rage. She couldn't look her father in the eyes. She wanted him dead just as much as the Company.
RENNY: But why? They were going to kill them no matter what. Right?

(MR. HOPKINS *removes the shades from his face.*)

MR. HOPKINS [SOURLY]: They could've easily killed them, Renny. I've seen them do things to people, innocent people. I knew exactly what was going to happen. The Company looked at it through uh—I guess—a broader view. Why destroy Leon's family by their owns hands when they had Leon to do it for them? It was the ultimate revenge, Renny, a man murdering the ones he loves. The thought alone of what Leon did to his wife and son was enough to make any decent man kill himself. That's one burden a man can't get rid of, even if he tries. That's the kind of burden, Renny, that stays with a man. . . *forever*. In a way, Leon wished they killed him that day. But they didn't. Then, the rage took over like a virus to a host. It's all Leon knew. He couldn't let Isabel and Dom die in vain. He knew what he had to do. And they never saw it coming.
RENNY: Did he seek revenge?
MR. HOPKINS: A man will do anything to avenge the ones he loved, Renny, even if it means going above the law. I'm sure you would do the same thing for Heather. Right?
RENNY: Did you ever think about contacting the police?

MR. HOPKINS [GRIMACING]: The police? Renny, the Company practically owned the police. Leon had nowhere to turn. He had to destroy them.
RENNY: Death Valley. He went to their main headquarters. I read about what happened—the fire. That was from Leon. Wasn't it?

(MR. HOPKINS *didn't comment on* RENNY'S *remark.*)

MR. HOPKINS: It was a secure facility, built like a military base, stashed deep in the desert basin of Death Valley. It didn't matter. He walked right through the front doors and killed them all, every last one of them—even children. There must've been over a hundred casualties. I happened to be there when the slaughter took place. I've never seen so much blood in my life. . . At night, I can hear their screams, their cries echoing across the hallways. The things Leon did to them, even the guards. The gaze was something else—cut through their visors like a knife cutting through warm butter. . . I watched them die, guards falling to their knees, blood streaming from every orifice of their face, screaming. I saw Leon turn a man to stone from head to toe and then chop off his arm with his own hand and use that arm as a club to kill another. I saw *men* shatter into millions of pieces like pieces of glass being thrown against the wall. I saw men turn to dust before my eyes. Never in my life, Renny, have I seen so much chaos, so much. . . horror. . .

(*He clenches his jaw; the sides of his old face flexing.*)

In order to destroy the Company, he had to become one of them. There was no other way.
RENNY: Become what?
MR. HOPKINS [CLEARLY]: A monster. . .
RENNY: And where were you when all of this was taking place?

MR. HOPKINS: I stayed out of the way. If Leon saw me, I knew I was as dead as every man, woman, and child before me.

RENNY: How did you manage to escape Leon's rampage?

MR. HOPKINS [QUIETLY]: I couldn't. . . I . . . couldn't hide any longer. When I found him in the basement, he wasn't the same person anymore. He wasn't even a human being. He had a face. . . he was. . . hideous, skin was different. . . like in Rural. I couldn't make out his whole face. He was standing there. I could see each breath he took. I told him it was over, to surrender. . . I begged and pleaded with him to leave.

(*His head falls forward into his curled hand.*)

I couldn't do it, Renny.

RENNY: You couldn't do what?

(MR. HOPKINS *pulls his face from his limp hand and turns his head over his shoulder.*)

MR. HOPKINS: I couldn't pull the trigger. So, I let him go. Later I. . . I found out that there was an explosion in Madison. When I arrived in Madison, there was nothing left of Leon's loft. Firefighters were pulling out tenants. All made it out alive, except one.

RENNY: Did they say how the explosion started?

MR. HOPKINS: They claimed it was from a gas leak, but right when I saw the fire, I knew what happened. I knew it was Leon.

RENNY: Why would he blow up his own home?

(*He pauses and thinks for a moment.*)

(MR. HOPKINS *hangs his head once more—the burden weighing it down. He sniffles the wet phlegm from the tip of his nose.*)

MR. HOPKINS: You know, Renny. . . *you know*. . .

(RENNY'S *eyes light up and then they slowly move toward* MR. HOPKINS. RENNY *sits back in his chair–slowly*.)

RENNY: I was just a kid when I first heard about the Red Strike, the thirteen Russians who took an entire courthouse hostage.

(*There's a tremble in his voice at first, then, eventually, the tremble eases.*)

At the time, I was probably five or six years old. At that time, Freeze had been around the block for a few years. So, most of the older kids knew about Freeze and I was always eager to find out more about him. I lived on the bad side of East Madison, Stoneharbor, which most locals called the *Armpit of Lansford*. Since my parents could hardly afford a roof over our heads, I had to walk to school, which was about four miles from where we lived. I knew very little of Freeze–only those rumors–until I met an older man, Mr. Buchanan, or [QUOTES] Bucky. [END QUOTES] My friends used to call him *Bow Tie* because he always wore a bow tie. He hung out on a bench that I used to pass on the way to school. One day, I saw Bucky reading the newspaper. I can't recall what the headline was, but I remember I saw that name, *Freeze*. I sat down next to this man and he told me stories about Freeze, what Freeze had done for Lansford, told me more about Red Strike and how it brought people closer together. I didn't even make it to school that day. . .

(*He smiles briefly. Then, the smile washes away from his face, leaving only a vacant expression.*)

Later on, I went to the library and found all of these articles on Freeze. I couldn't read too well. In the days to come, Bucky taught me how to read, even showed me his own personal collection that he had saved over the years, dozens of newspaper articles all from Arthur Mitchell to Craig Basse. Since Bucky didn't have any children, he decided to give me the articles. He told me to take good care of them and to pass them down to my kids and then my kids' kids and so on. That night—I remember—I read each article underneath my bed covers, a flashlight in my hand, my eyes glued to the paper; and from that point on, I dreamed about making it as big as Freeze. Over time, I realized there was no way I could turn into a role model such as Freeze, this beacon of hope. He was larger than life, and I was some stupid kid from Stoneharbor. Freeze had become a staple in Lansford. . . you know. . . native tongue. Whenever a conversation got stale, then that name would come up—always done so in a state of reflection—nostalgic, in a way. Then, there were the TV commercials [SMILING]. How could I forget?

MR. HOPKINS: I remember.

RENNY AND MR. HOPKINS [AT THE SAME TIME]: *Freeze* and think before you act.

MR. HOPKINS: The Anti-Drug Campaign.

RENNY: For a while, Freeze was the face of Lansford. All of a sudden, he disappeared from my life, from Lansford's life. Then, his name went silent. His name wasn't in the news, not in the newspapers. Strangely enough, he disappeared from the face of the earth. I remember I read about the accident at Death Valley, the death toll. Then, years later, the details were revealed. I didn't know if they were true or not. Feds said that Freeze was responsible. Moved his way up to number one on America's Most Wanted List. One day, a hero. The next, a terrorist, a traitor to our country. Then, there was a conspiracy theory saying that Freeze was framed to look like a criminal. Years went by. People just stopped talking about Freeze.

(*His eyes sharpen, voice too.*)

Then, out of the blue, I get an email from a man claiming to be Marcus Hopkins, Freeze's former partner, and now, he wants me to write a story on Freeze. [STRANGELY] At first, I think to myself: it's *too* good to be true. A story about the iconic Freeze. So, I decide to pay a visit to this Mr. Hopkins guy. Sure enough, he's right, right about everything, except for one thing: Freeze isn't dead.

(*He stands from the chair; his right hand tightens into a fist.* MR. HOPKINS *listens closely to the sound of the chair being pushed from underneath* RENNY, *two footsteps toward the bed, and then, lastly, pounding breath, now growing harsher.*)

A thick *silence* swelled over the conversation.

MR. HOPKINS: I'm sorry, Renny.
RENNY: Why—
MR. HOPKINS: It was the *only* way!

(*He turns around and faces* RENNY.)

RENNY: Why didn't you tell me—
MR. HOPKINS: If I told you the truth, Renny, then you would've never believed me.

Anne's face slackened in great surprise.
"Are you kidding me?" Anne said to herself as she turned up the volume on the laptop.

RENNY: Why did you bring me here?
MR. HOPKINS [LOUDLY]: I'm sorry, Renny.
RENNY [SEETHING]: Answer me! Why did you bring me here, Leon? What. . . what do you want from me?
MR. HOPKINS [WHIMPERING]: I must. . . I must get her back. *Renny.* Please. I know I've screwed up. Big time. I know. I. . . I don't have much time. Please, Renny. Help me.

RENNY: You lied to me!

(*Stricken with rage,* MR. HOPKINS *grabs a hold of his cane and takes a step closer to* RENNY.)

MR. HOPKINS: Then that makes us even, goddamn it!

(RENNY *shakes his head, face red.*)

RENNY: I never lied to you.
MR. HOPKINS: About *Heather,* Renny?   You didn't lie about her?
RENNY: This isn't about me! This is about you, Leon!
MR. HOPKINS: Bullshit! This story isn't about either of us.
RENNY: Then, what the fuck am I doing here! Tell me!
MR. HOPKINS: She. . . she despises me, Renny.

(*He staggers back over to the bed and sits down on the edge. Holds the cane in his lap.*)

I can't die knowing my own daughter despises me. I can't die like that. I know. . . you may not understand, Renny, because you don't have any children and you don't know what it's like to lose one of them.
RENNY: What do you want from me? Huh?
MR. HOPKINS: All I want is for her to realize that I was a good man, Renny; that I loved her, Renny, despite everything that happened to her mother *and* her little brother. I know she's out there, lost in a world she doesn't understand.

(RENNY *furrows his brows and leans forward.*)

RENNY: What are you talking about?
MR. HOPKINS: She knows you, Renny. She reads your magazine. . . *Flashback.*

RENNY: What?

MR. HOPKINS: Diego told me there was a way to reach her, to bring Chloe back. I never asked any questions. It was the *only* way.

RENNY: Only way for what?

MR. HOPKINS: To *save* her, Renny.

RENNY: Save her from what?

MR. HOPKINS: From herself.

(*Tension, so thick that* RENNY *can feel it pressing against his chest. Another long pause. . .*)

She's out there, Renny, alone, confused, living a lie.

RENNY: What makes you so sure?

MR. HOPKINS: Diego.

RENNY: What about him?

MR. HOPKINS: He. . . he's been watching over her.

RENNY: What?

MR. HOPKINS [STRESSING]: He said it was *the only way* for he to understand.

(RENNY *runs his sweaty palm over his mouth and sighs greatly.*)

RENNY [UNSTEADILY]: So, all of this, this interview, this was for your daughter? So, you used me?

MR. HOPKINS: No, Renny. Soon, everybody will know the truth about me, about Freeze. And it's up to you to choose whether or not you will cast me in a negative light. You, Renny, you once believed in Freeze. Believe in him. Believe in me, Renny.

RENNY [FLATLY]: How can I? After everything. . .

MR. HOPKINS: Put yourself in my shoes. What if the ones you loved were taken away from you? What if she was taken away from you? *Heather*. Renny? What would you do—

RENNY: —How did you do it?

MR. HOPKINS: Do what?

RENNY: How did you fake your own death?

(MR. HOPKINS *finally calms his breathing.*)

Tell me! You owe me that much. Leon, tel—

MR. HOPKINS: —I found one of them. He was still breathing, a guard from the Company. He had same profile as
me. Similar height and weight. I used the guard's body and
planted it inside my loft. I made sure the Company would
never identify the body. That way after the explosion they
would find the body and assume it was me.

RENNY: Why go through these extremes if the Company
was no longer a threat to you?

MR. HOPKINS: I might've destroyed their headquarters,
but they're still out there, waiting for me. I couldn't take a
chance of them finding me.

RENNY: And then you came here?

MR. HOPKINS [DESPAIRINGLY]: Yes.

(*He hangs his head once more, trying to imagine her face, his
daughter's face, Chloe.*)

Everyday, she's on my mind—my Chloe. Everyday, I wonder
whether or not she's standing outside in the courtyard as
she always did, looking up at me behind the window.

(*He follows the warmth and stares at the window, the place where
the sun lives.*)

I try to imagine her the same way before she ran away, her
face, smiling ear to ear, those two eyes staring up at me.
[SMILING] That *wasn't* the little girl who came back home
with us. The girl who came back wanted nothing to do
with me, Renny.

RENNY: Because of what happened in Rural?

MR. HOPKINS: Yes. [SIGHING] It was getting late in the
after noon. Chloe and I had a terrible argument. We
couldn't go a day without arguing. We cou. . . she said she
wanted me to d'. . . Diego chased after her, but she was too

fast for him. Chloe managed to escape through the woods. He couldn't keep up with her. . . it was raining that day too. And the ground was wet.

RENNY: Where were you when this happened?

MR. HOPKINS: I was weak, Renny. I spent so much energy trying to destroy the Company. When I came back, I was completely drained. Every *inch* of this place hurt me. I was in no condition to track her down. Diego and I drove around town the next morning. Chloe was nowhere around. Diego asked locals if they had seen her, if they had seen my Chloe, but they all gave him the same exact answer. After weeks of searching, we gave up. Surely, I thought the worst had happened to her. *Not* my Chloe. She was too strong like her mother. Numerous times, I tried to gaze myself. If I could make another man forget, then I could make myself forget about what happened in Rural. Was I wrong! It was so vivid, these images, the screaming, a river of snakes and blood, the *horror*, Renny. . .

RENNY: Did it work, the gaze?

MR. HOPKINS [VACANTLY]: No, Renny. It didn't work.

RENNY: Did you ever find Chloe?

MR. HOPKINS: No. We didn't. A year later after her disappearance, Diego and I drove to a drive-in movie theatre in Rural where Isabel and I had our first date.

(RENNY, *more engrossed than upset, sits back down in his chair.*)

RENNY: What movie?

MR. HOPKINS: *Dirty Dancing.*

(*A flash of a smile emerges from one side on his face.*)

RENNY: They don't make 'em like that anymore.

MR. HOPKINS: I will never forget. We shared our first kiss after the final song came on. You've seen the movie. You know the song I'm talking about.

RENNY: I do. . . [QUOTES] The Time of My Life. [END QUOTES] Billy Medley and Jennifer Warnes.

MR. HOPKINS: I kept her clothes too. I'll pull them out at times and smell them; the memories come back to me, so vivid as if I can touch them with my hand. The pain brought on from the loss of Isabel was too much to bear, Renny. So. . . I did the one thing I should've done years ago. Diego did all he could to repair the damage and scar tissue. It was already too late. I just. . . I just didn't want them anymore. I wanted to rid *this hell* from my body.

(RENNY *tilts his head in shock.*)

RENNY: What did you do?

MR. HOPKINS: I did. . . I. . . I did what I had to do, Renny. I couldn't live with them anymore. Losing my eyesight was the best thing that happened to me. Never have I felt so liberated. Living in darkness was the easy part. Your senses, tastes, smells, hearing, they compensate for your loss of vision. You learn how to see through sounds and smells. Somehow, there was still a little part of it left inside me, the gaze. When I would go out in public and surround myself with people, I could *see* their eyes—like tiny stars glistening in the darkness. Some eyes shine. And others don't.

(*He struggles to lift up his hand. When he finally does, he touches the backside of his neck.*)

Some of them pass like a breeze against the back of your neck. The hardest part, Renny, was trying to get her back in my life, finding a way to ask for forgiveness for what I did. I had no control in the course of her life until now, with you, *Renny*. All I want is for Chloe to forgive me for the awful thing I did years ago. That's why I need you. . . Renny. You said you've always wanted to write a story about Freeze. Well, this is our chance. . .

RENNY: What makes you so sure your daughter will forgive you?

(MR. HOPKINS *grunts as he stands and then hobbles to* RENNY.)

MR. HOPKINS: That's where you come in, Renny. You, Renny, you must be the one to write the story, my story, our story.

RENNY: What about Marcus? Your partner? What happened to him?

MR. HOPKINS: He's dead.

RENNY: How did he die?

MR. HOPKINS: Marcus came here years later after what happened in Rural. He asked me for forgiveness. I wouldn't give it to him.

RENNY: If you could never forgive Marcus for what he did to you in Rural, what makes you think your daughter will *ever* forgive you?

MR. HOPKINS [ABRUPTLY]: Because she has to, *she must.* Marcus had an opportunity to call it off, but he chose not to. Instead, it resulted in the death of my wife and son. I had a life, goddamn it! I finally found someone I could spend the rest of my life with! I was supposed to protect them from people like Marcus Hopkins! That man [GRIMACING] they took everything away from me. And that's why they *had* to die.

RENNY: Did you kill Marcus?

MR. HOPKINS: No.

(*A creak in the floor!* RENNY *looks over his shoulder and sees* DIEGO *in the corner of his eye.* DIEGO'S *standing at the doorway with both of his arms held by his waist side—his eyes shooting daggers at* RENNY.)

RENNY [ANGRILY]: Why am I here, Leon?

MR. HOPKINS: I told you. The story. It's all about the story.

RENNY: But people think you're dead. They'll never believe me.

MR. HOPKINS: Not if you tell it from Hopkins' point of view.

(*He finds* RENNY, *who takes a step forward into his arm length.*)

Come, Renny.

(*He grabs* RENNY *by the shoulder.*)

There's something I need to show you.

(RENNY *guides* MR. HOPKINS *to his wheelchair. He sits him down. Next,* RENNY *vigilantly peeks over his shoulder.* DIEGO *is no longer standing at the doorway.*)

RENNY: Where are we going?

MR. HOPKINS [STERNLY]: To the storage room. I believe you've been there before, Renny.

(RENNY *opens his mouth, but the words fall short.*)

Don't worry. The thing about muddy shoes: they always leave a trail.

RENNY: You're not mad?

(MR. HOPKINS *pats* RENNY *on the hand.*)

MR. HOPKINS: Of course not.

(RENNY *pushes* MR. HOPKINS *down the hallway.*)

The interview suddenly went dead silent, but the time on the player, Anne noticed, kept running as if whatever was left of the interview had been spliced. This wasn't the first time Anne had come across the varied time code. A couple of times—twice, she remembered—there had been changes in the time. She didn't think much of it, not at the time, but now, with her being so intrigued by Freeze's story, she wanted to know *why* that particular segment of the recording had been digitally snipped away as if it never existed at all.

9:25 PM

"THOUGHT you could use a cup," Florence said over Merrotti's shoulder as she held out a fresh cup of coffee, just the way the detective liked it, all the way black and hot enough to blister the roof of his mouth.

The detective, who had been rubbing his eyes for the past hour, turned his shoulder and eyed the cup for a moment.

"Don't worry," his partner said and handed Merrotti the cup of coffee. "I didn't poison it."

"How kind of you, Pam," he said and then blew the steam from the coffee.

Florence sat down on the edge of the desk as Merrotti leaned back in his chair and took a baby-like sip from the hot coffee. She closely studied her partner, his exhausted state.

"I'm worried about you, Devon," she said finally.

Merrotti smirked and placed the cup of coffee on the desk.

"Don't be," he said as he riffled through the crime scene photographs taken from Anne Roth's house, mainly of the perp. He nodded at the photos on the desk. "Still no ID on our guy. He's not in the database. No rap sheet. No records. No nothing." He mistakenly ran his hand over his bloodshot eyes. "The man's a ghost."

"I'm serious, Devon."

Merrotti pulled his tired eyes from the photographs and shot a glance at his partner.

"Relax," he said. "After this cup, I'll be doing jumping jacks."

"It's getting worse."

Merrotti squared his shoulders to his partner.

"What are you talking about?"

"You think I don't know about your drinking?"

Merrotti was at a loss for words.

"Come on, Devon," she said. "I'm not *that* stupid. I know all about it."

Merrotti shook his head and picked up the cup of coffee as he leaned back in his chair.

"I don't know what you're talking about."

Once more, he sipped from the cup.

"I haven't told anybody," Florence said carefully.

Merrotti turned away from Florence.

"Do we really need to have this conversation right now, Pam?" he said sharply and then glared at his partner. "We have four dead bodies, no lead what-so-fucking-ever, and your talking about issues that are completely irrelevant to the case."

"They're very much relevant, Devon," Florence said bitterly. "It affects the way you do your job."

"Well," Merrotti said as he placed the cup on the desk, "it's none of your business what I do with my personal life."

Florence leaned closer.

"It *is* my business, Devon," she whispered into Merrotti's ears only. "You're my partner. And I'm not going to sit back and watch you destroy yourself. I need you focused."

"I am focused!" Merrotti blurted out.

The sudden outburst caused a couple other cops in the vicinity to turn their heads toward the two detectives. Merrotti redirected his attention toward the eager cops, which, after receiving a frosty stare from the sulky detective, forced the cops to look the other way.

"I'm just trying to help, Devon," Florence said patiently.

Merrotti stood up and paced around the desk.

Florence stood to her feet.

"I was thinking about paying a visit to the morgue," she said.

"Good," Merrotti said suddenly. "Don't let the door hit you on the way out."

"Devon," Florence said sincerely.

She paused and thought about saying what she really wanted to say, which was that she cared about Devon.

After the long pause, Florence grabbed her coat and said under her breath, "Forget about it."

9:28 PM

ANNE fast-forwarded the interview until a voice finally came back on.

As the interview continued (this "Mr. Hopkins" character talking to Renny: *If the world find outs, Renny, then everything we've known, everything we've learned from years of research or studies would all be disguised as a myth, a legend*), she rewound the interview a few seconds before Renny's voice came back on.

RENNY: But how? It's not real. They're [STUTTERING] just myths, stories—
MR. HOPKINS: Stories have been handed down for many centuries, Renny. You're a writer. You should know that

there is always some truth in a story, even in the fictional ones.

RENNY: Say you're right and what you told me is true, then what?

MR. HOPKINS: If the world finds out, Renny, then everything we've known, everything we've learned from years of research or studies would all be disguised as a myth, a legend.

RENNY: So, how did you acquire this power?

MR. HOPKINS: Reach into my pocket.

(RENNY *reaches his hand inside* MR. HOPKINS' *left pocket.*)

No. The right one.

RENNY: This?

(*He pulls out an old, rusty Zigzags tin can and hands it to* MR. HOPKINS.)

MR. HOPKINS: That's it. That's where all the magic happens.

(*He opens the can, peels back the wax paper, and fingers around the inside until he finds a dried-up scale. He holds up the scale to* RENNY.)

When I was thirteen years old, a friend and I were playing hide and seek in the house. I never had any friends over. Never really had many to invite over. My father never let me. One day, he was gone on a trip. It was just Diego and I. The thing about Diego, if you beg loud enough, then he usually gives in. I showed my friend my father's collection, the lost artifacts, the treasures, what my father had brought back with him from his travels. Then, I showed him this.

(*He nods at the head inside the glass dome.*)

My friend dared me to eat one of the scales, so I did. I didn't discover what it had done to me until two years later. It just. . . happened.

RENNY: You're telling me you became this way from some dare?

MR. HOPKINS [SHAMEFULLY]: Yes, Renny.

(RENNY *lets out a sigh, a loud and exaggerated one.*)

It was already written.

RENNY: You believe in that, that we have no control over our fate?

MR. HOPKINS: I do, Renny. Too many things have happened in my life. I'd be a fool not to believe it.

RENNY: Then what about coincidences?

MR. HOPKINS: This was no coincidence. I. . . when Tammy died, I believe a higher power was punishing me, telling me that I would not be able to love another, that everything I would do *or* love would result in death. I didn't wake up that morning wanting to kill Tammy. I accepted what I did, and Chloe must understand that I was born this way, tha what happened to me wasn't by mistake or some *dare*; otherwise there's a possibility she will never forgive me. You must not put this in the story.

RENNY: You want me to lie?

MR. HOPKINS: Sometimes, you have to lie. Of all people, you should know this. Sometimes, the truth is too hard for people to understand.

A sudden *rustling*. . .

A couple of sharp thuds and grating clinks danced on the recording before the wave file came to an immediate halt.

Anne, still left in a state of disbelief, closed the file and opened the entry from earlier, the one from *10.17.2014.*

So, it's true about Freeze. In the back of my mind, I knew it was him all along. The moment I laid eyes on him, I knew. I never knew how much time away from loved ones could cripple a man. He's literally half the man he used to be. It's hard to even recognize him underneath that withered face, but it's him. I know it. I *feel* it. The way he speaks, what he has told me. I know it's him. Right now, I not only owe it to Mr. Dorsey to finish writing his remarkable story, but I owe it to myself. When I first came here, my intention was to write a story about Freeze and the life he and his partner, Marcus Hopkins, shared together. This is not a story about Freeze. This is a story about second chances, about forgiveness, about owning up to one's mistakes.

Everybody deserves a second chance. Right?

Three *knocks* on the door!

Anne closed the document and then the laptop.

"Yes," she said with a tremble in her voice.

"*Anne*," Jamie said softly from behind the door.

"Yes," Anne said once more, but this time she did so more curiously.

Jamie asked, "*May I come in?*"

Anne ejected the USB flash drive from the laptop and then placed the laptop aside.

Behind the door, a worried voice: "*Anne. . .*"

Another *knock* on the door, but this time softer.

"Coming," Anne said as she rolled out of bed and answered the door.

Jamie was standing there with her arms crossed over her chest. Her face was vacant, her wounded eyes speaking a come-hither tune to Anne; however, Anne was a bit dumbfounded from Jamie's aroused state.

"Is everything okay?" she asked.

Jamie bobbed her head as she unfolded her arms from her chest.

"Yeah," Jamie said shortly. "Would you like some company?"

Anne hesitated.

"Uhhh," Anne drawled. Then, a sudden, "Yeah. Sure."

She stepped out of the way and let Jamie into the bedroom.

They walked to the bed and then sat down, Jamie first and then Anne second.

9:58 PM

AFTER Florence left the precinct, she stopped at the morgue, which was located not too far from the precinct—about a ten to fifteen minute drive, depending on traffic.

There, she met the coroner, a scrawny man with green eyes and a cleft chin, which was partially concealed by a thin beard.

"If it isn't my future wife to be," the coroner said cheerfully as he briefly pulled his eyes from the corpse on the table.

"In your dreams, Terry," the detective said. "Ask me out when you finally win the lottery."

"Ouch," Terry said, wincing one side of his face. "That's cold, Pamela."

"What can I say?" she said as a smile grew somewhere underneath her stern face. "A girl needs reassurance, especially in this weak ass economy."

"Well, you can thank Shaw for that one."

Florence smacked her gums.

"Thought Shaw was your boy."

"Why?" Florence said snappishly. "Because I'm black?"

"Yeah," Terry said bluntly.

"Hey," she said, "how do you think I feel, Terry? I voted for that lying fool. It's not my fault he can't fix the economy. Isn't that the reason we voted for him to begin with?"

"That's why I voted for the man."

"Then, you're not the only one who got played, my dear."

Terry grinned as he walked Florence to another corpse at the other end of the morgue.

"So, where's your *other* boy?" he asked.

"Back at the precinct," she said quietly. "Had to wrap up some things." Before he could squeeze out another question, the detective cut him off, "What's the word on my stiff?"

10:03 PM

IN the corner of his eye, Merrotti spotted the young officer, Officer Cabrera.

"Brought the weapon Florence asked for," he said as he held up the evidence bag containing the bloody knife from Anne Roth's house.

Merrotti sipped from the coffee.

"Just missed her, pal." He removed his red eyes from the gore of the crime scene photos and turned toward the young officer. "I'll give it to her when she comes back."

The officer cautiously stepped forward and handed the evidence bag to Merrotti.

"Where did she go?" the officer asked.

"What's it to you, Cabrera?" Merrotti said sourly. "Why are you so curious about my partner?"

The anxious officer shrugged his shoulders.

"Not curious."

Merrotti closely eyed the officer.

"The morgue," he said.   "She went to the morgue."

As the young officer was leaving, Merrotti suddenly called out, "Hey, Cabrera!"

He turned around and walked back to the office.

"Yeah, Detective."

"You were working the night shift on Wednesday," he said. "Right?"

Cabrera didn't respond at first.

Merrotti waited for an answer.

"Yes," Cabrera said finally. "That's right."

"Did you see anything out of the ordinary?"

"No, sir."

"You sure?"

"Yes, sir," he said. "Nothing out of the ordinary."

"Had to ask."

"Sure." Cabrera paused. "Is that all?"

"Yeah," Merrotti said. "That's all."

10:05 PM

"YOUR Santiago fellow was pretty cut and dry," Terry said to Florence as he pulled back the white sheet from the corpse, not Santiago but the other one. "However, your mystery man is a different story. I was thinking more about this particular mark on his wrist." Terry showed her the tattoo on the corpse's wrist. "Then, it came to me. A few years ago, there was this thing on the Historic Channel about a group of rebels called *Ejército de Muertos Vivientes*. It stands for the Undead Army."

"Airsha-cito what?"

Clearly now: "*Ejército de Muertos Vivientes.*"

"Damn, Terry," Florence said surprisingly. "Didn't know you spoke Spanish."

"A little," he said. "My ex was from Puerto Rico."

Surprised yet again, Florence said, "Wow. Puerto Rico. Huh? Way to go, Terry."

"I have a weak spot for the *señoritas*."

"I'm sure you do."

"However," Terry said, "I never had much of a rolling tongue."

"Really?"

"It's true."

"Well," Florence said, "a lady likes a man who knows how to roll his r's."

"Are you flirting with me, Detective?"

"Of course not."

Florence couldn't help but grin.

"Anyway," Terry said as he carefully watched her grin become something beautiful, a smile, which, for Florence, was a shy thing—a recluse, in a way. Terry couldn't help but smile as well. "Where was I?"

"Some kind of rebels on TV."

"Right," Terry said. "Army of the Undead, Ejército de los Muertos Vivientes. They were like this legend around South America."

"*Undead*," she said strangely. "Okay. Like zombies. What does that have to do with my stiff? He's not gonna come back to life. Is he?"

"That would be ridiculous, Detective."

"Then, where are you going with this, Terry?"

10:08 PM

THREE more sips of coffee.

As the headache dimmed a little, Merrotti flipped through more photographs. He came across one in particular.

Intrigued by the photograph, he leaned closer and focused on the close up of the tattoo on the perp's wrist, those three lines, shaped like a capital E, and then a line running through the middle, the spine, and then, on the other side, the letter v.

10:09 PM

"SEE right here," Terry said as he held up the corpse's pale wrist. "There's the E for *Ejército*. Then, the M for *Muertos*. V for *Vivientes*. The Undead Army was basically a group of rebels who were trying to overthrow the government."

"So, freedom fighters. . . "

"Exactly," he said ecstatically. "They're from parts of Columbia, Venezuela, Argentina. However, the thing is nobody knew who they really were—farmers, carpenters, people like me and you, Florence, everyday men and women. *However*, what they do know is that it all started with a kid."

"A kid?"

"That's right," he said. "Took down an entire cartel."

"A *kid?*"

"Local, from a small town."

"So, a local hero?"

"That's right."

10:10 PM

BOTH Anne and Jamie stared into each other's eyes.

Anne thinking about her question: *Do you ever feel alone in the world?*

She didn't have a quick response to the question.

Finally, she shrugged her shoulders, pulled her eyes from Jamie, and said into her chest, "I don't know. Yeah. I mean. *No*, Jamie. I do feel like people only care about themselves." She turned to Jamie. "I care."

"I know you do, Anne," Jamie said as she grabbed a hold of Anne's hand. "That's why you're so special."

Her eyes fell upon her hand and then the USB flash drive inside.

"What is that?" she asked.

Anne looked down.

"It's nothing," she said.

Sternly, Jamie asked, "Is something going on, Anne?"

Anne hesitated. "No."

"You can tell me."

"You'll think I'm crazy."

"No," she said. "I won't."

Anne sighed. She looked Jamie directly in the eyes. "I think I'm in danger."

"What do you mean *danger*?"

"Because of this." She showed Jamie the USB flash drive. "I think people are after me because of this."

"A thumb drive?"

"It's what's on this drive."

"What's on it?"

"An interview," Anne stuttered. "I mean, lots of interviews."

"Okay," Jamie drawled.

"I knew it," she said suddenly. "You think I'm crazy."

Jamie slid her hand across the bed until her hand finally fell upon Anne's thigh.

"I don't think you're crazy, Anne," she said as she caressed her thigh. "You're a good person who's confused right now."

"You care about me," Anne said clearly. "Don't you?"

Jamie discreetly bobbed her head.

In her subdued manner, Anne witnessed Jamie
moistening her upper lip, the careful swallow as if Jamie was preparing to use her tongue in the moments
to come, and then, lastly, the hand patiently caressing
the inner part of her thigh. Anne moved her eyes
down to her lap, held them there for a second until
finally moving them toward her friend's hand, the
way it felt against her skin. Anne's eyes stayed there
for a couple of seconds, studying Jamie's hand and
watching it inch farther up her thigh. Her eyes pulled
away from Jamie's hand and slowly made their way
up Jamie's abdomen, across her pumping chest, and
then continued their trek up Jamie's body until finally
landing on those wounded eyes. For a second, the
two women both shared a stare: Jamie's more lecherous, predatory, whereas Anne's as vulnerable as a
prey. The innocence that was nestled sacredly inside
Anne striped away and was replaced with the lechery
which bedeviled Jamie.

In a sudden propel forward, Jamie kissed Anne on
the lips.

Anne's first reaction: sheer repulsion. Not a nasty
"*Yuck*," but, more or less, that crossing of a line.

Before Jamie could readjust her lips around
Anne's, Anne pulled her head back and studied Jamie's face, that lechery.

"What are you doing?" Anne said carefully.

The hurt from her eyes spread across her face.
"I'm doing what I have to. . . ."

On an impulse, Anne suddenly leaned her head
forward and kissed Jamie back. The kiss was rushed
at first, as if they were two spouses who routinely
smooched each other before heading out to work
every morning—as dull as watching a carwash.
Then, Anne pulled her head away and studied her
friend's face, as well as her flickering eyes. She kissed

Jamie yet again. The kiss eventually slowed its course, as if they were two lovers who hadn't embraced each other in years and they were now restoring the taste.

As quickly as she could, Jamie removed Anne's shirt while kissing Anne and then Anne, as previously with the first kiss, returned the favor and removed Jamie's shirt. Jamie followed by removing the black brassiere, exposing her perky cone-like breasts. She straddled Anne's body and traced her lips around her neck in search for her weakest spots, mostly residing behind her left ear. She moved her lips down Anne's plump breasts, but didn't spend too much time on them.

Next, Jamie worked down Anne's firm abdomen and, once she arrived at Anne's belly button, she removed Anne's pants.

With a grin, Jamie murmured in Anne's ear, "I like your innie."

Anne chortled, unsteadily at first.

"Thanks," she said as she cleared her throat.

She arched her hips upright and, with Jamie's help, slipped off her underwear as she raised both legs in the air.

10:11 PM

A sudden wave of panic rushed through the detective and sent him in a pale and fixed state. Merrotti's face went slack, eyes widened. He thought more about the break-in, the dead perp. He remembered Cabrera at the crime scene as well and how the young cop was digging through the perp's pockets, supposedly frisking the body, which seemed absurd to the detective; but at the time, he assumed it was from the officer's lack of experience. He didn't know exactly what Cabrera was doing, at least not until now when he focused on the tattoo, *that tattoo*, the same one he spotted during the exchange of the evidence bag. The detective only caught half of the tattoo behind the officer's sleeve, but nonetheless, it was enough for the detective to realize that Pam was in danger. Merrotti dropped the photographs and rushed from the office.

10:12 PM

"SO," Florence drawled, "are you're saying this man might be connected to this '*army*' you speak of?"

"I'm not a hundred percent sure, Detective."

"Well, as far as I'm concerned, Terry, this is between me and you," she said. "If Merrotti finds out, he'll think you're crazy. The million-dollar question, if you are right about this tattoo: 'What the hell is a bunch of freedom fighters from South America doing in Lansford?' Most importantly: 'What the hell do they want with a telemarketer from USR?'"

Terry said, "Beats the hell out of me, Detective."

"Okay," Florence said, thinking. "What else can you tell me about this Undead Army. . . "

10:14 PM

MERROTTI finally made it to the parking garage, only to find Cabrera's cruiser missing from the parking spot.

As the detective placed his hands over his knees and tried to catch his breath—the three flights of stairs did quite the number on him—he reached into his pocket and pulled out his cell phone. He dialed Florence's phone number, the # 1, on speed dial. The detective waited and waited, but he ended up getting Florence's voicemail.

What Merrotti didn't realize was that his partner had left her cell in the passenger seat of her car; but to Merrotti, he suspected that he was already too late and the worst had already happened.

10:16 PM

NOW fully nude, Anne, who was extremely bashful and embarrassed despite her friend's unclothed body, covered herself with her hand. Jamie gently removed Anne's hand away and nibbled, starting at Anne's foot and then worked her way to Anne's knee and then, from there, traced her lips to Anne's other knee in a horseshoe-like pattern. Jamie did this cycle, going from one knee to the other, panting over her bare flesh, until Anne couldn't resist any further. Anne ran her fingers through Jamie's greasy hair and then cupped the backside of her head with one hand while the other one played with herself. She guided Jamie's head upward and then, finally, placed her head between her thighs. Jamie settled her chin over the bed and made herself comfortable, as if she was going to be there for a minute: her *lips* squared with Anne's.

A couple of seconds into pleasuring Anne, now tugging at the bed sheets and ripping them from the mattress, she swiftly removed her tongue and walked her lips up Anne's abdomen. She reared back and suddenly bit Anne on the waist.

Anne violently recoiled her hips into the mattress!

"Ouch," she cried out.

"Sorry," Jamie whispered with a strange grin creeping over one side of her face.

10:24 PM

OFFICER Cabrera slipped past the morgue and snuck into a dark office area to make a call.

A man with a resonant voice, same one from the alleyway next to the Flying Wok, answered the phone, "How many are there?"

"So far, two, the detective and the coroner," he said quietly, occasionally peeking his head from the office. "They shouldn't be a problem, sir."

"Are you sure?"

"Yes, sir."

"Then, make sure it stays that way."

"Yes, sir."

10:27 PM

As she returned back to Anne's thighs and proceeded to pleasure her, a painful sensation rippled throughout Anne's body.

"Oh God!" she moaned.

With a mouthful of flesh, Jamie uttered, "You like?"

Anne moaned once more, "Oh God!"

"Yeah," Jamie uttered, her tongue penetrating deeper.

The pain was like a knife driving through Anne's insides. The feeling alone made her extremely nauseous. She arched her head forward, curious as to what exactly Jamie was doing. Her hazy eyes crossed Jamie, who, after intensely rattling her jaw like a maraca, raised her chin and smiled. There, she witnessed not Jamie's smile, but another smile. The person, who was slithering before her, was no longer a woman but a thin man with a gaunt face wearing an awfully wicked smile, *the* creature's smile. He straddled Anne's body. In return, she recoiled once more. Anne made an attempt to flee from the man, but the man forced her back onto the bed. He thrust his sharp and bony hips against Anne's. One thrust at a time, he sent warm jabs into the insides of her body, now throbbing like a pulse. And the peckerwood was hung like a horse too. Anne made yet another attempt to pull away from the strange man, but, with his bony palms, he pinned down her shoulders against the bed.

Throughout her the gauntlet of agony, Anne arched her head forward and looked below.

There, Anne witnessed the horror, blood spurting against the man's lower abdomen.

"*Please*," Anne begged. "*Stop. . .* "

Anne moaned the kind of moan that Jamie was reaching for.

"No!" Anne cried out once more.

Jamie penetrated deeper.

"I said, 'No!'"

Jamie suddenly pulled her mouth from Anne, who quickly slid across the bed and used the pillow to cover herself.

"What's wrong?" Jamie asked, wiping her mouth clean.

"It's not you," she said, struggling to look at Jamie. "It's me."

10:36 PM

AFTER running through three stoplights and speeding around two pedestrians, once actually mounting the sidewalk, Merrotti finally arrived at the morgue.

He cut off the engine and jetted from the car, not bothering to shut the door behind him.

On the way to the entrance, he found Cabrera's cruiser parked alongside the building.

10:39 PM

JAMIE crawled closer to Anne, who, in return, backed herself against the headboard.

"I thought you liked it."

"I did," she said. "I do. It's just. . . "

She mistakenly eyed Jamie, her body; and then, when she pulled her eyes away, she witnessed that creature standing at the edge of the doorway. He was standing there, naked, with a ring of fresh blood circled around his red genitals. A trail of blood was trickling down one side of his leg.

Anne shook away the stark image from her mind until the creature was no longer standing there.

Jamie glanced over her shoulder.

"What, Anne?" she said, closer now. "You can tell me."

She placed her hand over Anne's hand.

Anne retracted and sauntered to the bedroom window.

"I'm sorry, Jamie," Anne said quietly as she faced the window. "It's just. . . "

Jamie sat down on the edge of the bed with her hands in her lap.

"I don't know what came over me," she said, her eyes occasionally looking toward the floor. "But it was real, though. Wasn't it? Anne?" She raised her head and looked toward Anne and said optimistically, "It *was* real. Wasn't it?"

Anne turned her shoulder and said, "Yes. I just. . . "

Jamie dropped her shoulders.

"Just what, Anne?" Jamie said strongly. "You can tell me anything. We're friends."

"I keep having these kinds ah. . . I . . . don't know what they are. . . *flashbacks*, I guess."

10:42 PM

WITH vigilance, Merrotti entered the morgue, but he saw no sign of his partner.

He listened closely.

As he proceeded down the stale hallway, he heard a noise coming from the autopsy room near the back of the building.

10:43 PM

JAMIE asked, "What kind of flashbacks?"

"Memories, I think," she answered. "There was this man, a thin man. I think he did something bad to me when I was younger."

Jamie's face flattened. Her whole manner: stern and unyielding. She put on her shirt, stood up from the bed, and walked toward Anne.

"Bad?" Jamie said with a tiny furrow between her brows. "What do you mean?"

"I mean like. . . "

"Like he touched you?"

10:44 PM

AS Merrotti arrived at the autopsy room, he pulled out his gun, a Glock 19, from his shoulder holster and held it close by his side.

10:45 PM

IT took a few seconds for Anne to bob her head.

"I think so," she said finally. "I don't know. Times, I feel like. . . like a stranger in my own body, Jamie."

Jamie wrapped her arm around Anne's shoulder.

"I'm sorry things have been hard for you," she said tenderly. "I can't even imagine what you're going through. You know I'm here for you, Anne. You know this. . . "

Anne looked into Jamie's eyes.

"I know," she said. "Thanks, Jamie. I don't know what I would do without you. You've been a good friend."

For a moment, Jamie played with Anne's hair, mostly curling the ends around her fingertips. She made one last glance into Anne's eyes before kissing the side of Anne's neck. "No, Jamie," Anne said as her eyes fell downward onto Jamie's hands and then her wrists, mainly her right wrist.

Jamie pulled away.

"Okay," she said shortly.

Anne looked closer at the strange tattoo on Jamie's wrist. The tattoo was nothing like she had seen before; in fact, she was completely unaware of the tattoo.

Jamie followed Anne's eyes, which were both settled on her right wrist.

Once she realized Anne was staring directly at her tattoo, she flipped over her wrist and placed her hand by her side.

"Is something wrong?" she asked.

Anne shook her head.

"No," she said. "I just need some sleep."

Jamie ran her hand across Anne's back.

"Sure," Jamie said and cracked a smile before exiting from the bedroom.

10:48 PM

A commotion coming from the back of the room: *"Cabrera? What are you doing here?"*

Merrotti heard Terry's voice next: *"What the fuck is this?"*

Following the outcry, Merrotti heard two gunshots at first and then three more, which were much louder. He sprinted toward the back of the room. On the way, he heard, like the two gunshots prior, an additional three gunshots. He found Cabrera towering over Terry's curled body. The white coat that Terry was wearing slowly washed over with red. He finally spotted Florence, who was clutching her chest on the floor.

Merrotti aimed his gun at Cabrera.

"Freeze, motherfucker!" he shouted out.

Cabrera suddenly turned around, only to receive four bullets in the chest. He fell to his knees and then hit the floor with a loud thud.

Merrotti rushed over to Cabrera, whose eyes were closed. He kneeled down, pressed his fingers underneath his jaw, and checked for his pulse. He found one, faint and barely poking at his skin, like a fly trapped inside a snare drum.

Grimacing with anger, not pain, he kicked the gun from Cabrera's grip—far from the young officer's reach—and then ran over to Florence, who was taking her final breaths.

"Goddamn it," he seethed as he kneeled down and cradled his partner in his arms. "Pam!" Merrotti tightened his grip around Florence's body. He examined Florence briefly, her wounds. One of the bullets had caught the side of her neck, a main artery, which was now gushing blood. Another bullet had caught her in the side—missing her vest by inches—but wasn't as severe or life threatening as the injury to her neck. Merrotti tried to stop the bleeding with his hand, but it was already too late. Unless Merrotti had the proper tools, which he didn't (the only tools in the vicinity were used for autopsy and he didn't even know the least about them and, if he did, he didn't even know where to start), he knew that Florence was a goner from the moment he held her in his arms, but, as Merrotti was trained to do, he told Florence to hang on and, despite her injuries, to stay strong until help arrived. Merrotti didn't bother to call an ambulance or any kind of help for that matter. When Florence's condition worsened, each breath growing farther apart—the blood continuing to run from her neck and pool underneath the two of them—and then Merrotti witnessing Florence's eyes glazing over, he mourned her passing. Years had passed since he had shown any kind of emotion. For years, he wondered if he felt anything at all, and if the job had left him in a state of numbness, a disguised coma. Strangely, Florence found a peculiar tranquility in watching her partner's unraveling, the tears falling from his eyes, followed by a sudden cry, "Pam! Please! Don't leave me!" More tears escaped his eyes. More sobs. A sudden groan spilled from his chest. "Pam! Hang on! You hear me!" he cried, tightening his grip around Florence's shoulders. "You stay with me! Goddamn it!" In her passing, a phantom of a smile surfaced on the side of her face. Her eyes were still like a frame. Then, Merrotti felt the cold air release from her body, now a lifeless thing. He knew his partner had passed, both of her eyes had glazed over, and yet, for some reason, that smile found its way onto her face. Merrotti frantically glanced at the other body, the coroner, who wasn't breathing as well, and then Cabrera. There was no Cabrera. No blood puddle. No trail. The detective searched around the autopsy room, but Cabrera was nowhere in sight. Merrotti picked up his gun, gently rested his partner's body against the floor, and rushed from the morgue.

10:56 PM

THE young officer groaned as he slowly ripped off the bulletproof vest from his chest.

As Cabrera turned on the ignition and placed the gear in drive, he glanced through the rear view mirror where Merrotti was charging from the entrance of the morgue.

"*Mierda*," he fumed as he slammed his foot against the gas pedal.

Cabrera gunned the cruiser away from the vengeful detective, who, teary eyed, bloody, and stricken with rage, aimed the gun at the cruiser as it sped down the alleyway.

As Merrotti unloaded an entire magazine, a couple of bullets caught the rear window but didn't shatter the glass. One of them struck the bumper. However, none of the bullets hit his target, Officer Cabrera, or soon-to-be, The Dead Officer Cabrera. . .

11:01 PM

FOUR minutes after Merrotti called it in, the cavalry arrived at the morgue. Instead of dropping off dead bodies, they were picking up two. Two of their own. Three, if it was up to Merrotti.

11:03 PM

THE doorbell suddenly rang!

Anne, who was washing her face in the bathroom and preparing for bed, stopped what she was doing. She wiped the cream cleanser from her face and checked the hallway outside, only to find Jamie talking to a police officer at the front door. She quickly darted back into the bedroom and grabbed the knife from her belongings. She hurried back to the doorway and did so quietly. There, with the blade kept close to her body, she listened closely to what the officer was saying to Jamie—something like "Do you know this gentleman?" Like a skittish cat, Anne poked her head from the doorway and spotted Michael standing behind the officer.

Anne placed the knife on the dresser and stepped from the bedroom.

"What are you doing here?" she asked from the end of the hallway.

The officer let Michael through and said to Jamie, "We'll be outside if you need anything."

"Thank you, Officer," Jamie said as she stepped out of the doorway.

"I was worried about you," Michael said, as Anne exited the bedroom and walked to the foyer.

"You were worried about me?" Anne returned, almost in disgust. "If you were really worried about me, Michael, then you would've called me. . . "

Michael said patiently, "Can we talk about this outside?"

Jamie turned her shoulder away from Michael and without Michael looking, widened her eyes at Anne. She gave Anne a nod toward the door, motioning for her to go outside and join Michael's company.

After a moment of thought, Anne rolled her eyes and decided to step outside with Michael. They both hung out on the front porch, Michael pacing around and nibbling the inner part of his lip and Anne leaning against the railing with her arms crossed over her chest, giving Michael a penetrating, this-better-be-good kind of stare. Michael acknowledged the cruiser and the police officer getting back inside and then acknowledged Anne, that cold gaze.

"Jamie told me what happened," he said over an awkward silence. "I tried texting you, but you didn't respond."

Anne said suddenly, "No. You didn't."

"I did," Michael said, louder. "Like a thousand times."

"I'm not in the mood to argue with you, Michael," Anne said sharply. "I've been through too much shit. Okay? And you coming here doesn't help either."

"I didn't come here to argue."

Anne shifted her weight to one side of her body, hips arched.

She said, "Then, why *did* you come?"

Michael turned away from Anne and paced around the porch.

"Don't treat me like this, Anne," he said, his voice was restrained like a loose muzzle on a rabid dog.

"Treat you like what?" Anne returned, her voice gradually rising. "Do you know what I've been through the past twenty-four hours? Do you!"

Michael walked over to Anne and placed his hand over the side of her arm.

Anne shrugged his arm away.

"I deserve that," he said emotionlessly. "I know that. Anne, I'm sorry about what happened to your parents. I really am. But don't take it out on me."

"Why are you even here, Michael?" Anne said, uncrossing her arms. "I mean. *Really*. What do you want?"

"I want you to listen to me!" he barked.

"I *am* listening."

"You got it all twisted, Anne," Michael said in Anne's face. "What do *you* want? It seems like I can't do anything right anymore. I admit, Anne. I'm not perfect. So, why can't you just accept that?"

Anne didn't respond to Michael's comment.

"You know what I think, Anne," he said, even closer now, "I think you're more obsessed with the idea of having a boyfriend, than actually *having* one."

"That's not true."

"I've made plenty of mistakes," Michael said. "We all have."

"Least I own up to them, Michael."

Michael smacked his gums.

He said, "Don't give me that shit."

11:12 PM

NOT too far from Jamie's house, a black Lincoln parked alongside the curb.

The man in the passenger seat, the same man responsible for murdering Anne's foster parents—now dressed in all black, *not* in a police uniform—nodded at Jamie's house and then at Anne, who was sticking her finger in Michael's grill. The strange man told the driver to cut off the engine. So, he did.

Then, he pulled out his cell phone.

"We're here," he said on the phone. "What do you want us to do now?"

The Voice: "*Leave no witnesses.*"

"What about Karina?"

"*What about her?*"

"But you said—"

The Voice interrupted, *"What part of no witnesses don't you understand?"*

"Yes, sir."

11:13 PM

"SEE," Anne pulled away her arm, "right there."

"What?"

"That's the problem, Michael."

"Oh yeah," he replied, the tone in his voice more hostile than sincere. "What's the problem, Anne? You tell me because it seems like anything I do now doesn't please you."

"Right there," Anne said. "The way you talk to me, Michael. Nobody's forcing you to be here. So, *why* are you here?"

Michael smacked his gums once more and turned away from Anne.

"You act like the world is centered around you, Michael," she said. "And don't get me started on your work."

Michael planted his hands on his hips. His voice raised now: "And what about my work, Anne? I bust my ass every fucking day! Sorry I don't have a job where I sit on my ass all day and answer phone calls!"

"Very nice, Michael," she said sharply. "Maybe it's best we don't see each other anymore."

"I think you're right," Michael said and then bobbed his head like a bobble head doll. "I mean," he shrugged and then frowned, "I tried numerous times to fit you into my schedule, Anne, to make time for you," he said. "But maybe you're right. . . "

"I think you should leave, Michael," she said, her voice now sour. *"Please.* Don't make this harder than it has to be."

"Then, all of this," Michael grimaced, "this right here, this was all for nothing."

"Yeah, Michael," she said as she crossed her arms. "Now, that's something we can finally agree on."

Michael stepped forward, his right hand curled into a fist. He pressed his forehead against Anne's and tightened his jaw. Anne turned her head away as she felt his warm breath beating against the side of her neck. Then, a feeling came over her, one of those fight or flight feelings, that ride or die feeling, and it came on as quickly as a sneeze. She rotated her head back toward Michael, now inches away from his face; and she anchored her head downward, her narrow eyes brimming into her brows.

A *thud* from the street!

Both Anne and Michael directed their attention toward the door slamming shut. There were two men dressed in all black standing outside the cruiser. One of them was holding an object in his hand and pointing it at the windshield of the police car. The little dark object in the strange man's hand made a strange noise, which sounded similar to a foot kicking an aluminum soda can down a desolate road—similar to the noise Anne heard seconds before two men burst into her foster parents' house and killed them both. The bullet pierced the glass, but didn't shatter the glass completely. The cracks left behind from the bullet hole scattered outward across the pane of glass like tentacles reaching across a dark sea.

Two more of those metallic sounds!

Anne peered closer and realized the sounds were coming from a pistol with a silencer attached to the end of the barrel.

The cruiser door opened.

One of the cops rolled out of the seat and fell onto the street.

As the cop crawled away, the strange man walked behind the cop and shot him in the back.

Anne suddenly gasped and covered her mouth in horror.

"Back inside," Michael said as he hurried Anne into the house.

Jamie was casually perched at the counter with a cup of coffee in her hand.

Once she witnessed the two, as well as their horrified expressions, she eased away from the kitchen and sauntered into the living room.

Michael said feverishly to Jamie, "Lock the doors."

"Anne?" Jamie said. "What's going on?"

"They're. . . they're here. . . "

"Who's here?"

Anne cried, "I don't know."

Michael said to Jamie, "Whoever they are, they shot the two cops outside. . . "

Jamie gasped and scrambled to the living room window.

"Cut off the lights!" Then, she waved at Michael. "Hurry!"

Michael cut off the lights inside the living room and then rushed Anne into the guest bedroom while Jamie went upstairs and grabbed a wooden baseball bat from her closet.

Meanwhile Michael was holding Anne in his arms.

"I'm not going to let anything happen to you," he whispered in her ear.

In the corner of her eye, Anne saw a shadow creeping behind the window. The shadow disappeared as quickly as it made itself known. She turned back to Michael and gripped his arm.

"What about Jamie?" she asked, her voice trembling.

"Turn off the light," Michael said to Anne.

Seconds before Anne turned off the lamp on the nightstand as Michael demanded, the power to the entire house suddenly shut off!

"They cut the breakers. . . "

"Oh shit," Anne mumbled.

Michael scanned the bedroom for a moment, thinking about a place for Anne to hide.

After his brief survey, he realized it was either two places: the closet or underneath the bed. *If anything was to happen to me*, Michael thought, and they found Anne, she would never have a fighting chance underneath the bed.

He rushed Anne to the closet.

"Here," Michael said as he opened the doors. "Stay in here. I'll check on Jamie. If anything happens to me. . . "

Anne said while sniffling, "I'm so sorry, Michael. I never wanted to drag you into this. . . "

Michael kissed Anne on her wet lips, salty in taste from both the tears as well as the phlegm from her nose.

"I love you," he said to Anne. "I always have." He choked up for a second. Then, he cleared his throat. "I haven't been good to you, Anne. I realize this. But I can be a better man. You can make me a better. . . "

"Shut up, Michael," Anne said, the tears streaming from her eyes. "Please. Don't say that."

Michael sharpened his gaze.

"You're going be fine," he said, grabbing Anne's shoulders. "I promise. . . "

Anne said the words back to Michael, the words *I love you*, but only on impulse. But did she really mean the words? In the back of her mind, Anne wished to take the words back as soon as they mistakenly rolled from her lips. She never did, though. Instead, as a way of encouragement, she left the words with Michael, let him hold onto them, tightly in his chest, and protect them like a wolf to her cub. The words, as sacred as they were to Anne, were ones that Anne had never spoken before—at least never done so in a sincere manner. As far as she could remember, the words meant very little to her. Anne didn't exactly know how to love, and yet, having been raised as a teenager in a household brimming with love, Anne thought it was one of those impossible feats that she would never conquer because of a haunting uncertainty which crept into her daily life—a locked vault stashed deep inside her, guarded by the strange silhouettes that teetered through the lost memories of her childhood. If Anne only knew the combination to the lock, then she knew there would be a chance for her to love and to be loved. . . again. But the mystery of her dark past was the only barrier preventing her from bridging the gap between feeling and *not* feeling, belonging and *not* belonging.

As Michael left the guest room and checked on Jamie, who was hunkered next to the front door, Anne cowered in the closet.

"I see them," Jamie whispered to Michael.

"Got any other weapons in here?"

"There's a knife in the kitchen."

"They have guns."

Anne peeked through the crack in the closet and spotted the laptop on the bed. She hesitated at first, but then opened the closet, darted into the bedroom, grabbed the USB flash drive from the top of the nightstand, hurried back to the closet, and closed the door behind her. She raised her cold trembling hand to her face and studied it closely.

As Jamie squatted underneath the living room window, she shot a quick glance over the windowsill and found one of them creeping around the side of the house. Jamie raised her hand to eye level and then pointed at her eyes and then pointed at Michael. In return, Michael acknowledged Jamie, as well as her gesturing to the side of the house. Next, she held out her index finger, indicating the number one, and then both fingers, index and middle finger, indicating the number two. Michael, not knowing exactly where the second man was located, shook his head and shrugged his shoulders.

Suddenly, an elbow shattered the window of the backdoor.

Michael now motioned to Jamie.

Number two, he mouthed with his fingers holding up the number two.

"Backdoor," Michael whispered.

After two minutes of tense silence in the closet, Anne heard the stark sounds of a struggle: glass shattering; plates being smashed over the floor; furniture shifting across the living room; three loud thuds reverberating throughout the house from where Jamie missed the intruder, and then a soft thud from where she hit the intruder over the head. "Grab the gun!" Michael yelled to Jamie. Then, two muffled gunshots chirped throughout the house. Next, a loud thud over the hardwood floor! More sounds of struggle: Michael pleading with the intruder, "Please! Don't! *You. . .* " The words grew closer together, desperate now: "No! No! No! No! No! No!" Then, Jamie screamed, "Michael!" Four muffled gunshots! Each bullet struck the wall closest to the bedroom. Anne ducked and curled into a ball against the corner of the closet. Next, Anne heard Jamie crying out, followed with a grunt. There was a moment of silence and then a thunderous crash! The water spilled from the aquarium and soaked Jamie, who was now gurgling,

"*¿Qué estás esperando?* (What are you waiting for?)" Then, she roared: "You coward!" Another gunshot, but this time it was loud and deafening, not muffled as the ones before. Anne jolted from the sudden *boom* of the gunshot! She cupped her hands over her mouth and tried to fight back the tears, the sobs. Her jittery eyes shifted toward the crack in the door. A long shadow grew next to the doorway. Footsteps! The intruder inched into the guest bedroom. The man was dressed all in black, leather jacket, black jeans, dark slick-backed hair, like the shooter from the street. The left side of his face was bleeding badly. From what Anne witnessed, he could only see through one eye—the right one. Halfway into the room, he stopped in his tracks and turned toward the closet. Anne tightened her hand over her mouth. Her heart was racing uncontrollably, so loud and hard that she was convinced he could hear her heart, as before, beating away like a kick drum. The man in black walked directly to the closet. Anne quietly crawled to the center of the closet. There was no way of hiding, Anne knew. There was nothing she could hide under or behind like a large suitcase or whatever people usually crammed in closets. The closet was fairly empty. If this man opened the doors, then he would *discover me*. This, Anne was certain of. Therefore, Anne waited for the man in black to get close enough to the closet. Then, as he reached for the door-knob... *Bam!* She rammed her shoulder into the door, which caused the door to smack the man in black directly in the nose. He staggered backward as Anne made a run to the hallway. Three short strides into her escape, her head was suddenly yanked back! She screamed out in agony; and as hard as she could, she tried to tug and pull her head from the man's grip, but he had a death grip around her hair. A handful of it too! Anne reared her leg back and kicked him in the leg, precisely below his knee. In return, he shrieked. Anne didn't care the least about what she had done to this man, sending his knee ninety degrees in the opposite direction (part of the bone from his shin protruding from the side of his calf). She was too focused on the hallway to even pay attention. *If I could only make it to the hallway*, Anne wondered, then I *would have a chance*. The man loosened his grip. Anne jerked her head forward and released herself from his grip.

With a handful of Anne's hair, the man in black stumbled to the floor and grabbed his knee.

"You *perra!*" he screamed out. "Get back here!"

When Anne reached the hallway, she saw the aftermath in the living room. She rushed over to Michael, who was dead. He had a knife protruding from his chest. From what Anne saw, he didn't suffer. Then, there was the other shooter, who was lying next to the side doorway. He had a couple of bullets in his body, one in his head. Then, Jamie, Anne saw. She was perched against a homemade bookshelf, which was leaning like the Tower of Pisa. Her body was drenched in both blood and water. Shards of jagged glass and open books were scattered all around her.

Anne ran to Jamie, who was drifting in and out of consciousness.

"Jamie. . . "

Anne moved Jamie's head upright.

With her eyes partially closed, Jamie uttered, "I told you. . . I wouldn't leeee. . . "

Then, Jamie's eyes glazed over. Her head became heavy in Anne's hand.

Once Anne released her hand from Jamie's head, her head flopped over her shoulder.

"Jamie. . . " Anne cried, ". . . please. . . "

Anne turned her shoulder and saw the pistol next to the dead intruder. She picked up the pistol and stormed into the guest bedroom where the other intruder was sliding at a snail's pace across the floor.

As soon as he saw Anne storming toward him, he drew his pistol.

Anne aimed twice, fired once.

The bullet struck the man's shoulder.

Then, Anne kicked the pistol from his grip before he had a chance to draw the pistol.

She placed the pistol to his face.

"Who sent you?"

The man didn't respond.

Anne jammed the warm barrel underneath his chin, which caused him to groan.

"Who?"

Soon, the groan turned to a giggle and then a full laugh.

"You. . . you have no idea who you're messing with. . . "

Anne pressed the barrel harder against his flesh.

"Who sent you? Tell me!"

"Patience, Anne. . . "

Once more, Anne rammed the barrel into his chin.

"How do you know my name?"

The barrel was slightly lifted from the man in black's chin. The grip around the pistol eased a bit. The image of her foster parents, both bloody and still-faced, flashed through her mind. The deathly images sent streaks of anger throughout Anne's body, which caused the muscles in her body to tighten like a fist. She readjusted the grip around the handle.

"Are you the one who killed my parents?" she said, louder now.

"Go ahead," he said casually. "Pull the trigger. The way I look at it, I'm a dead man anyway. If you don't do it, then I will. . . "

Anne pulled the man closer and seethed, "ARE YOU?"

"Don't take it personal, kid," the man said quietly. "I was just following orders."

Anne's finger tightened over the trigger.

"Do it," he said, his voice growing. "DO IT!"

Anne peered into his red eyes—both red eyes peered back into hers. There, she witnessed the horrors that awaited the man, and then the man behind the curtains whose hands were covered in blood, a *faceless* man. He would come for him, *the faceless man*— no doubt—like a specter in the night, this man, this myth whose whispers ran far and wide through the back alleys of Lansford.

The man in black shouted, "KILL ME!"

If I didn't kill him, Anne thought, then he would kill himself. Why? Because of the failed mission? Was he expendable? And if so, would the person who was in charge actually kill his own employee for not carrying out a job? Which was what? To kill me? To kidnap me?

Who was this faceless man who waited behind the curtains, the man with bloody hands hiding in the shadows of night?

Anne suddenly released the barrel from his chin, grabbed the laptop from the bed, and stormed away.

On the way to the kitchen, she heard a scratching sound coming from the laundry room. There, she found Harley scratching his paws at the door of the kennel.

Anne opened the door for him.

Harley immediately hurried into the living room where his owner, Jamie, was lifelessly sitting against the leaning bookshelf.

Harley pawed at Jamie's leg and then groaned.

"Come on, boy," Anne said to Harley, grabbed Jamie's car keys from the kitchen, and exited the house.

On the street, Anne witnessed more carnage: the two police officers gunned down inside the cruiser.

A sudden gunshot came from the house!

Anne caught the end of the flicker from the gunshot behind the window.

Right then and there, she knew that the shooter meant every word that he had said, about this mysterious man behind the curtains, the boss man, so powerful and unforgiving that his own employee would take his own life in order to spare the hell that awaited him.

11:47 PM

SOMEWHERE along the outskirts of uptown Lansford, Cabrera parked the cruiser in an abandoned parking lot.

He removed a license plate from the trunk and then a full can of gasoline. He doused the entire car in gasoline, including the inside, and lit the cruiser on fire with a match.

Once the entire cruiser was up in flames, Cabrera walked a block until he reached a convenient store.

He found an unattended black sedan and then its owner—a male in his mid twenties—paying for his gas inside the store.

Without the young man paying attention, Cabrera removed the license plate with a screwdriver and screwed in a brand new one.

He tossed the old plate into the trashcan and stole the sedan without the young man knowing, at least not until he finished paying for the gas and found an empty spot next to pump #9 where his car used to be.

As Cabrera turned right onto Parker Street, an unmarked Crown Vic followed the young officer.

But at a distance. . .

PART THREE
EBB AND FLOW

CHAPTER 5

IT was a quarter past midnight, and Anne was driving in circles.

She turned on the radio, hoping to ward off the nausea with the sound of music. The attempt was *not* working; in fact, it had only made matters worse. In her second attempt, she cracked the window and hoped that the cool night breeze would rid the nausea. Again, the attempt was a failure. Her stomach was now talking to her in lengthy croaks. Her palms were both cold and sweaty. She turned off the radio and then rolled up the window. A tingling sensation suddenly crept into her chest and radiated across the surface of her entire body, which meant one thing, in fact, the *only* thing: whatever food Anne had inside her stomach was now making a tedious climb up her esophagus. Nature was going to run its course, she concluded, and there was no stopping it. The sensation gripped around her throat like a clasp and never let go. The saliva loosened and thinned in the corners of her mouth. She assumed, if she swallowed enough spit, the protein bar that she ate earlier would retreat to her stomach.

As before, the attempt was *not* working.

Without further delay, Anne gradually eased into the emergency lane.

"Wait here," she said to the dog, Harley, who was seated in the passenger seat like the gentleman he was, and parked the car on the side of the interstate. She bolted from the car—nearly getting sideswiped by an eighteen-wheeler zooming by—and vomited behind a guardrail. After that, most of the time was spent heaving spit and stomach bile. Her stomach, which was curled like a boxing glove, threw an onslaught of jabs to her chest. Six times, it went on like this for Anne, her stomach boxing the cavities of her chest until there was nothing left but pockets of air.

Once Anne was finished throwing up and now left in a pale and disheveled state, she cleaned the side of her mouth with her sleeve and emptied her stomach with a loud *burp*.

Next, she stumbled to the car like a sloppy drunk because, essentially, that was what it felt like to Anne after the adrenaline had finally worn off, as if she chugged a fifth of vodka and soon she was about to experience one helluva hangover.

12:33 AM

ANNE found this desolate parking lot outside a strip mall off Exit 9A. She parked the car two spaces next to a floodlight in the back of the parking lot where the light was bright enough to spot any vagrants or hoodlums or, even worse, any hired guns. The moment she found a comfortable position in the car seat— mainly her head rested against the backside of her hand, which was perched across the side panel of the driver's door—she closed her eyes. Harley, who was still seated like a gentleman in the passenger seat, kept a keen eye on the parking lot.

As the amber light cast from the floodlight brightened over her closed eyelids, two smooth hands gracefully ran through Anne's hair.

The amber light brightened, now warm and soft like the afternoon sun.

Anne slowly opened her eyes, both of them now tracing down her body and then her shrinking hands. She was holding this pink plastic comb in her small, juvenile hand and combing her dolly's bright yellow hair in her lap. There was a woman who smelled like roses sitting behind her. She was singing something soft and pleasing to her, but she couldn't quite make out the song, as it remained as gentle as a hum. She glanced up at the woman, only to feel the coarse paw of a dog brush alongside the top of her shoulder. The strange woman was hardly wearing any makeup, Anne saw through the young girl's eyes, and yet the woman was as gorgeous as an actress. Her face was long and narrow, skin bright and healthy, eyes dark and penetrating and yet comforting to gaze upon; and her eyes, Anne noticed, were smiling down at her in their own peculiar way. The woman had brunette hair flowing over her shoulder like a waterfall. The side of her face was glowing in a beam of sunlight cast from the window. Her eyes, Anne saw, comforting. She was sitting in a creaky rocking chair made from wicker and combing the girl's hair in fluent strokes. Like the dolly in her lap, Anne's lap, Anne was sitting in this strange woman's lap—her head resting against the top of her right breast, both eyes looking upward into the woman's eyes. Behind them, a weightless curtain was blowing ever so patiently as if time *didn't* exist in this world, this sanctuary of tranquility. A small statue of a Dalmatian was perched on top of an old television. Above the television was a juvenile painting of a leopard stalking through a jungle. *Or was it a tiger?* Anne couldn't quite tell. The song the woman was singing was no longer a hum. Her voice became louder over a growing beat, hollow and shaky like the tail of a rattlesnake.

The quivery beat became deafening—the woman's words now distorting from her ample lips. . .

Anne was yanked forward!

She flexed and stretched her hands until the feeling was back into her hands. Her attention was drawn to the street next to the parking lot and the pea green low rider cruising by with its stereo blasting as loud as a machine gun. She read the time below the dash-board, "1:17." Once more, Anne repeated the time, now in her head—*1:17*. She swore she got at least a half-night's rest, possibly squeezed in a good three or four hours of sleep, and yet she had only been asleep for no more than forty minutes.

She removed her eyes from the time and redi-rected them to the built-in navigation screen next to the center console. Except for her wide eyes, the rest of her face fell into a lifeless state as if the Grim Reaper himself had paid her an unexpected visit. As before, her palms became sweaty. Her forehead too. She didn't feel nauseous, although the feeling she felt was of great terror. The GPS had her precise loca-tion, she learned, *Grier Avenue*.

"Great," she said with frustration and then scanned the desolate parking lot.

There wasn't anybody in sight, which didn't seem so weird to Anne considering the time of night. She wondered if they could find her through this GPS de-vice. If they could find her at Jamie's house, then surely they could track Anne through this thing. She didn't want to take any chances. So, she did what she had to and ditched the car.

1:36 AM

EVENTUALLY, after hours of driving, Cabrera found a place to rest in a side alleyway in the small town of Reddington before he left the country.

As he started to doze off behind the wheel, the back door suddenly opened!

"*What the. . .*"

Cabrera grabbed the shotgun from the mount and turned around, only to receive a black gloved hand pressed against the side of his face. The hand redirected Cabrera's head toward the front of the vehicle.

"Now, take your hand off the shotgun," a resonant voice said from the backseat.

"*You*," Cabrera said surprisingly. "I thought. . ."

The Voice shushed the young officer.

"You didn't eliminate all witnesses."

Cabrera's hand still remained on the shotgun.

"I killed the two as I told you," he said.

"And what about the *other* detective?"

Cabrera stuttered.

"What other detective?" he said.

The Voice tilted his head to the side with amusement.

"The one who tried to kill you, Officer. . ."

"Right," Cabrera said, his throat tightening. A taunt sigh eased from his chest. "Long night."

"So. . ."

"I'm going to kill him next," he said with a tremble in his throat.

"Then, what are you waiting for?"

"There's too much heat right now," he said, louder this time. "When things die down, then I'll take care of him. I promise."

Cabrera's dumb eyes crossed the rear view mirror and settled on this man who called himself the Voice sitting in the backseat. He was dressed in *all* black and waited there as calm and patient as a saint with half of his face cloaked in shadows. The young officer never recognized the Voice's face—his profile for that matter. However, in the back of his mind, he knew what was coming next. In that final moment, Cabrera wasn't so dumb after all; in fact, he was brilliant. The young officer finally removed his hand from the shotgun and sat back in his seat, calmly like the stranger behind him.

1:48 AM

HARLEY sat guard next to the broken door while Anne washed up in an old bathroom in the subway.

There was no time to cry, Anne told herself once more.

Must keep moving.

So, she did.

2:04 AM

WITH a pocket full of loose change—mostly quarters she had collected from the car—Anne waited about ten minutes at a bus stop off Third and Tandy Street before the bus finally arrived.

When the bus arrived at the curb and the driver inside opened the doors, he told her without a second's hesitation, "No pets allowed, ma'am."

Anne begged the bus driver to let her in and then told him that her life was in danger.

From the looks of her disheveled state, the bus driver realized that Anne was either telling the truth and that her life was, in fact, in danger or she was just another one of them, a straggler who, over the years, he had learned to leave behind without feeling the least amount of guilt. Or a runaway, he wondered. They all had the same story, each and every one of them. Their parents didn't love them enough or they were too lazy to get a job; and, since they were so dependent on their parents, they latched onto the System.

She was different, he thought.

Once more, the bus driver studied Anne's face, the bloodstains on her shirt.

Since no one was riding and Anne was only going about six miles across the city—not only that, the pale, lifeless expression over Anne's face convinced the bus driver of her immediate danger—he decided to let Anne and Harley ride along.

2:11 AM

HALFWAY through the bus ride, it came to Anne's immediate attention that she was missing something important: the laptop!

She could visualize the laptop right there on the floor mat of the car, as well as the charger, which lay right next to the laptop.

Without speaking aloud, Anne cursed to herself and thought once or twice about hammering her fist into the back of the seat; but then, not too long afterward, her temper tapered off as quickly as it flared. There will be other ways to finish the story, Anne thought, there *always* is.

2:18 AM

THE bus came to a stop at Graham Park Street.

The driver told Anne to be careful and then said good night.

From there, she and Harley walked about three miles—mostly taking the shortcuts through backyards or alleyways and staying off the main roads—until they arrived at her foster parents' house. They entered through the back door with a spare key that Harold had hidden underneath a rabbit statuette. There was police tape on the doors, both the front and the back. Anne let Harley into the house first and then let him scope it out for any possible intruders waiting for her to show up. The house was clear, as she suspected. Now, somewhat relieved, Anne went to the kitchen and fed Harley a few slices of roast beef from the refrigerator and then fixed herself a glass of water. She only took a couple of sips before she started to feel sick to her stomach.

Once Harley finished scarfing down the beef, they went upstairs to Anne's bedroom.

On the way to the bedroom, she passed the foyer, the horror. She tried not to look at all the blood, which was as dark as tar from where the oxygen had gotten to it.

The lights were turned off, though.

Nonetheless, in the corner of her eye, she caught a glimpse of the blood puddles, the stains, the streaks across the walls, the great horror.

When Anne arrived at her old bedroom, she placed the gun aside and locked the door behind her.

Next, she wedged the desk behind the door for safety.

Harley jumped onto Anne's bed.

Anne followed Harley and slipped underneath the covers.

After Anne dozed off, which didn't take too long from her exhausted state, she had the same dream as before, the one from the car: a woman combing her hair while singing a song to her. Now, the song was more distinguishable. The song was *"Band on the Run"* by the group, Wings. She was halfway finished tying Anne's hair into a ponytail when a tall, handsome man with blonde highlights strolled into the living room and snatched Anne from the woman's arms. "Do you mind if I steal this little rascal from you?" the tall man asked before the woman even had a chance to reply. "I'm not done with her hair, Honey!" the woman shouted out as the man picked up young Anne and carried her through the house. "I promise I'll bring her right back!" The tall man lifted Anne in the air and pressed his lips against her skin and made farting sounds over her stomach. Anne giggled and cried out, "That tickles!" Laughing as well, the man carried her outside where a young boy—around six or seven years old—was dribbling a soccer ball on the parched front yard. The land was wide and open and stretched for miles into the parched desert. The distant horizon was marked with jagged mountains. "Come on, *Chloe!*" the boy said. "Let's play football!" He kicked the ball to Anne. In return, Anne grabbed the ball and threw it back to the boy. "No fair!" the boy shouted. "No using your hands." The tall man ran between the two, young Anne and the boy, and stole the ball before the ball reached the boy. "I bet you two can't steal the ball from me," he said and dribbled the ball around the two kids. As the three, the man and his two children, played ball in the front yard, a door opened from afar. Anne, chasing and laughing as she tried to steal the ball from the man, was caught off guard by the gorgeous woman, who was standing next to the front door. She stopped playing and looked to the house and then waved at the woman, who, in return, waved back at her. Suddenly, the woman's eyes moved to the left, to the long dirt road; consequently, Anne drew her eyes toward the dirt road. The man stopped playing as well and drew his eyes to the road and to the three black SUVs. The vehicles were driving fast, each one following dangerously close to one another. "Isabel!" the man shouted at the woman standing by the doorway. "Get the kids! Now!" Anne hurried toward the man. In return, the man was strolling closer to the dirt road. From afar, the woman shouted out, "Listen to your father, *Chloe!*" The tall man turned to young Anne, who suddenly came to a stop. "Everything's going to be okay, Chloe Baby. I promise. Now go!" Anne ran to the woman. The boy wasn't too far behind. "*Mom,*" Anne cried out, "what's wrong?" The woman returned, "Nothing, darling. Your father has to take care of business. That's all. Come. Let's go to the quiet room." Then, Anne pouted and said, "But I don't want to go to the quiet room." The woman replied, "Don't you worry, darling. Everything is going to be fine." Before the woman shut the door, Anne peered through the doorway. In the dusty front yard, the tall man was slowly backing his way toward the house. He looked over his shoulder and made eye contact with Anne. The two shared a long stare: Anne's face laced with fear, the man's... sadness. The emotion vanished from his face before Anne could make anything of it. Finally, he gave a stern nod to Anne. "Listen to *your mother, Chloe,*" he told Anne and then directed his attention to the three approaching vehicles. He stood defensively, contemplating his next move.

Suddenly, the door slammed shut. . .

Anne bolted upright from the bed!

She was sweating profusely, her throat closed.

Harley woke as well from Anne's startled response.

Anne, who was swallowing and doing everything she could to clear her throat, including massaging her throat, looked ahead at the bedroom door, which was *still* closed.

She rolled out of bed and checked the time on the nightstand.

The time read: 3:26.

Again, to Anne, it felt as if she had gotten a few hours of sleep and yet she had caught no more than forty minutes of sleep.

Frustrated from the lack of sleep, she strolled to the bathroom where she took a sip of water from the sink and then splashed her pale face.

On the second splash, her face went long. Her motions stilled, so much that she could hear her heart beating against her chest. She dried both hands with the hand towel, reached into her pocket, pulled out the USB flash drive, and held it close to her face.

She hurried into the television in the bedroom and turned it on. First, she started with the mainstream channels: CNN, MSNBC, and then, lastly, FOX.

With no luck, she flipped to the local news. She patiently watched a six-minute loop: one story, a mugging off Franklin Avenue; another, a fatal accident by a drunk driver; and then, at the end of the loop, a peppy meteorologist gave the forecast for the weekend.

Finally, a BREAKING NEWS report came on!

Dozens of news reporters, cameramen, and police officers were scattered around Jamie's house. The reporter for the local news, May Francis, was talking about the two dead cops as well as the four dead inside, one being the owner of the residence, Ms. Jamie Vasquez.

3:32 AM

DETECTIVE Sproles, another old dog like Merrotti, pulled the plastic gloves from his hands and stepped outside the house for a breath of fresh air.

If the night couldn't get any worse, a Crown Vic pulled up alongside the curb in front of Jamie's house.

Sproles walked back to the house and poked his greasy snout into the living room.

"Weathers," Sproles said from the front doorway, "look who decided to show up. . . "

The sergeant, Julius Weathers, stood up from his kneeled position, towered over Jamie's corpse for a moment, and then took a look outside.

"Who is it?"

"It's Merrotti."

The sergeant shook his head in disgust.

"I'll handle it," he said as he squeezed his way through the doorway.

Merrotti, still pale and red-eyed from the previous events, stepped out of the vehicle and made his way to the house.

Before he could reach the porch, Weathers stopped him.

"What part of *go home and cool off* don't you understand, Detective?"

"Where is she, Jules?"

"Did you hear what I said?"

Merrotti interrupted, "Where's the girl?"

The sergeant surrendered with a sigh.

"Can't find her," he said quietly.

Merrotti followed, "Where is she?"

"Her friend, Jamie Vasquez," he said, "her car's missing." Weathers read from his pocket-sized notepad. "It's a two-thousand twelve burgundy Ford Taurus."

"Any witnesses?"

"Yep," Weathers said. "One. Next-door neighbor. Said he heard gunshots. Then, saw the Taurus drive off. Couldn't make out the make or model, but he's pretty sure it was Ms. Vasquez's car."

"Did he say who was inside?"

"Said it was dark." Then, Weathers patted Merrotti on the shoulder. "Go home, Devon. Get some rest. You've had a long night. . . "

"I heard about Johnson and Murphy," Merrotti said sincerely. "How many others?"

"Six bodies altogether, including Johnson and Murphy," he said. "One, we think is self inflicted."

"Murder-suicide?"

"Looks that way," he said. "Two of them had same tattoo as before, the one on the wrist."

"Cabrera," Devon grimaced, "he had a tattoo on his wrist as well."

"*Get this*," the sergeant said after he blurted out *Oh*. "So too did the friend."

"Anne's friend?" he said. "Jamie?"

"Yep," Weathers said, his eyes narrowing. "Apparently, Ms. Vasquez worked with your girl. Practically inseparable. Ms. Vasquez was shot and killed. She took one to the chest. Then, Ms. Roth's boyfriend, Michael Duncan, was stabbed to death."

Merrotti asked, "You check that name Vasquez?"

"Haven't got that far, Detective," the sergeant said, "but we're on it."

"Do you have any idea where she could be?"

"There was a shootout between the boyfriend and the intruder in the living room and then a scuffle ensued in the bedroom," Weathers informed Merrotti. "Think your girl was hiding in the closet when it all went down. Tangles with the other intruder. Then, she messes him up good. I mean *good*. She gets scared. Drives off. Then, the guy puts a bullet in his head. Aside from blowing half of his face off, he certainly doesn't appear to be a lowlife like Santiago or that other guy. If these guys are pro like you've been saying, then this is just the beginning. . . "

Merrotti whispered, "What the hell has she gotten herself into?"

"Could be a witness to a crime," Weathers said, thinking out loud. "Don't know."

"Doesn't make any sense," Merrotti said to himself as he pulled his head away and thought about the next course of action. "Did you put out an APB on Anne Roth?"

"Go home, Devon," the sergeant said, more sternly now. "I'll let you know if anything comes up."

"What about the girl?"

Weathers said, "We'll find her. It shouldn't be that hard, Devon. All we need to do is follow the wake of dead bodies." The sergeant tapped Merrotti on the arm. "*Now*, go home. That's an order."

5:08 AM

NOT too long after Anne realized what she had to do in order to keep herself safe, she was rifling through old clothes in the closet. Anne wasn't so picky when it came to picking out an outfit. She grabbed a handful of tee shirts and sweaters that she used to wear in high school and crammed them in a duffel bag—mostly black tees tagged with lyrics from rebellious anthems or holey band tees that she wore during her goth and punk rock phase in middle school or sweaters that were two sizes too big. Surprisingly enough, the clothes fit.

After she was done packing, she moved the desk from the door and went to her parents' bedroom. There, she grabbed as much jewelry as she could get her hands on—a couple of old necklaces and bracelets. Then, the crème de la crème, Harold's Rolex. She placed the jewelry, as well as the expensive watch, in a small handbag. In her final survey, she came across a phone, Harold's phone. She had left her smartphone at Jamie's house and she assumed the police were going through it at this very moment. Anne considered taking the phone with her, but then thought about the GPS device in Jamie's car. It would be a very bad idea, Anne concluded, taking Harold's phone. If they could track her through GPS, Anne figured they could easily track her on the phone as well. The same went with credit cards or debit cards or anything purchased with plastic. Using a plastic card would be the same thing as Hansel leaving behind a trail of breadcrumbs. Then, she thought more about the house. It wasn't safe here anymore. This place would be the first place these men would look, she told herself, *not* the last, as she guessed a couple of hours ago. It was only a matter of time before more of them showed up, if not here, then wherever she went.

With that in mind, she left the phone behind, as well as her wallet, and decided that it was best to travel solo—no electronic devices, no credit cards, no dog, no distractions.

On the way out, her eyes fell upon the bottom drawer of the dresser. She didn't know exactly why, but on impulse she opened the drawer. The feeling she felt when she opened the drawer was the same one she used to have while driving and listening to music. Her body was there in the driver's seat—both hands steering the wheel, eyes steady on the road—but her mind was not. It was as if part of her body was operating on autopilot, and her mind had journeyed elsewhere. She kneeled down and pulled out the contents and did so automatically. When that peculiar feeling went away, she wondered why exactly she had opened the drawer. Why this one? Anne had everything she needed: jewelry, clothes, a *gun*. But why this drawer? Then, it hit her! More stuff, she thought, meant more things to pawn away. *Right.* Anne soon realized that wasn't the case at all. She mindlessly pulled out dusty stacks of bound papers, documents, reports, letters, and folders with the name DIANA HAILEY ROTH on the front. Then, clinical notes, she discovered, as she browsed through the stack.

Anne skimmed through doctor's notes from Dr. Charles Lowe.

"Lowe," Anne said to herself.

That name *rang a bell.*

She read the doctor's notes to herself, "*Patient suffers from PTSD.*" She pulled the note away and then thought to herself: *Posttraumatic stress disorder*, the same exact thing soldiers were diagnosed with after coming home from serving a tour overseas. Anne had never been in the army or the marines. She had never served a tour overseas. But she *had* been overseas—*yes!* Anne remembered sitting next to a window and looking down at the water below—*the whitecaps*, Anne remembered, like tiny stars twinkling in the dark sea. And there was a war, Anne remembered, an old war. Perhaps the oldest. And it wasn't a political war. It wasn't a religious war. The war that Anne battled, she learned after skimming through a few more notes, was tougher than any war known to mankind: the war waged inside the mind. Mono versus Mono. There were personal notes on a piece of notebook paper: *"The man who adopted Diana didn't leave behind any bread crumbs for me to find. Either he's been doing this for a very long time or he has connections in the services or, worse, she made up this man, Louis Bringer, a personal tormentor— possibly schizophrenia—but we'll run further tests."* Anne flipped another page: *"He calls her Sugar Pie. Tall, around six foot, two inches, lanky, crooked teeth. Always blinking, she says."* The thought alone of this strange man's description sent a warm ripple throughout Anne's body, starting from her gut. She could see him, the lanky man the doctor had described in his notes, blinking his eyes as if his mind was always running, always talking to her when, in fact, he remained silent. More notes, this time jotted down from a session on 6/21/2002: *"Diana's having the nightmares again. Talks frequently about the bright lights and cameras. He made her play dress-up in front of the cameras and told her to put on a smile for the camera. That one word, cheese, she says, plays out in her mind like a merry-go-round. Then, he would make her take off her clothes and touch herself, 'the place where babies live.' She told him that she didn't want to hurt the babies. He said, 'Babies like it when they're touched.' She said sometimes the babies get mad and draw blood. At times, she said, there would be others there in the room, much older than her age, some of them grown adults, standing behind the bright lights. Most of them watched her touch these 'babies.' Other times, they would get involved. Whenever they were asked to touch Diana and her babies, they would wear masks over their faces."* She flipped through more clinical notes. *"The nightmares are getting worse."* More personal notes, this time from 8/2/2002: *"Diana tried to take her own life last night. She snuck into her foster mother's purse and ingested over a dozen Hydrocodones. She was rushed to the hospital where her stomach was pumped."*

Then, she remembered. . .

. . . *the darkness*, as cold as a winter's night, and then tiny bright lights flickering all around her, and then, unexpectedly, wheat fields, miles and miles of wheat fields. There was a dog—a golden retriever, she remembered—and it was prancing alongside her as she walked through the wheat fields. Then, the wheat turned from gold to ash gray. There were sounds of cold things, sounds of machines and beeps and synthesized chirps. Both Harold and Molly were standing above her. Both of them were crying. Molly had taken the incident the hardest, Anne remembered.

Then, finally, Anne came across the very last entry from Dr. Lowe's notes: "*Harold agreed that we conduct the ECT. First treatment will begin on Monday.*"

Anne pulled the paper from her face and said, "ECT?"

She placed the stack of folders and notes back into the drawer, went to her bedroom, and logged into the computer. She opened the search engine and typed the letters, *ECT*, into the search bar.

<u>Do you mean</u>. . .

The first result: *Electroconvulsive therapy*.

She pulled herself from the computer's screen.

It was a dream, she thought.

Wasn't it?

Anne reached back as far as her mind could take her, a place inside the cold darkness, and found a tiny glimpse of light past a lightning storm. Not a sun, she visualized, but something else. She stretched her thoughts—*her arm now*—and reached into the thick gray clouds. Another tingling sensation ran through her body. The hairs on her arm erected like quills on a porcupine as violent streaks of lightning danced and crawled over her bare arm. She stayed with the light behind the gray, focused on the light, brighter now. Not a sun, Anne kept telling herself, but something else, something. . . important—*yes!* Then, the light grew wider and then farther apart on the ceiling above. From the darkness, she found herself in a lit hallway. She glanced down at her hand, smaller in size, and then Harold's hand gripped in hers. He was walking beside her through a stale hallway. There was a blanket of fog covering the floor. A couple of strangers dressed in all white, unsmiling, were walking with her as well. The wheels of a gurney were rolling beneath her. There was also a faint odor of excrement in the air. Anne wondered if it was coming from the fog. A voice: *"It's for your own good, sweetie."* She turned toward the voice, Harold's voice. *"They will make the nightmares go away. I promise."* Then, he asked her: *"Do you want the nightmares to go away?"* The words literally fell from her parched lips, even as she sat in front of the computer's monitor, "I'm scared." Harold said, *"There's nothing to be scared of, Anne."* He tightened his grip around her hand. *"You are the strongest girl I've ever known. I love you. I love you so much."* He ran his finger down the side of Anne's face—a warm and tiny thing. A tear balled up in her eye and then, eventually, fell down her cheek.

Anne suddenly touched the side of her face, fingering the same tear that dropped from her eye years ago. They always tasted the same, the tears. She wiped the tear away from her face and logged off the computer.

5:42 AM

WITH a set of car keys in her hand, Anne went to the garage where Harold's Mercedes was parked. She opened the passenger door and let Harley ride shot-gun.

5:44 AM

ANNE drove to the neighbor's house. She didn't know much about the neighbor, only that her name was Denise Wilkesboro and that Denise was a single mother with two kids, very friendly, enormous heart, definitely not the type who would call a shelter and have the dog put down—at least that was the impression Anne had gotten when she first met Denise. She worked at home, Anne remembered. She didn't remember what kind of job, though; but nonetheless, she made a decent salary. No pets from what she recalled. *Harley would be in good hands*, she thought.

Anne parked the car in front of Denise's house and left the engine running. She walked Harley from the car and tied his leash around the front door handle.

"You'll be safe here, boy," Anne said to Harley and petted the underside of his chin. "This is going to be your new family now. They'll take good care of you. Okay?"

Anne hugged Harley and kissed the top of his head.

Harley groaned, looked up at Anne with puppy eyes as he had a tendency to do, and sat down on the front porch.

"You be good for me," Anne said and walked away.

Harley suddenly barked.

"*Be* good. . ."

While walking away, Anne carefully placed her finger over her mouth and hushed the dog. Harley made one last attempt to run away, but the leash yanked him back and kept him on the front porch.

Anne simply got in the car and drove off into the night. She didn't pass one cruiser, and if she did, she assumed she would be pulled over. So, she kept to the back roads all the way to the Madison Library.

Since the public library wasn't going to open for two more hours, she drove to the nearest coffee shop, a local dive called Roast Café, and bought a cup of coffee, as well as a blueberry muffin. She drove back to the library, where she nibbled on her muffin and sipped from her Guatemala coffee, until the library opened.

8:01 AM

ANNE was the first one to enter the library.

After she greeted the librarian with a short, *"Good morning,"* Anne went directly upstairs to the computer station. She found a computer located in the back of the room, facing the window.

She sat down in front of the computer and inserted the flash drive into the port on the back of the CPU.

The first thing she did was open the *Journal Notes* folder.

Then, she double-clicked on the next journal entry, *Journal Entry 10.18.2014*, and read to herself.

Saturday morning. First decent sleep I've gotten since I arrived at Leatherby Manor. No nightmares. No dreams. My mind was too tired to trigger nightmares or dreams. I only caught about four or five hours, but it was better than no hours. Woke up next to the same driver's license Leon showed me when I first arrived at Leatherby Manor. The name and address: Marcus Hopkins, 23B San Rigo Park, California. Sex: M. Ht: 6-04. Eyes: BRO. Hair: BRO. The race on the license was either scratched away with a razor or simply faded away over time. The corner of the photograph was peeled far enough for me to remove the

photograph from the driver's license. Last night, Leon
told me that the photograph was taken from a guard who
worked at the Company. He had the similar profile as
Leon, or at least what I could remember. I looked closer at
the photograph and noticed that the guard had green eyes,
not brown as the license read. Leon had blue eyes as well,
or at least used to. I peeled away the photograph of the
guard and then the *real* Mr. Hopkins was revealed. He
was black. Never would've thought that one, although the
"part" hairstyle was a dead giveaway now that I think
about it. I don't know too many white fellows who wear a
part anymore. That was the look in the 80's. White *or*
black. Didn't matter. Marcus was a handsome man, rigid
jaw line, keen eyes. Reminded me of the actor Philip Michael Thomas. That would be Tubbs from *Miami Vice* for
those of you who are still popping pimples. I'm more confused as to why Leon left the ID on the nightstand for me.
Or was it Diego? Leon and I are scheduled for a late
morning interview. I don't plan on asking him about the
ID. For the first time since I've been here, I actually have
butterflies in my stomach. A part of it is because the cat is
now out of the bag and Mr. Hopkins is, in fact, Freeze. In
a way, I understand why Leon decided to disguise his
name from me. He looks at least twenty years older than
Diego and yet Diego is his elder. I doubt it had anything
to do with the avocados, but I could be wrong. Leon said
his body started to age after he lost his vision. Makes
sense. The pain and stress of losing his family was too
much for him to handle. It's weird saying this, but I feel
relieved that Leon came forward and stopped pretending to
be Mr. Hopkins. Now, I look forward to further conversations with the man, the legend, who was once known as
Freeze.

Anne scrolled down the next page in the document
and read a couple of lines before closing the window.

Those lines: *I overheard Diego talking on the telephone.
He was talking about a girl.*

Since Anne was now starting to get the hang of the timeline (and not to mention, at the very edge of her seat from the reading), she knew it was best to stop reading before anything was spoiled. She grabbed a pair of headphones from the main station—a pair of clunky things that looked like two soda cans attached to a flimsy boomerang with a worn piece of duck tape holding the lousy thing together—and opened the next interview on the drive, *Interview #7.*

MR. HOPKINS: I've been meaning to ask you, Renny. Have you come up with a title yet?
RENNY: *Title?* A title for what?
MR. HOPKINS [LOUDLY]: For the story, of course. Have you come up with a title for the story?

(RENNY *grins and readjusts himself in the chair.*)

RENNY: As a matter of fact, I have. I know it's way too soon, but I think she's a keeper.
MR. HOPKINS: I've always enjoyed reading the titles of your stories. You have to have that, that *hook* like that one. . . Cast From the Heavens: *The Celestial Renegade.*
RENNY: Ah! Yes!

(*He chortles briefly.*)

The story I did on the great Starlet Rollinson, singer of the once popular band from the Nineties, Mona's Arch. That was a fun interview.

(MR. HOPKINS *leans forward, now closer.*)

MR. HOPKINS: So, do you mind telling me? About the title? I promise I can keep a secret.
RENNY [TEASINGLY]: It's not really a secret. Well, you know what I mean. . .

MR. HOPKINS: I suppose I should know a thing or two about keeping secrets.
RENNY [CHUCKLING]: That's right.

(*He contemplates for a moment whether or not he should tell* MR. HOPKINS *the title.*)

RENNY: I was thinking about. . . [SUDDENLY] Nah! I shouldn't!   It might be bad luck or something.   An omen. . .
MR. HOPKINS: Don't be so ridiculous, Renny. I thought you didn't believe in that kind of stuff.

(RENNY *shrugs his shoulders.*)

RENNY [BLUNTLY]: A Week With Mr. Hopkins.
MR. HOPKINS: *A Week With Mr. Hopkins?* Huh? [GRINNING] I like that.
RENNY: Well, it's a work in progress.
MR. HOPKINS: Sounds like a winner to me.
RENNY: We'll see. Okay! So, first, since I know now who you really are, let's start out by talking about your childhood, if that's okay with you.
MR. HOPKINS: What is there to tell? I didn't have much of a childhood.
RENNY: How about where you grew up?
MR. HOPKINS: I grew up right here in this very mansion, in the East Wing. Since I didn't have a mother in my life, or much of a father for that matter, both Calvin and Diego were the closest figures I had to a parent.
RENNY: Because your father traveled a lot?
MR. HOPKINS [SOLEMNLY]: Yes.
RENNY: Anything else you care to share about your childhood?
MR. HOPKINS: Stories.

(RENNY *leans back in his chair and crosses one leg over the other.*)

RENNY: Let's hear them.

MR. HOPKINS: I mean, the stories you read. Bedtime stories. When it came to bedtime, if Calvin was busy with chores or whatnot, Diego would read me lots of stories, mostly stories about my father, his adventures. After Calvin died—

RENNY: Calvin? The butler before Diego? The one who died of pneumonia?

MR. HOPKINS: Correct.

RENNY: Where was your father when Calvin passed?

MR. HOPKINS: Somewhere in Tunisia, I believe.

RENNY: Did he know about Calvin?

MR. HOPKINS: He knew. He couldn't stand to see Calvin like that. Calvin—in a way—he was like an older brother to him. But. . .

(MR. HOPKINS *lets out a sigh. Then, places both hands over the blanket on his lap.*)

. . . But I never understood why my father would just leave Calvin like that, especially after everything they had been through. It didn't make any sense to me.

RENNY: Your father sounds like a complicated man.

MR. HOPKINS: Enigmatic. You know, before Calvin. . . before he passed away, he told me that my father had not been the same since my mother died. There were times, many times I wondered if he hated me. I guess I reminded him too much of himself. . . I'm sure you felt the same way about your father.

RENNY: Well. . . I don't think he hated me. All he wanted was for me to do good in life.

MR. HOPKINS: It's funny, Renny, how the things that you experienced as a young child come back to haunt you as a parent. You do everything in your power not to be like your father. You even convince yourself over and over again that you're not going to be that man. Then, it just happens. Next thing you know, you *are* your father.

(*He turns away from* RENNY *and takes a moment to catch his breath.*)

RENNY: Leon, you were nothing like your father. You were *there* for Dom and Chloe. Then, things just happened. Things you had no control over.

(MR. HOPKINS' *attention remains on the wall.*)

MR. HOPKINS: I got word of his passing around the peak of my career. I did the job. [SHRUGGING] Had to. The city needed me. People needed me. And I couldn't show any signs of weakness, especially to the ones who wanted my head stuffed and hung on a mantle. Thankfully, if it wasn't for that one rookie cop. . . Officer Devon Merit, no, Merrotti, Devon *Merrotti*—yes, that was his name—then I very well would've be joining my father that day.

(*He turns back around toward* RENNY.)

I wasn't myself, clearly. My game was off, which meant the gaze was off. It was low key. Had one unit with me. Word on the street: there was a cocaine laboratory in operation directly underneath Grand Park Street. If I knew we were going to be in the sewers, then I would've worn something a little more appropriate.
RENNY: Just curious. What were you wearing, if you don't mind me asking?

(MR. HOPKINS *arches his head backward, thinks for a moment.*)

MR. HOPKINS: Silver blazer, black silk dress shirt, thousand dollar cuffs made from twenty-four karat gold, a new pair of alligator-skin shoes.
RENNY: You always knew how to dress.

(*He gives* MR. HOPKINS *a once over, starting from* MR. HOPKINS' *pale blue sweater to his chocolate brown leather slip-ons.*)

Still do.
MR. HOPKINS: I figure if I'm going to go out, I better do it in style. Right?

(RENNY *chuckles yet again, this time louder.*)

RENNY: Right.
MR. HOPKINS: You should be telling that to Sophia. She's the one who picks out my daily attire.
RENNY: Well, she has good taste.
MR. HOPKINS: Thank you, Renny. I like to think so.
RENNY: No problem.
MR. HOPKINS: So, where was I?

(RENNY *glances down at his notes.*)

RENNY: Ah, the sewers.
MR. HOPKINS: Right. The sewers. We were walking right into a trap. One of their junkie buddies gave them a heads up and told them we were on the way. They were waiting for us before we even showed up. I remember two officers were killed that night. Six injured. One in critical condition. If it wasn't for that one police officer—*what was his name?*
RENNY: Merrotti?
MR. HOPKINS: Yes! Merrotti! If it wasn't for Officer Merrotti, none of those men, including myself, would've made it out of the sewers alive.

—

Anne suddenly pressed the PAUSE button.

"Merrotti?" Anne said to herself. "Where have I heard that name before?"

She thought about his title, a police officer.

Then, the strange man's identity came to her.

"The detective," she said to herself and then hit the PLAY button.

MR. HOPKINS: I had already taken out eight of them. I was in the middle of using the gaze when suddenly I heard that reverberating click of a hammer right next to my ear. My heart sank to the bottom of my chest.

(He struggles to raise his arm. He finally lifts his trembling hand and holds it next to his ear.)

And then [QUOTES] If it isn't Lansford's Knight in Shinning Armor. [END QUOTES] I heard two gunshots. I thought he killed me. Literally saw my entire life flash before my eyes. My childhood. My adulthood. There was this beautiful woman, Isabel. Then, two angels, Dom and Chloe—they were the last ones I saw. I've never even met them before, and yet they were there, Renny, in my thoughts. I wondered to myself: except for these people, these strangers whom I would soon grow to love, would they miss me?
RENNY: Would who miss you?
MR. HOPKINS: The people of Lansford. People, in general.
RENNY [EXCITEDLY]: Of course, they would. You were the Great Freeze!
MR. HOPKINS: Sure, Renny, they would miss me for a day or so, perhaps mourn me for a couple of weeks, months, or a year. Then, a couple of years would go by, and I would be a forgotten memory.
RENNY: That's the world we live in now. We live in a country that's slowly becoming A.D.D.

MR. HOPKINS [PASSIONATELY]: No, Renny. You can't blame people for their own mistakes. We *all* make mistakes in life. Mistakes do *not* define us. They pave roads for us, new and better ones. We are a species that is capable of committing terrible acts; and yet, on the other hand, achieving great wonders. That is what makes us so extraordinary. *That*, Renny, is what connects us. You. Me. . .

(*He points across the hallway.*)

. . . Diego. Sophia. It is the world, Renny, the world that molds us into the human beings we want to be.

RENNY: And did you want to be Freeze?

MR. HOPKINS: No, Renny. I *never* wanted to be Freeze. At first, I enjoyed the fame. What young man wouldn't? Then, the fame turned me into someone I didn't want to be.

RENNY: Which was?

MR. HOPKINS [SOMBERLY]: A puppet. It turned me into a puppet, Renny.

RENNY: I think we're all *puppets* in some way or another whether we like to admit it or not. We are copies of a copy, *puppets* lacking any structure or substance. We take everything at face value. We lack imagination.

MR. HOPKINS: Not true, Renny.

RENNY: Face it. We've become cynical, hollow creatures who only care about one thing and one thing only: ourselves.

MR. HOPKINS: Have you always been like this, Renny?

RENNY: Like what?

MR. HOPKINS: You would think I, being a blind man, would have nothing but ill will toward the world. For you, Renny, it sounds like the shoe is on the other foot.

RENNY: What exactly does that mean?

MR. HOPKINS: You sound like a cynic.

RENNY: I *am* a cynic. This world has made me a cynic.

(*He clears his throat. Then, hangs his head. Just for a moment. He looks up at* MR. HOPKINS. *A look of frustration on his face.*)

But like you, Leon, I never wanted to be this way.

MR. HOPKINS: Then don't.

RENNY: It's hard not to be cynical when we walk around like zombies, desensitized. . . uneducated. You walk around the streets of any big city and ask the average person what year we first landed on the moon or who the 36th President was. I mean, is this stuff relevant? [HE ANSWERS] Of course, it is.

MR. HOPKINS: Sometimes we forget the things that matter the most. Other times we choose to forget. It's easier, Renny, to lose ourselves in fantasy than it is to cope with reality. The question you should be asking: How do we learn how to live effectively without learning from the mistakes we made in the past?

RENNY: Good question.

MR. HOPKINS: Most of us drift through life without any meaning—like shadows always searching for light in a place which has *no* light, only numbers and codes, deception and illusions. The only way to find the light is to destroy the darkness; otherwise, the darkness will always find you, and it will always *win*.

(*He moistens his mouth and then clears his throat.*)

One day, I believe, we will see each other in the light. It won't happen today or tomorrow. It's going to take time for people to come together. And people *will* come together, Renny, if it's from the accumulative effects of a certain event or tragedy. People *will* come together. Throughout history, the human spirit has *always* prevailed. That, Renny, *that* is what makes us so extraordinary, so *unique*. And the spirit must go on. It *will* go on.

RENNY: And what if it doesn't? What if we're just laying the groundwork for our own extinction?

MR. HOPKINS: People are scared of change. Me, I was scared of change—terrified! You believe that? Freeze? Terrified? I was terrified of settling down with a woman. *But* in our own worst fears, we find out who we really are; and when I found Isabel, I found myself. And I. . . I never would've found my Isabel if it wasn't for that one man, Merrotti, Officer Merrotti.

RENNY [CONFUSEDLY]: Then, what really bothers you? Why don't you think people would miss you? Is it because of what happened in Death Valley?

MR. HOPKINS: No, Renny. What bothers me is that. . . at that time, I wished I could've done more with my life. I could've made a greater mark on the world, especially with what I possessed. Helping out the LPD was one of the best things I did, but it was also the worst.

RENNY: Worst? How?

MR. HOPKINS: When JeneCorp partnered up with the LPD, they wanted to turn me into a god, controlling who lived and who died, Judge, Jury, and Executioner. I couldn't be that person, Renny. Not anymore. All that mattered in those final moments where my life flashed before my eyes was making sure I *stayed* alive.

RENNY: What happened after you heard the gunshots?

MR. HOPKINS: I turned around—my ears still ringing—and I saw Officer Merrotti standing right there. His hands were shaking. Looked as if he just shit his pants.

(*He giggles for a second and then shakes his head.*)

RENNY: First time pulling the trigger? Huh?

MR. HOPKINS: That's right. I thanked him for saving my ass and then I finished the job.

RENNY: Sounds like you had a guardian angel looking over you. Maybe your father put in a good word for you.

MR. HOPKINS: Yes, Renny. I'd like to think so.

RENNY: I remember reading about that in the newspaper. Cops seized like—
MR. HOPKINS: Two hundred and forty pounds of cocaine. Biggest bust in the history of Lansford.

The interview stopped.
Anne opened another interview, *Interview #8*.

MR. HOPKINS: Did you enjoy the lunch?
RENNY: I did. It was delicious. Thank you.

Anne fast-forwarded through the first part of the interview.

MR. HOPKINS: His name was Jesse Vanderbilt, single father with two girls. He was holding a gun to a bank teller's head. He never saw me in line, of course. Otherwise, I reckoned Jesse Vanderbilt would've thought twice about robbing the bank.

(*He removes the shades from his eyes, exposing his eyeless face.*)

I removed the shades from my face and looked into his eyes. I gazed him. Accessed his *hippocampus*, part of the limbic system, which deals with memory. There, I saw his memories with his children, their births, first birthdays, and then I saw a desperate man who would do anything for them, even it involved committing such a horrible crime or putting other people's lives in jeopardy. I kept gazing and cut right through his *amygdale*, the emotional part of the brain.

(*He points to the back of his head.*)

Mr. Vanderbilt immediately put down his gun and cried, I mean, like a baby. Then, he walked right out the front door. I didn't go after him. No reason to. I didn't do anything. I just let him go.

RENNY: What's it like?
MR. HOPKINS: What's *what* like?
RENNY: When you gaze somebody.

(*With assistance from his other hand,* MR. HOPKINS *holds up his hand, his fingers rubbing against one another. His skin sounds like paper.*)

MR. HOPKINS: Have you ever lit a match in your hand and let the fire burn all the way down until it reaches your fingertips.
RENNY: Yes.
MR. HOPKINS: That's what it feels like, only throughout your entire body.
RENNY: Then, it must hurt?
MR. HOPKINS: You have no idea.

Once more, Anne fast-forwarded through the recording until she reached the four-minute mark.

MR. HOPKINS: To be honest, I don't even know what that word means anymore. So many people have so many different interpretations of religion, so many messiahs or gods or deities.
RENNY: Then, *spiritual.* Yes?
MR. HOPKINS: Before I discovered what I was capable of doing to another person. Very much. Yes. Still am. Think I have Diego to thank for that.
RENNY: Is he spiritual as well?
MR. HOPKINS: Don't know. We never really talked about that stuff. He would read me stories from the Bible or Qur'an or Bhagavad Gita—the *Gita*—or even stories from his culture. We never really deciphered the stories. We just let them be whatever they wanted to be. But I enjoyed them, enjoyed listening to him read them. That's probably why I've always been fascinated with different cultures, the gods they worshipped. Call Him what you like, Renny, God, the

Almighty, Buddha, or Vishnu. . . The *fact*: nobody really knows the truth about life after death or how we came to be here on this earth. Was it God? Evolution? These are both convincing arguments, one side may be more convincing than the next or vice versa. I. . .

(*With both hands, he points to his chest.*)

. . . I believe it's good to *believe* in something. Don't you think?

RENNY: Do you believe in tolerance?

MR. HOPKINS: A man who criticizes another man's beliefs or non-beliefs only does so because he is threatened. You can do all the research you want or try to find the answers to our origins, as my father tried, but it won't change the way we look at faith. Faith is personal. Faith is foundation. Faith is *you*. Even if you don't believe in a god, then I think it's good to believe in something, *anything*. Your church, your temple, your mosque, your synagogue, any place of worship, office, work, home, *anything*. As a matter of fact, it doesn't have to be a building or structure at all. It can be here, Renny. Yourself. *Believe* in yourself.

(*He places his hand over his chest, his heart. Then, he carefully searches for the glass of water. He finds it, finally. He takes a sip from the glass of water and then he places it back on the coaster next to him.*)

When a preacher, minister, or a man of the cloth makes *money* or profit from teaching the word of God, then it's not genuine. A man of faith is a humble man. In most, if not all, circumstances, he is a poor man with rich values.

RENNY: You mean an author?

(*He suddenly chortles.*)

MR. HOPKINS: Sure. He can be a writer. But you and I both know, Renny, many writers have too many demons.

RENNY: I got one out of two, I suppose.

MR. HOPKINS: And which is that?

RENNY: The one about being broke.

MR. HOPKINS [AMUSINGLY]: What do you expect? You live in New York City.

RENNY [UNCOMFORTABLY]: Good rent is hard to find.

MR. HOPKINS: And how about the other?

(RENNY *hesitates, but doesn't respond to the question at first.*)

You don't have any values?

RENNY: I have my moments.

MR. HOPKINS: Well, a man of faith could very well be a writer or an artist or musician or even a person who lives off the land like a farmer or fisherman.

Again, Anne fast-forwarded through the interview.

(MR. HOPKINS *laughs, a wet and phlegmy one.*)

RENNY: Oops.

MR. HOPKINS: You write a lot in your journal?

RENNY: I do.

MR. HOPKINS: About me?

RENNY: You. The world. Things that happen each day.

MR. HOPKINS: Ah ha! So, that's why I always hear that clicking noise. And I thought I was going crazy—like a mouse talking to me.

RENNY: That would be me.

(SOPHIA *walks in behind* RENNY.)

MR. HOPKINS: Enough about this stuff, Renny. Let's take a break and then we'll get back to business.

RENNY: Sure.

Another *click*.

RENNY: We were talking briefly about the Pope earlier. He was a man who grew up with humble beginnings; and you, on the other hand, were—don't take offense—born with a silver spoon in your mouth. Correct?

MR. HOPKINS [JOKINGLY]: That's one way of putting it. Unfortunately, I didn't come from humble beginnings like Pope Joseph.

RENNY: So, tell me. Why do you say [QUOTES] unfortunately? [END QUOTES] I know people who would kill to grow up in a place like this, myself included. You were one of the [QUOTES] *fortunate* [END QUOTES] ones.

MR. HOPKINS: I didn't learn anything about life and the beauty of people until I left Whisperfront. Throughout my entire childhood I lived in a bubble. The only outside world I knew came from the artifacts and remnants of ancient cultures. My father used to take pictures everywhere he visited. One in particular: the Parthenon in Greece. To see the picture of Iktinos and Kallikrates' work was one thing, but to experience what they felt, to smell the same exact air they breathed, to hear the sounds they heard, to taste the ocean they tasted, to amerce yourself in that environment, Renny, was a completely difference experience. It's like you became a piece of them, if only for a short while.

RENNY: A picture will never serve justice to the real thing. Even half the pictures out there, all photoshopped, it's hard to tell what's real or not.

MR. HOPKINS: Photoshopped? You mean like a Polaroid?

RENNY: No.

(*He smiles, widely.*)

Photoshop. It's a photo editing software. A lot of celebrities use it to alter their appearances.

MR. HOPKINS: I don't know anything about that non-sense. I could care less. I was never photoshopped. What you see is what you get.

RENNY: I wish it was like that, but the world has to keep spinning.

MR. HOPKINS: All I'm saying, Renny, is that when that bubble burst and I was forced to leave Whisperfront, I discovered the greatest discovery of all time.

RENNY: Which is?

MR. HOPKINS: Patience, Renny. Without patience, there is no reward in life.

RENNY: Interesting. . . So, would you say you were *content* in Sri Lanka?

MR. HOPKINS: I wouldn't say content. I was. . .

(*He pulls his head away and thinks about the next word.*)

. . . Hungry. I was hungry.

RENNY: Hungry for what?

MR. HOPKINS: Hungry for life, for meeting new people, for talking to new faces. After I met Marcus, I was pulled from that world. Along the road, I sort of lost myself. I *lost* my patience. When I became Freeze, I wanted everything all at once, the cars, the women, fame. Then, when I met Isabel, I was thrust back into that life. I rediscovered my patience.

There was a five second gap of silence.

Anne fast-forwarded the interview until there was a sudden spike in the volume.

She pressed the PLAY button and listened to the rest of the interview.

RENNY: —ive in an age where a person's fame is merited on how many scandals or how many times they've been in the headlines.

MR. HOPKINS: What's that one saying about publicity?

RENNY: Any publicity is good publicity.

MR. HOPKINS: Yes. That's it.

RENNY [AGGRESSIVELY]: I get suckered into it myself—writing confessions, sharing them on the Internet, expressing personal opinions or emotions to a machine, *not* an actual person—sure, there's a person on the other end—but, in the end, it's a computer, phone, whatever—a void is what it really is. One big ass void sucking me in.

MR. HOPKINS: What about your journal?

RENNY: Like I said, I get suckered into it. It's hard to hold back sometimes. It's become a problem.

MR. HOPKINS: The best way to fix a problem: start at the source. Are you a slave to the machine or are you a master to it? The choice is yours. It's *that* simple.

RENNY: I wish it was *that* simple.

MR. HOPKINS: If you get comfortable in sharing your feelings with this machine, Renny, not an *actual* human being, then how are you supposed to live life with another human being? How are you supposed to love another? By doing this—in essence—you are rewiring your brain. Are you not?

RENNY: I don't know. *Maybe.* Yeah.

MR. HOPKINS: I think you're problem is, Renny, is that you don't give people a chance. The whole Internet thing, it will come and go as most things do. Diego, however, has his own personal views about the Internet.

RENNY: And what does Diego think of the Internet?

MR. HOPKINS: He looks at it more like a tool.

RENNY: Like any tool, it can be used for good or bad.

MR. HOPKINS: I agree.

(*His face suddenly lights up.*)

Moderation.

RENNY [LOWLY]: Yeah.

(*He hangs his head from the comment. Then, a brief silence over the conversation.*)

MR. HOPKINS: Remember, Renny, the wolf.

(RENNY *doesn't respond.*)

Is something wrong?
RENNY [DEJECTEDLY]: Sometimes the wolf gets tired of hanging out with other wolves. Sometimes the wolf just wants to hang out with the sheep.
MR. HOPKINS [QUIETLY]: I see.

Another strange *click* and then distortion in the interview.
About three seconds later, the distortion finally cleared away and Leon's voice came back on.

MR. HOPKINS: Like you said, Renny, things happen to us, things that question our own upbringing, our own belonging, things that open our eyes—some things we can try to explain and others will *never* be explained. Before I lost my sight, I witnessed the signs around me—the little things, Renny, pushing me toward *this* or *that* direction, guiding me, in a way—as if everything, the whole universe was connected and my path had already been written for me. The questions we should be asking ourselves: Do we really know the truth about the universe? Or do we simply see what our eyes want to see?
RENNY: Nothing is certain.
MR. HOPKINS: The truth, Renny. If you slice me open, I will bleed the same color of blood as you or any other man, woman, or child. We are *who* we are, Renny. We don't get a say in the matter. Most importantly, our history does *not* determine our fate. Yet, our history teaches us how to take control of our fate.
RENNY: So, you think being blind was your fate?
MR. HOPKINS: Yes, Renny. It was *my* purpose.
RENNY: So, the young outcast who was you years ago was always destined to be blind?

MR. HOPKINS: *Yes*, Renny. I know it's hard to understand. But yes. *He was.* What happened to me happened for a reason.

(*He takes a sip from the glass of water.*)

In this life, you have to learn how to *hate* in order to love. Without hate, Renny, you will *never* learn how to fight. And if you don't know how to fight, you will never understand how precious life can be. And *life*, Renny, life is worth fighting for. All of us, no matter where we come from, who we are, what we do, all of us should be treated with equality and dignity, two qualities *worth* fighting for. It's up to you, Renny. It's up to you to choose whether or not you hate for the right reasons.

(RENNY *bobs his head, thinking.*)

We can't change the past, and if we could, Renny, and we were given ah—I don't know—a time machine—
RENNY: Time machine?
MR. HOPKINS: Again, I have Diego to thank for that.
RENNY: H.G. Wells? Huh?
MR. HOPKINS [SUDDENLY]: Ah! That's right!

(*The excitement causes* MR. HOPKINS *to cough. The coughing spell lasts for a couple of seconds.* RENNY *gets up out of his chair and helps wipe away the phlegm from* MR. HOPKINS' *chin.*)

RENNY: Are you okay?
MR. HOPKINS: Fine now. Thank you. What I'm trying to say is that if we were to travel way back in time and redirect the course of our history, the life we know would cease to exist. The progress we've made would be for nothing. The human race is an incredible species—no doubt—but we are, indeed, *a work in progress.* There is still a chance for us, for

you, Renny. Like young Cathy, the girl I met in town, eager about life. Do you remember?

RENNY: The one you talked to on the bench outside the grocery store?

MR. HOPKINS: Yes. *Her.* She can be a role model for her generation and next generations to come. All that matters is the now, the actions we take in order to prevent us from falling back into the same situations that divided humanity in the past. As I was saying earlier, Renny, we have to *respect* ourselves in order to respect others.

RENNY: So, back on the record. . .

MR. HOPKINS: I was wondering when you were going to pull me from my soapbox.

(He coughs violently and then uses the tissue on the nightstand to wipe the secretions from his lower lip.)

RENNY: You okay?

MR. HOPKINS [FAINTLY]: Still dying.

(He laughs, provoking more coughing. Again, he uses the tissue at his disposal.)

RENNY: I like our conversations.

MR. HOPKINS [GRINNING]: Me too, Renny. You're not so bad yourself.

(He places the damp tissue in the trashcan next to the bed.)

RENNY: So, after you married Isabel—with all the fame and glory, I'm sure you had plenty of women practically throwing themselves at you—were you faithful to Isabel?

MR. HOPKINS: To Isabel, I was. I would never look at another woman the same way. She was everything to me, the one woman who finally set me straight. She was mine, Renny. And I. . . I was hers. If you spend too much time longing for someone special, then you might miss out on the one who really matters. You might not even know it when you see it. Isabel was a graceful woman. She had a natural beauty about her, not like some of the women I've been with who were all about big *hair* and lots of makeup. She never wore makeup or wore her hair big, but she was extremely easy on the eyes. Not afraid to wear a pair of blue jeans too.

(*The thought of Isabel makes him smile.*)

Believe it or not, she didn't even like me at first. She thought I was conceited. Imagine that one. Just another city boy who thought he knew it all. I didn't blame her. But I kept hanging around.
RENNY: Why?
MR. HOPKINS: *That*, Renny, I can't explain. Polarity, I suppose.
RENNY: You were opposites?
MR. HOPKINS: Like day and night.
RENNY [WISELY]: Day needs night as much as night needs day.
MR. HOPKINS [SLOWLY]: Yes.
RENNY: So, you hung around. I take it Isabel got under your skin.
MR. HOPKINS: Like a splinter. The more I got to know Isabel, the more beautiful she became.
RENNY: She was your hole in one.

(MR. HOPKINS *smiles again. Then, nods his head.*)

MR. HOPKINS: After I got to know Isabel, I knew she was the one. I don't think she felt the same about me, even though I could see it in her eyes. You know. *The light.* She definitely had her guard up, as any woman should. One thing I did know: I couldn't do to her what the Company wanted me to do.
RENNY: And what exactly did they want you to do?

MR. HOPKINS: Persuade her to move.

RENNY: Move where?

MR. HOPKINS: I don't know. Anywhere but Rural.

RENNY: All because of the oil?

MR. HOPKINS: That's correct. They wanted me to gaze her. I would never harm a single hair on her head, Renny. Then, after what happened in Rural. . . the incident. . . a part of me died with her. I'm sure you can understand why I didn't want to be Freeze anymore.

RENNY [JUBILANTLY]: But you had everything a man could ever want: women, money, fame!

MR. HOPKINS: I didn't have it all, Renny, not until I met Isabel. The money, *the fame*, all of that nonsense didn't mean a damn thing when I met Isabel. Those things. . . they were the furthest from my mind. The fact: Isabel stripped everything away from me, stripped me to the core, and showed me who I really was as a man, as a lover, as a father.

(*He holds up his left arm.*)

Here. Give me a hand. Will you?

(RENNY *carefully cradles* MR. HOPKINS' *body and then carries him to the wheelchair.*)

Sophia is going to have a fit once she finds out you're doing her job.

RENNY: It's the least I can do.

(*He secures* MR. HOPKINS *in the wheelchair.*)

MR. HOPKINS: Where was I?

(RENNY *pushes* MR. HOPKINS *closer to the window. Then,* RENNY *slides his chair next to the wheelchair.*)

RENNY: You were talking about Isabel.
MR. HOPKINS: Right.

(*He tries to steady his breathing.*)

You feel the urges with beautiful women, the instant gratifications. You're having a great time. You feel like you're the luckiest man on earth because you're making love with a natural goddess.

(*He readjusts himself in the wheelchair and then takes a moment to catch his breath from the previous move.*)

Then, Renny, they ask you for something. It always starts with them asking you for something like a necklace or a car or it even might come as a suggestion, but they don't really *ask you*, more or less, they give you a hint of what they really want. Then it turns to more things, more stuff to make them look pretty, stuff to fill the emptiness inside them. Over time, you realize, Renny, they don't love you. Never did. All they want is—

(*He shrugs his shoulders. It hurts him while doing so.*)

Stuff. They just want stuff. That's all they want. You know what kind of stuff I'm talking about.
RENNY: Oh yeah. I know.
MR. HOPKINS: Then, these women start to think outside the box. They finally grow a brain and use their imagination—or what little imagination they have. How do I get money from a wealthy celebrity without coming off as another freeloader? [ANGRILY] I was so damn naïve at the time.
RENNY: You're talking about like a gold digger?
MR. HOPKINS: Gold digger? *No.* A freeloader.
RENNY: Okay. So, was that what you were looking for, for love?

MR. HOPKINS [SOLEMNLY]: Any man who is *not* in love is always looking for love, whether he likes to admit it or not. It's like trying to go against a primal force of nature. It's why we're here, Renny. It's why we are here on this earth, to love and to be loved. Isabel was my love, my only true love. And then when we had Dom and Chloe, they were my barometers, my two little angels showing me what kind of man I should be.

RENNY: And what kind of man was that?

MR. HOPKINS [SERIOUSLY]: A humble man.

The tears unexpectedly glazed around Anne's eyes.

MR. HOPKINS: I swore to myself that I, from that point forward, would put them first no matter *what* I did.

RENNY: But you were loved by hundreds, thousands, millions!

MR. HOPKINS: You're not getting it, Renny. Those people, they loved Freeze, *not* Leon Dorsey.

(He sniffles. *There were no tears, though, none that he could muster from the severe damage to his eyes. Just a wet nose.*)

After I destroyed the Company, I couldn't even recognize the person who was looking back at me in the mirror. I was hideous. I had become everything that I feared the most. I was turning into *her*, you know. Even my. . . my hair. I could feel it crawling over my scalp as if it was alive. Then, *that fire*, a constant fire burning inside me. I didn't want them anymore. I just want to be with my Chloe one last time, to tell her that I'm sorry.

RENNY: You will, Leon.

(He *leans over the armrest and touches the top of* MR. HOPKINS' *hand.*)

MR. HOPKINS: The worse feeling a man can ever experience is never saying goodbye to a loved one.

(*He turns to* RENNY.)

One day, they're there. So close you can touch them. The next, *gone*. You never have a chance to tell them how much they mean to you, how much you love them. They're gone like dust in wind.

RENNY [TEARFULLY]: What is your fondest memory you have of   your daughter?

(*A smile forms on the side of* MR. HOPKINS' *face.*)

MR. HOPKINS: She always had this fascination with animals, mainly mice. When she was little—three or four, I believe—it was insects, grasshoppers, beetles, fireflies, *baby snakes*. Once, she had a thing for those bugs that make a lot of noise.

RENNY: June bugs?

MR. HOPKINS: That's it. June bugs. Anything with more than four legs—or no legs—she would keep them in these mason jars with holes poked in the top. You know, so she didn't kill them.

RENNY: Gerbils were big when I was a kid.

MR. HOPKINS: I don't think we had any gerbils. Maybe she did, though. She'd always sneak her pets into the house without us knowing about them.

RENNY: A tomboy?

MR. HOPKINS: She was. Yes. She definitely took up after her old man, but she was sassy like her mother.

(*He catches his breath for a second; the thought of his daughter nearly knocks the wind out of him.*)

When Chloe turned six, she got into mice. She would even catch them in the backyard. Isabel used to get *so* upset. She didn't like mice at all, especially in the house.

RENNY: But you didn't mind?

MR. HOPKINS: Me? Of course not. Just seeing the smile on Chloe's face when she played with her mice was enough to melt your heart. One day, I took Chloe to the local zoo. They didn't have many animals there. A couple of giraffes. A zebra. They did have these great big African bush elephants. Isabel knew one of the zookeepers working there and asked if we could get a closer look at the elephants. She let Chloe pet the elephant. Something happened. All of a sudden, the elephant flung its trunk at Chloe. I pulled her out of the way in the nick of time. The elephant rampaged through a highly electrical fence.

RENNY: You're kidding?

MR. HOPKINS: True story. Eventually, the zookeepers caught up with the elephant. They had to put it down. Later that day, I saw on the news that the elephant trampled a pedestrian and left the poor man with severe head trauma. I never told Chloe about what they did to the elephant. I knew it would upset her.

(*He pauses for a moment. Thinks more about Chloe.*)

After the whole ordeal, I knew there was something special about Chloe.

RENNY: Special? How?

A sudden *click* startled Anne!
She tilted her head in confusion.
Another one. . .
Anne rewound the interview a couple of seconds and heard that same click over again.
Finally, Renny's voice came back on.

RENNY: After you, you know, after you lost your sight, did you ever try to explain to Chloe about, you know, about your powers?

(MR. HOPKINS *turns motionless and listens closely.*)

MR. HOPKINS: I'm afraid I'm going to have to retire for the night. We will finish the story tomorrow. I promise.

(DIEGO *enters the bedroom, startling* RENNY.)

RENNY: Are you sure?

(*He stands from the chair as* DIEGO *walks by.*)

MR. HOPKINS: Yes. I'm sure.

(DIEGO *walks behind the wheelchair and pushes* MR. HOPKINS *toward the doorway. On the way,* MR. HOPKINS *reaches out his frail hand, now waving.* RENNY *grabs a hold of* MR. HOPKINS' *hand. He doesn't shake it. Instead,* RENNY *holds* MR. HOPKINS' *hand for a moment and then finally lets go.*)

Goodnight, Renny.

Anne rewound the interview and listened to the elephant story once more. Bits and pieces of that one day at the zoo suddenly came back to Anne (memories of the same tall man—who, prior to the story, only lived in her dreams—standing next to her, more detail upon his face, high cheek structure, shiny skin, lush wavy hair with blonde highlights, as well as the elephant, its beady eyes, its pupils swelling like tiny black balloons, its haunting screech, its trunk swinging at her, this tall man barely pulling her out of the way); and then, at that moment in time, Anne knew exactly who "Mr. Hopkins" was even though his true identity had been revealed prior to the recent interview. She put the pieces together earlier that morning, but the story about the elephant confirmed her deepest suspicion.

With a deadpan expression on her face, she closed the interview and opened the same journal entry from before, *Journal Entry 10.18.2014*, and scrolled down to the place where she left off, about the "girl."

I overheard Diego talking on the phone. He was talking about a girl. "The girl," he specifically said. He called her Anne. I couldn't quite make out the last name. Whoever this Anne girl is, I feel that her life may be in grave danger. The more I stay here the more I feel as if my own life may be in danger. If Leon can't get in touch with his daughter, possibly this Anne girl whom Diego spoke about on the phone, then I believe Diego will resort to extreme measures in order for Leon to fulfill his final wish before he dies. I don't know how much Leon has left in him. He is becoming weaker by the day. Today took a lot out of him. The pain brought on from the absence of his daughter is, by far, stronger than the cancer itself. The story *must* be finished.

Anne stopped reading; in fact, she stopped everything and sat in front of the computer with that same deadpan expression. The only thing that Anne kept on doing was breathing, and she couldn't very well stop doing that.

Before she could finally gather herself, that feeling was upon her, the three o'clock feeling, and yet, as both of her eyes mechanically crossed the time on the upper right-hand corner of the screen, she realized it wasn't even high noon. As with the past stories and what they had done to Leon, the feeling nearly crippled Anne.

She retraced her thoughts. Another sequence of images, so stark and terrorizing, flashed through her mind. The first images: young Anne running away from Leatherby Manor, through the tall grass and into the dark woods; and then Anne glancing back, only once throughout her escape, and then witnessing a bald headed man with a pencil-thin mustache chasing after her but unable to keep up with her, for she was too fast for him.

The images came together now in full sequence. . .

Eventually, after miles of dodging trees and leaping over falling trunks, she excited the woods and crossed the edge of a coastal town. Each image in her mind was like coal to a fire. *The smell of diesel gasoline was in the air—the fumes, she choked on. Then, she felt droplets of water hit her leg during each pass of a vehicle.* The images now grew farther from one another: Anne searching for food in an old parking lot; the gnawing in her stomach growing larger and heavier; dumpster diving behind a restaurant with a colorful sign of a cartoon character with a round hamburger patty as a head; sleeping behind cabs of freight trucks; feeling vibrations—bad ones; listening to the *hisses* and *pops* coming from the trucks—startling at times, like little robots speaking in their own unique language; yearning for sleep but getting none; the bones inside her body aching from weeks of traveling; gathering several full trash bags at rest stops and, without the truck driver looking, stuffing them against the back of the cab, which helped with the vibrations.

The images came closer together. . .

A coarse hand suddenly reached out and rescued her from her most vivid nightmares and grabbed her by the forearm. The shadowy man behind the hairy club-like arm was the size of a black bear—now screaming out, "Gotcha!" She moaned from his firm grip. Then, the heavyset man tossed her on the side of the road. She choked yet again on the fumes as the truck went speeding down the highway. Walking, Anne suddenly remembered as she focused on the road, walking for miles along the side of a dark road. She stayed close to the memory, recent now. *The night was bright and beautiful.* How could Anne forget? *The stars clearer than ever. The moon cast its pale light over the calm road.* Once or twice, she questioned whether or not she was caught in one of her dreams. But as with all dreams, eventually the dreamer had to wake. What happened next was something Anne had never expected—not even in her wildest dreams. *Her legs were extremely sore, but the sight alone of the night sky was enough to mask any pain in her body. Then, she heard it, a truck whizzing closer. Smaller than the one she had ridden on across the South. She turned her shoulder, only to witness the two headlights bearing down on her. The voice of a man singing to a Top 40 song on the radio built over the sound of a throbbing engine. Anne didn't know which way to move from the two lights. Her only maneuver was to backpedal, and so she did. The ground below her was now soft and squishy, not hard like the asphalt. Then, she heard the same man, the one behind the steering wheel, screaming to the top of his lungs, "Deer!" The blood punched like a thousand fists against her veins. She let out a sudden grunt from the pit of her belly. Before she could make sense of what had happened to her, the ground in which she stood on gave way. For the slightest moment, gravity ceased to exist. Her eyes were staring directly at the stars. Then, the pale light swirled above her, the moon passing in intervals. Dampening now. Then, gravity set in, and she was falling back to the earth. Once more, the blood punched through her veins, but this time she hardly felt a thing. However, she did hear the loud cracks beneath her, which sounded like handfuls of dry pasta being snapped in two. From there, the numbness gripped her body like a giant hand; and then came the darkness and the ominous hum of silence. Two warm fingers pressed against the side of her neck and pulled her momentarily from the darkness. "Oh fuck!" the man slurred to himself. "What da fuck have I done?" The man was arguing to someone. But then, after her wandering eyes crossed the staggering man towering over, young Anne realized the man was only arguing to himself. "I'm fuckin' screwed!" he cried out. "I can't! You gotta! But she jus' a lil' gurl! I CAN'T! They'll lock you away for good! FUCK!" The same two warm hands lifted her broken body from the side of the road.*

Anne didn't remember much during the car ride, only the sounds of the drunk same man sobbing like a girl, a *rusty door squeaking* open, and then the *soothing and yet repetitive sound of ocean waves* crashing against the shore. Again, those same two hands, now as cold and sweaty as melted ice, cradled her lifeless body.

The next thing Anne remembered was the frigid water, her entire body submerged in it. . .

The blood poured from her body, staining the water with clouds of bright red. Beyond the red clouds and into the darkness of the abyss, she witnessed something incredible: hundreds of jellyfish glistening like city lights, each one carrying a different light or sparkle, each one shaped differently.

Now, from here, the young girl didn't quite know where her dreams began and where they ended. She descended into the school of jellyfish; and yet, instead of feeling the dreadful sting of jellyfish, she felt the complete opposite. The jellyfish wrapped Anne in their tentacles and gently carried her to the surface of the water where, eventually, Anne drifted to the shore and lay unconscious in the damp sand until a bearded man found her body. Anne didn't remember much about the man, only that he reeked of brine and had a beard on his chubby face. She remembered *the lights, how bright and glorious they were, not from the jellyfish but from the ones haloed above the bearded man. The lights changed in size and then in brightness. The bearded man had gone away and was replaced with another man wearing a surgical mask over his face. Then, more bodies,* the girl realized, *cloaked bodies exiting from the lights, and like the man before her, they too were wearing surgical masks. From there, each day ran into the next. She heard the same noises day in and day out, the machines, the chatter in the hallways. She received the same visitors, all of whom were dressed in those same white gowns as before. To her, these people remained distant, alien-like. Then, she was walking again, now on her own, through the very hallways where the chatter was more clear. Others like her, other patients, she saw. Next, they put her in the company of other girls her age but she talked to none of them.* In one room, which was always off limits, she remembered a pale boy named *Sam, whom the girls had called Tentacles from all the tubes running in and out of his body. All of the girls giggled at the boy, but not* Anne, *not her. Whenever the adults weren't around, she would poke her head inside the young boy's room. There were machines everywhere, all ranging in pitch from beeps to buzzes. The boy never said anything to her or anybody else for that matter. Instead, he would smile and give her a thumbs up. Before too long,* Anne remembered, *she was pulled from the stale environment and driven to a more "suitable" place. A wide faced woman dressed in a burgundy suit was introducing her to a lanky man with a thin beard and glasses. "Dee, Sugar," the woman said warily, "this here is Louis. Louis is going to take extra special care of you." The strange man shook the woman's hand.* Anne remembered the strange man's eyes, *especially his eyes,* and how they appeared as if they were *talking to her when, in fact, they weren't talking at all. "Thank you so much for doing this, Chelsea. Ever since. . . " He choked up for a second and then broke down in tears, his hand cupping his eyes. "There, there," the suited woman said and rubbed the man on the back. "Thank you so much." The man kneeled down to her—his eyes not showing the least amount of red in them as she expected—and then introduced himself. His hands were as cold as ice,* Anne remembered, *the hands of a dead man, but as* soft and smooth as a woman's. He said to her in his smoker's voice, "You're so pretty." Then, his two bony fingers grazed across her knee.

There was a skip in the sequence of images, but Anne stayed with the images as much as she wanted to block them out.

Now, she and the strange man were in another room. . .

They were seated on the edge of a bed—the strange man seated right next to her. The room was both quiet and tense like a doctor's room. Chelsea was nowhere around; in fact, she was gone for good. The curtains on the windows were closed. Then, Anne recalled the blue flowers on the wallpaper. Roses, Anne remembered, blue roses. Everything in the room was so pristine like a dollhouse. The strange man's wife sat down next to her, which caused her to shift farther down into the bed. The woman was as pale and gauntly as a stiff, her voice was thick and rich, and yet her eyes were dark and beady like buttons. "Go," the man drawled. "But Louis, we said—" the woman returned. "I just want ten minutes alone with her. To get to know her a little better." The woman's brows furrowed, her eyes narrowed as well. "Louis, I thought we were done with this shit." Before she could finish the rest of her argument, the man barked, "Get out of here!" She flinched from the man's screams. Next thing she heard was the sound of a door slamming shut. The room grew more tense. His eyes trailed down over hers. His breath was heavy and warm—like the fumes of a car. Even his queer eyes were beating like a pulse. His cold hand grazed across her knee yet again as if the first time he had done it never gave him the hint that she was certainly not interested in whatever carnal acts or desires the man had up his sleeve. That icy hand redirected its course and slowly trailed up her thigh. "What are you doing to me?" she asked innocently. The man shushed her and removed the strap from her dress. "I'm going to make you feel good," he said as he undressed her. While he removed her underwear, he nibbled on *the side of her neck. Soon, the nibbling turned more aggressive from kissing to biting; but he never pierced her skin.* Next thing Anne remembered *was the bare man lying on top of her—biting her at times—an extremely sharp pain suddenly streaking throughout her entire body like bolts of lightning, and then the blood. There was so much blood.*

Before the red could wash over her eyes, Anne suddenly jolted from her seat.

"Oh god!" she cried out.

The same stabbing pain from her groin was still there, she noticed, but much more faint. She quickly removed the headphones from her ears, pushed them aside, and hurried to the nearest bathroom.

Once inside, she made sure to lock the door behind her. She splashed her face with cool water and tried to make sense of the perverted images in her head. Was it a dream or was it a memory? She forced herself to ask the question over and over. It certainly didn't feel like a dream, she wondered. Her earliest memories were of Harold driving her home from the "hospital." Before that, it was like one gigantic jigsaw puzzle. Some of the pieces fit together, pieces like her *running in the woods* or *riding in the back of trucks* or *living with a strange couple* (something not right about them, especially that one man). She remembered another woman, her first foster mother, Chelsea. There were other girls, none of whom she had gotten along with. Then, there was that one *couple,* mainly the strange man who collected plastic dolls, which Anne didn't think too much about. She assumed they were for her to play with. Then, *the wife,* Anne guessed, was gone most of the time. She rarely saw the woman; in fact, she only saw her on weekends. There were photographs of another girl in the living room, she remembered; and every time this woman would bring up the girl's name, the strange man would get upset. Then, after she experienced this new pain daily—the *camcorders scattered around the basement*, the *flashes of cameras* as strange hands touched, fondled, and poked at her private parts, the other *silhouettes* standing behind the bright flashes like cloaked monks, the *hundreds of photographs of young girls like* Anne posted on the walls around her, all of them dressed in little to no clothing—Anne was back doing the one thing that she was good at, which was running. Anne remembered breaking through a boarded window, climbing and crawling around sharp glass, cutting her forearm during the fall, and then running as fast as her legs could take her. She pushed through the pain and ran as if she had a purpose. A couple of cars pulled up next to her and asked her if she needed any help, but the words were bunched in her mouth like a spool of yarn. She couldn't explain them even if she tried—it was as if she had a mouthful of peanut butter. Then, she ran and, as before, ran as far and fast as her legs would take her. Eventually, after her legs had given out, she found a place to hide, a filthy restroom in the back of a rundown convenient store. *The blood*, she witnessed as she hid behind the graffiti-covered stall, *the blood running down her legs after she ran.* There was so much of it. That night, she slept underneath an old bridge in a park and dreamt of cloaked monsters with hands like tree branches stretching out to her and prodding at her, creeping up her bare legs, the tips of the branches as sharp as claws. She slept with the monsters until the morning sun cast them away. *Two women*, Anne remembered, *walking along a path spotted her.* They asked her what her name was, where her parents were, and what she was doing out here alone, but she was too frightened and cold and traumatized to answer. A police officer picked her up from the park and took her to a place where there were other police officers. Then, the vicious cycle started over yet again. She was back in another foster home, only this time with a couple who paid little to no attention to her. They had a sixteen-year-old son, an ill-tempered punk who was always yelling at them. On many nights, she would wake to the sound of a door slamming or loud thrash metal. At times, she wondered what she was doing there. The noise wasn't what bothered her the most. It was *the smell*: the combination of potpourri, which smelled as sour as rotten milk, and cigarette smoke. And the entire house reeked—even the furniture and every little thing the smell had touched, including the inside of the microwave. Anne lived there in that smelly ass house for a couple of weeks until another couple adopted her—an older couple. The woman in charge of placing her in the previous home had erased them from the records—it was as if those couple of weeks never even happened. For Anne, they *did* happen. These people were nothing but unsatisfied customers who treated her as if she was a defective product; and then, like all defective products who didn't live up to expectation, she was returned back to the store—that was exactly how she felt, as if she didn't belong in the care of others, and yet, she remained with all the other defective products. Then, there were the leery shoppers who weren't cut out to raise a child. Finally, there was Harold and Molly, the older couple. Anne had no recollection of them at first—that was their first encounter. All Anne remembered, from the time spent with her last foster parents—the ones from the smelly house—to the long drive home from the hospital, was a violent electrical storm—the veins of lightning streaking across an ocean of blackness until the prodding and pricking had faded away into a dull nothingness. It didn't take long for the storm to pass;

and when it did, a ray of sunlight dawned over her open palm and everything was okay. Her bedroom— *my bedroom*, she remembered, the faces of models on the walls, the posters.

Anne arched her body downward and once more, splashed her flushed face with water.

10:23 AM

AFTER Anne composed herself, she was back on the computer in no time.

With the headphones around her head, she read the following entry, *Journal Entry 10.19.2014*:

Sunday. Possibly my last day here depending on how the final interview goes. Leon wasn't in the mood to do the interview this morning. By no means is he a shrinking violet when it comes to expressing his views, as I have learned these past couple of days, but I need to reel him back into the relationship with his daughter in order to make a convincing story. At times, Leon gets sidetracked with talking about other things, which makes me wonder if the story is about Anne or if its about life lessons in general—kind of like a *How-To-Guide* on how to live a meaningful life. At the end of the day, the story is for her, regardless if this thing gets published or not. As of now, I'd say it's looking very unlikely, but I've been in hotter water. With that said, Leon and I planned on wrapping up the final interview later in the afternoon. After lunch, I killed time by wandering around Leatherby Manor. While I was walking back to my bedroom, I couldn't help but overhear Diego talking to Leon. I tried to get a better listen. Next thing I knew, I heard a metal tray crashing to the floor. I rushed to the door and peeked inside, only to find the lunch that Diego brought Leon on the floor. Diego was screaming at Leon, "It's the only way!" Leon was crying as well. His hands were covering his face. I couldn't make out exactly what Leon was saying, although I did hear my name somewhere in his cries.

To Do List:
1. Finish the interview
2. Submit everything to Edie no later than Monday morning
3. Hand in first draft by Tuesday
4. Final draft done on Thursday
5. FRANTIC FRIDAY!!!

She scrolled down the page and read the next entry on the page.

Leon canceled the interview for this afternoon. So far, the day has been a complete wash. Frantic Friday is looming around the corner. If I don't have the story in Edie's hands by at least Wednesday, then I'm afraid I will possibly be out of a job.

Anne scrolled farther down the same journal entry from *10.19.2014*.

Couldn't sleep. I stretched my legs by mostly pacing around my room. I did that for about an hour or so until I finally decided to venture outside. I was as skittish as a squirrel. Every noise, every little creak or crack in Leatherby Manor, sent me into a state of high alert. Without getting spotted by baldy, I came across something that I had never seen before in the study. So, naturally, the Sherlock in me poked its tiny head. On the desk, I found many photographs piled on top of one another like a pyramid. One set of photographs was bound by a pink barrette. The others were scattered every which way. Not sure if they were put there on purpose *or not*. I pushed aside the photographs and came across the same photo album that Leon had showed me the other day. Inside, there were many pages of pictures of Leon's family, mainly Polaroids of Chloe and Dom—physical Polaroids you could actually touch. The kids in the pictures looked like any other kids,

at that stage in life where they haven't really developed
any distinct characteristics that made them stand out
among the other kids. I wasn't the least interested in the
photo album. I was more intrigued with the other photographs, the ones of Chloe as an adult. She is an incredibly
beautiful woman and smart as a whip from what Leon has
explained. When I asked him how much he knew about
his daughter today, Leon only gave me the same information any worm like Stew could find on the Internet. Chloe
changed her name to Anne. She was working as a telemarketer for USR. Not happy with her life. From the photos, she had a little bit of both her mother and father in her.
From the nose up, she looked more like Leon—except for
the hazel eyes—and from the nose down, she looked like
Isabel. But like I said to Leon before, a photo can "never
serve any justice." As I was meandering throughout the
study, I heard a door open behind me. I noticed Leon
standing there with this strange look on his face, as if he
broke the TV remote and then blamed it on the dog; and
now, he was ready to give his confession. He wasn't in his
wheelchair, I noticed, which was rare—the guy's courage
and strength never ceases to amaze me. I asked him what
he was doing up so late. He said that he had become a
night owl over these past few years. He told me that he
was meaning to give me these pictures, but he had forgotten. I acted like I didn't know what Leon was talking
about. I forget at times that Leon's ears have now become
his eyes. We talked mostly about Chloe and what they
used to do together, the games they played, hide and seek,
football. I asked him about football. Never really struck
me as a game kids normally play. Then, Leon reiterated
"football, *real* football," he said, where a person used a
foot and not a hand, not American football, soccer, I realized. He ranted about the interests of America and how
the arts had been neglected like this very place, how people only cared about playing video games and watching
porn, how one day we would resort back to cavemen—"a
bunch of savages," Leon told me—and, years from now,
how every single country will surpass us. I didn't know

what had gotten into him or whom Leon had been talking to. These ideas were clearly not his own. He wasn't his usual optimistic self—that tender man I had grown to greatly admire over these past few days—which made me wonder if it was Leon who was actually talking or *this cancer* inside him. Also, there was something off about him, I noticed. He was more aggravated, more discouraged. However, as much as the old Renny wanted to agree with Leon on *all* these topics, I wanted to stay optimistic despite my previous views on the matter. The fact: Leon could be right. *Could.* We are becoming a less educated nation, but we *don't* have to be a less educated nation. Now, we choose whether or not we want to expand our way of thinking. People may not be reading anymore. This isn't new information. We'd rather read blogs, than a book. If you show a kid a book, he'll probably ask you, "What is this thing?" or "Where do I press?" The more time I spent with Leon, the more these critical issues came to the forefront. On any other day, Leon would've told me that there is a *chance* for us, that playing a moderate amount of video games will enhance our way of thinking during critical situations, or that playing sports when we're young will teach us how to work or communicate effectively as a team. We are a country that doesn't like being told what to do. At times, we can be indecent. We can be crass. We can be feisty. But at the end of the day, put aside all the bullshit, I think most of us want to love or want to be loved. That is what being human is all about. So, I didn't know where all of this was coming from. Toward the end of our conversation, Leon pulled me closer and told me that Diego had gone too far with getting back his daughter. I told him about the pictures. Several of them appeared as if they had been taken from a distance, like a private eye had taken them. I asked him if he knew about this, about the pictures. He denied any involvement. There was only one person behind it all, I knew. Before I left, Leon showed me a secret room in the study. He told me to grab the hardback, Melville's *Moby Dick*, from the shelf. So, I did. I handed the book to Leon, but he didn't appear the least interested in the book. He said, "Press the red button." I did a double take on *Moby Dick*, and then, after I realized what he was talking about, I pressed the button on the shelf. One part of the shelf slid open and revealed another door. My stomach was in complete knots from the anticipation. We walked into the secret room. Having grown up during his prime, it was a dream come true—Freeze's own memorabilia room. Inside, there were the toys he collected, the same ones I used to play with as a kid, framed photos of Freeze working with law enforcement, posters from his modeling days—most of them still rolled up and kept in their packages—the many books on Freeze, several editions of *Gaze*, the newspaper articles from Arty, even trading cards on Freeze as well as the criminals he had put away behind bars. Lastly, I found the key to the city on the wall. Still in a state of awe, I asked Leon why he kept it all. He said, "To remind me who I used to be." He was ashamed for what he did to Chloe, and in that shame, he removed the two culprits from his life, which were the very eyes Daniella had given him, but, Leon went on to note, he was *never* ashamed of who he was. "I had to be Freeze because I had to learn how to be Leon Dorsey," he said. I stayed in the room for a little longer until Leon decided to get some shuteye. He ended the conversation by telling me to keep an eye open and then finished with goodnight.

After reading the journal, she closed the document and opened another one, *Journal Entry 10.20.2014*:

Woke up extra early to finish our final interview. I told Leon I overheard Diego talking on the telephone. He mentioned his daughter's name, *Anne*, not Chloe. Now, I am certain about Diego. But has he gone too far as Leon had said last night? Either way, let's ready the presses. I got a story to tell! I can't wait to get back to New York where I can finalize this baby and hand it over to Edie. Somehow, I need to find a way to email Edie the story in case anything happens to me. After all, this story is my baby and

I'll do anything and everything to protect it and make sure it gets the proper attention.

As soon as Anne finished reading the *last* journal entry, she minimized the document and opened the interview, *Interview #9.*

As she played the interview, she couldn't help but notice the date of the file. She stopped the recording and examined closer. The date was earlier in the week, in fact, from the eighteenth of October, not the twentieth as she suspected.

Anne pressed the play button and listened closely.

First, Interview #9 started out with Leon's distorted voice, saying something like *pay* and then *shush,* which Anne concluded, after listening to the recording several times, was the word *patience.*

Eventually, the distortion tapered off and the interview came back on.

Then, Renny's voice:

So, what did you want to be when you grew up?

(MR. HOPKINS *thinks carefully about his answer.*)

MR. HOPKINS: An astronaut.
RENNY: An astronaut?
MR. HOPKINS: I've always wanted to be an astronaut.
RENNY: *Why* astronaut?
MR. HOPKINS [WEAKLY]: I think every kid wanted to be an astronaut at the time. I was around the age of eight when we first landed on the moon. I remember watching it on television. It was my dream to do what those men did. I just wanted to grow up, be an astronaut, and not only go to the moon, but also explore the universe.

Strange, she wondered. There wasn't much shock and awe in the interview, at least none that Anne had gathered so far.

Anne kept listening, though, hoping that the interview would pick up speed.

RENNY: Did you play any sports?

MR. HOPKINS: I liked to play sports for fun. Diego always said I had an arm like DiMaggio. But sports really wasn't my thing.

RENNY: You were a stargazer.

(*A faint smile emerges onto* MR. HOPKINS' *slack face.*)

MR. HOPKINS: Every night, I would look up at the stars and wonder if there was a kid like me who was out there light years away from this place, all alone on the other side, looking up at space and wondering the same thing.

RENNY: So, you do believe there is life out there in the universe?

MR. HOPKINS: We can't be the only ones, Renny. I believe there is life outside earth, life *still* waiting to be discovered, *or* possibly life that is so far beyond our intelligence, Renny, that it doesn't want to be discovered.

RENNY: Why don't you think it wants to be discovered? If there are other life forms out there. . .

MR. HOPKINS: Any outsider can look at the history of mankind and see our pattern. We migrate, we settle, we conquer. It's been going on like this for centuries.

RENNY: Do you think it will ever change?

MR. HOPKINS: Should it?

RENNY: I'm asking you.

MR. HOPKINS [STERNLY]: No.

RENNY: Why?

MR. HOPKINS: Because the world needs *bad* guys as much as it needs good guys. We need them because they remind us of the virtues of the human spirit.

RENNY: Like Freeze, he needed his enemies as much as they needed him.

MR. HOPKINS: Precisely.

(MR. HOPKINS *readjusts in the wheelchair and does so with a grimace.*)

Back to childhood. When I was a young boy, the idea alone always intrigued me, the singular idea of *not knowing* what was out there. I used to always question my father about things such as the universe. Are we alone? And if not, is there life out there beyond the stars? That sort of thing.

RENNY: And was your father a religious man?

MR. HOPKINS: If he was, he never showed it. He was more of a man of science.

RENNY: But you never wanted to be like him. Is that right?

MR. HOPKINS: I *always* wanted to be an explorer like my father. Then, after a while—after hardly seeing him—I didn't want to be anything like him anymore.

RENNY: Did you lose interest?

MR. HOPKINS: I never *lost* interest. I just never wanted to be like him.

RENNY: Clearly, you weren't that way with your children.

MR. HOPKINS: No. We saw the world together, all four of us did.

RENNY: Did you ever fear for their safety?

MR. HOPKINS: No. *Never.* Dom was a baby. And Chloe, she loved to travel with us. We never told her about the Company. Traveling from country to country felt normal to her. Second nature.

RENNY: I'm sure that was rewarding and yet difficult at the same time, having your children travel with you?

MR. HOPKINS: More rewarding.

(He *smiles from ear to ear—the pain melting from his face.*)

The good thing about being young, and me having grown up around all of these artifacts, is that the mind can take you as far as you let it. When all four of us were traveling, it was as if I was a kid all over again. However, when you get older, you get stuck in these certain roles. It's like a switch gets flipped on inside you and your sole mission is to raise that child and to protect that child and no matter what, you will *never* let anything bad happen to that child.

RENNY: Your father, how did he handle you always questioning him? Did he ever get upset?

MR. HOPKINS: More annoyed, I suppose. If he asked me to do something, I would ask why. If he said because I said so, then I would ask why again until he gave me a reasonable answer.

RENNY: Like you mentioned earlier, you were hardheaded.

MR. HOPKINS: I was a little bit. It's good to be that way when you're young. It's good to be curious. My father and I never got along. You know this. But I loved him, as much as I didn't show it. And even though he was never around most of the time, I always thought about him, where he was, what he was doing, or wondering what present he would bring me when he came home.

RENNY: You mean like an artifact?

MR. HOPKINS: When I was around eleven, my father brought home a bracelet for me. He said it belonged to the Pharaohs.

RENNY: When I was eleven, I think I got a baseball glove.

MR. HOPKINS: I guess that's the difference between you and me, Ren—

The interview abruptly cut off.

In a frantic state, Anne searched for the rest of the interview. She went through every nook and cranny of the flash drive but couldn't find it. The more Anne thought about the interview, as well as the strange clicks and stops during the interviews, the more she wondered if there were parts of the interviews that weren't meant to be heard. The more Anne thought about it, about the *clicks*, the *clippings*, the *fuzzes*, the *distortion*, she realized that something just didn't seem right.

For about ten minutes, she ended up rooting through the entire flash drive, opening files she had already read and listened to. She finally came across the one folder that she had neglected the most, the *Miscellaneous* folder. She opened the folder; and as soon as she did, she remembered another folder called *Open*. Surely, it had to mean something.

A clue. . . something. . . anything!

She quickly opened the folder. There, a Quick-Time video called *Urgent* was revealed before her eyes. She read the date of modification: October 20, 2014 8:37 AM. She opened the video and then clicked on the fullscreen button on the bottom right corner of the player.

"*Renny*," Anne uttered as she witnessed Renny, *her* Renny, sitting in front of an old bookshelf. He was sweating bullets, Anne noticed, and his eyes were filled with both terror and panic. Occasionally, he was shooting glances to a person behind a camcorder, but to Anne, the person remained as dark and distant as a shadow. There was also a cut, Anne noticed, on the top of his head. The cut wasn't bleeding; how-ever, she could see a trail of blood next to his temple and around his left ear. "Hello, Anne," he said. His voice was trembling. Hands too. "My name is Renny Jacobson, and I'm a contributing editor for *Flashback* magazine. As you may already know, I was flown to Whisperfront, Maine, to conduct an inter-view with a man who went by the name, Marcus Hopkins. If you have been following along and listen-ing to all of the interviews on this flash drive, then you know that Mr. Hopkins is *not* who he says he is. His real name is Leon Dorsey, and he is your father, Anne. He is dying, and he needs your help." Another unsteady glance behind the camcorder. "I assure you the interviews that have taken place this past week are the confessions of a desperate man who is trying to reach out to his daughter. You, Anne, you must come before it's too late." Renny hung his head. He ran his trembling hand across his forehead and wiped away both the sweat and the dried blood. He pulled his eyes back to the camcorder before him. "I know we have never met before, but you are the only person who can save me right now."

"*Save you* from who?" Anne said to herself.

"If you have gotten this far, then maybe you're willing to go a little farther," Renny said unsteadily. "I can't tell you the precise location of where I am because I fear that the wrong people may come across this drive. Only you know where I am. If you have been reading the entries and listening to all of the interviews, then you know exactly who you are now." His voice grew louder, higher. "Please, Anne. My life is in danger. If you contact authorities, I will be killed. If you contact *Flashback*, I will be killed. If you contact anyone, you get the point. Right now," he swallowed a dry lump down his throat, and, while doing so, he shot another unsteady glance behind the camcorder, "right now, the only person you can trust is yourself. I hope this drive finds you well. Be careful. Watch your back. Don't trust anyone." As the shadowy man made a move toward the camcorder, he cried out, "*He's coming for yo—*"

The tripod fell, which caused the camcorder to shake violently.

Then, the video scrambled. The sound spiked and distorted, which caused Anne to fling the headphones from her ears. Strangely, though, the time on the video kept running. She turned down the volume and carefully placed the headphones back over her ears. She fast-forwarded until another video appeared in front of her. The video was taken from Renny's very first interview. On the screen, she saw this man (an older white man, *not* black) whom she had been listening to for the past couple of days. She pressed the PAUSE button and took a good look at the old man in the wheelchair. Anne couldn't recognize the older man; in fact, he appeared nothing like the man from her dreams.

Anne closed the player and opened the *Study* folder from Photos. She scrolled through the JPEGs and made sure she didn't miss any. The photos Renny had discovered in the study were taken from a distance, as Anne had determined the first time around. Some of them were taken when she was leaving work, eating lunch with Jamie outside a local diner, or having a drink with Michael. This whole time, she realized, *he* had been following Anne. But who? Then, why, Anne wondered, why would he try to *kill* me? Most importantly, why would he want to kill Renny?

She removed the headphones from her ears, ejected the USB flash drive from the CPU, and gathered the rest of her belongings.

On the way to the exit, Anne passed the periodical section.

After the thought came as sudden as a chill, she walked to the nearest computer and out of curiosity, typed the name LEON DORSEY into the search bar. There, she found many articles, most of them, as figured, based in the periodical section of the library. Anne jotted down MO - 123 on a slip of paper and walked back to the periodicals. There, she found the letters MO. She removed a couple of magazines from the shelf. The magazines were old and crinkly and sticky—from 1986 to 1989, Anne read. On one particular magazine, *The Lansford Lowdown*, there was a picture of Freeze on the front cover. She gazed over the front cover, Freeze's face, *her* father's face. It was him, she realized, the same tall man from my dreams, my memories.

Anne placed the magazines and newspaper articles back into their proper place.

And like that, she was out the door.

11:19 AM

THE first thing Anne did after she left the library was drive straight to the nearest pawnshop, a small hole in the wall called Lucky's Jewelry and Things, located in the lower bowels of Lansford.

As with the library, Anne was the first civilian of the day.

Lucky himself, Earl Lucky, but most simply knew him best as "Lucky," was flipping through the morning rag and working his way through his second cup of coffee that he recently brewed himself in the back of the store, even though he was still using the same dirty cup from the local convenient store, 24/7.

"Hello there, Missy," Lucky said as soon as Anne entered the pawnshop.

His lazy eyes flickered at Anne and then rested over the *Sports* section.

Anne strolled right up to Lucky and placed a handful of jewelry on the counter.

Somewhat startled, as well as taken back from Anne's directness, especially at such an early hour of the day, Lucky placed the newspaper aside, eyeballed the jewelry below, and said cautiously, "Okay." He rolled his tongue around the inner part of his lip. "Let's see what we got here." He carefully eyed the necklaces between his fingers. Most of his interest was on the gold watch, Harold's watch, the Rolex. He placed the watch underneath a large magnifying glass. "How much you looking to get for all of these?"

Anne thought briefly, mainly about how much the plane ticket was going to cost her and then whatever expenses she was going to have after the flight.

Then, she replied sharply, "Four hundred."

"Well, I can give you two for the watch," Lucky said after he cleared his throat. "These other pieces." Again, Lucky rolled his tongue underneath his bottom lip and kept it there while he thought to himself. "I'd say twenty a piece for the necklaces." He separated the necklaces from the bracelets. Next, he mentally counted each necklace and bracelet. "Ten for the bracelets. So, we're talking about three-forty altogether."

"I can do three-forty," Anne said and then reached around her backside and pulled out a pistol.

Lucky flinched and nearly spilled coffee over his shirt.

Anne asked, "How about a gun?"

"Whoa there. . . "

Lucky raised one hand in surrender.

Once Anne placed the pistol on the counter, Lucky leaned forward and grabbed the pistol. While doing so, he kept an eye on Anne, making sure she didn't pull out anything else that might scare the shit out of him, and then he turned on the safety. Lucky scanned the pistol in his hand, checked the chamber, and then the magazine inside.

"Nice weapon you got here," he said with a smirk. "What's a pretty girl like yourself doing with a fine weapon like this?"

"Don't let the looks fool you."

"Sure," Lucky stuttered. "Okay."

"How much for the gun?" Anne asked.

Again, her voice was sharp and direct.

"Sure," Lucky stuttered. "Let's see. . . a gun like this goes about five-six hundred dollars on the market. But I got to make a little profit. How about two hundred?"

Anne peered into the clerk's heavy eyes. Her eyes sharpened and then brightened like a sunray. In return, Lucky's eyes faded a little in both color and energy. His face fell into a lifeless manner.

"Three hundred," Anne said, her eyes never leaving the clerk's eyes.

"I can give you three hundred for it," Lucky drawled.

Anne reached out her hand.

"Then, it's a deal."

Lucky shook Anne's hand.

"Deal." He robotically opened the cash register and then robotically handed Anne six hundred and forty dollars, three hundred and forty for the jewelry and then three hundred for the pistol.

12:04 PM

MERROTTI'S cell phone suddenly rang!

The weary detective answered the phone before it rang a second time.

"Merrotti," he said.

"Devon," the sergeant said, "Got good news. Reddington Police found Cabrera."

"Is he dead?"

"Found him in a car with fake tags," he informed. "Strangled to death like the others."

The sergeant continued to inform the detective about the officer, his state, the stolen car; but the detective completely zoned him out. He hung up the phone and tossed it aside and stared down at the dried blood on his hands, Florence's blood. He finally turned on the faucet and washed the dark blood from his hands as quickly as he could with a bar of soap. He even grabbed a steel wool pad from beneath the sink and scrubbed away the blood from underneath his fingernails until the blood was gone. But the blood was *not* gone. It was *still* there, Merrotti sensed, in the cracks of his fingernails, in the places he could not reach with a steel wool pad.

Still dressed in the same clothes from last night, the ones covered in blood, Merrotti stepped into the cold shower and, as the water rained down upon him, he fell into the tub and wept. This time, there was no fighting back the tears. He let them run as freely as the water before him.

12:52 PM

AFTER Anne left Lucky's, she drove to Conway International Airport, which was only about fifteen miles away, but with midday traffic, it took her about forty to fifty minutes to get there. She arrived at the airport around twelve-thirty in the afternoon, but it took her about ten minutes to find a parking spot in the Terminal B parking lot. The inside of the airport was more crowded than she thought. *Friday*, Anne remembered. What better day to fly than on a Friday? The past two days had gone by so fast, with everything that had happened. She knew she couldn't drive there. She *could*, but the drive would take way too long. By then, who knows what would've happened to Renny? Would he be alive or dead? Did it matter? How about her father? Was he really dying or was it a front? Anne decided to wait in the back of the line like everyone else. While waiting in line, she could feel their beady white eyes pounding down on her. The thought alone of people staring at her caused her to sweat and turn pale. Then, that three o'clock feeling was upon her, even though it was only one o'clock in the afternoon. However, the feeling was different, more severe as if she knew exactly why the feeling was upon her and yet she couldn't control it. She reached for the anxiety pills in her purse but came up empty. A creeping suspicion came over Anne. Did I grab them from the bathroom before I left Jamie's house? She opened the purse and dug through all the crap inside. The pills were *not* there!

"Shit," she uttered as the coffee cake in her stomach started to make a climb from her stomach.

There was a moment where she thought about hurling on the person in front of her in line (a young businessman dressed in a suit that cost more than her monthly house payment). For the past ten minutes while the line was moving as slow as the DMV, the arrogant businessman had been checking out every single woman who appeared in his range of vision. On several instances, his eyes did pull-ups—checking out the derrière on one busty lady and then beaming down the cleavage on another. If there was anybody to hurl on, she thought, what better candidate to hurl on than Mr. Hungry Eyes himself. Anne never hurled on the jerk, even though she thought about doing it on more than one occasion. She kept the coffee cake inside. Same with the coffee. What better place to keep it? The only thing that kept Anne in line was the thought of Renny and how, if his life was really in danger as he had said in the video, she needed to get there and get there fast.

Anne finally arrived at the checkout counter.

The clerk greeted Anne with a closed, fraudulent smile.

"How may I help you?" the clerk asked.

For a second, Anne completely forgot where she was going.

Then, her destination came to her after the clerk repeated, "Ma'am?"

"One-way ticket to Bangor, Maine," Anne said and placed the duffel bag next to her feet.

1:11 PM

ONCE Merrotti was all cleaned up and dressed in a pair of new clothes that Florence had bought him last Christmas—a casual dress shirt with the sleeves rolled up to his forearms, black slacks, one size too small, and then suspenders with gold clips—he eyed the outfit in the standing mirror and gave a contemporary shrug of approval.

Next, he sat in his study and replayed the recent events in his head.

Cabrera was dead, the detective now knew, but he wasn't working alone.

Who was running this operation?

All fingers pointed toward Anne Roth's direction, Merrotti realized. Her foster parents, Harold and Molly Roth, were wealthy but squeaky clean. As far as Anne's upbringing, there was a gap in the timeline, mainly surrounding her birth and then her childhood. He thought more about these tattooed gunmen. Whoever these men were, they either wanted something from Anne or Anne *was* involved, in fact, neck-deep; and yet she didn't even realize it until it came knocking on her doorstep. Either way, something had to be done.

With this in mind, Merrotti reached down to the bottom drawer of the desk. The door opened, revealing the metallic-like visor, second-generation, next to a flask of bourbon. He pulled out the flask and gave it a once over before tossing the thing in the trash. Then, he directed his attention back to the visor. As with the flask, he pulled out the visor but never tossed it in the trash. Instead, he stared at the visor. Another event was brought to mind, only this was from a long time ago—over twenty something years, in fact. He remembered the day as if it was yesterday, in the sewers, the scumbag creeping up behind Freeze. He pulled the trigger, first ever in his early career. The scumbag let out a sudden gasp and fell to his knees. There, the young cop watched the life exit from his body. Freeze spun around and said, "Thanks, kid." Merrotti didn't even know what to say. Like many residents of Lansford, he too was a supporter of Freeze; and like most, if not all supporters, he too was left star-struck from the presence of the great Freeze. Later that day, Freeze bumped into Merrotti at the precinct and shook his hand. To Merrotti, it was the greatest gesture of his life, shaking Freeze's hand. The next thing that came out of Freeze's mouth was something Merrotti would never forget. "I owe you one," he said, and then, "one day I will repay you." Merrotti pulled his thoughts away from the past memory and continued to stare at the visor.

He said to himself, "Where are you when I need you the most, old friend?"

Merrotti placed the visor back into the drawer.

Next, he decided to empty every flask, gallon, and bottle of alcohol from every nook and cranny in the house. Merrotti ended up filling two garbage bags worth of alcohol.

Once he was finished and both garbage bags were dumped on the side of the road, Merrotti drove back to the precinct.

2:03 PM

SINCE Anne's flight was three hours away from departing, she made a pit stop at a bar called Chasers. She did her best to try to escape the televisions, but they were everywhere. Before the renovation in 2011, the airport was somewhat quiet and tolerable. Now, there were televisions around every corner, outside newsstands, multiple flat screens inside restaurants. At the bar she ordered a gin and tonic. The bartender asked her if she wanted to keep her tab open. Anne declined and used the money she had leftover from the plane ticket to pay the bartender—nine dollars for the drink and the six dollars for a tip. She took her drink and sat down next to the window where there were no televisions, only the murmurings of an exuberant sport's commentator from a distance and a large glass pane separating her from the airplanes parking or idling outside the terminals. Halfway through the gin and tonic, her stomach began to unknot a bit. A waiter stopped at her table, placed a two-page menu—food on the front and cocktails on the back—in front of Anne, and asked her if she wanted anything to eat. Anne skimmed through both sides of the menu while the waiter stood patiently with both hands crossed over his waist. The waiter didn't mind waiting since there were only two people in the restaurant: Anne and a heavyset man sipping from a beer and watching highlights from Spo(r)tLights on one of the many televisions. Anne ordered a Western omelet with grits and then another gin and tonic, since the first one was so delicious and soothing to her stomach. It didn't take long for her food and drink to arrive, no longer than five minutes. She ate quickly. She didn't pay attention to the television or the man at the bar or the waiter prepping the other tables.

Once she ate as much as her stomach would let her, she pulled out from her duffel bag a magazine that she bought at the newsstand. The magazine was *Flashback*, the September issue. On the cover was a close up of a badly scared face man who appeared as if he suffered from severe acne at a young age. The man was dressed in an orange jump suit. His name was Simone Drake, but most knew him as the "Ballantyne Butcher." The contributing editor of the article was Paul Clifton, who, besides Renny Jacobson, was another writer she followed. In 2008, Drake was charged with first-degree murder and sentenced to life in prison. In the span of three years, he killed over thirty-eight people, all males ranging in age from twenty-five to thirty. In those three years, young men were afraid to leave their homes. And if they managed to leave their homes, the butcher was always on their minds. The butcher got his name from exactly that: he worked at a local meat house and served human meat to the wealthy high society of Ballantyne. Hence the name, Ballantyne Butcher. At the time, it was a huge deal. The media was all over the small town of Ballantyne, Ohio, like black on licorice. Now, as with most happenings in the media sphere, one week the Butcher was hot and then the next, the Butcher was not. She remembered what Renny had talked about in the interview, calling America ADD. Anne thought that perhaps this was one of those cases where it was best forgotten. As with the menu, Anne skimmed through the article.

4:58 PM

BY the time five o'clock rolled around, Anne's plane was starting to board.

Anne shouldered her way into the plane, located her seat, stowed her luggage in the overhead bin, and sat down in her seat, which happened to be a window seat—Anne's favorite seat on a plane. Then, as always, the nerves kicked in once more. The gin and tonic helped calm the nerves. Nonetheless, the nerves were still there, lingering around like a cold during winter season.

One other passenger was already seated in her row. The passenger was an older man with gray hair. The man didn't say much to Anne, only the common greetings: "Hello" and then "How you doing?"

As Anne took her seat, she watched a group of stragglers wander into the airplane. The entire time, she hoped that none of them had the seat next to her. The last thing Anne wanted right now was to create small talk with a stranger. She could imagine the conversation. The passenger: "Where you headed?" Then, Anne: "Whisperfront, Maine." Passenger: "Business or pleasure?" Anne: "Business," she would say. Passenger: "So, what kind of business?" Anne: "The rescue business." The passenger would probably laugh or try to act as if he or she was interested in the conversation. From there, Anne could only see the conversation going south. It wasn't that Anne didn't mind small talk; in fact, sitting next to a stranger in complete silence would be more uncomfortable than not breaking the ice early in the encounter as she had done with the old man seated in the aisle seat. If the old man decided to spark up a conversation with her, then it wouldn't seem strained, as if the old man had being mapping out what to say during the flight. The conversation would come natural, not forced. Just Anne's luck. One of stragglers squeezed her way through the row and then sat down next to Anne. She was in her mid-teens. At first, Anne thought she was flying all by herself, which she thought was pretty brave for a girl her age. Then, she saw an anxious mom sitting two rows ahead making frequent glances to the young girl seated next to Anne. The girl didn't even acknowledge Anne; in fact, she had a pair of white ear buds in her ears and was staring down at a reality TV show playing on the smartphone in her hands. At least she didn't have to worry about creating small talk with the girl; in fact, Anne didn't even have to worry about anything. It would be as if the girl didn't exist at all, as if she was trapped in her own little world and the people around her were nothing but apparitions or mere obstacles to walk around.

And Anne didn't mind.

Didn't mind one bit.

5:06 PM

OUTSIDE Terminal E, Diego was standing next to the payphone. He picked up the phone and made a call.

His assistant, Jasmine, answered the phone.

"Jasmine," he said, "everything is going according to plan."

"Where is she?"

"She's on the way," Diego said. "Call Richter and tell him to prepare the jet."

"Yes, sir," Jasmine said and hung up the phone.

6:13 PM

AFTER Anne's trail went cold, Merrotti resorted to knocking on doors. Forget about relying on technology, cameras, or credit card charges. They were nice resources, especially for an old dog looking for a face. In today's world, Merrotti realized, every single person left a trail either on the Internet or at the grocery store, whatever. If it wasn't through a credit card, then it was always through something: fingerprints, facial recognition through surveillance videos, traffic cameras, or cell phones. Every now and then, an old dog like Devon Merrotti liked to do things the old fashioned way.

With Florence's death put behind him, Merrotti knocked on every door in and around Anne's neighborhood, places she frequented like that one café on the corner of Park Avenue called Beret, and asked the locals if they had seen Anne. Lastly, after two hours of questioning, he stopped at Mr. Reyes's house directly across from Anne's house. The house was registered to a one Martín Reyes, but he wasn't home on the day of the breaking and entering last Wednesday morning. Mr. Reyes didn't have any sons or daughters. He wasn't married either. Merrotti went through his notes and read them carefully before knocking on the door. There was a woman living there at the house with Mr. Reyes, Merrotti read, *his girlfriend*. Her name was María, Spanish for Mary. Other than that, there wasn't any other information on the woman.

After three attempts at knocking, there was still no answer. There was one light on inside, Merrotti noticed, but nobody appeared to be home.

As the detective turned away from the door and decided to walk back to his car, he caught a movement in the corner of his eye. He suddenly shot his eyes toward the inside of the house and saw a silhouette of a woman inching behind a wall.

Merrotti walked back to the front door.

Instead of knocking, he rang the doorbell, not just once, but twice.

A third time. . .

A *click* from behind the door!

The door slowly cracked open, but the woman inside kept the chain on the door.

"I'm Detective Merrotti with the Lansford Police Department," Merrotti said as he displayed his badge to the woman through the crack. "May I have a word with Mr. Reyes?"

The woman shook her head *no*.

"Is Mr. Reyes home?"

Again, the woman shook her head.

"You must be Mary," Merrotti said. "*Correcto*."

The woman hesitantly bobbed her head.

Merrotti asked nicely, "If you would, ma'am, can you please open the door?"

María was slow to open the door, now in its entirety. She remained defensive, half of her stubby body hidden behind the door.

"Sorry to disturb you, ma'am," Merrotti said as he placed the badge on his belt. "I've been in the area asking your neighbors about a young lady who is wanted for questioning. Her name is Anne Roth, your neighbor." He reached in his pocket, which caused María to flinch. "I," Merrotti paused and keenly watched the woman, "I have a picture here of what she looks like." He carefully pulled out the picture, which was taken from Anne's MyCircle page, and showed it to the jittery woman. Merrotti studied the strange woman's fidgety movements: the tremor in her hand and lips, the pulse in her unsteady eyes, the inflated nostrils, and then the bead of sweat crawling down the side of her face. At first, he really didn't think anything of her unsettled state, at least not until she raised her hand to wipe the bead of sweat from her brow. Being a cop who—at times—made people nervous, especially people who were doing something they weren't supposed to be doing, even if it was as banal as not tipping the pizza guy or, like Mr. Reyes's girlfriend, being extremely defensive, Merrotti received this sort of behavior a lot. In all odds, the detective wondered, she was illegal or she recently bought a pizza and forgot to tip the deliveryman. In a perfect world, Merrotti would've been as wrong as the next guy. María finally shook her head *no*. Merrotti thanked her for her cooperation. At that moment, she wiped her forehead clean and revealed the tattoo on her wrist. Merrotti kept his composure, kept a still of the tattoo in his mind's eye, said goodnight to Mr. Reyes's girlfriend, and then proceeded to his car parked on the side of the road. Not once did he fully turn around to Mr. Reyes's house, at least not until he arrived at his car and noticed Mr. Reyes's girlfriend peeking through the curtains. He suddenly put the two clues together: one, the tattoo on her wrist, which happened to be the same one on the other perps; and then, two, this María woman peeking through a window. He turned around and looked toward Anne's house and then turned back around to the woman, who had a perfect line of sight on Anne's house.

A sudden gust of wind blew through Merrotti's hair.

"It was you," he whispered, as a cool chill moved underneath the gooseflesh of his skin. "This whole time, you've been watching her. . . "

Without drawing too much suspicion, Merrotti glanced back at Mr. Reyes's house where his girlfriend had already closed the curtain. The detective did nothing out of the ordinary. He casually got back in his car and drove off.

6:26 PM

ANNE'S neighbor, María, picked up the telephone and dialed a number.

6:27 PM

AS Diego waited inside the parked vehicle on the tarmac outside Kelley Pines, his phone rang. He looked down at the number, which read PRIVATE, and then answered the phone before it could ring a second time.

"Yes," he answered.

"*La policía*," María said on the other end.

"What about them?"

María said in perfect English, "They know."

"Did they come in?"

"No."

Diego sighed loudly.

"Detective Merrotti," he said mistakenly.

"*Sí.*"

"Follow the plan," Diego said casually and hung up the phone. Then, he said to himself, "Never trust a cop who has nothing to lose."

Before Diego exited the car and entered the private jet, he reached inside the back of the phone, removed the battery, and tossed it onto the tarmac.

7:21 PM

MERROTTI pulled the car next to the curb and parked in front of Angry Ale Saloon, a local bar not too far from the precinct. The bar appeared fairly crowded, which was not out of the ordinary for a Friday night. He couldn't help but look up at the glowing red sign on the façade of the building. As the red filled his eyes, he thought about the vow he made to himself. It wasn't going to be one drink, the detective knew, especially with the bar being crowded and all. There would be other temptations: a local patron wanting to buy a round for the *Great* Detective Devon Merrotti; a young puma being dared into hooking up with the old dog, mainly for bragging rights. The list went on and on, but one thing was straight: one drink would lead to others, as they always did. Then, Merrotti thought about Pamela, his sweet and sassy Pamela. What a woman! As much as Merrotti couldn't stand her at times, he missed the hell out of her. The thought alone of his partner being killed erased all thoughts about having a drink. He slammed the gear in drive and drove back to Anne's neighborhood.

7:38 PM

MERROTTI parked close enough to see Mr. Reyes's house. The lights were off, which made him wonder if Mr. Reyes's girlfriend, María, had already skipped town or if she had called it a night.

10:12 PM

OVER two hours had passed and still nothing.

Merrotti finally decided enough was enough. It would take hours, possibly even days, for him to get a search warrant from the judge.

The detective stepped out of his car and then checked the round in his chamber before he walked an entire lap around Mr. Reyes's house. During the walk, he looked inside every single window. Not once did he see a person inside, no María, no Martín Reyes; in fact, he didn't even see a single piece of furniture. No couch. No bed. The house was completely gutted!

With this in mind, Merrotti walked to the front door and pulled out a bobby pin from his pocket.

As he went to pick the lock on the door, he realized there was no need.

The front door was already unlocked, which caused Merrotti to draw the gun from his holster.

With extreme caution, Merrotti entered the dark house. All five senses now enhanced: sight, smell, taste, hearing, and touch. The air, Merrotti noticed as he sniffed the foyer and rolled his tongue over the bottom part of his lip, reeked of bad body odor. His eyes were peeled open. Eventually, both of them adjusted to the darkness. But he couldn't see a damn thing. His ears were opened too. But he couldn't hear a damn thing as well, only a faint ringing in his ears from old age. First, he checked the same front window that Mr. Reyes's girlfriend, María, had been looking through. He peeled back the curtain. Just as he thought: *perfect line of sight*. The detective directed his attention to the carpet below and found three dents from where a possible tripod had been stationed.

Next, he checked every room in the house, including the kitchen where he found a couple of candy wrappers on the granite countertop.

Lastly, he checked the guest bedroom.

At that moment, those cop instincts came to him! His heart nearly skipped a beat, not only from the dark silhouette standing in the middle of the room, but also from the tiny red flash in his eyes.

"*Freeze*," Merrotti hissed as he aimed the pistol on the dark silhouette. "Make one move and I'll put one between your eyes."

Merrotti blinked his eyes several times, but the red line, as narrow as a strand of hair, ran across his entire vision.

As with the faint ring in his ears, he couldn't help but wonder if his eyes were now failing him as well—the red, he wondered, could've been from the bar. Nonetheless, in these tense moments, his thoughts ran in milliseconds and each second counted.

Before he could think more about the red light, he blindly reached for the light switch on the side of the wall.

He finally found the switch and turned it on. The red light vanished and revealed not a person, but a sculpture shaped like a person.

The sculpture was alien-like, skeletal, and made from tarnished metal—very similar to the one from Jamie's house, Merrotti realized, that strange thing in the garage.

Both of its arms were held in front of its lanky body as if the sculpture was handing the detective a gift.

There was nothing inside the sculpture's palms.

He carefully stepped into the guest room.

Halfway into the room, Merrotti realized there was something inside the sculpture's palms: a tiny black box about the size of a jewelry box.

"What the fuck is this shit. . . " the detective uttered to himself.

Merrotti stepped even closer to the sculpture. At the five-foot mark, his foot triggered a bulb to suddenly light up the inside of the black box!

The detective froze in his tracks.

All the blood escaped from his face, now leaving it pale and ghostly.

He lowered the pistol to his side—the pistol now trembling in his hand. He slowly turned his head toward his right at the open closet where a mound of

C4 explosives rested. He didn't exactly know how much C4 was there, as it nearly filled half of the closet, but surely enough to level an entire fucking house.

Next to the C4 were these wires, all running into the plastic explosives, as well as a control box with a red beam running horizontally across the room, the very same beam Merrotti had just tripped. . .

CHAPTER 6

THE flight altogether lasted a little over five hours, approximately four hours in the air and then the rest of the time on the tarmac—twenty minutes waiting for the plane to finally take off and forty minutes waiting to deplane. The stewardess only made two rounds during the flight, once to hand out water and beverages and another time to hand out small bags of trail mix.

After Anne exited the airport, she jumped in front of a man approaching a taxi and slammed the door in his face.

As the taxi drove off, Anne didn't feel a hint of remorse for stealing the man's ride. She felt *nothing*. The taxi dropped her off at the rental car station where she rented a green Mercury Sable without insurance—the cost alone to insure the car would've left her penniless, but money was the last thing on Anne's mind right now. She was down to thirty-seven bucks after she rented the car. Just enough to get by until she reached her destination.

When Anne arrived in Whisperfront, it was past midnight and she could hardly keep her eyes open. The area was unfamiliar; however, some areas she remembered from her childhood. She recognized a couple of family-owned restaurants that she used to eat at when she was younger. Everything else had changed. There were more Holiday Inns, more Best Westerns, and tons of Sky Brew coffee shops on every corner, Anne saw. She ended up stopping at a local convenient store for a cup of coffee. The last thing Anne wanted to do was draw any suspicion, but she didn't know how much longer she could drive like this throughout the night. The words were right there on the tip of her tongue, ready to leap into the clerk's ears. Anne gathered her change; and just as she was about to ask the clerk, a burly man dressed in a camo suit swung open the door and made quite a ruckus while doing so. The customer waited by Anne as she placed the rest of her change inside her pocket. As she made her way from the checkout counter, the man behind her hawked up a loogie from his throat without even covering his mouth—part of the phlegm projected onto Anne's shoulder. What made matters worse was that the man didn't even apologize or, *worse*, didn't even acknowledge what he had done. Anne's eyes trailed down below the counter. There was a shelf of batteries, air fresheners, candy bars, etc. In the midst of these knickknacks, there was a USB flash drive. She pulled out the flash drive from her pocket and compared the two. They were identical, Anne realized. She quickly grabbed the USB flash drive from the hook and placed it on the counter before the burly man behind her could pay for his gas.

"I would like to buy this too," she said suddenly as the man behind her was making his way toward the counter.

He did this thing where he took a step back, shifted his weight to one side of his body, sighed, and then, most importantly, smacked his gums.

Anne never picked up on the other things the man did, except the smacking of his gums. *Oh*, she heard that. She most definitely heard that. She paid for the USB flash drive; and as she was collecting her money, she shot a glance at the man, who was now staring at her ass. Once he got caught, his eyes shot up at Anne's eyes. His lecherous stare turned into an ugly glare. However, the man never said one word to Anne, even though the words were right there on the tip of his tongue.

12:23 AM

As Anne waited next to an unmanned pump, she placed the cup of coffee on the top of the rental car, removed the USB flash drive, discarded the rest of the package—the cardboard and plastic and whatnot—threw it into the nearest trashcan, and then slipped the brand new flash drive into her right pocket, whereas the other flash drive, the one with Leon's story, stayed in her left pocket.

Meanwhile, another *ring* of a bell!

The same burly man from before was exiting the convenient store.

On the way to his peacock blue truck, which was parked in front of the gas pump adjacent to Anne, he mumbled the words *stupid bitch* under his breath. Again, as before, he was making quite a ruckus everywhere he roamed: coughing and spitting, his boots dragging against the damp asphalt below. Then, as he approached the truck, he started to blatantly pack his smokes against his palm. He stopped at his truck, and like before, shot another glare at Anne. He shook his head in disgust and then, as before, hawked up another loogie. He spat the loogie in Anne's vicinity, but it never really came close to hitting her. After that, he removed the filler cap and inserted the nozzle into the tank and began to fill up the truck with regular gasoline. If the situation couldn't get any worse, the reckless bastard lit up a smoke right there next to the pump.

As Anne made her way back to the rental car, she peeked over her shoulder and caught the man littering the film, as well as the aluminum paper from the cigarette pack.

Anne paused and redirected her body toward the burly man.

"Sir," she said, "you dropped something."

"Aw lemme guess," he said bluntly with the lit cigarette dangling from one side of his mouth. "You're one of them leftwing, liberal, think-she-knows-it-all yahoos who thinks they can make a fuckin' difference, who thinks they can tell me what to do, who thinks their shit smells sweeter than mine!" He removed the cigarette and let out a noisy exhale from his mouth. "Believes in global warmin' and that kind of baloney." He took a step closer to Anne, both of his shoulders reared back in offense. "Aw why don't you do yourself ah favor and mind your own fuckin' business. . . "

Anne boldly stepped closer to the burly man.

"I'm going to ask you nicely," she said calmly. "Please pick up your trash and put it where it belongs."

"Hey," he said, grabbing his crotch, "bite me, lady."

The burly man got back into his truck while the gas was still pumping into the tank. He left the door cracked open, hung out his foot, and again, said those same two words under his breath, the words *stupid bitch* while taking a drag from the cigarette.

Anne stormed over to trashcan, grabbed the squeegee from the cleaning station, and strolled toward the truck.

She broke off the wooden handle from the squeegee against her knee and tossed the remains in the back of his truck.

"Hey," Anne called out, "bite this, asshole!"

The burly man lazily turned his shoulder.

Then, once he saw what was coming directly his way, his eyes suddenly swelled with fear.

Next thing he knew a wooden handle was flying his way, not just once, but twice! Hell! Three times to prove her point!

The cigarette smashed against his face—the tip exploding into a cloud of flaming ash—and then leaped from his gaping mouth onto the passenger seat where it eventually burned a hole right through the upholstery.

Anne ended up breaking his snout, in fact, splitting the greasy, pimple-covered thing in two pieces, and then breaking his teeth, mainly the front four, including his incisors, which had trickled from his mouth, down his chin, and into his overalls. Blood gushed like a perforated hose from his nose. He tried to catch as much blood as possible, but the slippery thing kept squirting out blood as if he had an endless supply of it.

As she did with the other remains, Anne tossed the bloody wooden handle in the back of the man's truck, got into her car, and drove off. She drove about three feet before she realized the coffee cup was still on the roof of the car. She came to a gentle stop, retrieved the cup, and then drove off.

12:43 AM

On the way out of the parking lot, Anne spotted a distant lighthouse, which was settled over a rocky cliff. *The lighthouse,* Anne remembered. Then... *running* through the red dusk and well into the dark night. The lighthouse ... it was there—guiding me away from him and *toward the main street.* She remembered he was right on her tail. And it was getting darker outside. Then, she spotted that beacon of light flickering through the tree branches. She followed the light until she reached the main roads. By then, he had given up on her. Even the smell in the air was that *same* smell, Anne remembered, the smell of car fumes and the sea. Then, she reached the open sea; and from there, she traveled down the jagged East Coast and along the Gulf of Mexico until one clear night two strange lights forced her into years of darkness. In time, Anne crawled from that very same darkness and found herself right here, right now, in Whisperfront, Maine, as a woman with purpose.

Anne finished her cup of coffee and drove to the black and white checkered lighthouse. She got out of the car, the ocean breeze blowing all around her. She stood in front of that ominous lighthouse and looked north. Not too far from the lighthouse, there was an old pier. Anne remembered sitting at the very edge of that same pier and crumbling the leftover breading from fried mushrooms into the gaping mouths of sturgeon below (if it wasn't the breading from mushrooms, then it was other appetizers like rolls or lump crabmeat from a crab cake or anything that she could stuff into a napkin). If there was any kind of escape as a young girl, then this was about as good as it got— feeding fish. Anne remembered he would be standing not too far from her, keeping one eye on her, making sure she didn't do anything juvenile like fall in or, even worse, jump in; but to young Anne, she knew nothing more about this man who never smiled, other than he being her chaperone. She moved her eyes south, to that same dark road, and then west, to the dark woods. There, in her long study, she found yet another light glimmering from a distance.

1:08 AM

"WHAT seems to be the trouble, Floyd?" Deputy Wallace asked the clerk.

Floyd, the clerk, who was standing outside the convenient store, pointed at the burly man with the bloody towel pressed against his face.

"Ask Bernard here."

The deputy retorted, "I'm asking you, Floyd. What did you see?"

The burly man, Bernard, blurted out, "That bitch cold-clocked me outta nowhere! Broke my fuckin' nose!"

"All right," Deputy Wallace said loudly. "One at a time." He turned to Floyd. "Is this true?"

"I only caught the end of it," Floyd said. "They were going at it for a minute. I believe Bernard said something to the woman. She didn't like it one bit, clearly. I saw her grab the squeegee. Next thing I know, she was hitting Bernard in the face with it. Then, she drove off."

"Did you get a license plate number?" the deputy asked.

"Nope," he said. "But she wasn't from 'round here."

"How do you know?"

"First time I've ever seen her face."

The deputy asked, "And what did she pay for? Gas? Food?"

Floyd thought for a second.

"Ah," he drawled, "coffee and then," he thought again, "then a thumb drive."

"Thumb drive?"

"You know," he said, "like a USB thingy for the computers."

"If you don't find that bitch, then I will," Bernard suddenly cried out over the deputy's shoulder. "You got that, Deputy."

"Easy, Bernard," Deputy Wallace said patiently and then pointed at Bernard's nose. "Let me do my job. In the meantime, you better get that looked at it. *You* got that?"

Bernard didn't respond.

"Bernard," the deputy said as he sharpened his eyes, "either go get that looked at or go home. Understood?"

After a long stare-off, Bernard shook his head and stormed back to his truck.

The deputy directed his attention back to Floyd.

"So," he said, "you got a surveillance tape I can look at."

Floyd motioned to the inside of the store.

"Right this way, Deputy. . . "

1:29 AM

ANNE made a right on Foxhole Lane and stayed on Foxhole until she finally reached King's Drive. She stopped at King's Drive and gazed down the desolate road. Instead of turning on King's Drive, she decided to stay on Foxhole until she reached a dead end. The area didn't look familiar. There were a couple of houses on the street, but most, if not all of them, were ranch style houses. No mansions as described on the USB flash drive. She decided to drive back to King's Drive. Again, the area didn't look familiar. The woods to each side of her looked like any other woods. Plus, it was still dark outside. She had roughly five more hours before daylight. She kept driving, though, searching for a distant memory. . . anything! She drove up a winding road. One thing that came to mind was a hill. She remembered running down a hill and tripping several times during her escape. The idea alone gave her a sense of reassurance, as if she was on the right track. *Any second now*, Anne kept repeating to herself. Strangely enough, she stopped trying to recreate the images of her past and focused on Renny's words. He talked about a road in his journal entry. He described the road as a snake's tail with *as many potholes as a Detroit expressway, bending each way as he and Diego ascended to their inevitable doom* or something like that. The drive became bumpier, rougher. Many roads had potholes. The average road was known to have potholes, Anne concluded. But to have lots of potholes, she realized, enough to mention them in a journal was substantially odd. There were many potholes in the road, enough for Anne to think: a *lot of freaking potholes*. The realization that she was on the right track now was clear to her. The thought alone sent a rumble through her stomach. The coffee that she downed was starting to swim laps inside her body. Her throat tightened ever so slightly as if a hand had a firm grip around her neck. She carefully breathed in through her nose and out through her mouth and thought about something different other than hurling over the steering wheel. Of course, she thought about running. She didn't know where she was going or what she was going to do when she got there, wherever *there* might be. She just ran through a world of blackness with an occasional obstacle here and there, and then the nausea tapered off.

Ten minutes into the drive, she passed at least a dozen mailboxes on the side of the road. She stopped at each mailbox and looked up the dark driveways. The houses were invisible from the street. She didn't know if she had time to check out each house. Nothing came to her, no memories. Renny described the house as a mansion with a fountain in front. *Apollo*, she remembered. Anne kept driving on King's Drive. Each mailbox she passed was getting farther and farther apart. More money, Anne thought. More land. More money and more land meant bigger houses— *mansions*, she assumed. She stayed on King's Drive until she reached another dead end.

Within the half-mile stretch, she passed three mailboxes and none of them brought any memories to her. She decided to park the car on the side of the road. She had a good feeling about the area, but she had no idea where to start. So, she started with the first mailbox, the last one on the left. She cautiously strolled up the dark driveway. Halfway up, she spotted the house. The house was no mansion by any means. However, there was an unpaved road that stretched behind the house, which Anne thought was strange. She didn't recall Renny mentioning anything about a house or a street that stretched behind a house. So, she nonchalantly walked back to the car.

On the way back, she heard a noise growing louder above her. The noise turned rhythmic, throaty. She peered up at the dark sky. The noise grew louder now, nearly deafening! Then, Anne saw it, a tiny yellow light beaming over the treetops. The first thing Anne thought of was the police. Then, her worse fears turned to the hired guns. The first two Anne remembered: two amateur gangsters with in-

credibly bad aim. The next two: two cops with incredibly good aim. Then, the next: two don't-fuck-
with types who meant business.

The helicopter flew directly past the house and
started to make a descent not too far behind. Anne
rushed back to her car and followed the helicopter.

With the headlights still cut off despite the night
darkness, she drove up the driveway and then cut
across a patch of grass before making her way down a
bumpy gravel road, which cut through the woods.
The bright spotlight glimmering above the trees, as
well as the pale moonlight, cast enough light below
which enabled Anne to stay on the road and not wind
up in a ditch. She rode along the road for about a
quarter of a mile until she finally reached a paved
road, which was veiled with maple trees on each side.
In spite of the night darkness, the road was the exact
same one from the photographs on the USB flash
drive. That, Anne remembered vaguely. The road
revealed a silhouette of a mansion. Most of the lights
were turned off. She parked the car in front of a cast
iron gate, which, like the road, was identical to the
photograph she saw from the flash drive. She quickly
got out of the car and tracked down the helicopter,
now starting its final descent in an open field. Anne
tried to make out the person in the helicopter, but it
was too dark and too far away.

As soon as the helicopter touched down, a man
dressed in black stepped out. He gave a half-ass sa-
lute to the pilot and then stormed toward the mansion
as the helicopter ascended and flew away into the cool
night sky. Another memory suddenly came to Anne.
Although the mansion was much smaller than she
imagined from the time she was a young girl, the
mansion was exactly the way she remembered: that
statue of Apollo in the front, same one from the flash

drive; the courtyard with glass walls; and then that open field. She remembered playing in that same field with her little brother and her father. The three of them would always play the game, *Tag! You're it!* Her father would always tag her. The thought alone of them playing tag played in slow motion in her head: her chasing her father and then him trying to avoid being tagged. Anne moved her eyes to the woods where she spent most of her time after her little brother's death. The only company she had were the animals around her and the winds behind her.

3:08 AM

A rickety wooden door opened from above the stairs and cast a narrow light across Renny's covered face. The door was the same one which had been haunting Renny for these past few days. He didn't exactly know when that rickety door opened or closed and when *or* if it opened, what creatures were let inside. Many times he wondered about the darkness, how long he could survive trapped in the darkness. The darkness was a whole new creature, the slyest one of them all, with an innate talent for casting out its most wicked friends.

The door's squeak pierced through the hollows of the basement and ripped Renny from his sleep.

Shaking from the constant state of paranoia, Renny uncurled himself from his fetal position and looked up at the dim light, but could barely make out a presence from the bag over his head.

Carrying a paper plate with a ham and cheese sandwich that Jasmine had whipped together in the kitchen, Diego revealed himself in the pale hallway light. He tediously walked down each aged stair until he arrived at the bottom where Renny anticipated the shadowy man's arrival.

In defense, Renny held his bound wrists—both fists tightened—in front of him. He couldn't move his hands at least three feet in either direction, for both of them were bound by heavy shackles wielded from iron—lost artifacts from the late eighteenth century, as Diego had earlier explained—which were chained around a metal post in the middle of the basement.

Diego shuffled closer to Renny, causing him to flinch.

Frightened, Renny muttered through the white bag over his head, "Who's there?"

"It's only me, Mr. Jacobson," Diego said casually.

He removed the bag from Renny's head.

Renny's hazy eyes rapidly flickered around the room until they settled on Diego.

"Why are you doing this to me?" Renny cried as his eyes adjusted to the darkness.

"It's almost over, Mr. Jacobson," Diego said, his glossy eyes like marbles glistening in the faint hallway light. "Promise."

"Soon, they'll come looking for me," Renny said feverishly.

Diego kneeled down and slid the plate closer to Renny.

"Eat," he said sternly.

Renny flinched once more.

After a moment of silence, he carefully ran his bloody hands along the coarse floor and fingered the cold sandwich. He grabbed one half of the sandwich and squeezed it in his hand.

Renny shouted, "Go fuck yourself!"

Then, he flung the balled up sandwich at Diego.

At the very last second, Diego tilted his head to the left and avoided being hit by the sandwich.

"Behave," he said as Renny, in return, hung his head and then wept, quietly at first.

"Why are you doing this?" he whined.

Diego towered over a shrunken Renny.

Then, Renny begged with his head down, "Just let me go. *Pleeeeeease.* I promise. I won't tell anybody."

"Patience, Mr. Jacobson," Diego said from above. "At the rate you're going, you'll be dead by the time they find you. That is if they do *find* you."

"*They'll find* me," Renny said, his voice trailing off. "They have to. . . "

"You?" Diego said amusingly as he kneeled back down to Renny's level. "I doubt it. Tell me, Mr. Jacobson. Why would they want to find a nobody like you?"

Renny looked into Diego eyes and saw something ugly riddled inside them.

"Wha. . . wh. . . what about Leon's story. . . " he said hesitantly as he tried to catch his breath, ". . . you owe him that much. . . "

"Exactly how many times do I have to tell you, Mr. Jacobson?" Diego said sharply. "There is *no* story. There *never* was."

Renny blurted out, "What about Anne?"

Diego inched closer, his voice now raised, "*What* about her?"

"She knows about this place. . . Mr. Hopkins. . . and the Company. . . "

"Yes," Diego said. "I believe she does. But why would a confused girl like Anne share her father's sad story with the world?"

Renny didn't answer Diego's question.

"For money?" Diego said, louder now. "Huh? For fame?" He furrowed his brows. "Please, Mr. Jacobson. Anne is just an ordinary girl who doesn't know who she is. If bringing her here makes the old man happy before he dies, then so be it. He'll be dead within weeks." He glanced around the basement. "And all of this," he showed Renny, "will be mine."

"What do you want?"

"The thing about cancer, Mr. Jacobson," he said curiously, "once it sinks its teeth in you and grabs hold, there's no releasing it."

"I thought you were his family. . . "

"Family?" Diego shook his head while slapping his tongue against the roof of his mouth. "No. He's *not* my family. He *never* was. My real family died a long time ago."

"I. . . I don't understand. . . how could you. . . "

"You see, Mr. Jacobson, in my country, we call it *estafador*," he said over Renny's shivery voice. "You might know them as swindlers, con artists."

"So what!" Renny suddenly cried out. "This is all about you robbing an old man on his deathbed! Huh? Are you that fucking pathetic?"

"Easy, Mr. Jacobson."

Then, Renny: "Why don't you do Leon a favor and just put him out of his fucking misery! What are you waiting for?"

"I could've killed Leon a long time ago," Diego said intensely. "I could've slipped poison into his soup or smothered him with a pillow while he was sleeping. I could've done numerous things, but I chose not to." He leaned even closer to Renny, close enough for Renny to feel the warmth of his breath against his sweaty face. "What do I look like to you, Mr. Jacobson? A coward?"

Renny seethed, "Precisely."

"Nah, Mr. Jacobson," Diego returned. "I'm no coward. I'm like you. I'm a realist."

"You don't know me. . . "

"I know enough." Diego retraced his thoughts—*the con*. "If there was one thing Leon taught me over all these years," he said, "it was patience. I knew in order to pull off this con, it would take *a lot* of patience."

"What did you do?"

Instead of answering the question, Diego drifted into thought.

"My father was a man of few words," Diego said, his voice tamed. "You see, Mr. Jacobson, where I come from a man is never asked to explain himself, even to his wife. He never talks about his problems, his issues. From an early age, a father teaches the son what it takes to be a man. The father is like the priest of the household. It's who we are, Mr. Jacobson. It's in our makeup. But I feel like there's something I need to get off my chest, something I've kept inside for a very long time." Then, Diego paused for a moment. He breathed carefully. "Not until now. If you think about it, Mr. Jacobson, love, in a way, is another form of insanity. Makes you blind to the truth. And Leon," Diego shook his head, "he was blind even before he lost his sight." Bitterness ran deep throughout his voice. "Old fool. By then, it was too easy. I knew if Isabel was torn from his life he would only destroy himself. I knew it wouldn't be so quick, though. I knew it would take time and *patience*, lots and lots of patience. And what he did with his eyes. . . " Diego tilted his head as a grin slipped across one side of his face, ". . . I never saw that coming." Then, his eyes flared like a madman. "Tell me, Mr. Jacobson. Have you ever watched a man wither away?" Another grin. "It's quite fascinating."

A tense silence. . .

"Marcus *never* ratted out Leon. . . " Renny's voice slowly trailed off as his head fell into deep thought.

The first thing he thought about was the framed picture Leon had showed him on the first day of his arrival and then the note on the back. The two were
friends—like *blood brothers*, Renny thought. He pulled
his eyes upward and then kept them on Diego's eyes,
the devil's eyes. "Why did you do it? He looked up
to you, you coward! You fucking coward!"

"You don't understand," Diego said and tapped
Renny on the forehead. "Do you, *Renny*? This was
never about Leon. This, Renny, this is about the
blood that has been spilt by thousands of innocent
men and women across my country." The veins
swelled above Diego's temples, rage filled his eyes.
"For years," he fumed, "your leaders have been sup-
plying the most dangerous cartels across South America with weapons and ammunition, the very same
weapons used to murder the innocent and spread tyr-
anny across my country, the very same weapons that
murdered my entire family." His eyes sharpened.
"You have no idea what it's like to be alone, to live on
the run, to constantly look over your shoulder. The
hardest part, Mr. Jacobson, is knowing that you are
going to die. They could find you in the middle of the
night while you're sleeping. They could grab you
while you're eating. And you pray, Mr. Jacobson,
that it'll be quick and painless, but it's *not* going to be
quick. It's not going to be painless. They want to
watch every drop of blood spill from your veins as
they rip you apart piece by piece. They want to
watch you suffer." Diego's thoughts drifted back to
that one day in the Inca temple, the day the white
man came and rescued him from the demons of the
night. "Then, he found me. Peter. He gave me a
life, but it never got rid of the guilt of what I did to my
family. Eventually, my guilt turned to anger. And for

years, I concealed that anger deep inside until I finally found a way to set it free."

Renny asked, "So, what does Leon have to do with this?"

Diego answered, "It's what Leon possesses."

"Money?"

Diego shook his head yet again.

"*No*," he said mischievously. "Something more valuable than money, Mr. Jacobson."

"You don't have to do this. . . " Renny begged. "Please, Diego! Of all people, you should know that people *do* change. . . sometimes. . . they change for the better!"

Diego didn't respond to Renny's remark.

"We will find a way to make it work, Diego, and we pick ourselves back up as we always do!"

"That's the best you can do, Writer," he said, emphasizing the word *writer*.

"Please, Diego!" Renny begged. "Your. . . your friend—Emilio, right? He taught you how to read because he saw something in you, Diego, something good. We all go through hard times. We all do things that we have no control over. We all *lose* people we love, the people who make an impact on our lives; and in their deaths, they teach us how to become stronger, *not* weaker."

Diego turned away and thought briefly about Renny's comments.

Renny said, louder now, "Think about the human spirit, Diego! It will *always* need stories! It's what keeps us together! It kept us together during the Great Depression, and it will continue to do so through this. . . this age of. . . of vanity!" He held his bound hands in front of Diego. "Good stories like Leon's will come along as they always do, Diego, and they will inspire us and make us better as human beings. We don't have to continue along this path of uncertainty anymore. There's still a chance for us, Diego." He reached out to Diego and cried, "We have so much potential, Diego. You know this. . . this country has so. . . so much. . . potential. . . Give us a chance. . . "

"Renny, Renny, Renny," Diego said surprisingly, "I think you've been listening to the old man's bullshit for too long. I can't believe Leon actually thought he could turn some smug writer from New York into an inspiring voice." He shrugged both of his shoulders. "And it worked," he carefully eyed Renny, "to *some* degree. You and I both know, Renny, that this country has had its reign. Unfortunately, that reign is now over. . . "

Renny shouted, "Listen to me!"

"Listen?" he said charmingly. "I've listened long enough. Your leaders must be held accountable for what they've done to my people." Diego now leaned closer, eyes widened. "For too long, I've sat back and watched these corrupted politicians and bureaucrats lie to our faces!"

"Then, we can *change* that! Damn it!"

"That's all you people talk about," Diego returned. "Yet, you never do a damn thing about it. If you want to change, then change. . . "

"We can!" Renny cried out. "We will!"

"It's too late," he said quietly. "Leon might've proven to me that the world can be a better place or given me *hope*—if that is such a word—but after the years I've spent living here in your country, I've only realized that there is no hope for you people. You Americans have lost *touch*, lost *passion*, lost the *will* to stand up for what you believe in. Sure, Renny." He shrugged his shoulder. "There may be," then, frowned, "a few of you still out there who fight for a valid cause." He carefully eyed Renny. "And I applaud you. But this has been going on for way too long. Now, it's time to put the final nail in the coffin."

"Why, Diego?" Renny said as he kneeled upright.

Diego returned, "If you only knew the things that went on behind the curtains, what your leaders have done to my people all for political gain." His tone shifted, quieter now. "But then again, the people of your country wouldn't even care if they knew what took place."

Renny yelled out, "*People change,* Diego! Please!"

"You people, you haven't *been* where I've been." Diego grimaced. "You haven't *seen* what I've seen." His eyes widened again, now sinisterly. "I've *stared* into the eye of Agatha, and she stared right back at me. She showed me your country's fate. Nothing good remains of it."

"If the world finds out what really happened to Leon, what the Company made him do, what they did to him. . . " Renny pleaded, ". . . then he can be a symbol, Diego. He can inspire us to rise again, to be better men, *stronger* than ever!"

Diego turned away once more.

"They will find me," Renny said again. "You know this. And when they find me, the world will finally know the truth about Leon."

"Your story will never see the light of day."

"They'll find me," Renny said desperately. "They have to. . . "

"Tell me, Mr. Jacobson," Diego interrupted, "who would look for you in a place like this?"

"*Edie,*" he said suddenly, "Edie will find me. . . "

"Your editor?"

Renny didn't respond.

"Five foot ten, dark hair, slender built, attractive?"

Renny paused, his face slackened.

"What did you do to her?" he asked, louder now. "What did you do to Edie?"

Diego frowned.

"The same thing I'm going to do to you, *Renny*," he said.

Renny flinched as Diego stood up.

"But not yet," he said calmly. "I still need you for one last thing. That is if things get out of hand. Then, once I'm done with you, you'll be as dead as your friend, Edie."

Diego walked away.

As Diego made it halfway up the stairs, Renny shouted out, "It was you! Wasn't it?"

Diego paused on the staircase and then turned his shoulder.

"You sent the email?"

"Who else do you think it was?" Diego said scornfully. "Leon? You really think that old man had the stomach to plan this whole thing out? All he cares about is his daughter, *not* you, not anyone else."

Renny asked, "Then, what do you care about?"

Diego never answered the question.

"Diego?" Renny screamed. "Answer my question! What do you care about?"

In return, Diego walked back up the stairs and closed the door behind him.

3:42 AM

ANNE spent a little over an hour wandering through the dark woods until she managed to find an opening in a chain-link fence. The sight of the old fence brought back more memories. She remembered making that same opening many years ago with a pair of bolt cutters she stole from the storage shed next to the garden.

Once Anne exited the woods, she sought cover behind a large oak tree. There, another memory flared from the sight of a handmade swing—two ropes attached to a 2x8 piece of treated wood sawn into a two-foot length seat—dangling from the sturdy tree branch above. Her father, Anne remembered, made that very same swing for her years ago. She remembered the day he built it, and how excited she was that day, especially after all of the traveling they had done after Isabel's second pregnancy. Anne was around four years old at the time, and her family was currently passing through Segovia, a city outside Madrid, when things started to get a little hairy. They ended up retreating to Whisperfront for the weekend—as they always did when things got a little too hairy—until the Company lost their trail. That Friday night, Leon didn't sleep a wink. Instead, he spent all night making that very swing, but Anne knew nothing about this. When Anne woke, there it was hanging from the tree—that swing. Then, days later, they were doing what they did best: bouncing around from one country to another.

3:43 AM

DIEGO stood behind a hallway window in the upper West Wing and watched Anne sneak her way across the lawn.

"Impressive," he said to himself.

3:46 AM

ON the way to the mansion, she passed the Apollo statue in the front. She studied the statue for a moment and after a close examination, determined that it was, indeed, the same one from the photographs.

She proceeded toward the front entrance of the mansion.

Before she knocked on the door, she suddenly paused. . .

3:47 AM

As Diego walked into Leon's bedroom, he made a last second rearrangement of his black tie.

"Master Dorsey," he said at the doorway and then walked toward the large garden window. "She's ahead of schedule."

Leon's breath went faint for a second.

"Tell me, Diego," he said from the bed. "What does she look like?"

Diego opened the curtain, which gave way to the pale moonlight above. He glanced once more at the front lawn and then toward the fountain but couldn't find her anywhere in sight. Diego turned toward at Leon.

"She's just like you imagined, Master Dorsey," he said.

"You did it, Diego," Leon said weakly. "You did it. . . "

Diego thought carefully, not about Leon's comment, but what Renny said to him in the basement.

"Leon?"

"Yes, Diego."

"Will God ever forgive us for what we've done?"

Leon said solemnly, "If my Chloe can't find it in her heart to forgive me for what I've done to our family, then why does it matter?"

Leon rolled his head to the left of the pillow, away from the window.

Diego stopped what he was doing and listened closely!

"She's here," he said to Leon.

"Whatever you do," Leon said, "stall her. She can't see me like this."

"I'll tell Sophia that you're ready for your bath."

Diego made an exit.

"Diego. . . " Leon said, as Diego was about to close the door.

"Yes."

"If I doubted you at all. . . "

"You had your reasons, sir."

As Diego made an attempt to close the door, Leon said, "You think she remembers me?"

Diego nodded.

"How else would she find her way back here?" he replied with a question of his own.

As Leon reflected over the question for a short while, Diego finally closed the door behind him.

3:50 AM

ANNE approached the massive front door, tried to open it. To her surprise, it was unlocked.

As soon as she pushed open the door, the very same door inside her mind opened as well. It was a red door as small as a door on a dollhouse, and yet the memories that had been locked away inside were as vast as the universe. The feeling that she had known all too well—that three o'clock feeling— suddenly burned bright inside her and remained nothing more than the ashes of what was left behind. Every image from her past was given both life and color; and from there, she connected each shard of shattered glass from a life once held inside a jar left to preserve in utter darkness.

As Anne closed the heavy door behind her and took a step into the foyer, she could feel the memories pressed against her face. So long it had been, Anne wondered, so long that she couldn't exactly remember the last time when she was here. Nonetheless, she had been here before, *right here*. There were faint reminders all around her: the stale and dusty smells of Leatherby Manor; the famous paintings on the walls, sculptures, which were no longer decorated throughout the mansion, as she had seen from Renny's photos. She opened more doors and then closed the doors behind her and stepped into another room, as open as a gallery, revealing the horseshoe-shaped staircase. She stopped in the center of the main room and couldn't help but wonder if it was her footsteps or someone else's making tiny echoes. Then, the footsteps tightened in depth, thinner and yet louder. Anne turned her shoulder and saw an expressionless man dressed in a pristine black suit approaching her. He was wearing white gloves, *not* black. At first glance, she knew exactly who the short man was. The last time she had seen that man was over fourteen years ago and yet, strangely, he hadn't aged much. He looked about the same except for a couple of gray hairs on his mustache. The last image of him was a scowl on his face as he was chasing her through the woods.

Diego walked through the foyer and greeted Anne.

"Welcome to Leatherby Manor," he said calmly.

Anne didn't respond.

"It's been a long time," he said. "You must be exhausted from your travels."

Anne nodded at Diego.

"I see you haven't changed much."

"Same goes for you, only taller."

Then, he studied Anne for a moment.

She didn't know what to say to Diego. She was, in some respects, still in a state of shock.

Diego stepped closer.

"Would you like for me to take your jacket?"

"Enough with the reunion," she said suddenly. "Where's Renny?"

"Mr. Jacobson is not here."

Anne furrowed her brows.

"Not here?" she said. "What did you do to him?"

He replied, "I sent Mr. Jacobson home after he got what he needed from your father."

"Save it, butler," Anne said, her voice trembling. "Tell me where he is?"

"I told you, Anne," he said, remaining calm. "He's not here." He extended his arm. "How about an old tour of the house? You've been gone a long time."

Anne replied, her voice sterner now, "Not long enough."

"I'll see to it that you didn't come all this way for nothing," Diego said patiently. "You and I both know you didn't come here just for Renny Jacobson. So, you might as well make yourself comfortable—"

"So, you let him go?" Anne said over Diego's voice. "I'm supposed to believe that? What about that video he made?"

"Well, we had to get your attention somehow."

"We?"

"Renny and I," he said. "The video was his idea, actually, plan B."

Diego's comment made the blood boil in Anne's veins—the blood, she remembered. He had a cut on his head. *That*, she knew.

"Come," Diego said, once more extending his arm. "Your father has been looking forward to this day for a very long time."

"And where is he?"

"He's currently resting," Diego answered. "Come," he said and rotated his body around. "I'm sure you have a lot of questions."

Anne was hesitant to follow.

Diego held out his hand.

Finally, Anne walked with Diego to the right of the main room, in the living room, where Diego sat down with his legs crossed in a leather chair.

Anne didn't bother to sit as Diego had instructed.

Instead, she paced around the lit fireplace.

"I insist," Diego said and pointed once more to the couch.

As before, Anne was hesitant to follow along with Diego's demands.

She finally sat down on the couch.

"Would you like a cup of tea?" he asked.

"Yeah," Anne said. "Whatever."

Diego raised his right hand in the air.

Shortly after, his assistant, Jasmine, strolled into the living room with a tray of hot tea. She placed the tray on the coffee table between the chair and the couch.

"Thank you, Jasmine," Diego said, carefully eyeing Jasmine.

In return, Jasmine nodded her head at Diego and went on her way.

Diego asked, "Would you like sugar with your tea?"

"Sure," Anne said slowly.

Diego grabbed the spoon and scooped one cube of sugar from the tiny bowl. He placed the cube in the cup. He kept placing one cube after another—three exactly—until Anne finally said, "Enough."

He handed the cup of tea with a stirring spoon to Anne.

"Be careful," he said. "It's hot."

Anne grabbed the cup of tea from Diego and sipped cautiously.

"So, how was the trip?" he asked while watching Anne sip from the tea.

"I'm the one who's going to be asking the questions here," Anne followed. "Start with the helicopter."

"What helicopter?"

Anne sharpened her gaze at Diego.

"Ah," he said strangely. "*That* helicopter. As you already know, Anne, your father is a sick man and he doesn't have much time left to live. The helicopter delivers proper supplies and medicines used to keep your father alive. Plus, if anything was to happen to Master Dorsey, well, we have the helicopter at our disposal."

"Seems kind of extreme," Anne said. "Don't you think?"

"If there's one thing I've learned about your father: everything is extreme with him," he said. "Another toy to add to his collection, I suppose."

"Let's cut the crap, Diego," Anne said and pulled out the USB flash drive from her right pocket. "Why do people want this so badly?"

"Right," Diego said mischievously as he carefully eyed the flash drive in Anne's hand, "the package."

"Package?" Anne said mindlessly. "What package?"

"The one in your hand, of course," Diego said casually. "My men intercepted the flash drive in the mail. Then, you picked it from one of their pockets, just as planned."

"You?" Anne said as she furrowed her brows.

"What other way was there to bring you here, Anne?" Diego said and then casually sipped from the cup of tea.

As he lifted the cup to his lips, his cuff barely lowered from his wrist, revealing the same tattoo that Anne found on the same men who murdered both of her foster parents, as well as Jamie and Michael.

"Harold. . . " Anne fell into a trance. "*You*," her eyes narrowed, "it was you. This whole. . . " her voice slowly rose in anger.

As Anne stood to her feet, a dizzy spell forced her back on the couch. First, she grabbed the top of her forehead. Then, she grabbed the cup of tea, but did so heedlessly by spilling some of tea over the table.

"Are you feeling well, Anne?" Diego asked as he leaned forward.

"I'm. . . "

"Would you like to lie down?"

"Nooo," she slurred and grimaced slightly. "Wha did you do t'me?"

Anne's eyes grew heavy.

Her head swayed back and forth.

Then, her eyes eventually rolled into the back of her head.

Anne flopped forward. . .

Before she crashed through the coffee table, Diego quickly swooped in and caught Anne and then gently placed her back on the couch.

2:21 PM

BEHIND the darkness of her eyelids, Anne smelled a scent of sharp cologne.

She opened her weary eyes, only to see a blurry face looming over her in a ray of sunlight.

Once her eyes adjusted to the daylight, she scurried toward the headrest of the bed.

"*You*," Anne said, her lips shivering. "What did you do to me?"

"You passed out, Anne," Diego said as he was seated by her bedside. "Luckily, I was there to catch you. Otherwise, you would've banged your head against the coffee table. So, if I were you, I would be a little more grateful for being alive."

"You're a monster!" Anne blurted out. "You... you killed my parents! Michael! And Jamie..." Anne remembered the tattoo on Jamie's wrist, the same one that she saw on Diego's wrist, "... she was working with you?"

"I *will* explain, Anne," Diego said.

"Start with my parents..."

"It wasn't my intention for your foster parents to be murdered," Diego explained. "Those men I hired were there to merely scare you." He momentarily hung his head and could hardly look Anne in the eyes. He said quietly, "I should've known not to trust them, Anne. They acted like... like savages." He looked into Anne's eyes. "I can't tell you how sorry I am for your loss," he corrected, "losses, but you have to realize," his voice grew now, "Anne, the only way for you to remember who you were and who you are was for me to put you in a situation that tested your will to survive. I had to recreate your memories. I had to force you to live on the run..."

Anne suddenly cried, "Why are you doing this to me?"

"Anne, I know what happened to you after you ran away," Diego said carefully, "I know how the police found you, the treatments. I know everything."

"Did you know what that man did to me?" Anne said. "I was only ten years old..."

"Yes," Diego said, "I know all about him."

"Then why would you want me to remember the horrible things that man did to me?" she asked. "Let alone, what my father did..." Anne suddenly changed her tone from whiny to stern, as if a switch had been flipped on deep inside her, ". . . just answer this one question: Was he involved in any of this? My father?"

"He came to me," Diego said, thinking back to that one day. "He was dying. He asked me to find you. 'Whatever it takes,' he said. For months, I looked for you. Then, about a year ago, I found you. You owned a house, had a job, boyfriend. But it wasn't you. It was all a cover.

"You don't know the first thing about me. . . "

"I know you walk around like everything is okay when, deep down, you are alone and confused and scared," Diego said. "What kind of life is that?"

"I was happy," she said, sniffling. "I had people who cared about me. . . "

"Maybe so," Diego said. "But you *weren't* happy." Anne made an attempt to retort, but Diego quickly interrupted, "I know more about you, Anne, than you know about yourself. You must realize I couldn't just bring you in," he said. "No. You needed a little 'push.' You had to learn who you were on your own. Then, I thought about the one thing that came second nature to you, when survival instincts come to fruition." Diego paused. "Running," he said clearly. "Your entire life you've been on the run. It was all you knew. And now, memory erased, living the American Dream, settled in a new house. You actually think you can go back to that life? Running is all you know. It is all you'll ever know—"

"You *don't* know me," Anne said snappishly.

Diego ignored Anne.

"Your father asked me to find a way in," he said casually. "So, I did. His name was Renny Jacobson."

"Let me get this straight," Anne said seriously. "My dying father came to you and asked you to find me. So, you did. And for the past year, you've been stalking me."

"If that's the way you want to put it. . . "

Anne stumbled from the bed.

"Easy now," Diego said.

She backed her way to the window.

"You told your friend, Jamie, that you were sick and tired of going through the motions everyday," he said as he stood, as well.

"She wasn't my friend. . . "

"'*Lost*,' is what she told me," Diego said over Anne. "Am I not right?"

Anne didn't answer.

"That day you ran away, your father searched the entire country looking for you," Diego said, easing closer to Anne. "After a while, he just gave up. I asked him if I could help, if there was anything I could do to spare him from the misery that you left behind. He simply gave up on life. Once, he tried to kill himself. Took a handful of painkillers. Never killed him, though. Just knocked him out for an entire week. I'm sure you never heard about that in the journals you read or the interviews you listened to."

Anne remained quiet.

"After he was diagnosed," Diego said, "he finally accepted what he had done, to Isabel, to Dominic, most importantly, to you. They told your father he had only had a few months to live. I knew it was a death sentence, but your father surprised them all. Even surprised me. That's when he came to me. Asked me if I could track you down."

"So," Anne said bitterly, "so you found me. Here I am. What now? You actually want me to forgive him after what you two have done to my family. He's as much a part of this as you are."

"But your father doesn't know what happened, Anne, to Harold, to Molly, to Michael." He walked around the edge of the bed, closer to Anne. "Let me ask you a question. Did you really love your foster parents?"

Anne retorted, "What kind of question is that? Of course, I did."

"And why did you love them?"

"Because they took care of me."

Diego shrugged, easing closer.

"A nurse can take care of a patient," he said, "but do all nurses love their patients?"

Anne didn't answer the question.

"Your father loved you more than Harold and Molly loved you," Diego said bitterly. "More than the world itself! Tell me. What kind of parents would zap a little girl's brain until she felt absolutely nothing at all?"

Anne asked, "Do you have any children?"

"I do not," Diego answered.

"Then, how can you possibly know what it's like?"

"You're right," he said softly.

Anne tried to fight back the tears.

Diego stepped even closer.

"Get away from me!" She suddenly backed away until she found herself against the window. "Take me to Renny!"

"I told you, Anne," he said. "Renny is *not* here."

"I don't believe you!"

"I never said it was going to be easy for you," he said. "I apologize for all the," Diego paused and thought carefully about his next words, "for the theatrics, but it was the only way for you to understand who you were and who you'll always be."

Anne cleared her throat, straightened her posture.

"And who is that?" she asked.

Diego pulled out a picture from his pocket, which caused Anne to flinch. He stepped forward and handed the picture to Anne.

"Jaelene *Chloe* Dorsey," he said clearly.

The name suddenly came back to Anne, mainly that one name, Chloe—the final piece of the puzzle. Anne knew there would be other puzzles. Life was fruitless without them. But this one, her birth name, was the greatest puzzle of them all, and right now the greatest puzzle she would ever know. Ever since the time she returned home from the hospital, the name Chloe had remained only a word hanging on the tip of her tongue. Even if the name had been spoken in public, Anne always knew there was something special about that one name in particular; and just when a glimmer of light would cast upon that name, *Chloe*, its origins, its two convivial syllables, it would crumble away into the crevasses of her mind, only to resurface later in time.

My name was Chloe, she said to herself.

Anne looked down at the photograph of Leon and herself. At the time the photograph was taken, Anne was only eight years old. The two of them were sitting on the front porch glider. Leon had his arm wrapped around young Anne, who was smiling from ear to ear. Leon was beaming too.

The sight of the photograph drew more tears to her eyes.

"He never stopped loving you, Chloe," Diego said. "For so many years, he lived with so much hate inside him. For so many years your father lived in denial. Eventually, he realized it was he who drove you away from here. The thought alone of losing you made him sick. Once he accepted what he had done, the hate turned into something else. . . " He searched for the right word once more, ". . . something *incredible*," he said shortly.

With her eyes narrowing, Anne said to Diego, "After all you've done, why should I trust anything you have to say to me?"

"It's up to you to choose whether or not to trust me," Diego said, his resonant voice trailing off as he walked over to the bedroom door, opened it, and then stopped at the doorway before he turned his shoulder.

There, in her blank stare, Anne recognized Diego for who he was, a man of many faces and many sleeves, the hawk-eyed man burning the candle at both ends, the puppeteer pulling the strings behind the curtain, the Voice making the late night calls, the director staging the scene as it had been written in a screenplay, the faceless man closing doors and opening others. For Anne, as ambitious as this plan had sounded, it made sense. Like Renny wrote in a journal entry, *not perfect sense*, but some kind of sense. This man, whom she had only known for a few years—and even in these years, Anne knew him best as her chaperone or her father's butler, the man who never smiled and only responded with "Yes, Master Dorsey" or "No, Master Dorsey" to the questions he was asked—would go so far as to direct another individual to take his or her own life after the job was finished in order to make her remember her past. . . Exactly how much *power* did this man have?

The memory alone of the desperate man at Jamie's house begging for Anne to pull the trigger glistened in her eyes.

"When you're ready to see him, Anne," Diego said, pulling Anne from her thoughts, "his bedroom is the last room on the right."

Diego left the door cracked open and then exited the bedroom.

Anne glanced down at her hands, both of them trembling violently. She tried caressing the tremble from her hands, working the tension out as a masseuse would do, but both the excitement and the terror were too great.

2:58 PM

ANNE stared out the bedroom window for several minutes until she finally made up her mind.

At the very end of the hallway, a door was left cracked open. It just so happened to be the last door on the right, her father's room, as Diego had told her. She looked around the quiet hallway and found nothing that caught her interest, except for the quietude of the hallway. Diego was nowhere around, nor were any of his aides or assistants. It was just Anne and the ghosts of Leatherby Manor.

She proceeded toward the last room on the right.

The closer Anne walked toward the room, the more the nerves churned inside her. Her palms grew sweaty; and even then, she had to constantly wipe the sweat from her hands. The blood emptied from her face, leaving it pale and clammy. Her armpits, as well as the mustier regions of her body, became damp with beads of sweat. Even the walk became arduous. Her limbs, nearly paralyzed.

When she arrived at the master bedroom, her thoughts raced. What if he really had absolutely nothing to do with it? What do I say. . . what about *his eyes*. . . were they like dark voids. . . *would he be able to recognize my voice*. . .

Calm and resolute, Anne pushed open the door and was greeted by a woman dressed in a black dress, the same woman from before, Jasmine, and then another woman, Sophia, who was dressed in jade-colored scrubs, dark hair tied in a pony-tail, well-fit.

Jasmine introduced Sophia to Anne.

"This is Sophia, your father's nurse," she said vacantly.

Sophia smiled and reached out her hand.

"Hi," she said. "I've heard a lot about you. It's a pleasure to finally meet you."

With a vacant expression, Anne shook the woman's hand.

"Your hand is freezing," Sophia said merrily.

In return, Anne didn't say anything at all.

Before an awkward silence took hold, Jasmine interrupted, "We'll leave you two alone."

The two women exited the room in single file.

Anne waited until the women were gone before walking farther into the bedroom. She rounded a corner and found an old man slouched over in a wheelchair, which was parked in front of the garden window. His head slightly twitched from the sluggish, nearly soundless squeak along the hardwood. Then, finally, he rotated his head toward the window.

Anne didn't even think too much about the word.

Yet, it spilled from her mouth like a droplet of water from a leaky faucet.

The old man at the window didn't turn to her voice, *that one word*. Yet, he stayed there in the same exact position.

Anne crept closer.

She said once more, louder now, "Dad?"

The old man mechanically turned around as if the muscles in his neck were made from sticks.

"Chloe?" Leon said finally, his voice filled with great curiosity. "Is. . . is that really you?"

Anne faced Leon, who was wearing his daily sunglasses.

Leon reinforced his grip around the armrest of the wheelchair and pinpointed the voice.

"It's me," Anne said quietly as she approached Leon.

As Anne cautiously stood several feet away, she studied her father: his withered body, the outfit—a beige sweater worn open and then a black collared shirt with a pair of loose black pants to match—the wrinkles on his face, the gray hair—or the lack of—as well as the tremors in his bones. Even the smell, Anne gathered, was foul but fairly tolerable. The age, however, was something that Anne couldn't quite gather. He looked twenty to thirty years beyond his actual age—a frail old man, as she had learned from the recent interviews. For a moment, Anne wondered if it was actually her father, Leon Dorsey. The last memory she had of him was from this very room. He was sitting against the base of the bed, a photo of her mother gripped in his hand. He was much taller back then and incredibly handsome too; and he had beautiful wavy hair, which after several months, started to thin and fall out from all of the stress and misery, which now she could totally relate to. Molly's comb, Anne remembered, the one passed down to her, had more strands of hair on it each day; and it had gotten so bad lately that pulling out her hair had become a hobby. But that one question cut the deepest: *How could a once healthy man have aged so fast?*

Anne recalled the interviews, mainly that one in particular.

"Chloe!" Leon suddenly cried as he reached out his free arm. "It's really you. . . "

Hesitant at first, Anne retracted a little.

Finally, she stepped forward and hugged her father. She could feel his weak, trembling bones against her torso. Subtly, she attempted to pull away from her father. Leon held on tightly to Anne as if he was clinging onto a cliff. His bones, mainly his scapula, humerus, radius, and ulna dug into the side of Anne's ribcage, but Anne fought through the sting.

"I've missed you so much," Leon cried. "For years, I've looked for you. I. . . I. . . I knew I would find you. I just knew. . . "

"I'm here now," she said quietly, trying to hold back both the tears and the anger. "I'm here. . . "

"Please," Leon said urgently, "can you lay me down?"

"Lay you down?"

"Yes."

Anne looked around the room and asked, "What do I do?"

"Push the chair closer to the bed."

Hesitant, Anne walked behind Leon.

She made an attempt to push the wheelchair, but it didn't budge.

"Unlock. . . the wheels. . . "

Anne glanced down and saw that the wheels were locked.

She unlocked them with her foot and then wheeled Leon to the bed.

When they arrived at the bed, Leon lifted his arm.

"Here," he said. "If you can stand me up, I can do the rest."

Anne unpeeled the blanket from the bed.

"Thank you," Leon said as Anne waited for further command. "Now, slip your shoulders underneath my arm."

Anne leaned forward. Leon wrapped his arm around her neck. Then, he counted to three, and when he got to three, Anne lifted his frail body from the wheelchair (he wasn't that heavy, she learned, literally half the man; however, it wasn't the weight that bothered Anne). She guided him to the bed where she carefully placed him on the bed.

Next, Anne guided his feet onto the bed and slid his body away from the edge of the bed.

With her hand cradled behind his head, she gently placed his head on the pillow.

Lastly, she slipped the blanket over his body.

"Thank you, Chloe," Leon said sincerely. "Thank you so much. I'm afraid I haven't felt," his breath labored, "so much excitement since... I... I can't even remember when..."

Once more, Anne carefully studied Leon.

"It's really you," she said, noticing the glazed patch of tears around the right side of his nose. The tears, however, weren't falling from his eyes. She looked closer and said, "Tears."

"The lacrimal gland on my right side is still intact, but it was severely damaged," he said faintly. "If I cry hard enough, the tears come..."

Intrigued, Anne pointed at Leon's sunglasses.

She asked, "Can I see?"

Leon was at a loss for words.

"Your eyes?"

"Of course," he said and removed the sunglasses from his face. He handed the sunglasses to Anne, who then placed them on the nightstand.

Once more, she studied her father's face, but this time with mild disgust. He had no eyes as she had learned through Renny's interview. But to see it in person... The skin underneath his eyes—or where his eyes used to be—was dark and wrinkly. His eyelids were wrinkly too. There was scar tissue around the socket, mainly from where Leon's fingernails had gouged out his eyes. Part of the lacrimal gland was barely intact on the right side.

"Does it hurt?" she asked.

"No," he answered.

"I don't know what to say," Anne said.

"You don't have to say anything, Chloe."

"*Anne*," she said suddenly. "My name is Anne."

"Right," Leon said softly. "I forgot."

Anne shrugged.

"Sorry."

"No." Leon groaned as he repositioned his body on the bed. "You don't have to be sorry, Anne. If anybody should be sorry, it's me for what I did to your mother and Dominic." He cried once more, but the tears never came. "I. . . I wasn't there for you when you needed me the most. . . "

"So it's true," Anne said sternly. "You're Freeze."

"Your mother and I kept it a secret from you two," he said. "We never wanted you two to know the truth about who I was. Someday, though, someday I knew you would find out." Leon suddenly cleared his throat, which sounded wet and gravelly from the mucus draining down his throat. "I know what you may be thinking: How did I become this way?" he said closely to Anne. His face lifted with excitement. "I take it you listened to all of the interviews. . . "

"Most of them," she said. "Yeah."

"Then, you know why I look like this."

"Yes," she said solemnly. "You did this to yourself."

Leon said, "And there's nothing I can do to change that, Anne. *But* there are some things I can still change." He extended his hand across the mattress. Anne was slow to grab it. "What I said in the interview, to Renny, to you, it was all true. Every word."

"Except for you pretending to be Marcus Hopkins."

"You must understand that it was the only way he would conduct the interview," he said. "Otherwise, he would've never come here."

"So, you lied to him?"

"I had to, Anne."

Anne thought about Leon's comments, which aligned with what Diego had told her prior to the re-union with her father. Still, she wrestled with another question in her mind, the one that had plagued her thoughts ever since Diego exposed his master plan to Anne.

Leon said, "I asked Diego if there was any way he could find you."

"He told me."

"He did?"

"A few minutes ago," Anne said. "Yeah."

"I never told him how to do it," Leon said. "I didn't want to know. Though," his breath labored once more, "he did tell me about what happened to you, what that one man did to you. I would've pro-tected you from people like that. . . "

"People?" Anne retorted, releasing a little bit of the anger from her voice. The anger was nestled inside her, as warm as a furnace. "That man wasn't a per-son." Then, Anne's voice climbed: "He was a mon-ster!"

"I know he was, Anne, but I don't have murder in my heart."

"What about this Company?" she replied. "What you did to them?"

"They *were* monsters—"

"And the man who did this to me?" Anne said, the anger burning slowly inside her veins. "He doesn't qualify?"

The thought alone of this man, Louis Bringer, touching Chloe in that way sent a ripple of anger

throughout Leon's body. He too shared the warmth
of Anne's rage, but he never let it take hold. Leon
grimaced for a second, but as he had trained himself
over the years, he let the anger pass.

"I'm not that man anymore," Leon said. "I'm so
sorry for what happened to you, Anne. If I could go
back in time, I would. But I can't, Anne. You understand. We can't. . . "

As with Leon, Anne grimaced as well.

The grip around Leon's hand grew slightly tighter.

"So, you weren't involved in Diego's plan?"

"*No*, Anne."

"Did you know what he did?" Anne asked, now
holding back the anger. "Diego? Do you know what
he did? And don't lie to me."

"He didn't hurt you?" Leon asked suddenly. "Did
he?"

"Were you in on it or not?"

"No," Leon said sincerely. "All I want is for you to
understand how sorry I am. I'm *so* sorry, Anne, for
what I did to you, to your mother, to Dominic. I'm
sorry."

"You want to talk about being selfish," Anne said,
recalling one of the interviews from earlier, "you took
everything away from me——"

"I'm so sorry, Anne. . . please forgive me. . . "

Anne said desperately, "Don't lie to me."

"The only person I lied to was myself," Leon said.
"For years, I thought that one day you would come
back into my life and everything would be okay like
before, that we would move on from the past and that
awful thing I did. Days drew on. . . months. Then, I
waited and. . . waited. I waited for so long." He
stopped and caught his breath.   Then, breathed
slowly. "The hardest part was not knowing where
you were. Thinking if you were dead, if someone had

abducted you. I couldn't bear bringing more pain to the people who I cared about the most in my life. So, I did what I had to do." Leon brought himself back to that one day in Rural, the agony he had felt was like no pain he had ever felt before. The toughest part about ripping out the eyes was getting a good grip on them. He tried over four times until he finally got several fingers around the eyeball, as well as the muscle, both as slick as jelly, and then, after that, he yanked and tugged as hard and quickly as he could as if he was ripping off a Band-Aid. "I thought. . . " he said to Anne, ". . . I thought it would make it better. . . I thought it would make the pain go away. . . "

"And did it?" Anne asked.

"Yes," he said. "I was finally a free man and yet, with you gone from my life, I was a man without purpose. Stuck here like a bird with clipped wings."

"You clipped your own wings, *not* me."

Leon hung his head for a moment.

"I know I did," he said sorrowfully.

"When I ran away things happened to me, bad things, unspeakable things, but. . . " Anne took her time. Her breath was slow and heavy like an old, neglected engine. ". . . But I survived, and I found a new home. I was raised by good people. They are now. . . they *were* the only family I knew, and they were," her eyes narrowed like blades, "murdered by that son of a bitch. My friends too, murdered. All of that was taken away from me because of what? Because you wanted to say that 'you're sorry.'"

"I am, Anne," he exclaimed, which caused a sudden cough. "I had no idea Diego did that to you. If I knew that. . . that Diego was going to resort to these. . . extreme measures, then I would've never agreeeeed. . . I. . . " His breath grew heavier, ". . . I caaaaan't die knowing that you. . . you still have malice in your heart for what I did in the—"

"What if you just left me alone?" Anne said vacantly. "I would've never remembered what happened to me, what happened to us. I would've lived a normal life."

A tense pause was created from the *what-if* question.

Once more, Leon carefully slowed his breathing as Sophia had taught him.

Finally, he said, "You can never live a normal life, Anne."

They both waited in the same tense silence.

"What do you mean?" Anne finally asked.

"When Diego told me about what happened to you after you ran away, I asked myself: Many years from now, what if her memory comes back?" he asked himself aloud. "By then, I will be long dead. And you'll need to know the truth about who you really are. . . that way you will never make the same mistakes as I did."

"Mistakes?" she said confusedly. "What do you mean?"

"You have it inside you."

"Have what?"

"You know," he said. "The gift."

Anne thought about the gift. Her father mentioned this "gift" throughout the interviews. "The gaze," Anne remembered, that was what he called it. The gaze wasn't even acquired from his bloodline, Anne discovered, but, in fact, acquired from a ridiculous dare Leon had made with his friend. The sound bite was supposed to be deleted from the USB flash drive, but it wasn't deleted. It was there for her ears to hear.

"How do you know?" Anne asked after some thought.

"When you were little, you got mad at Dom for stealing your dolly," Leon said as he cracked a smile. "Do you remember the time when your mother and I took Dom to the emergency room because he hurt his finger?"

Once more, Anne thought for a moment.

Then, she drawled, "I remember."

"Dom lost part of his finger," Leon said. "Do you remember?"

Again, she drawled, "Yes."

"It wasn't from that truck," Leon said. "It was from you, Anne. *You* turned his finger into stone. We told the doctors that Dom was messing around with one of those trucks, you know, the ones with concrete inside them. . . "

"A concrete mixer," Anne said vaguely. "I remember."

"He accidentally stuck his finger into the asphalt." While Leon explained, Anne retraced her thoughts to that day Dom was rushed to the hospital. Little Dom was at it again. The little squirt was picking his nose and then flicking boogies at her. He stole her doll when she wasn't looking. Then, she remembered one boogie had landed directly on her cheek, a real nasty-looking one, as big as a grain of rice, with dried blood and tentacle-like nose hairs coming out of it, as if the thing had come straight from a cesspool of toxic ooze. The first reaction: Anne cringing in great repulsion. Second reaction: her face as red as a fireball. *"They did all they could to save the finger,"* he said. "But they ended up having to remove part of Dom's finger." Then, Leon reached out and grabbed Anne by the forearm. The feel of his cold, bony hand grabbed her attention. "If anyone finds out about you, Anne, about what you can do, they will come after you as they did with me. And this time, they *will* kill you. I don't want you to go down the same road as I did. *Please*, Anne. That road is filled with nothing but pain and sadness. Do you understand?"

Anne removed Leon's hand from her forearm and walked toward the window.

"I don't know if I can ever forgive you for what you did to them, but," she said, her eyes glazing over, "I can try. That's all I can do right now. I can try."

Leon coughed loudly.

"Please do me a favor." A string of saliva ran down the corner of his mouth. "In the bathroom," he said faintly and then pointed to the bathroom across the room, "there's a box of tissues. Would you grab it for me?"

Anne walked to the bathroom where she found a tissue from a box on the vanity.

Behind Anne perched a row of shelves, the first section holding most of Leon's medicine. She recognized a couple of the names from the medicine bottles, mainly the anxiety pills, as well as the painkillers, which Leon had a lot of—even the hardcore stuff. A few bottles of Levaquin were there to treat Leon's frequent urinary tract infections. The other medicines were for the cancer, Anne supposed. Each pill, Anne saw, the size of a bullet. The second shelf held containers of plastic gloves, masks, vials, syringes, catheters, and many other medical supplies Anne had never seen before. Next to the shelves were dozens of boxes, all carefully stacked in order from largest to smallest. She read the names on a couple of the boxes, one called *Pro Advantage* by LBM, and then *Milestone Medical Group*, each label addressed to the mansion's address, 1412 King's Drive, Whisperfront, MA. The boxes were filled with the same stuff on the shelves: bandages, catheters, and whatnot. Next to the boxes were cases of *Ensure* and other types of canned protein shakes.

As Anne made her way back into the bedroom, her eyes caught a glimpse of a dark object behind the toilet. She took a double take and then walked to the vanity. Behind the toilet was a triangular piece of black plastic. Anne was more or less intrigued by the plastic debris.

Possibly from a smartphone?

She reached down and picked up the debris.

"SAM," she read the lettering on the side of the plastic.

She pocketed the piece of plastic and scoured the crime scene.

"*Anne. . .*" Leon said from the bedroom.

"Coming," Anne said mindlessly as she checked in and around the vanity.

Next, she checked the side of the vanity. There, she found a smudge of blood on the line of calking. The blood could've come from anywhere, Anne mused, from Leon or his pretty nurse, Sophia. She couldn't help but wonder about where the blood really came from, which happened to be the first person on her mind, the only person. . .

With this in mind, Anne walked back into the bedroom and assisted Leon. She wiped the saliva from the side of his chin and tossed the damp tissue in the trashcan.

"Thank you," he mumbled.

Anne sat down in the chair next to Leon's bedside.

"Diego told me about Renny," she said bluntly. "He said he sent Renny home. Is that true?"

Leon's demeanor suddenly changed from pleasant to stern and quiet.

3:29 PM

DOWNSTAIRS in the lower West Wing, Diego was staring at an old picture. In the golden frame there was an old black and white photograph of his family—his original family, that is. The sides of the photo were crinkled from where Diego had kept it in his pocket for so long. He had come from a big family, Diego did, three older brothers, as well as four older sisters. Diego, of course, was the youngest.

Diego gently placed the framed picture back in its proper place on top of the dresser and then strolled toward a standing mirror on the other side of the room. He stared at the mirror, making sure his black suit appeared flawless, no hairs or fibers. He checked his pencil-thin mustache and, like the suit, made sure it was straight and orderly.

Next, he carefully slipped on a pair of black leather gloves, not white.

Last but not least, he walked back to the dresser, opened the top drawer, and pulled out two wooden handles, which were both attached to a piano wire. He placed the device in his pocket and proceeded to the basement.

3:32 PM

"YESTERDAY afternoon I heard a noise coming from the bathroom," Leon said to Anne. "We were wrapping up our last interview. Renny told me he had to use the restroom. Then, I don't know, he was gone. That was the last time I spoke to him."

Intrigued, Anne said, "He never said goodbye?"

"No," Leon answered. "He just. . . "

"Just what?"

"Disappeared," Leon said.

Anne placed her hand along her temple as she lowered her head and thought about the recent exchange. . .

3:34 PM

RENNY grunted in agony as he tried yet again to free himself with the pink barrette that he stole from the study. He took a break from trying to free himself and tried to make out his surroundings, anything that could help him with his escape, but all he saw was pitch black. He thought about what Diego had said to him early today. It was only a matter of time before that door opened. The next time it did, Renny knew, it would be the last.

3:35 PM

"I asked Diego about Renny," he said after Anne sat him upright against the headboard of the bed. "Where did he go? Why would he get up and leave without saying goodbye? We only spent a week together, but in that week, I got to know Renny more than most friends do in an entire lifetime."

Anne asked Leon, "What did Diego say?"

"He said Renny was feeling under the weather and that he had to get back to New York."

"Do you believe him?"

"Diego has been with me ever since the beginning," Leon said. "He's taken good care of me. He's been like family. It doesn't make any sense why he would lie about Renny's disappearance. Maybe. . . " Leon's voice weakened, ". . . Renny wasn't who I thought he was. Maybe he was another smug writer who got what he wanted for a story and then, the next thing you know, he's gone, never to be heard from again." Leon turned his head toward Anne. "He could've said goodbye. Right?" He reached out and searched for Anne's hand. She made it easier for Leon by grabbing his frail hand. "You won't do that to me. Will you?"

Anne was slow to answer.

"No," she said, her voice uneasy. "I won't." Anne cleared her throat. "Dad. . . "

Leon's face lit up.

"Yes, Anne."

"What if. . . " Anne said, ". . . what if something happened to Renny? What if Diego was responsible for his disappearance?"

"Diego wouldn't do that!"

"How do you know?" She removed her hand from Leon's hand and paced around the bed. "We're talking about the same man who was in charge of hiring assassins to kill my foster parents *and* my friends. Didn't this man use to work for the cartel?"

"That was a. . . " Leon sighed and then patted the top of Anne's hand, ". . . I always wanted to believe that there was still some good left in Diego, that he and I could live a meaningful life together. But I think all the good left in him died a long time ago."

Anne asked, "Why do you say that?"

"Ever since I came back to the mansion," he said, "when I brought you back home with me after the you know, after the incident, Diego, he wasn't the same. It was like *he was*. . . " Leon traced his thoughts back to that one day he walked in on him meticulously cleaning the glass casing, which enclosed the head of Agatha, making sure it didn't have any marks or smudges on it. Diego paid Agatha at least five visits per day, Leon remembered, spraying the casing with cleaner, making sure the glass was spotless, and Leon couldn't help but wonder if it was he who caused Diego to be like this. After all, it was *he* who told Diego to watch over Agatha, as well as his father's possessions, and it was he who told him to make sure nothing ever happened to them. So, Diego did, and he kept waiting for Leon to return. One night, he walked in on Diego gaping into the vacant eyes of Agatha as if her dead gaze had drawn him in like a mosquito to a zapper. "... *Like he was* on a mission," Leon said finally. "Before I came home, we would talk about stuff. He used to always enjoy listening to me talk about my Freeze days. When I came back, it was all business. He'd tell me about the world, current events, and get upset at times about what was going on in the world, extremely critical. Something changed inside him. I don't know what. But *something* had changed. . . "

3:43 PM

THE basement door in the East Wing slowly opened, but Renny was nowhere to be found.

As Diego stood at the top of the landing, his body as dark as a silhouette, he called out, "Mr. Jacobson. . . "

With the piano wire gripped tightly in his hand, he walked down the wooden staircase. He finally reached the bottom, only to find a white bag, a pink barrette, and empty shackles on the floor. There was no Renny.

Diego stood there—his hands gripping tighter together, so tight that the leather cracked in his hands. His eyes shrank as well, tiny crow's feet marking the corners of his face.

3:45 PM

ANNE leaned over Leon's bedside and grabbed his hand.

"Come back home with me," she said tentatively.

"There's no point," Leon said, his voice cracking. "This is where I belong."

"This place is a tomb," Anne said. "Lansford has some of the best doctors in the country."

"Anne, I don't care about doctors anymore," he said before Anne could say another word. "I was raised here and I *will* die here."

"What if what you said about Diego is true?" Anne said closely. "Who will watch over this place?"

Leon didn't have to think long for his answer.

"You," he said. "You will."

Anne said confusedly, "Me?"

"Originally, Diego was going to have all of this," he said. "But *you*, it should belong to you, Anne." He readjusted his grip around Anne's hand. "You can have it all, every square inch. I'll have Diego call the lawyer tomorrow."

"But Dad," Anne said, "I don't care about the money. I have a house, a job. I can't leave all that behind. . . "

"It's not too late to start over, Anne."

As Anne fell deep into thought, mostly thinking about her mundane life back in Lansford, how miserable she actually was, and then thinking about starting a new life right here in Whisperfront, a distant *clank* suddenly interrupted her train of thought.

"What was that?" Anne said quietly, the color of her skin turning pallid.

"I believe it came from the storage room."

Anne released Leon's hand and stood up from the chair.

"Please, Anne," Leon said, "stay with me. . . "

Starting over, she thought once more.

If there was a chance you could hit the reset button in life, would you?

"Anne?"

"I'll be right back," she said sharply. "I promise."

"If Diego did harm Renn—"

Anne interrupted, "Don't worry. I'll be fine."

Once more, she heard another noise, which sounded like two pieces of metal being struck together. She left the room while Leon remained on the bed. She walked down a narrow hallway until she reached the same room that she had woken up in. Another noise, Anne heard, but this time it sounded as if it had been made accidentally. She followed the noise to a room farther down the hallway—possibly this storage room that Leon was talking about. The door was opened, but no lights were on inside. The only light was from the doorway, which cast a sharp beam of hallway light over the burgundy carpet.

Anne turned to her right and flinched from her own reflection!

The reflection, she noticed, except for her gleaming eyes, was dark and distorted and shaped like a spoon.

She inched toward the strange reflection, which returned back to normal size, and found over a dozen old mirrors, covered in a thick layer of dust, all varying in shapes and sizes, perched against the wall.

Anne walked back to the center of the room.

Then, a *rustling* noise to her left. . .

Behind a manikin of an African tribe leader stood Renny with a samurai sword gripped tightly in both of his trembling hands. He was sweating profusely. His breath was extremely heavy as if he had finished running a marathon. His skin was bloodless, as well, from the terror. His swollen eyes, the left one covered with a fresh bruise from where Diego had beat him on the head with his fist, followed a slowly moving silhouette inside the dark room. Anne examined the many statues scattered around the room, the busts, the manikins, and the paintings, the same ones she had found on the USB flash drive. The storage room was identical to the one on the flash drive—a "museum," as written in the journal entries.

As Anne spotted the same glass case at the very end of the main aisle, the sunlight eased from the overcast sky and cut through the distant window and splashed over a long blade, as sharp and tiny as a glint of light in the corner of her eye.

By the time Anne spun around, it was already too late.

The blade suddenly came across her bare throat and settled there along the flesh of her neck.

Anne gasped in great horror!

"*Who*. . . who the fuck are you?" Renny whispered sharply into her ear.

Anne's limbs went numb and heavy.

Her knees about gave way.

She cracked open her mouth to answer Renny's question, but the words somehow fell short.

"Answer me," Renny hissed as he pressed the blade harder against her neck.

"Anne," she uttered, her throat bobbing three times, twice upward and then once downward. "My na. . . naaa. . ." her lips trembling, ". . . name is Anne."

"Anne Roth?"

Anne listened closely to the man's voice behind her.

"Um," she stuttered, "yea. . . "

The voice, she thought, from the recording.

Renny carefully removed the sword from Anne's neck and spun her around.

"Renny?"

"How long have you been here?"

"I just got here not too long ago," she answered as she noticed the cuts and bruises over Renny's face. There was also a dried string of blood caked around his left nostril. "What happened to your face?"

"The butler," he said.

"Diego?"

"That's right," he said. "Diego."

"Why did he do this to you?"

"Because he's an evil son of a bitch with a lifelong vendetta against America," Renny said, trying to catch his breath. "That's why."

"I don't understand," Anne said confusedly. "What does he want?"

Renny threw his head in a nod and pointed behind Anne at the preserved head inside the glass dome.

"*That.*"

Renny looked closer and realized that there was no head inside the glass dome.

"Where?"

In a trance, Renny said, "It was there. . . "

"The head?"

"Yes."

"What is it?"

"You mean," Renny paused, "you don't know who it is?"

"Should I?"

"If I told you, you'd never believe me. . . "

"Try me."

Before Renny could utter another word, Diego said from the shadows, "Go on, Renny. Tell her."

Renny quickly grabbed Anne's arm and took a couple of steps back as Diego casually walked from the shadows.

"Get away from him," Renny said to Anne.

Diego asked calmly, "Nice sword. The Japanese call it the 'katana.' It dates back to the Muromachi period."

"Take another step and I'll cut your fucking head off."

Diego smirked, a dreadful, sinister thing.

"As you wish, Mr. Jacobson."

"What's going on here?" Anne said to Diego. "Renny told me you tried to kill him. Is that true?"

"Yes," Diego answered without giving the question any thought. "You know I couldn't let him leave here with all he knows. . . about your father. . . "

"So, you used him?"

"Of course I did," he said as he pointed at Renny. "Do you really trust this man? Do you, Anne?"

Anne shot a glance at Renny.

"This man is a journalist," he said to Anne. "He's paid to lie, Anne. Once your father is gone, he will make up whatever story his magazine wants in order to fulfill its personal interests. Would you want your father's story written by this man? Him! *He* will exploit your father and tell the American people exactly what they want to hear, that your father was a traitor to our country—notorious crime fighter turned criminal. Is that what you want?"

"He'll write about the truth," Anne said and once more glanced at Renny. "Won't you?"

Wiping the sweat from his forehead, Renny bobbed his head.

"If he does, Anne, if he does write about 'the truth,' then you must know that once people find out about this place, they will tear it down until there's nothing left of it."

Anne asked, "What makes you so sure?"

"Think carefully about this, Anne," Diego said. "Regardless of all that has happened, many years from now people will forget about what happened at Death Valley and remember your father as a hero, a man who stood up against the filth of Lansford. Do you want to tarnish your father's legacy?"

Anne didn't respond.

"Well, do you?"

"You should've thought about that before you decided to betray my father."

"*Betray* is a strong word to throw around, Anne," he said.

"Then, why exactly did you bring him here?"

"We brought Mr. Jacobson here to make *you* understand, Anne," Diego answered. "Don't you see? The only way you would be able to reconnect with who you were in the past was to recreate the past, to keep you on the run. But you already know this, Anne."

"We?" Anne said. "You said my father wasn't involved. He said so himself."

Diego's eyes widened—like the smirk, sinister things.

"He was *very* much involved, Anne."

"He's lying!" Renny blurted out as he shielded Anne with his other hand. "This piece of shit is behind it all!"

"*We*," Diego said over Renny's voice as he stepped closer, "we knew that you would be so frightened, Anne, so much that you wouldn't even trust anybody—not even the police, not even the weasels who worked at his little magazine."

"And then once you're done with Renny," she said, "then he's expendable like the rest of them, like those men you hired, like Jamie, like my father." Grimacing, Anne seethed, "Isn't that right, Diego?"

Diego never responded to the question.

Instead. . . "You must've been around eight, nine years old at the time when Marcus came to me," he said in a state of reflection, his face more relaxed. "You and your father were in Rural. Prior to Rural, he jumped around so much that I lost track of where he was. During his success as Freeze, he would pay frequent visits and check up on me, see how I was do-ing. And then, he stopped coming." Diego sighed heavily. "When you spend a lot of time alone, Anne, your only enemy is yourself. If it wasn't for what Cal-vin had told me the day before he died, then. . . " Di-ego paused, his eyes like tiny sabers, ". . . then *you*, Anne, you would've never existed at all." Diego opened his eyes and looked around the room in fasci-nation. "He was right, though, Calvin. This place *is* special." His manner was casual now, not as intense. "Marcus asked me about Leon's whereabouts. He told me they wouldn't harm Leon. But what they planned on doing to him would be worse than death. I couldn't let that happen. So, I sent Marcus on his way and told him to never come back, and if he did, there would be consequences."

Renny shouted out as he aimed the edge of the sword at Diego, "He's lying to you, Anne!"

"The journalist?" he said amusedly. "Calling me a liar?"

"He killed Marcus because Marcus was going to tell your father the truth about this son of a bitch," Renny told Anne.

"You're right about one thing, Mr. Jacobson," Di-ego said loosely. "I did kill Marcus for what he did to

Leon and his family. Any person in my position would've done the exact same thing."

Out of breath, Renny said, "He's lying, Anne—"

Diego interrupted, "Put the sword down, Mr. Jacobson."

Renny never did. He tightened his grip around the handle.

Diego directed his attention back to Anne.

"Anne," Diego said patiently, "do you think I would harm your father after all the years I've serviced him, doing dishes, preparing meals, doing the laundry. . . "

Renny eased Anne behind his body.

". . . Do you know what it's like to kill your own flesh and blood, to watch the pain wash over their eyes?"

Anne didn't respond.

"Do you?" he yelled, which caused both Renny and Anne to flinch. "I took a vow! I would never kill your father!"

"No," she said, now with clarity. "You just slowly killed him." Anne stepped away from Renny. "Right? All you did was make my father kill himself by ripping away the people he cared about the most. When he finally found happiness, you stole it from him because you were jealous. That's what *you did*." The tears filled her eyes. The tears now hardened like glass. "You knew this would happen to him. . . "

Renny took one step closer to Diego.

"Go ahead, Renny," he said haughtily as he held out his arms. "Make your move."

Renny grabbed Anne and stepped away from Diego.

"I never make the first move," he said, his breath labored from the adrenaline racing through his body.

"Of course, you don't," Diego said and grinned. "You're a writer who hides behind a computer all day and takes pleasure in ruining people's lives by exploiting them to the public and then when it comes to being accountable for your words, you find other places to hide." Renny couldn't believe what he was hearing from Diego. One minute praising writers and the next, blaming them for all of society's faults. Diego's eyes fell upon the glistening sword before him. "Like the katana. And you call me the coward? In my country, we have a name for you people. A *cobarde*. That's all you are, Mr. Jacobson, and that's all you'll ever be. . . "

In a heap of rage, Renny leaped forward with a thunderous grunt and swung the sword at Diego.

"Renny!" Anne screamed as she reached out to Renny.

Diego swiftly moved from the course of the samurai sword and pulled out the piano wire from his back pocket.

Once more, Renny struck at Diego, but Diego, in return, lassoed his wrist with the wire.

In the blink of an eye, he yanked the sword from Renny's hand.

4:31 PM

I took a vow, those were the words he thought he heard across the hallway.

Then, after that, the words *I would never kill your father*.

Leon listened closely, but the words were now muffled.

"Anne," he mumbled and struggled to rise from the pillow. "Is that you?"

No response.

"Wha. . . " he said, now angrily, ". . . what's going on?"

Again, there was no response.

Leon heard more yelling across the hallway, but he could only make out bits and pieces. He pulled the covers from the bed, blindly felt the air beside him until he came across the cane that was leaning against the nightstand, and staggered through the bedroom. Even taking a single step felt like dragging around a twenty-pound ball and chain around his ankle. He finally made it to the very edge of the doorway where he grabbed hold of the wall. By then, the bloodcurdling cries, as well as the frantic screams, had faded. He heard other sounds now, thuds, as well as moans.

"Anne?" he groaned as he hobbled down the hallway.

Suddenly, he heard Anne shout out the name *Renny*.

Following the cry was a loud thud against the floor. Having lived without eyes for so many years, Leon's other senses compensated like the sense of smell, hearing, and, most importantly, the sense of touch. Below his feet, the floor rumbled. In the subtle rumbles, Leon heard two men wrestling. One of the men gained the upper hand and pinned down the other man.

Panicking now, he hurried his pace, nearly tripping along the way. He closed in on the sounds, now more evident, the sound of a man choking to death.

Once Leon arrived at the source of the commotion, Diego was already on top of Renny. And by then, Renny was already dead. His death wasn't quick by any means. He struggled to his very last breath. Diego, who had both of his knees pinned against Renny's shoulders, released the handles of the piano wire. He took in a deep breath and embraced the warm blood dripping from his face and chin. To the left of Diego, Anne was lying on the floor from where she was thrown against one of the many columns in the room. Her head hit twice, the first from where her head had caught the initial impact of the column and then the second impact from where she fell like a rock against the floor.

Leon could feel the tension in the air pressed against his face.

"Anne?" he said warily as he staggered into the room.

Diego rose from Renny's lifeless body and casually walked toward Leon.

"It's Renny," he said, out of breath.

"Diego?"

"I found him in the gallery," Diego said as he slowly approached Leon. "He had a sword in his hand. He said he was going to call the cops and report a kidnapping. I told him he was free to leave. He snapped, Master Dorsey," he said, the tone in his voice was of great concern. "He. . . he came at me with the sword. I had to protect myself."

"What did you do, Diego?" Leon asked, struggling to stand on his feet.

Diego rushed toward Leon, who legs were wobbling. He grabbed Leon underneath the arms and held him upright.

"He's dead, sir," Diego said to Leon. "I'm afraid I had no other option. He was going to kill me."

A grimace rose upon Leon's narrow face.

"*You*. . . " Leon seethed, "you should've let him . . . Why, Diego? Now, everyone will be looking for him."

"But, Master Dorsey," Diego said abruptly. "I can fix this. I can dispose of the body. If anybody asks, then. . . then we will tell them we dropped him off at the airport. . . "

A sketchy voice from behind the column: "*He's lying. . .* "

Both Diego and Leon directed their attention toward the voice, Anne's voice. She was slow to stand to her feet.

Grabbing the knot on the side of her head, Anne used the column to stand upright.

"He's been holding Renny captive this entire week," she said as she staggered toward the center of the room. Her eyes sharpened over Diego's. "He may be able to fool an old blind man, but he can't fool me. He's been using you from the very beginning, Dad, using Renny, the others. . . "

"Anne. . . wha'do you mea—"

"Diego was behind it all," she said angrily as she pointed at Diego. "Go on. Ask him about the time Marcus came to visit you."

"I know what he did, Anne," Leon said gravely. "I was there."

"I'm talking about before," she corrected. "Marcus wasn't the one who told on you. Renny said it was *him*, Diego."

"Diego?" Leon said as he suddenly turned toward Diego's direction. "What? Why?"

Anne said loudly, "Tell him, Diego."

"What is she talking about, Diego?"

"Marcus wasn't the one who told the Company about your whereabouts," Anne said before Diego could utter a word. "It was him. . . right there. . . " she paused to catch her breath, ". . . this whole time. . . he played you, Dad. . . "

"Diego," Leon said surprisingly, "is this true?"

Diego didn't respond.

Leon cried out, "Is it true, goddamn it!"

He tried to remove his arm from Diego's grip, but Diego had a firm grip around Leon.

"Let. . . let go of me. . . *Diego*. . . "

He tried once more to pull himself from Diego.

Louder: "You're hurting me."

"Let him go," Anne said, squaring her shoulders to Diego, "or else. . . "

"Or else what?" Diego said with that same sinister thing on his face. "What are you going to do, you bitch?"

Anne squared both of her shoulders to Diego and stood defensively with her hands curled into fists. Her narrow eyes glistened. Beads of sweat raced down her forehead. The pale and sickly skin around her eyes turned dark. But her eyes, they grew brighter and fiercer. Something had clicked on inside her, a switch! Anne couldn't explain the feeling that she felt, a feeling opposite to what she felt day in and day out, that feeling of emptiness. This was different. Her skin felt as if it was on fire, and it all started after the blow to her head.

"Stop it. . . " he said as his throat suddenly double clutched. ". . . Wa. . . what are you doing? Stop. . . "

Diego let go of Leon's grip.

Leon's legs buckled.

His arms bolted outward. One of them managed to catch the wall behind him.

Before he could fall, he grabbed hold of the wall and fell to his knees.

Diego: "Stop it!"

Leon peered through the hazy darkness and saw two tiny lights glistening like two headlights.

"*She's doing it*. . . " he said under his labored breath.

With her hair gusting all around her head as if each strand of hair was alive in its own way, Anne dug the soles of her shoes into the floor and braced herself.

"Dad. . . " she whimpered, ". . . what's happening to me?"

"Breathe, Chloe," Leon said to Anne. *"Breathe."*

Diego's shriek echoed throughout the mansion.

"Dad!"

Leon yelled out, "Breathe, Chloe!"

As Diego lifted his arm to his face and covered his eyes, his fingers tingled—that familiar pins and needles feeling he knew about all too well. Then, strangely, the feeling tightened over his hand. That strange sensation prodded at him, sharper, harder. His hand suddenly became cold and stiff. The muscles in his entire arm stiffened as well. Then, it happened! It all started with the hair on his arms, which turned as hard as bodkins. The hair was first and then it was his skin. Once it reached the skin and then the nerves, the pain was excruciating. His skin turned gray, starting at the very tips of his fingers and then it spread to his fingernails and then his knuckles and then his wrist. By the time the gaze reached his wrist, his entire hand had been turned into stone.

Like Leon before him, Diego dropped to his knees—but without anything to embrace himself against.

"It's impossible. . . " Diego cried as he shielded his eyes with his good hand.

Before the gaze could take his entire forearm, he stumbled toward the doorway and ran away.

Out of breath, Anne fell to her knees and grabbed the side of her temple as the blood in her veins started to cool a bit.

"What. . . " she gasped and then cleared her throat and gagged a couple of times, ". . . whaaa. . . what da hell. . . jus' happened to me?"

"Breathe slowly," Leon said faintly. "It takes time to clear from your system."

"What is hap. . . "

"*Breathe*, Anne!"

She used the column behind her to stand to her feet. She did as her father had instructed and breathed, now slowly.

Once she caught her breath, she staggered to Renny's lifeless body and checked if Renny was still alive. She concluded he wasn't after she carefully pressed her ear against his gaping mouth and then searched for a pulse on the side of his bloody neck. She felt neither a breath nor a pulse. Then, she did what any person in her shoes would have done and closed his eyelids and crossed his arms over his chest. To her right, she heard a sudden grunt. She turned and saw Leon clutching his side. Anne rushed toward her father as quickly as she could without tripping over Renny's body.

"Are you okay?" she asked, embracing her father.

Leon responded with a nod of his head.

"Now," he said to Anne, "now, do you believe me?"

"I always knew there was something wrong with me. . . "

Leon grabbed Anne by the shoulder.

"There's abso. . . " Leon trailed off as he grabbed his chest with his other hand, ". . . na. . . nothing wrong with you!"

In a trance, Anne's eyes moved toward the floor.

Leon said once more, "Do you understand me?"

Anne bobbed her head and said, "We need to get out of here."

"Please. . . Anne. . . " Leon groaned, ". . . I don't know how much longer I can. . . "

"Yes," Anne said, catching her breath. "We can do this. Do you know why? Because you're Freeze, goddamn it."

Leon grimaced yet again.

Anne wrapped her arm around his loins and pulled him up to his feet, but Leon's weak legs quickly brought him back to the floor.

Fervently, Anne rallied, "Let's go, Freeze!"

She tried yet again; and while doing so, they both let out grunts, Anne's sharp and distinct while Leon's deep and gravelly. Anne instructed Leon to grab hold of the doorway and he did so as if he was clinging onto dear life.

"Wait," Leon said suddenly.

"What is it?"

"If what you said is true. . . then Diego. . . he won't leave without Agatha."

"Agatha?"

"The head. . . by the window. . . " Leon said, ". . . in the back."

"I already checked," Anne said. "It's not there."

"What do you mean?"

"I mean it's not there."

She confirmed that the head was not there as she scanned around the room.

As Anne pulled her eyes back to Leon, she spotted two strange statues in the corner of her eye. She took a second look at the statues, only to realize that she had seen them before. The last time Anne had seen the statues was back in Rural; and at the time, she was too distraught and sickened to even look at the things. She got a closer look at the statues, two of them, one of a gorgeous woman shielding her face in agony and another, a young boy stilled in a running stance. The sight of the statues brought back a wave of memories, none of them good.

Anne said to Leon, "Can you stand on your own?"

"Only for a minute," he said carefully.

She left Leon behind and walked toward the statues.

"Where are you going?" Leon said despairingly.

Anne didn't answer. Instead, she kept walking toward the statues. She reached the two and examined them briefly before she touched the side of the statue's face, the woman's face, her mother's face, Isabel. She was wearing the same exact clothes that she had died in. There was even blood over her collar from where one of the Companies' men had struck her in the side of the head with a pistol. She pulled her attention to the young boy, her brother, Dominic. He too was dressed in the same clothes he had died in: a *Ninja Turtles* tee shirt that matched a Leonardo watch and a pair of jean shorts that were one size too big for him. Anne's eyes crossed his hands, especially that one hand, the one missing the finger.

A grunt from behind caused Anne to turn around.

"Dad. . . " she said as he stumbled toward Anne.

Anne grabbed Leon before he fell.

"What are you doing?" she asked.

"You see them," he said. "Don't you?"

"Yeah," Anne said and helped Leon to the statues. "You kept them."

"Yes," Leon said solemnly. "Before I became ill, I came in here every night."

"Why?"

"I always thought there was a way back for them, for Dom and your mother," he said quietly. "I thought whatever the gaze could do, it could easily undo. I also kept them to remind me. . . "

"Remind you of what?"

Leon paused as he hung his head in misery.

"Dad?" she said closely. "What?"

"I kept them to remind me of what love once felt like," he said with his head down. "They were my everything, Anne. You are *my* everything. And you're all I have left."

"Are you saying what I have inside me, this power," Anne said clearly and looked into her mother's stoned eyes. "If it is a curse, then there must be a way to reverse the spell."

"No, Anne," Leon said, pulling his head upright. "I've tried. It doesn't work."

"Then, what are you saying?" Anne said. "I can do this to a human being, even someone I love deeply?"

5:33 PM

"*AGARRA tus cosas*," Diego barked as he stormed through the kitchen.

"Diego," Jasmine said in awe as she noticed Diego nursing his other hand, which was wrapped in a bloodstained towel.

She rushed through the kitchen.

Then, Diego cried out before Jasmine could examine his injuries, "That's an order!"

Jasmine stepped away from Diego and grabbed her belongings from her room, as he had demanded.

Diego placed his stone-hand on top of the kitchen counter and unbuttoned the three middle buttons from his dress shirt with his other hand, the good one.

5:34 PM

"I'M afraid so," Leon said after careful deliberation. "That is why you need to learn how to control it, Anne. The main thing: nobody must ever know who you are and *what* you can do."

Anne turned away from the statues.

She said to Leon, "I take it this head has something to do with what we are."

Leon barely nodded his head.

"Then," she said composedly, "it must be destroyed."

Again, he nodded his head, but this time more confidently.

5:35 PM

WITH his stone-hand rested inside the unbuttoned part of his shirt—the shirt acting as if it was a sling—Diego pulled out his cell phone from his pocket and dialed a phone number.

Another man picked up on the other end: "*Hola.*"

"Lucas," Diego said, out of breath, "there's been a slight change in plans."

5:36 PM

"WHAT do you think Diego's going to do with it?"

"I don't know, Anne," Leon said carefully as the thought slowly came to him. It was such a distant thought, one that Leon hadn't thought of in a very long time. Nonetheless, the thought greeted him like an unwanted guest. Leon remembered a conversation he and Diego had years ago, way before Leon had been diagnosed with cancer. Diego told Leon a story, a tragic one about his family in Venezuela and what he was forced to do to them. "Whatever he plans on doing with it," Leon said clearly, "it can't be good. You must stop him before it's too late."

"*We* will stop him," Anne said. "We're in this together. Remember? He murdered Renny."

Leon cut in, "But that's not what he's going to do to us." He placed his hand over her shoulder. "Come," he moaned. "I need my chair. . . "

Anne turned her shoulder and glanced at Renny's body.

"What about Renny?" she asked over her shoulder.

Leon replied, "Leave him. There's nothing we can do."

5:39 PM

THEY barely made it back to the master bedroom without the old man keeling over from excitement (after all, the past two weeks, mainly the week prior to this week, had been the most action Leon had experienced in many years—in some way or another, it had made him feel more alive and energetic than all of those years mopping around Leathery Manor). From the commotion downstairs, Anne figured that Diego was still here, but she didn't know exactly where.

The first thing Anne did was help Leon to his wheelchair. Secondly, Leon asked her to do him a favor, which was to empty out the urine bag strapped to the side of his leg. Anne had no choice in the matter, even though emptying out urine bags wasn't quite her forte. Leon informed Anne about the urinal in the bathroom. She asked what it looked like. "Like a pitcher for iced tea, only made of plastic," Leon described. Anne didn't have much trouble finding the urinal. She lifted up Leon's loose pant leg and emptied out the urine from the bag and dumped the urine into the toilet. Anne was immediately praised with another thank you from her father.

Leon pointed to the dresser at the other end of the room, but Anne was suddenly caught off guard by the slam of a car door outside. She peeked through the window and checked the driveway. Both cars, the Jaguar and the Rolls Royce, were still parked in the driveway. The trunk door of the Jaguar was opened, but Anne didn't see any sign of Diego.

"He's still here," she said to Leon.

"Of course he is," Leon said. "Diego won't leave until he ties up loose ends."

"Loose ends?"

"Us," Leon said. "We're the loose ends."

Anne pulled herself from the window and wheeled Leon to the far dresser. On top of the dresser was an old vinyl player, which looked about as ancient as the relics from the previous room they were in. Next to the dresser perched a shelf of records from Classical to Motown, some still wrapped in loose film. Her father didn't strike her as a Marvin Gaye fan (Anne saw that one record, "What's Going On," protruding from the edge of the shelf), but then again, Anne hardly knew anything about her father other than what she had discovered on the flash drive.

Leon reached up to the top drawer but struggled to open it.

"Give me a hand," he said to Anne. "Will you?"

Anne opened the drawer for Leon.

He sorted through the neatly folded white tee shirts until his hand crossed a rusty Zigzags can near the bottom of the drawer.

Anne asked, "What's this?"

He pulled out the Zigzags can and showed it to Anne.

"Do you trust me, Anne?" he asked.

"Yeah," she said.

Leon opened the can, peeled back the powdery paper inside, and revealed five yellowish-brown snake scales, which, to Anne, appeared like old fingernails.

Next to the scales, she saw, was a silver key attached to a chain. There was a letter and numbers on the key, but Anne couldn't read them from where she was standing. However, she was more interested in these scales.

She ignored the key and took a closer look at the scales.

"What is that stuff?"

"Scales."

"Snake scales?"

"Yes," Leon said tentatively.

He extended the can toward Anne.

"Here," he said. "Take one."

Anne was hesitant at first.

"Go on."

"But. . . "

"Trust me," Leon said.

She reached inside and grabbed a scale.

Once more, her eyes crossed the key.

Anne asked, "What's the key for?"

Leon ignored Anne's question, closed the lid, and inserted the Zigzags can into his pocket.

"May I?" he said as he held out his palm.

Anne carefully placed the scale in Leon's palm.

With his index finger and thumb, he picked up the scale.

"This is the only way you can defeat Diego," he said. "By ingesting this scale, you will have twice the power you already have."

"I have to eat that?"

"I know how this may soun—"

"Ridiculous," she interrupted. "It sounds ridiculous. . . "

"It's the only way. . . "

Anne turned away.

"Anne," Leon said from behind, "it's the *only* way."

"If it's the only way," Anne turned back around and faced Leon, "then let's do it."

Leon pointed in the vicinity of Anne's mouth.

"Open your mouth."

With his hand, he searched for Anne's mouth, which was already opened.

Right before he placed the scale on top of Anne's tongue, she closed her mouth, pulled back her head, and said, "You never answered my question."

Leon lowered his hand and sighed.

Again, she asked, "What's the key for?"

"I was hoping to discuss the key with you later," he said, "but since you've asked, I will tell you." He paused and then, finally, pulled out the Zigzags can from his pocket. "The key is for you, Anne."

"I told you I already have a house."

"It's not for a house."

"Then, what's it for?"

"A safety deposit box."

"For what?"

"I can't tell you what's inside the box," Leon said. "Only you can be the one to find out for yourself. *However*, I will tell you this." The thought of that one man and then the awful thing he did to his daughter caused his heart to race. He carefully calmed his breathing. "There," Leon said carefully, "there are only two reasons why people run, Anne. They're either chasing someone or someone's chasing them. In time, you're going to have to make a choice, Anne. Either you run or you don't. I will tell you right now." He leaned closer to Anne. "Running will get you nowhere," Leon said. "Look where it got me. *Look* where it got us."

"You hardly know anything about me," she said, her voice cracking. "And now, you. . . you. . . "

"I know that searching for answers in the bottom of a bottle will get you nowhere in life," Leon said. "I know there's more to life than feeling sorry for yourself. Diego," another pause, "Diego told me about you, how you're always hanging around bars, told me about your drinking, how you're always 'looking' for somebody. The only answer you're going to find in the bottom of a bottle is a reflection of your own self. It's time to move on with your life. Don't make the same mistakes I did."

Anne grimaced.

"You were never there for me when I needed you the most and now you want to give me life lessons?"

"I'm here *now*, Anne," Leon said loudly. "Aren't I?"

"How can you—"

"Diego found him."

"Found him?" she said. "Found who?"

"Louis Bringer."

Anne clenched her teeth.

"Why are you telling me this?" she seethed.

"Because there's going to come a day, Anne, when you're going to have to look the devil directly in his eyes," he said, "and you're not going to like what you see." Leon placed the Zigzags can on his lap, and with his free hand, he grabbed Anne's hand. "The first step into moving on with your life is to accept who you are. Don't let anybody tell you any differently. You hear me?"

"What's in the box?" Anne said dourly.

"Answers," he said bluntly and handed Anne the Zigzags can. "Main National Bank, Port Row Street, a couple of miles outside the city of Sanford. Password: Anodes." Then, he spelled out each letter for Anne, "A-N-O-D-E-S. Anodes"

"Anodes?" she said. "Why Anodes?"

Leon paused for a moment.

"Maybe," he said in a trance, "maybe because I've always wanted to go there."

Anne finally grabbed the can, but Leon never let go.

"*Move on*, Anne," he said as he let go of the Zigzags tin can.

She eyed the can closely and then placed it in her back pocket.

"Are you ready?" Leon said as he lifted up the scale.

Anne asked, "Are there any side effects?"

"Yeah," Leon said sternly. "You turn into a grumpy old man."

Anne stepped back.

"Kidding," he said flatly.

Leon's shoulders deflated.

"Nice one," she said with a ghost of a smirk flashing across one side of her face. "Okay." Anne sighed. "I'm ready."

Leon placed the scale on the tip of Anne's tongue.

"Now, swallow." Leon's hand ran down Anne's chin. He noticed that she didn't swallow. Either she was too afraid or she couldn't muster enough saliva in her mouth to swallow the dried, coarse thing. Leon said once more, "Trust me."

Anne reared back her chin and swallowed the scale down her throat. Even though Anne didn't have a clue as to what dirt tasted like, she assumed it tasted just like this or at least around the ballpark. And even when she swallowed the scale, it was sharp and jagged and burned all the way down until it reached her gut.

"Okay," she said as she cleared her throat. "Now what?"

"Give it time."

"How will it make me feel?"

At first, Leon didn't answer.

Anne asked once more.

Then, he finally said, "Unstoppable. . . "

6:04 PM

As Anne and Leon rode the elevator to the first floor of the mansion, the sun was already setting.

Once they reached the first floor, Diego was standing in front of the fireplace with his back facing them.

He was no longer dressed in his typical butler getup: a black sports coat with coattails, black tie tucked underneath a silver vest, white dress shirt, and white gloves.

Instead, he was wearing a pair of black steel boots, black cargo pants, black long sleeve shirt underneath a black jacket with a shoulder holster around his torso—the zebrawood grip of a pistol protruding from his left breast.

Diego heard the soft ding of the elevator, but not once did he turn to acknowledge the two, father and daughter.

His left arm was held inside a splint that Sophia had thrown together.

"He's here," Anne whispered closely to Leon. She spotted a beige-looking bag, which was about the size of an average head, resting on the fireplace mantle. She could only assume that the head, Agatha's head, was inside. She whispered once more, "I think I see the head."

"Stay close to me," Leon said as Anne wheeled Leon into the living room.

"What took you two so long?" Diego said pompously as he stared at the fire below.

"Had to put on some makeup," Anne said sarcastically.

Diego mumbled, "How lovely."

"Surprised you're still here, Diego," Leon barked. "All this time. After all we have been through. . . "

"I'll only tell you this once, amigo," Diego said with his back still turned to both Anne and Leon. "Take your daughter and go back to bed and die in peace."

"Not before you explain to me why you sold me out!" Leon cried out, his hands shaking. "After all these years," he coughed, "this is how you repay me?"

"Shouldn't it be the other way around, Leon?" Diego returned fiercely. "Everything that *I* have done for you. I took care of you when all of your loved ones abandoned you, including that one standing right next to you. Where was she when *you* needed her the most?"

They didn't answer, neither Leon nor Anne.

"I was always there for you," Diego said over the silence.

"I know you were, Diego," Leon said gently. "And I am so grateful to have had a friend like you. Tell me. . . *why* did you do it, Diego. . . *WHY*. . . "

Diego turned his head slightly.

"You had your vengeance, Leon," he said over his shoulder. "Now, let me have mine. . . "

"Please, Diego," Leon said, his voice strained and gravelly. "Remember the vow you took? Remember? Remember Calvin. It doesn't have to be like this. . . "

Anne leaned over her father's shoulder and whispered into his ear, "He's wearing some kind of helmet."

"Calvin is dead to me," he said and turned around to face both Anne and Leon. "And soon, so will you. . . "

Diego displayed the new gear that he was wearing, a custom made visor, which the Company had made for him as a present commending him for all of his cooperation.

"Let me ask you something, Anne," he said teasingly. "Do you know why police officers wore visors when your father worked with them?"

Anne didn't respond.

"Well, I tell you," Diego said as he paced around the fireplace. "It was your father's second time working with the force. He did so well the first time that they called him back for a second." As Diego had a tendency to do at times, he clapped his tongue against the roof of his mouth. "Big mistake," he said quietly. "Your father arrived at the scene of a crime. One of Lansford's own accidentally shot a pedestrian, a mother of two, during a chase. Later that night at the hospital, the mother died from the gunshot. Leon was called to convince the witness that Mrs. Brown—the mother—didn't get shot by a cop. Yet, the perp who was being chased by the authorities killed Mrs. Brown because she was simply in the way." While Diego was telling the story, Leon hung his head in shame. "Leon arrived at the scene, cool and calm and collected as always. *Freeze*." He smirked from the name *Freeze*. "After he works his magic on the witness, a seasoned cop, Officer Banning, says something to Freeze. Freeze doesn't like it. Not one bit. So, Freeze looks the officer in the eye. Officer Banning's lips turn to stone. Right there! In front of everybody! Even the commissioner! The damage didn't look so bad on the outside." Diego chortled as he imagined Officer Banning in his mind, a man who appeared as if he was wearing gray lipstick. "At least not to some. *However*, on the inside, Officer Banning's entire jaw had been turned to stone. He couldn't talk. And even if he even if he tried, every word was muffled by the sounds of two pieces of stone clacking together. As a result, Officer Banning had to be fed through a feeding tube. He never left his house. His only friends became the four walls around him. It was as if he was locked in a prison. Officer Banning ended up quitting the force. Three months later, he decided to put a bullet in his head." Diego raised his good hand. Pointed his finger at the side of his temple. Anne glanced over at Leon, who still had his head held downward. "After Banning's death, they issued these babies," he tapped the visor, "to every police officer. If Freeze was going to be on the scene, then you *had* to wear your visor. The point of the story: these people needed your father so much that they were willing to spend the taxpayer's hard earned money as a 'precaution.' It was almost like having a rabid dog around. If it bites its master, then you lock it up in a kennel, as any right person would do. Then, if it bites its master a second time, then you put a muzzle on it and prevent it from harming others. A third time, well, you get the point. I knew the Company wouldn't have been so. . . " he thought carefully about what word to use, ". . . *lenient* as the force was with Leon."

"My father made his mistakes, Diego," Anne seethed, her hands curling into fists. "But he was given a second chance to start over and he created a family of his own, a new life. And then, you took all of that away from him. My father was all the family you had and once you saw him with a family of his own and you were out of the picture, you decided to betray himm—"

"—Why does it matter anymore?" Diego suddenly interrupted. "When Leon dies, all of this," he looked around the living room, "all of this will be mine."

"Think again, Diego," Leon said abruptly. "You honestly think I would hand all of this over to you after what you've put me through! I'll make sure you don't get a single penny!"

"Well, you can forget about calling up Lawyer Bill," Diego said coyly. "He will no longer be in the. . . picture. . . "

"What did you do?"

"Let's just say. . . " Diego paused, ". . . well, Lawyer Bill had himself a little tumble. But don't you worry. My guys are all over it."

"You won't get a damn thing," Leon said in agony. "I'll make sure of it. . . "

"It's already done," Diego said casually. "All you have to do now is. . . " he shrugged, ". . . die."

"I have a new deal, Diego." Leon grunted softly. "Leave now and we'll spare your life. . . we'll go our separate ways and forget all about this. . . "

"You and what army," he said as he bravely stepped closer to Anne, whose eyes were now glowing. He tilted his head in curiosity, his good hand easing behind his back. "Her? That pathetic thing you call a daughter?" His voice grew bitter, raspier. "I've waited an entire lifetime to possess this power," he nodded at the bag on the mantle, "and I'm not going to let some ornery bitch get in my way!"

Diego grabbed the piano wire from his back pocket.

In two swift movements, he swung the piano wire around Anne's neck—one handle intertwining around the wire and then locking around her throat.

Anne reached at her throat and tried to squeeze her fingers underneath the wire before it was too late, but the wire was too hard and thin to ease her fingers underneath.

While Anne gasped and choked and dropped to her knees, Leon barked, "What are you doing? If it's me you want dead, then kill me goddamn it! Leave her alone!"

Diego grinned wickedly.

"Two heads are better than one," Diego said as he leaped over Anne's body and pulled back on the wire.

Anne's face slowly turned red and then purple. The veins in her forehead swelled.

There was a noise coming from above, a pulsating sound, and it was getting louder!

Diego looked to the ceiling above.

"Sounds like my ride," he said to himself.

Before Diego choked her to death, Leon grabbed the cane holstered along the side of the wheelchair, pinpointed the grunts and groans, and rammed his bony shoulder into Diego, which caused Diego to drop the piano wire. Anne freed herself from Diego's legs. She removed the wire from her neck.

While Anne coughed and gagged and tried to get air back into her lungs, Leon, once more, charged at Diego, but Diego, more aware now, shoved him aside.

Leon stumbled and tripped and hit his right side along the sharp corner of a table.

With a piercing moan, he fell and made a loud *thud* over the floor.

Diego turned to Leon, who was now motionlessly lying on the floor. His bruised hand was clutched over his side, precisely around his liver. He flipped open the visor and tended to Leon. His facial expression went from solemn to furious. His eyes flared, dark and fiery.

"Look at what you. . . " Diego said to Anne. "You bitch!   Look. . . at. . . what. . . you. . . made   . . . me . . . do. . . "

As Diego stood to his feet, the side of his head was greeted by the metallic end of the cane. The visor took most of the blow and then the side of Diego's hip as it struck the hard slate surrounding the fireplace. A small section of the visor was cracked and chipped away. One of Diego's eyes was left exposed. The other one shielded by the visor.

Anne darted toward Leon, who was still moaning.

"Dad," she said and lifted up his shirt. The wound over his side had instantly turned from red to purple. She noticed the severity of the blow, the dark color spreading over his papery skin. She reached down and wrapped her arm around Leon's upper body. "Come on," she grunted, as she made an attempt to lift up Leon, "work with me, Dad!"

Leon used the cane for extra support as he staggered to his feet; the right side of his body was limp and numb.

As they took a couple more steps from the living room, Diego suddenly grabbed hold of Anne's ankle.

She stumbled, which caused Leon to stumble as well. He braced himself over the cane. The injury overtook Leon so much that, once Anne fell from his grip, he fell as well, but over the couch. Once more, Diego tugged on her ankle. The third tug sent Anne flopping in the air. Her hands flung out beneath her, as her face came driving to the floor. Her hands and chin took most of the fall. One of her teeth in the back of her mouth had chipped from where her chin smacked the floor.

Before she could recover, Diego climbed his way up both of her legs. She did all she could to kick the furious man off, but he threw aside each leg that came flying his way.

Anne managed to sneak in one blow to his stomach, which momentarily winded Diego.

In these few moments of recovery, she crawled away from Diego.

Leon barked from behind, "*Use it*, Anne! Use the gaze!"

Anne tried to use the gaze as Leon had told her, but the visor was making it more difficult to look into Diego's eyes. Part of the visor was cracked, she saw. She knew she wasn't as talented as her father when it came to using the gaze. She didn't know where to begin, how the gaze worked, or if the gaze came out naturally through concentration. Anne gave it a try on the little part of eye that was showing through the visor. Her eyes honed in on Diego's eye, that little part of it. It was like trying to thread a needle with arthritic hands.

"I can't," she cried out as Diego stood to his feet.

As he loomed over her body, Anne searched for a weapon around the living room. Surely, she couldn't defeat him with her own hands. He was much too powerful for her. And the gaze wasn't working. Then, a tiny glint in the corner of her eye. . . Anne turned and spotted a brass fireplace set next to the fireplace. She saw that one piece with the sharp end—the poker. She made an attempt toward the poker while Diego was still regaining his strength. She reached for it, but he kicked away her hand at the very last second, sending her body into the fireplace. The logs inside suddenly broke loose. A cloud of fire chips rushed into the air like fireflies. Anne's sleeve caught on fire. She quickly rolled from the fireplace and patted out the fire before it could spread over her entire arm.

Then, Diego picked up the poker.

"Looking for this," he said sinisterly as he waved around the poker.

Just as Anne put out the fire from her sleeve, the tip of the poker came whizzing by. She ducked out of the way before the sharp end could strike her dead. Diego swung three more times at Anne. On the fourth attempt, the poker caught the side of Anne's arm. Anne bellowed, but she pushed through the pain as he swung once more. Anne ducked and dodged. And then again. She rolled out of the way from the oncoming poker and picked up a lamp from the table. Diego swung at Anne yet again, but she stood her ground and knocked away the poker with the lamp. She grabbed the cord on the lamp and swung at Diego. The prongs hit the side of Diego's head, dazing him. Then, she swung a second time, a third. On the fourth attempt, the cord managed to wrap around his throat. The prongs locked around the cord, securing the cord around Diego's throat.

"Taste of your own medicine," she said as she yanked back on the cord, which sent Diego to his knees.

She dropped the lamp and pulled tighter on the cord with both hands. Instead of trying to squeeze his fingers inside the cord before the cord could choke him to death, he grabbed the cord and yanked it from her hands.

Now weaponless, Anne stood with her fists ready.

Diego charged at Anne and slammed her to the floor. He pinned Anne down with both of his knees and wailed on her. In his assault, Anne did all she could to protect her face. At the same time, she reached out for things to throw at Diego. One of them included a fiery log from the fireplace. A piece of it struck Diego in the side of the head, which loosened and shifted the visor from his face.

His eyes were now exposed underneath the visor!

But Anne was too dazed from the barrage of blows.

While Diego continued to punch Anne across the face, the carpet suddenly caught fire from the fiery log.

Next, the fire spread toward the couch. By the time the fire reached the couch, the fire spread like dominoes, spreading from one piece of furniture to another. Leon felt the heat pressed against his face and backed away from the fire.

While crawling away from the fire, he felt an object slide behind him. He blindly ran his hand across the hardwood.

At the same time, the flames grew all around Diego as he curled his bloody hands around Anne's throat.

Diego closed both of his eyes, making sure the gaze didn't penetrate them.

"Time to die. . . "

As her face turned blue, Anne gasped for air.

"You see, Anne," Diego seethed. Eyes still closed. "All I have to do is close my eyes. And when I open them, you will be dead."

Diego's eyes suddenly bolted open.

He gasped, his shoulders shot upright—both hands releasing from Anne's throat.

Slowly, his eyes trailed downward to the edge of the poker protruding from the upper left side of his chest, just below the clavicle. His hands hovered around the poker. The visor slipped from his head, and he fell forward. Anne moved before Diego's body could land on top of her. She pushed his lifeless body aside and found Leon hunched over in front of the fireplace.

"Did I get him. . . " he said faintly.

"Yeah," Anne said as she tried to catch her breath.

Leon breathed a sigh of relief.

"Not bad for a blind man," Anne said as she managed to stand to her feet.

The fire spread along the walls now.

"Let's get out of here before this place comes down on us."

". . . Good idea."

As Anne tended to Leon, she noticed the wool bag on the mantle.

She asked, "What about the head?"

"We'll take it with us," Leon said.

Anne grabbed the head from the mantle—grimaced from the harsh smell emitting from the bag—picked up the cane from the floor, and then walked Leon from the house.

On the way out, Anne grabbed the car keys of the Rolls Royce from the kitchen counter.

6:41 PM

BY the time they made it to Rolls it was dark outside, and half of the mansion was engulfed in flames.

"What do we do now?" Anne asked Leon as she heard the sound of a helicopter behind the mansion.

Leon thought for a moment.

Finally, he said, "The well?"

"What well?"

"The one you used to play around," he said.

She followed suit and thought for a moment, mainly about this well.

6:43 PM

SHERIFF Lucas Navarro was no longer dressed in his typical beige sheriff's attire. Instead, as with Diego, he was dressed in an all black militant outfit.

As he anxiously waited inside the running helicopter (the nurse, Sophia, was already seated in the back of the chopper, this time her scrubs were gone and she was dressed in black militant attire, as well as the same black boots as Diego), he looked south and found a darkened figure stumbling from the burning mansion. Another figure, who was carrying a duffel bag, quickly followed. Eventually, the two darkened figures were revealed in the light cast from the rising flames: one was Jasmine and the other Diego. Jasmine swooped in beside Diego's right side, his good side, and kept him from falling over as they walked together to the helicopter.

In one last motion, Diego spun around, stopped for a second, and watched Leatherby Manor burn.

"*Señor*. . . " Jasmine said from his side.

Right then, Diego's eyes glazed over.

But he never shed a tear.

Not one.

"Let's go," he said to Jasmine.

They finally arrived at the helicopter.

Grabbing the wound along the left side of his chest, Diego said to Jasmine after she tossed the duffel bag inside the back of helicopter, "*Siga el plan original* (follow the original plan)."

Jasmine returned with a nod of her head and backed away from the helicopter.

Diego opened the door to the cockpit where Lucas was waiting behind the cyclic stick.

"Thank you for your service, Lucas," he said as he pulled out a pistol from the holster and aimed the barrel at Lucas's head.

6:45 PM

"I used to throw pennies down a well when I was a little girl," Anne said to Leon.

"That's it," he said tiredly. "Can you take me there?"

"Sure," Anne said. "Can you make it?"

A sudden gunshot rang out underneath the same pulsating sound of the main rotor blades!

"Diego. . . " Leon said under his breath.

Anne wrapped her arm around Leon and walked him to the Rolls.

6:52 PM

ON the short drive to the well, Anne cracked open the windows to help air out the car from that awful smell emitting from the bag. She didn't know exactly what the smell was, nor did she really care at this point.

When they arrived at the well, which had been boarded up for safety purposes after a bad storm about two years ago, the helicopter had taken off behind the flaming mansion.

As Anne helped Leon from the backseat, the two couldn't help but look to the sky.

"Where's he going?" she asked, as she guided Leon to the well.

"Don't know," Leon said as he propped himself upright with the cane. "The head," he said weakly. "Throw it in."

Anne placed the bag aside and removed the loose board from the opening, which caused a rusty nail to drop into the well. The fall was so far down that Anne never heard a splash or a thud or even a single sound for that matter.

Curious, she gazed down into the hole and couldn't even see the bottom. All that remained was a void of darkness fading into oblivion, which made Anne wonder about the darkness and how strange it was, if the well, in fact, had any bottom at all, or if the other end of the well wound up in China. She heard about these rumors as a child, not about the well, but about digging holes into the ground, and if you dig a hole far enough into the earth, then you could possibly wind up in China. These, of course, were only rumors. But still, it made Anne wonder about the unavoidable "what if." She put aside her suspicions and picked up the dirty wool bag from the ground.

As Anne was about to open the bag, Leon said suddenly, "Anne, throw it in!"

Without hesitation, she leaned over the well and dropped the bag into the hole.

Anne said suspiciously, "And the flash drive?"

She pulled out the USB flash drive from her right pocket, not left.

"That story was for you, Anne," Leon said. "For you and no one else."

"So you were in on it," Anne said clearly. "You said you weren't involved."

Leon said, "Diego told me the plan was to scare you. He never told me about your foster parents. . . or your friends. I swear, Anne. . . if I knew what he was gonna do, I would. . . I would've never agreed. . . you have to *believe me*. . . you must. . . "

Someone had to be held accountable, Anne knew. From the looks of her father, Anne knew she couldn't grill him any longer, as much as she thought about it: grilling her old man, as a detective would do to a suspect in an interrogation room. Leon was in no condition to argue or explain his story right now. In his view, the story had already been told. And it was up to Anne to believe it or not.

"Whatever you do," Leon breathed slowly, "you mustn't let anyone else see it. . . "

"Shouldn't the people know about what the Company did to you? What they did to us?"

"If they find out about me, then they will found out about you, Anne," Leon said as he shook his head. "I don't want that. *You* don't want that. . . " he tried to catch his breath, ". . . never, Anne. Never let them take what's inside you. I want you to promise me. . . "

"I promise," she said soon after.

She turned her attention to Leatherby Manor, which was now completely engulfed in flames.

She thought carefully about whether or not to dispose of the flash drive.

After she finally made up her mind, she smashed the flash drive from her right pocket over a rock and tossed the remaining pieces of the drive into the well and then placed the board over the hole. She guided Leon back to the car and helped him to his seat.

As he sat there moaning and grimacing, she carefully lifted up his shirt and examined the mark over the right side of his body. It didn't look good, Anne realized as she directed her attention to her father's face, the deep lines running through it. The lesion had spread from his liver to his chest. Anne knew her father didn't have much time, but she didn't want to tell him something he already knew.

7:18 PM

BY the time the two made it to the front gate, Leon was already out of it. The first thing Anne thought about when she saw her father in the rear view mirror was that he was dead and she never got that chance to say goodbye to him.

"Dad," she said as she looked in the mirror.

Leon slowly rolled his head over the headrest.

"I need to get you to a hospital."

"No," Leon groaned.

"But you'll die. . . "

"There's no comin' back fro'this," Leon mumbled. "You and I know. . . "

The gate automatically opened once Anne pulled the car closer.

"When you were a lil' girl," Leon said as Anne sped down the unpaved road, "I used to take you. . . to this spot on the beach. . . remember?"

"Pirate's Cove," Anne said as she witnessed each grimace in Leon's face caused by each subtle bump in the road. "I remember."

Leon grimaced severely and grabbed his side from another bump.

He said intensely, "Take me there!"

"Are you sure you want this?"

"Yes. . . " Leon coughed, ". . . they'll never find me there."

"What do you mean?"

Leon grunted and said to Anne, "You know this is a one-way ticket, dear. . . "

7:28 PM

As Anne made a left on Ocean Front, she passed two wailing fire trucks.

In the backseat, Leon was fading in and out of consciousness.

"Don't die on me just yet," Anne said as she glanced in the rear view mirror.

"Anne," Leon uttered, struggling to hold up his head, "I want to gi. . . give you something." He reached his frail hand inside his pocket and pulled out a silver bracelet. He reached around the driver's seat, but his strength was too weak to hand his daughter the bracelet. With one hand on the steering wheel, Anne reached around the seat and grabbed it from her father's weak grip. "This bracelet belonged to'ur mother. I want you to have it. . . "

Anne pulled her eyes from the winding road ahead and glanced down at the bracelet in her palm.

"It's beautiful," she said. "Thank you."

"So, tell me about yourself, Anne," Leon said softly as he grimaced once more. "Do you have a boyfriend?"

Anne hesitated to answer.

Once more, her eyes crossed the rear view mirror.

"No," she said with a sigh. "I mean, I did before all of this happened to me."

"Sorry. . . "

"Don't be," Anne said coldly.

"Are you happy?" He corrected, "Were you happy?"

Anne thought about the question.

"Yeah," she said with her voice cracking. "Well, I mean," she cleared her throat, let out another breathy sigh, and then shrugged, "that's what Harold asked me before he died."

"Was Harold your boyfriend?"

"Foster parent," Anne said and paused in thought. After she reunited with her father, Anne remembered, she told him that her foster parents were the *only* family she knew, the only family she had ever known— that was before she realized who she was and what she was capable of doing to another person. "I. . . " Anne said, her voice trembling, ". . . I thought I was happy." The tremble went away. Now, her voice was clear. "Now, I realize exactly who my real friends and family are. Harold and Molly, my foster parents—don't get me wrong—they were good people." She shot another glance in the mirror. "But I don't think raising a teenager was a solution to their failing marriage. They provided for me. I'll give them that. They gave me my space. Never hovered. But at times, I felt like I was getting in the way."

"They did what they could, Anne. . . "

"I know they did," Anne said and changed her thought.

7:46 PM

THE flames were too great when the firefighters arrived at the mansion. They did all they could to extinguish the fire.

Right now, the only thing they could do was watch it burn, all of it, straight to the ground.

7:48 PM

"THE first time I met Michael, my boyfriend," Anne said to her father, "I was completely in love with him. I thought. . . I thought I was out of his league." Anne shook her head, *not* in disgust, but from her recent naiveté. "He was way cooler than the other guys. I *thought* Michael loved me. After a few months into our relationship, I found out he was seeing other girls. And Jamie. . . " Anne paused yet again. She said in contempt, "I should've known."

Leon asked, "Who's Jamie?"

"Nobody," Anne said sternly. "She's nobody." Then, another sigh rolled from her lips. "These people, my foster parents, Michael, all of them turned out to be the wrong people for me."

"Nobody. . . nobody's perfect. . . "

"*You* were perfect," Anne said, the tears falling from her eyes. "Our family, we were perfect." She tightened her hand around the steering wheel. "You know. . . when you're born into this world, you don't get a chance to pick your parents. But if somehow, there was a chance where you could pick, I would've picked you and mom any day of the week. So, I don't know how to answer that question: *Am I happy?* I suppose all my happiness died in Rural." She shot her eyes, now sharpening, toward the mirror. "I *hated* you so much. You know that." The tears raced down her cheeks, now like tiny fists. Anne seethed, "I couldn't even stand the sight of your face. For so long, I wanted you dead. . . "

Leon said quietly, "I'm sorry, Chloe. . . "

Anne drifted into a daze.

"My name was Chloe," she said mindlessly.

"You're my Chloe." Leon suddenly moaned, clutching his side. "You'll always be my Chloe. . . "

Anne grimaced as well, but not from the pain.

"Maybe there was one thing Diego did right," Anne said with clarity as she nodded her head in agreement. "I didn't know what true love was until the night those two men came to my house and tried to kill me. At the time I ran away, I didn't want to believe that you had anything to do with it and that it was this Company you worked for—they were to blame for mom's and Dom's death." Anne moved her eyes from the road to rear view mirror. "I'm sorry that I abandoned you when you needed me. I didn't," Anne wiped the tear from her eye, "I didn't realize how much you loved us. If I could redo the past, I would. . . in a heartbeat. I would've stayed here and taken care of you and moved you away from this place. . . away from Diego. . . "

"Don't be sorry," he said, his voice rattling. "Please. . . "

Anne glanced in the mirror.

". . . Take a good look," he said abruptly. "This is what feeling sorry for yourself will do to you. A regret is like a cancer and it will eat away at you until there's nothing left of you but a woman running from her own shadow."

Anne sniffled and cleared the tears from her face.

"We're almost here," she said vacantly as she witnessed the sign for Pirate's Cove.

12 MILES, the sign read.

For Anne, twelve miles seemed too long.

8:06 PM

"GOT a live one over here!" the young firefighter shouted out as he kneeled over Lucas Navarro's body.

The closest firefighter, a veteran named Whiskers, darted to the body.

He kneeled down next to the other firefighter and examined the gunshot wound over Lucas's face.

The firefighter's jaw lowered in shock.

"Holy shit," he mumbled.

The young firefighter asked, "What is it, Whiskers?"

"It's Sheriff Navarro. . . "

"Are you sure?"

Whiskers turned toward his other colleagues.

"Ambulance!" he yelled. "Hurry!"

8:15 PM

WHEN they pulled up to Pirate's Cove, Leon was already passed out.

Anne parked the car in the graveled lot in front of a large dune, hurried from the driver's seat, and checked on Leon in the backseat.

"Dad," Anne said as she shook Leon's shoulders. "Wake up. . . we're here. . . "

Leon was unresponsive.

"Come on, Dad," she said once more, "Wake up. Please, Dad. . . "

Leon nudged his head toward Anne's direction.

"Izzy?" he mumbled.

"It's me," Anne said. "Chloe."

She helped Leon from the backseat. His body was heavy, and he wasn't helping her out that much. She walked him along a wooden pathway that led them to the secluded beach. To the right of the beach was Pirate's Cove, a massive rock along the rugged shore that formed an arch over the ocean. Once they reached the sand, the walk was extremely arduous for Leon. He could hardly take one step into the sand before stumbling to his knees. They ended up resting halfway toward the cove in the sand. The tide was feet away from their bodies. Even the sound of the ocean water splashing against the shore created hypnosis for Leon.

"I can't," Leon groaned as Anne tried once more to carry him toward the cove.

Anne fell to her knees as well and sat beside Leon, who was embracing the ocean breeze.

"Fine," she said as she combed Leon's hair with her hand. "We'll just rest here. How's that sound?"

With the last bit of strength in his body, Leon lifted up his hand and touched Anne's face, her cheekbones, her nose, her chin, her forehead.

Anne stared into Leon's eye sockets; and, for the slightest moment, she saw him with two eyes, the two blue eyes that she remembered looking into when she was a young girl, the two calming eyes of a father who would do anything for his little angel, even if it meant tearing out his own eyes to prove to her how sorry he was for the hideous thing he had done to her family.

A smile stretched across his face.

"There you are. . . "

The tears filled Anne's eyes. She couldn't hold onto them any longer. Yet, as before, they ran down her cheeks.

"Promise me, An. . . " Leon uttered, his hand falling from her face.

His voice faded, so too did that smile.

"Yeah," she said suddenly, sniffling the loose phlegm from her nose.

"He. . . he can. . . can't find meee. . . "

"Who? Diego?"

He muttered, "Yeaaaasss. . . Dieeeee. . . gooo. . . "

"I promise," Anne said clearly.

"Don't let him find meee. . . " Leon said under his breath, ". . . or the others. . . "

With his slack jaw opened wide, his head slowly flopped back.

"Others?" Anne said as she tried to hold Leon's head upright. "What others?"

She received no response from her father. His entire body went lifeless. Anne let go of her father's head, hugged his frail body as tightly as she could, and cried into his shoulder.

Once her tears had run dry, Anne released her father from her grip. While doing so, she felt something hard and pointy pressed against her breast. She reached inside her father's inner pocket. There, Anne found a pair of vintage sunglasses without a single scratch on them. The spotless shades were nothing like the ones her father wore in the mansion: those big, bulky ones. These were sleek and shiny, like the ones he so famously wore during his prime—the upper right corner of the lens read, "VBANS." She read the name of the sunglasses to herself—the same exact ones her father used to model—and wondered why he kept them on his person this entire time. Anne placed them back inside his sweater's pocket. Minutes went by before Anne finally came to terms with the passing of her father. The only thing she could now think of was the promise she made to him. They couldn't find his body, Anne thought, *he* couldn't find his body—*he*, as in Diego. Since Leon had already made up the will for Diego, as well as Diego's confederates, Leon's maid, Jasmine, and his nurse, Sophia, there was no reason for her to pursue the will since there would be repercussions. There would be tests and lots of questions. They would have to match her DNA with Leon's dead body and so forth. Who could she trust by then? What if they linked her father's DNA to Leon Dorsey? In most cases, they would. And what if the Company had his DNA stashed away in one of their unknown facilities (that is if they were still around)? There were so many situations, as well as questions for Anne to think about, so many loopholes *and* answers, ones Anne could've easily missed if she wasn't careful enough. Either way, Anne would have to take Diego to court. *That*, Anne knew. Most likely, he had already left the country (after all, Leon's bank accounts were all held offshore, scattered over a dozen countries). It was only a matter of time before Diego received a fat paycheck in the mail. And if he did pony up, he would have his own attorneys, whom, for all Anne knew, were hired guns disguised in suits and polished ties. The risk was *too* great, she knew, and all for what? A small fortune? If Anne didn't relinquish her father's dead body, it would take the state at least seven years to declare her father "legally" dead since there was no evidence or proof of his body, which meant no assets or funding for Diego or his crew's operation. Diego had waited nearly an entire lifetime for Leon to divulge his money, as well as possessions, including Leathery Manor, which was now left in a mound of rubble. What did another seven years matter?

Anne finally made up her mind and carried her father to Pirate's Cove where she rested his body over a flat boulder.

9:35 PM

WHILE Anne stood outside the Rolls, she faced the three options she had before her: bury the body, burn the body, or call the police. Anne knew the third option was clearly out of the picture and yet, for the longest time, she contemplated going to the nearest payphone to call the police. She remembered exactly what her father had told her, about his identity and how she needed to protect it from the public, mainly Diego. She reached in her left pocket and pulled out the real USB flash drive, same one Diego had mailed to her. If I call the cops and *tell them about Diego*, would the whole cat-and-mouse chase happen all over again? What if the Company was still out there hiding in the shadows, waiting for Leon's heir to come forward? If they *are* still alive and they do find out about me, Anne asked herself, then they will come after me. Burying the body was the best option, Anne thought. They would never know—that is if I bury the body *deep enough*. But then again, there would be nothing left of the body if she decided to burn it. Then, Anne thought more about the supplies she would need. She would need firewood, of course. She would need to make a nice bed for the body. In order to make a bed of wood, she would need plenty of sturdy wood. And she couldn't make several trips from the convenient store to the beach. She would also need lots of gasoline, matches, of course, and a shovel to clean up the bones. But how much gasoline would Anne need to burn through an entire human body? Not a question she asked herself on a daily basis. Then, she thought about the first idea: burying the body. All she needed was a shovel and maybe a blanket or tarp to wrap the body in and then a spot with loose dirt—possibly in the woods—to bury the body. She didn't have to worry about finding a spot to bury her father's body. Most of the surrounding area around the beach was wooded and miles away from civilization. What it really came down to was *time* and *decay*. So, with that in mind, she decided to go with the first idea, which was burying the body. She drove to the nearest convenient store, a hole in the wall called Q's, which was roughly sixteen miles away from Pirate's Cove. Anne could barely afford the shovel, as well as the tarp, with the leftover money she had from the pawnshop, but it was *just* enough to get by. After she bought the proper supplies, she drove back to Pirate's Cove. She let out a little air from each tire on the Rolls before driving on the beach. The last thing she wanted was to carry his body all the way across the beach. When she got there, his body was still perched against the rock—in the same exact position as she had last left it.

She carried his body to the car and placed it on the tarp inside the trunk.

Once the body was loaded in the back, Anne drove from the beach. She drove about nine miles north of Pirate's Cove until she reached a lush wooded section along the coast. It took Anne most of the night to dig the hole—roughly two hours.

When the hole had reached an ideal depth— around three to four feet—she couldn't dig any farther. The ground below her was rock solid from the previous freeze and both of her hands were sore and blistered. She wrapped her father's body in the blue tarp that she had bought from Q's and dragged the body to the bottom of the hole. She said her final goodbyes to her father and christened the goodbye with a kiss along the center of his forehead.

Right before she covered his body with dirt, she removed the shades from the inner pocket of his sweater and, after a moment of thought, decided to keep them, not to remind her of her father and who he once was, but to remind her of the power she now held within her very eyes. As Leon had done after he discovered his ability to turn a living, breathing human being into stone (even now, to Anne, the idea alone seemed so farfetched), Anne couldn't help but ask herself the one question: Was the gaze a gift or a curse? Only time would tell. . .

CHAPTER 7

EVER since Bonnie and his two children, Sebastian, six, and Octavian, four, died in the devastating flood brought on by Tropical Storm Adel, which had swept over the northern part of Maine in the fall of 2006, killing eighteen people, including his wife and two children—all three of their bodies were never recovered by state police, only the sodden mini van that they were washed away in—Nicky Eugene Fincher had become overly fascinated with the idea of death; as a matter of fact, after six years of what Nicky called "chasing," death had become all he knew. From 2006 to 2008, Nicky searched for his family, but he ended up falling short. Two long years of searching, but finding nothing, did quite a number on him, mentally and physically. He didn't exactly know if they were buried by the flood or if their bodies were carried into the Atlantic by the raging waters (and now they are perched on the ocean's floor like the Titanic) or if scavengers had picked their bones clean. Nicky always wondered "what if." What if they were still out there? Not out there, as in alive—Nicky knew they were as dead as the Sixties—but *out there*, Nicky wondered, as in drifting through another realm where we remain nothing more than shadows to them.

In the fall of 2008, the course of Nicky's life had led him directly into the paranormal after he witnessed his first death: an older man who was involved in a car accident. Name was Corbin Belafonte, the local barber who could cut a mean hairdo. No relation to the famous singer. Mostly popular among the old timers. Nicky just so happened to be at the right place at the right time on that one particular day. Mr. Belafonte's car hit a slick spot on the road. The car hydroplaned. The front end caught a telephone pole, splitting his station wagon in two pieces— literally. Part of the windshield severed Mr. Belafonte's main artery. The only way Mr. Belafonte could've survived was if there was a surgeon on sight. No surgeon, only one of the many widowers of Whisperfront who tried to keep a dying man comfortable before he was welcomed into the Pearly Gates. Mr. Belafonte never suffered. Nicky did all he could to stop the bleeding with his shirt, but, unfortunately, the local barber bled out minutes before an ambulance arrived. In those final moments of Mr. Belafonte's death, Nicky saw something that he couldn't explain, something that would change the course of his life forever. Not only did Nicky see it with his own eyes, but he also felt it—a presence beyond our scope of rationalization. Nicky liked to think of them as spirits towering over him, as if a door opened—if only for a second—and exposed Nicky to another realm that waited for him on the other side of our own realm. *That*, to Nicky, was the crème de la crème of chasing: watching a spirit exit from a body—like the spirit was attached to an invisible string in the clouds or wherever and there was a force on the other end of the string pulling it directly into this other realm. For Nicky Fincher, there was nothing like it: watching both eyes fixate; and then, the air leaving the body; and finally, that thing with the invisible string. Most townspeople of Whisperfront thought Nicky was off his rocker. When asked why Nicky did it, why he enjoyed capturing death, he could never put words to it even if he had one too many at the Rabbit Hole. Instead of finding a rock to crawl under after the great flood and then—if things couldn't get any worse— Mr. Belafonte's death, he embraced it, *death*. Hooked like a junkie to a fix. "I mean," Nicky would always say, "we all die at some point. Really, it's the only thing we all have in common. So, why the hell run away from it? People take pictures of babies after they're born. Why not take pictures of people after they die?" He was very much the Lydia Deetz of his time, only without the darkroom, as well as the black makeup and funeral clothes. He was also known as a *nimrod* (that means skillful hunter, but others had different meanings for the word). He and his two dogs, Smiley, originally named Coon, a white English Cocker Spaniel with two black eyes, who was acquired six years ago after Coon had bitten his master while his master was trying to separate Coon from another dog at a local fare (the master ended up with sixteen stitches on his face—and after the whole mess, Coon was driven about fifty-eight miles north into the countryside outside Whisperfront where he was dropped off at a doorstep; Master had gotten word from town that the owner of the house was an outdoorsman and liked to hunt), and Biscuit, his other dog, Bonnie's dog, a miniature poodle who was occasionally called Snuggles from the TV commercials, lived off a four-acre piece of land to the west of Whisperfront. Nicky once dragged Biscuit along for a hunt after Bonnie's passing, but the little squirt wasn't worth a damn when it came to retrieving a duck or whatever bird Nicky was hunting. Biscuit was a very gay dog, the kind that operated on batteries. Unlike Coon, Biscuit enjoyed playing with the ducks rather than retrieving their bloodstained carcasses for dinner. So, that day when Coon found Nicky or, better yet, Nicky found Coon, it was a blessing in disguise. Even though Coon looked exactly like that, a giant raccoon, and it was the name on his tag, Nicky decided to change the spaniel's name to Smiley because the dog always looked like it was smiling at him. Besides, if Nicky and Smiley went into town and Nicky started yelling out, "Coon! Get over here!" or "Sit, Coon!" Nicky assumed the local brothers wouldn't be too fond of the dog's name, or even worse, think that Nicky was yelling at them. So, whenever he wasn't hunting bird, Nicky was hunting dead bodies, human bodies that is—"*chasing*," that's what he called it. From there, he gutted out the garage and created his own HALL OF DEATH: gunshot victims, stabbings, car accidents, freak accidents (one time a young man, Derek Lynch, was riding on his moped down Wally-bird Lane when a three foot pipe suddenly fell from a truck and went through the young man's motorcycle helmet, piercing his skull). Whisperfront wasn't a dangerous city by any means. There were crimes here like any other city. But whenever there was a crime or accident, it was a big deal; and Nicky became almost like a historian in a way, keeping track of every death that took place in Whisperfront. Some people hated him, thought he was more or less a discourteous man. Some, even a nuisance. Others were terrified of him, wondering if when they died, Nicky would be hovering around like the Grim Reaper, ready to take their final snapshot and post it on that wall with the others; while others figured it was his way of coping with the loss of his wife and kids. Either way, if someone died in *or* around Whisperfront, then most likely Nicky had a photograph of it.

At a quarter past seven, Nicky was brought to King's Drive by an old dispatch, a classic 187 over his police scanner. There was a fire, Nicky heard, which he had never encountered ever since he started photographing the dead. According to the dispatch, the sheriff of Whisperfront, Sheriff Navarro, had been shot in the head at Leatherby Manor; and possibly more dead bodies were inside the estate. Nicky heard of Leatherby Manor, the big fucking house off King's Drive, the one where the recluse, Marcus Hopkins, lived with his manservant. Nicky knew nothing about Mr. Hopkins other than he was a man like himself: shunned and always frowned upon whenever he came into town. Nicky Fincher, of course, had his many suspicions, as most people did about Mr. Hopkins, but what Nicky Fincher was about to discover next would be one for the records.

7:17 AM

WHILE the sun cast its red light upon the dark sky, the local authorities, including Deputy Levy Wallace, were combing the outskirts of the charred remains of what used to be Leatherby Manor when one of the deputies cried out from the woods.

As the others rushed to the woods, Deputy Lance Horton was helping a frightened Jasmine from behind a tree stump. She was severely shaking, her hands especially. Her knees and shins were muddy. Her face, mainly her cheeks, was covered with dark shades of soot. The shock, the deputy knew all too well, consumed her eyes.

"Does anyone speak Spanish?" the deputy asked the others.

7:23 AM

NICKY parked his truck behind the last fire truck in front of Leatherby Manor.

One of the locals had told the deputies about Nicky and his dog, Smiley, and how, even though the dog wasn't a bloodhound, he was pretty good at locating things, especially dead things. Nicky had also gotten word from one of the deputies that so far the firefighters found one body inside Leatherby Manor. Nicky was dying to get a picture of the charred body or even a glimpse of it. Possible male, the deputy told Nicky, but they couldn't determine the identity of the body until it was safe for investigators to enter. In the meantime, the deputies let Nicky and his dog loose and gave them permission to scour the estate for any other trails.

They first started their search toward the East Wing of Leathery Manor, but the trail went cold.

When they came across the West Wing of Leatherby Manor, Smiley picked up a faint scent in the air. Nicky and the dog zigzagged their way across the lawn until they finally came to rest at a well that had been boarded shut.

At the well, Smiley nearly tugged his master to the ground from the potency of the stench. The remaining deputies rushed toward the sound of the barking spaniel and then his master calling out, "I got something over here! Hurry. . .

9:03 AM

AFTER catching about five solid hours of rest in the car, Anne arrived in Lancaster, a small town outside Sanford, Maine—precisely, at the Main National Bank off Port Row Street.

Once the bank opened for business, she strolled directly inside and asked to speak to the person in charge.

9:23 AM

WITH the supplies they had at their disposal, the local construction workers jerrybuilt a rig (basically a piece of rope with Nicky's wireless camcorder attached to the end, which fed to a small boxed television). They lowered the camcorder into the well—vigilantly watching the grainy monitor while doing so. The only light cast into the darkness was the pale glow of the camcorder; and even then, it was extremely hard to make out the surroundings. When they reached the bottom, the light from the camcorder shone on an object protruding from the opening of a bag. The entire crew, Nicky included, got a closer look on the monitor. Nicky was flabbergasted, the crew as well. The old spaniel was right. There was something in the darkness, Nicky and the others realized, something round and decayed with two tiny voids where a pair of sunken eyes used to reside.

9:28 AM

ANNE got back into the car, pulled out the CD from the case and held it closely.

On the disc, the words *FOR YOUR EYES ONLY* were written in a black Sharpie.

She slid the CD into the player and pressed the PLAY button.

A distortion at first and then a voice came on, Leon's voice. . .

"Hello, Chloe," Leon said, *"if you're listening to this, then I am already dead and you know exactly who you are. . . In the next couple of days, a writer named Renny Jacobson will be visiting me to conduct an exclusive interview. For the sake of protecting my identity, I will pretend to be Marcus Hopkins, my former partner at JeneCorp, a dangerous company that will do anything to find you. In these interviews, I plan on revealing my story to you, Chloe. But, if you have gotten this far in the time-line, then you should already know this by now. In time, you will learn more about me on this CD and you will know why it is quintessential that not only my identity, but also YOUR identity, remains a secret. I'm sure you still have many questions. I promise I will cover most, if not all of them—about the gaze, the ABCs on how to use it properly, but most importantly, how to live a productive life with these remarkable powers you now harness. Before we begin, I'm sure you're probably wondering about the address on the piece of paper. . . "*

Anne looked down at the piece of paper that she recently grabbed from the safety deposit box and un-folded it.

The address: 76541 HARRIET FALLS LANE.

"Mississippi," Anne read to herself.

10:12 AM

IT took them about an hour to bring in a crane from Newtown, the town over.

Once they set the crane outside the well, they ended up using a hook to fish out the strange bag below (along with the help of the feed from the camcor-der to the monitor as they had done the first time around; otherwise, it would've been done with blind luck).

When Deputy Wallace carefully unveiled the contents of the bag, Nicky was, without a doubt, left beyond words. In all his years of chasing, he had seen some pretty nasty things done to the human body: mutilations and lacerations, which, except for a few miracles here and there, almost all of the time resulted in death. At times, the extent of these injuries exposed the vital parts that man kept sealed behind the flesh. The only key to opening the flesh: a sharp blade, a piece of jagged glass, or, in Mr. Lynch's case, an industrial-sized pipe. However, in *all* his years of chasing, Nicky Fincher had never come across a decapitation.

11:43 AM

JUST when the crew was about to break for lunch, Smiley picked up yet another trail from the same exact scent of the corpse's head, but this time it was coming from the garden behind the house. Nicky pulled the other remaining deputies together and rushed to the garden where Smiley found a particular spot: a six-foot by two-foot bare section where beets had already been harvested. Nicky told the deputies that he was certain that the owner of that very head was buried underneath this very garden.

After some convincing, not only from Nicky, but also the dog, who couldn't stop barking, the deputies got their shovels and started digging. The second they started loosening the damp soil, the same horrendous stench from the bag only tripled in potency as it emitted into the air. One of the deputies excused himself, for the smell was too foul and pungent. But they kept digging until the owner of the head was revealed. Sure enough, the old spaniel was right. . . but almost. One of the deputies struck a hard surface while another one unearthed the origin of the stench. Instead of finding a corpse missing a head, the old spaniel found two! One of the bodies was in the early stages of decomposition, a few days old—seventy-two hours old, give or take—past rigor mortis, considering the moist environment, female from the looks, and, not to mention, headless too. The skin of the body had a greenish tint to it, they discovered, as well as blisters from where the gases inside the body had broken through the flesh. And the smell! The smell caused the deputies to gag, even Nicky himself. As for the other body, the weary deputy brushed the dirt around with the flat side of the shovel until the other body was revealed in its entirety. There was nothing left of it but a skeleton, years old—ten years, give or take. There were no marks on the bones caused from blunt force trauma, only the small chip along the humerus from where the careless deputy had struck it with the tip of his shovel.

"Looks like we found the owner of the head," Nicky said to the sweaty deputies.

Deputy Wallace, with his face left in the same shock he witnessed in Jasmine's face, turned to the other deputies and said, "Why the hell would someone cut off the head, only to bury the body later?"

"Got me, Wallace," a deputy said, out of breath.

The deputy said over a tense silence, "I think it's time we bring in the big guns."

1:46 PM

DEPUTY Horton was still figuring out how to properly word the recent news that he received from Deputy Chaplin.

He spotted the deputy storming through the sheriff's office.

Deputy Chaplin pulled Deputy Horton aside.

"Do you want me to tell him?" she asked.

"No," Deputy Horton said. "I'll do it."

As Deputy Wallace made his way through the booking area, Deputy Flint, with the phone pressed against his shoulder, said to the passing deputy, "Sir, ah got a Mr. Dill on the phone. Says it's ah important."

Deputy Wallace ignored the deputy and continued walking down the hallway. Then, he said over his shoulder, "Tell him he's gonna have to wait in line like everybody else."

He noticed another deputy, Horton, who was now trying to keep pace with the deputy.

"Any word on Navarro's condition?" Deputy Wallace said as he proceeded toward the interrogation room where Jasmine was currently waiting. In his hand he carried a plastic evidence bag with piano wire inside, the same wire used to kill Renny.

"No word yet," the deputy said. "Last I heard he was still in surgery."

"Well, keep me posted."

"Will do, sir."

He followed the deputy to the interrogation room on the other side of the office.

"When *they* get here," the deputy said with a tremor in his voice, "they'll catch this guy. Right?"

"Let's hope so, Lance," the deputy said to himself.

They arrived at the interrogation room where Jasmine was seated across another deputy.

As she was sipping from a cup of coffee, Deputy Wallace peeked through the open blinds and carefully acknowledged the nervous woman. As before, both of her hands were shaking. As of now, the deputy couldn't quite tell what to think of this woman. He wondered if she was scared of this strange man whom the other deputies were gossiping about, this Mr. Reyes (when she was asked why she didn't report him sooner, she had no answer), or if she was still shaken up from the fire. Either way, the deputy realized, Jasmine was the one person responsible for breaking the case wide open.

The deputy said with a nod, "And her? What's her story?"

"She's one of Mr. Hopkins' maids."

"Just one of them," Deputy Wallace said. "She wouldn't know where the others might be. Would she?"

"Don't know, sir."

"So, what else does she know about this Mr. Reyes?"

"Martín Reyes," he elaborated for the deputy. "She's saying he's the one who shot the sheriff in cold blood and then burned down the house."

"And the three stiffs?"

"Strangled them with that piano wire, except for the woman."

"Any ID on the woman?"

"Not yet," the deputy said. "Apparently, this Reyes guy suffocated her with a bag and then buried her body in the garden—that is before he decided to cut off her head." The deputy shrugged. "She also said one of the bodies was Renny Jacobson, a writer from New York."

The deputy furrowed his brows.

"You mean the one who went missing?"

"Yep," the deputy said. "That's the one."

"You sure?"

"That's what she's saying."

"If that's true, then what are the odds that the woman is the other one who was reported missing?"

"Ah, I'd said very high."

The deputy sighed, *hmmm*.

"Crimes of passion," he mumbled as he glanced down at the evidence bag in his hand. He directed his attention back to Jasmine. "So, anything else on Martín Reyes?"

Deputy Horton said, "Get this. The 'butler,' she said."

"Butler?" Deputy Wallace said with confusion. "You're shitting me."

"Shit you not," the deputy said and then grinned. "It's like our own little *Clue*."

"You think that's funny, Deputy," Wallace said sternly as he shot daggers at the young deputy. "This isn't a game. Your sheriff is in the hospital right now fighting for his life. If I were you, I would put a lid on that wise mouth of yours. You got that?"

"Sorry, sir," Horton said, as he dropped his head. "Won't happen again."

Deputy Wallace glared at a deflated Horton and then looked over the deputy's shoulder at the other discouraged deputies around the office.

Finally, Deputy Wallace asked Horton, "Anything else on this butler?"

Deputy Horton reached into his pocket, pulled out a notepad, and read the address to the deputy.

"He lives in Lansford, sir," he said to the deputy. "1876 Tuttle Drive."

"Lansford, huh?" Wallace said as he noticed the tremble in Horton's hand. "Long way from home." Then, he followed with a question. "What the hell is he doing all the way out here?"

"I had Arlene notify the Lansford Police Department. . . "

"Okay."

"They said there was nothing left of the house."

"Nothing left?" Deputy Wallace squared himself to Horton. "What do you mean?"

"There was an explosion."

"What kind of explosion?"

"Don't know," Horton said. "All she said was that when the firefighters arrived, there was nothing left of Reyes's house. It was completely leveled. They said they also found a person two houses down from Reyes's house. Burned to a crisp. Neighbors were ah awakened by the explosion and then heard the sound of glass shattering. They checked out the noise, only to find a body in their living room. Crashed through the window. He's in critical condition right now. Can you believe that?"

The deputy asked, "Did they identify this person?"

"Yeah," Horton said surprisingly. "A cop."

"Cop?"

"Detective," he corrected, "with the Lansford Police Department."

"Shit," Deputy Wallace said, as he ran his hand across the backside of his neck. "Here." The deputy handed Deputy Horton the evidence bag. "Take care of this," he said. "Will ya?"

"Ah, what about her?"

As Deputy Wallace walked away, he said over his shoulder, "She looks like she could use another cup of coffee."

Just as he rounded the corner, Deputy Horton suddenly called out from behind, "There's one more thing. It's probably nothing. Angie said she found pieces of plastic near that well. She thought maybe it might've come from ah the construction workers—"

Deputy Wallace said hastily, "Get to the point."

"A USB flash drive," the deputy said. "Shattered to pieces. But like I said, it's probably nothing."

2:09 PM

IN the hallway, Sergeant Weathers pulled the doctor aside from the hospital room.

"What's the news, Doc?" he asked.

"Well, we finally got him stable," the doctor said, "which is the good news. Bad news: Mr. Merrotti suffered third degree burns over ninety percent of his body. The man is strong as an ox. Never in all my years have I seen a man with such a will to survive."

"But will he live, Doc?"

"Yes," the doctor said. "He'll live, but after this, he'll wish he died in that explosion."

The sergeant grimaced, all of the anger bottled inside him channeling into his jaw muscles.

"So," he said shortly with both hands placed along his hips, "what's our next step?"

"Well, if he can remain stable in the next twenty-four hours," the doctor said, "then we'll transfer him over to the Burn Center in Jester. They have an excellent facility over there. They'll take good care of him. Until then, Sergeant, there's really nothing we can do for him."

2:18 PM

DEPUTY Wallace pulled up to the LazyDay Inn, a motel off Whisperfront Highway. Outside the motel waited the owner of the motel, Mr. Dill—a "gumma" was what the locals called him, which was a person who wore dentures. Mr. Dill, unlike most who had flocked south during the winters and north during the summers, was one of the few who was born and raised in Whisperfront. He was a red-cheeked man who went through a drastic change after having learned about his thyroid condition: changed diet, cut out the smoking, and then slimed down from a size 39 waist to a size 34.

"This better be good, Jay," the deputy said as he approached the motel.

The motel owner nodded upward.

"How's da sheriff?" he said in his gravelly voice.

"Not good," Deputy Wallace said and then nodded at the worried motel owner. "So what is it, Jay? Got a lot on my plate."

"A couple of days ago, I read about the two people who went missing," he said. "Both from New York."

"Right," the deputy said. "Two writers. I've heard."

"Well, gee, then I'm sure you aware, Deputy," Mr. Dill said, "I called that Sheriff Navarro and told him that the man came by here. The woman I've never seen, but the man. He stayed here alright."

"The sheriff never mentioned anything to me."

"I called him," Mr. Dill returned. "He said he would look into it."

"When was this?"

"I believe it was last Tuesday or Wednesday."

"Well, which is it?"

"Ah Tuesday," Mr. Dill corrected.

"You sure?"

"Ahm tellin' you, Deputy," he answered. "I ask him his business. Said he's writing a story at Leatherby Manor. I ask him, Mr. Hopkins? He looks at me strangely like he slipped his tongue and then all of a sudden he changes his story. Says Mr. Hopkins was a friend of his, and that he's doing a story on the brutal wintas in Whispahfront. Sounded bogus to me, but he was a nice fella, and I didn't think too much of it. Anyway, the otha day I saw his face in the papahs. Said he was reported missing. Find out he's from the big city, a hotshot writa for sum magazine. So, I call up da sheriff and tell him 'bout this guy. Navarro told me he would handle it."

Deputy Wallace lowered his head and mainly wondered about Sheriff Navarro and how he always kept him informed, even about the most trivial matters, especially in a small town that hardly received crime. The sheriff never told his deputy about Mr. Jacobson. Didn't even mention his name. The past two weeks the sheriff had been acting strange, to say the least. Not showing up. Not answering calls. Always putting off stuff. Disappearing for hours at a time. So, naturally, the question replayed in the deputy's mind: *What was Lucas hiding from me?*

"So, how many nights did this guy stay here?" the deputy asked over the momentary silence.

"Jus' da one night."

"Tuesday night?"

"That's right," Mr. Dill said. "I was jus' wondering, you know, if what happened earl'r this morning—you know, with that wicked fire—if it might've been related. Business gets ah kinda slow around this time of year and my mind gets racing. Jus' thought you should know."

"No, Jay," the deputy said suddenly. "Thanks. I appreciate it."

Mr. Dill replied, "Any time."

Another silent pause in the conversation.

"You know," Mr. Dill said, breaking through the cold silence, "I thought 'bout becomin' a cop once."

Deputy Wallace pointed over his shoulder.

"Gotta run," he said as he made his way to the car. "I'll get up with you later."

Mr. Dill waved his hand and said under his breath, "Yeah. Whateva."

2:38 PM

ON the way back to the office, Deputy Wallace received a call on the radio.

"Deputy Wallace," the dispatcher said on the other end.

"Go."

"They're here."

The deputy sighed and tried to release the nerves from his stomach.

"I'm on my way," he said and suddenly did a U-turn on the main road.

2:46 PM

DEPUTY Wallace arrived at Leatherby Manor where a team of men and women dressed in blue jackets with yellow FBI lettering were scattered throughout the entire lawn. Most of the traffic was centered around the two dead bodies, which were covered in the garden. The others were inside the mansion, which had been cleared for entry.

Two deputies greeted Wallace.

"That was quick," Wallace, looking around Leatherby Manor.

The deputy said, "What do we do?"

"Set a perimeter," Wallace said. "Make sure no press gets in. Got it."

"Yes, sir," the deputy said as Wallace made his way to the garden.

On the way, two other individuals, both dressed in suits, greeted Wallace

"You must be Deputy Wallace," the FBI agent said.

The deputy gave him a once over. The agent was much taller, about four inches. He had light skin, well-groomed, dark eyes. Then, the other agent, like his partner, was dapper as well, red hair parted to one side of his scalp, green eyes, freckles.

After the quick study, Deputy Wallace finally shook the agent's hand.

"I'm Agent Karp," the agent said as he displayed his FBI badge in the wallet. Then, he pointed to his partner, the red haired man. "This is Agent McClintock."

The deputy followed with another handshake, this time coming from the other agent.

"Nice to meet you," he said and then glanced at the others in FBI getup. "When we asked for help, we didn't expect so many people. . . "

"Well," Agent Karp said, "we're very thorough, Deputy."

"I see."

The other agent followed, "We heard that one of your own was gunned down and is now in the hospital. Is that correct?"

"That's right," the deputy said. "Sheriff Navarro."

"Sorry to hear," Agent Karp replied.

The other agent asked, "You think you might know who did this?"

"We have a woman in custody right now," he said. "Says a man named Martín Reyes was responsible."

"And what's the relation between the two?"

"She's the maid," Deputy Wallace said. "He's the butler. I know that. . . " he cut off the agent before he had a chance to respond, ". . . it sounds nuts. But her story adds up."

"We'll find whoever's responsible for this," Agent Karp said. "He's got nowhere to run. And if he so much as shows his face in public—which, if he's smart, he probably won't—well, we'll catch him. . . "

The deputy's eyes lit up.

"One more thing," he said as he reached into his pocket. "I had one of my men check it out. Her name is Anne Roth, wanted for questioning by Lansford Police Department. It's probably nothing, but Ms. Roth roughed up one of the locals last night. Messed him up bad too. We're talking about a former All-State Offensive End." The deputy pulled out the picture of Anne. He unfolded the piece of paper and handed it to the agent. The black and white picture was a still taken from the convenient store's surveillance camera just above the checkout counter. The picture was dark and fuzzy, but, still, it was clear enough for the two agents to make out. "I just thought it was kind of odd. This young lady strolls into town like she's got a purpose, wanted by police. Local man says something to her. She doesn't like it. She breaks his face and then drives away into the night. Doesn't happen very often 'round here. This is probably the most excitement we've gotten in a long time." He pointed at Leatherby Manor behind the agents. "Then, this. Just doesn't make sense."

"Do you mind?" the agent said curiously as he held up the picture.

"Sure," Deputy Wallace said. "Keep it. I got copies back at the office."

Agent Karp secretly handed the picture to Agent McClintock.

"So, what are you going to do with the stiffs?" the deputy asked before the agents could follow up with a question of their own.

"One of them is getting pretty ripe," the agent replied. "I take it you have somewhere to keep them overnight."

"Of course," the deputy stuttered. "There's a morgue not too far away—ten minutes. The roads are pretty greasy out there. So, about fifteen minutes tops."

"Very well."

The deputy cleared his throat.

"Anything you need," he said anxiously. "We're here to help."

"Thank you, Deputy," Agent Karp said and forced a smile onto his face as his partner placed Anne's picture inside his left pocket.

3:53 PM

As the head surgeon, Doctor Ministry, removed the bloody gloves from his hands, he glanced up at the clock on the wall and called Lucas Navarro's death at precisely three fifty-three in the afternoon.

3:56 PM

Doctor Ministry stepped out of the operation room and walked toward Deputy Wallace, who was pacing back and forth in the hallway.

As soon as the deputy witnessed the expression on the surgeon's face, he knew exactly what had happened to Lucas before the surgeon even had a chance to tell him.

4:01 PM

THE surgeon, as well as the nurses, gave the deputy some time alone with Lucas's body before they cleaned the body and transported it to the morgue.

"I'm sorry this happened to you, Lucas," Deputy Wallace said solemnly as he reached below and grabbed Lucas's cold hand.

As his head fell downward on the operation table, the deputy paused and looked even closer at the strange marking on Lucas's wrist.   He carefully flipped over his wrist and examined the strange tattoo. . .

5:32 PM

IN the morgue, the two agents from Leatherby Manor, Agent Karp and Agent McClintock, were looking over the three corpses: one, a female, half-decayed, severed head—the head resting normally where any ordinary head would rest, which was above the neck—another one, a skeleton, male, no marks or broken bones over the skeleton other than where a careless deputy had chipped the humerus with the tip of the shovel; and lastly, a crisp body as black as coal.

"So," Agent Karp said as Agent McClintock carefully unpeeled the sheet from the skeleton, "you sure that's what the machine said?"

"When is the machine ever wrong?"

"Ninety-nine percent?" Surprised from the recent discovery, Agent Karp shook his head. "That's what it said?"

"Yep."

"Huh?"

Agent Karp followed with a snort.

Then, he said to himself, "What are the odds?"

"Well, she got homesick," Agent McClintock said. "Who knows?"

He grabbed a pair of tweezers from the tray beside him and removed a fragment from inside the skull's right eye socket.

"So," Agent Karp said, "is it him?"

Agent McClintock placed the brown fragment, as tiny as a breadcrumb, inside a glass jar, closed the lid, and said vaguely, "Won't know until the test results come back."

"How long will that take?"

"Could take a day or two." The unsmiling agent examined the skeleton some more, mainly the height. "From the looks, no. Not tall enough."

"How long you think he's been dead?"

"Ten years, roughly."

"And how about them?"

He glanced at the two other bodies on the tables.

"Let the Feds deal with these two," Agent McClintock said callously. "You know they're always looking for something to do."

He inserted the jar into his pocket and then covered the skeleton.

Meanwhile, Agent Karp pulled out a notepad from his coat's inner pocket.

"Now, back to business. . . " he skimmed over the list of names, ". . . got a few here."

"Any good ones?"

"One or two." He eyes landed on *one* name at the bottom of the page. "There's one here, local nut who likes to take pictures of crime scenes."

"Interesting."

"It could work."

"We'll make it work," he said. "And a motive?"

"The man's a nut," Agent Karp said. "Shouldn't that be enough motive?"

"All right then," Agent McClintock said casually. "How do we do this?

"Paper, rock, scissors?"

"You know I hate that game."

"Right," Agent Karp said sardonically. "You *hate* everything, McClintock."

"What do you say we. . . " he hung onto the word *we* as he reached into his left pocket and pulled out a quarter, ". . . we do this the old-fashioned way?"

Agent Karp sighed.

Then, his partner said, "Heads or tails?"

6:58 PM

DEPUTY Wallace and Deputy Chaplin were the last two left in the office. Wallace asked the remaining deputies to go home, except for Deputy Horton, who was currently driving to Hooper's to fetch a box of sweets to go along with the recently brewed coffee. The mood around the sheriff's office was quiet and somber. Most of the time was spent talking about Lucas and how, despite his many faults, he was a good sheriff and did a lot for the town. He had no family, at least not in Whisperfront. The office was his home away from home, which very well meant the deputies were like his family. There was something on Deputy Wallace's mind, though.

When the deputy finally decided to ask, the door swung open.

"That must be Lance," Deputy Chaplin said to herself as she stood up from the desk. "Finally. . . "

Deputy Chaplin noticed the vacant expression on Deputy Wallace's face. She followed the deputy's eyes toward the front door. There, she found two men dressed in black suits, nearly the same outfits as the two agents earlier that day—Agent Karp and

Agent McClintock. They were casually approaching the front desk.

"Can I help you?" Deputy Wallace said as he approached the two strange men.

Both of the men reached into their inner pockets and then pulled out FBI badges.

They displayed the badges for the deputy.

"I'm Agent Schuster from the FBI," one of them said.

Then, the other one: "Agent Porter."

Baffled from their appearance, Deputy Wallace replied, "I had a chat with two of you guys earlier this afternoon—Agent Karp and the other, McClintock, I believe."

Both baffled as well, the two agents turned to each other.

Agent Schuster said, "We don't know about any Agent Karp or Agent *McClintock*."

"Is this a joke?" he asked.

"You tell me, Deputy."

Deputy Wallace placed his hands over his hips.

"What's going on here?" he asked curiously.

7:48 PM

HUNCHED over in his cubicle, Stewart checked the time on his watch.

"What's taking her so long," he said to himself.

9:52 PM

DEPUTY Horton peeked outside the front window of the sheriff's office and found the deputy sitting alone on a bench.

"Go home," the deputy said as he poked his head through the cracked door. "You're now a sheriff."

"Deputy, Lance," Deputy Wallace said, "as far as we both know."

"It's been a long day, *Deputy*."

"Not long enough," Wallace said quietly as he took a drag from the cigarette.

Horton grabbed his heavy coat from the holder and stepped outside.

On the way to the bench, he pointed at the cigarette in the deputy's hand.

"Do you mind?" he asked.

Wallace reached into his breast pocket and pulled out a pack of Cherry smokes. He extended a cigarette from the pack, far enough to where the deputy could put his fingers around the butt. Horton placed the cigarette in the corner of his mouth and sat down next to Wallace on the bench.

Wallace already had a light ready for him.

He lit the cigarette for the deputy.

"Thanks," he said.

The deputy responded with a nod of his head and then watched Horton inhale from the cigarette.

"What a goddamn mess. . . " Horton said, as the smoke eddied through his words.

"Tell me about it," Wallace returned.

"So," Horton said, "what do we do now?"

"It's out of our hands, Lance."

"Who do you think they were?"

"Don't know."

"Homeland Security?"

"Doubt it."

"CIA?"

"I don't know, Lance," Wallace said, as he stared straight ahead into the woods behind the parking lot. "Whoever they were, I'd say they got exactly what they wanted."

"But Arlene said they were wearing FBI jackets," Horton said abruptly. "She said there was a whole team of them. *You* were there. *You* saw them."

Wallace shot his narrow eyes at the dumbfounded deputy.

"What do you want, Lance?"

He shrugged and said in return, "Ah, what'd you mean?"

"I mean '*what* do you want?'"

Horton thought for a second.

"Answers," he said after a moment of silence.

"Well, you and me both," Wallace said. "I'm afraid I'm fresh out of answers." He breathed in the chilly night air and then blew it out through his nose the same way he did with the smoke. "*What* I do know. . . " he turned his narrow eyes toward the deputy, ". . . we're not alone."

"Sir. . . " Horton said, as Wallace moved his eyes back to the same dark woods.

"I'll tell you, Lance," the deputy said vacantly, his eyes sharpening. "There's something dark out there. We've only seen a glimpse of it. *But* something tells me this isn't the last time we'll see it."

Horton leaned forward.

"You okay, sir?" he asked.

Wallace ignored the deputy's question and walked back into the office.

As Deputy Horton was about to put out his cigarette, he found a folded piece of paper on the edge of the bench—precisely where Wallace had been sitting. He turned toward Deputy Wallace, but the deputy had already walked into the office. The deputy's eyes were drawn back to the bench, to that crinkled piece of paper. *The paper*, he thought, *so familiar*. He picked up the piece of paper. Unfolded it. Just as the deputy had suspected, it was a copy of the same grainy black and white surveillance video still that the deputy had handed out earlier throughout the office. Why the deputy had so much interest in this particular woman was beyond Deputy Horton.

As the deputy pocketed the piece of paper and then smothered the cigarette butt on the sole of his shoe, he suddenly heard the shatter of glass coming from the side of the sheriff's office. The sound was small and airy, similar to a glass animal balloon being dropped from a distance. Nonetheless, the sound was loud enough to grab the deputy's attention.

Horton's first suspicion: *just another drunk who had one too many*.

Then, he heard another shatter of glass.

Louder and fuller, like a pane of glass shattering.

"What the hell?" Horton said as he gradually stood from the bench.

He eased around the office and found himself in an alleyway—only a damp orange light from a floodlight calling attention to the clutter left behind from a recent refitting a couple of months ago.

Now, two soft *clinks* danced behind a pile of garbage!

Galvanized chains, Horton perceived, from a destroyed chain-link fence that he and Chaplin had tossed away during the refitting.

More sounds, rustles and whatnot, but the deputy couldn't quite tell what they were. However, he knew exactly where they were coming from. Horton located the sound, or better yet, sounds, which were coming from behind the dumpster.

Surely, the deputy thought, it was just a cat rummaging for a late night snack *or* it very well could've been a drunk, like the scraggly alley cat, rummaging for leftover food, *for* drink, for whatever drunks do at night. Whisperfront sure did have its share of them, both cats and drunks; and every now and then, they had a peculiar way of acting like raccoons late at night whenever businesses closed shop. The town also had its share of left-wing artsy-types who liked to scavenge for things like junk or scraps for an art project.

The deputy pushed aside his thoughts as he arrived at the dumpster.

Nothing.

No cat.

No drunk.

No Picasso.

Only obsolete computers, monitors, and electronic equipment, as well as the faint stench of dog shit in the air.

"The hell with this," he uttered.

As soon as Horton spun around, he found a shadowy man standing motionlessly behind a telephone pole. The man, the deputy saw, carried no expression, no movement, a man shielded by the night.

Again, the deputy flinched from the strange presence.

"Damn it," he said as he grabbed his chest. "You scared the shit outta me."

The shadowy man took one step forward and then, as before, remained still, quiet, and armless.

Horton's right hand cautiously lowered to his waist, near the leather holster.

"Levy?" he said curiously and peered closer.

The shadowy man grew an arm from behind his back. A pistol with a long barrel was drawn from his side.

On impulse, Deputy Horton drew a pistol as well, but not quick enough. The deputy's pistol got halfway from the holster before the shadowy man put a bullet through the center of his forehead. The deputy's head flung backward in a wicked nod. The pistol slipped from his hand like yolk from an eggshell.

As the deputy's head violently recoiled forward, his body flopped forward as well, and then he fell to the ground. The shot had gone unnoticed by any deputies or civilian in the area—unheard, for that matter—for it sounded as soft and dainty as a finch's chirp or, as Anne had distinguished prior to Michael's death, like a foot kicking a soda can down a desolate street.

Then, the shadowy man took another step forward into the beam of light cast from the floodlight above. He was dressed exactly like that, like the shadows—the light only exposing his hazy eyes as well as the pistol dangling below his black gloved hand, a Beretta 92FS with a suppressor on the end of the barrel.

He exited the alley with graceful strides and then strolled directly into the sheriff's office, revealing his attire: a black shoes, black tie, black suit—an agent's suit.

Five seconds after the agent entered the sheriff's office, a couple of muffled screams cut through the night and then nine more of those same *chirps*—each one coming in intervals of three.

Then, after the chaos was over, there was an eerie silence. . .

10:13 PM

EXCEPT for the janitor, Hal, who operated like a clock, Stewart was the very last employee in Flashback's offices, which was quite a rarity since Stewart was always the last one to clock in and the first one to clock out.

Once Hal made his final round through the office, Stewart managed to sneak inside Edie's locked office.

He piddled around Edie's office for a couple of minutes—mostly riffling through trivial novelties inside Edie's drawers or snooping around Edie's sentimental belongings on her desk such as framed pictures of her and her aunt Rene, a breast cancer survivor, as well as her Great Dane, Eureka, whom she had more pictures of than her own nephew—before he finally logged into her computer.

Next, he opened the homepage on the screen and pulled out a neon green sticky note with the password, *BlueElephant00*.

10:19 PM

INSIDE the control room, the agent pushed aside the dead deputy who was seated in front of a row of monitors, pressed the EJECT button on the top of the video recorder, and removed the CD from the tray.

10:24 PM

SEATED at a bar in Manhattan, a high-end restaurant called 101 Fuji, Carol, Executive Editor for *Flashback* magazine, constantly checked the smartphone in her hand.

The bartender, a young buck who had been stalking Carol the second she strutted into the restaurant, asked her if she would like another drink. The question went through one ear and out the other. He patiently waited behind the bar, a lecherous look on his face, until Carol observed his queer presence.

With her hazy eyes widened, she stuttered, "Yes." Then, she followed more easily, "Can I help you?"

Acting as if she hadn't heard the question the first time around, the bartender asked once more, but this time louder.

"Oh. . . " Carol blurted out.

She glanced down at the sweaty drink in her hand, a half-empty vodka and club soda.

In two gulps, she downed the rest of the drink and ordered another.

10:27 PM

WITH a loud sigh, Agent Karp stepped into the vehicle and planted himself in the passenger seat.

"How'd it go?" Agent McClintock said as his partner placed the surveillance CD on the center console.

Agent Karp didn't answer the question.

Instead, he glared at Agent McClintock and said, "Drive."

10:49 PM

TWO drinks later, Carol's phone finally rang.

She checked the phone, the caller, *Stew*.

"About damn time," she said before Stewart had a chance to say hi, hey, hello, or whatever greeting Stewart preferred to use.

10:51 PM

AFTER walking a quarter of a mile through dirt and gravel, Agent Karp arrived at a ranch style house in the middle of nowhere.

"*Make it quick this time*," he mumbled what Agent McClintock had said to him in the car. Then, he followed with a retort of his own, "*I'll give you a fucking horse to eat, you arrogant fuck. . .* "

Agent Karp stopped at the very edge of the driveway and spotted a truck parked at the other end.

There wasn't another house for miles—three, to be exact, as Agent McClintock informed Agent Karp before he was dropped off. On each side of the house was roughly an acre of land, mostly flat, except for a hill in the backyard, which trailed off into the woods that surrounded the property. Next to the house was an old wooden tool shed, and next to that was a rust-colored 1969 Impala that had been gutted from inside out, the backseat used as a lounge chair for the front porch while the rest of the car parts were sold to the nearest junkyard.

Agent Karp removed a pistol from his holster, the Beretta 92FS, and then untwisted the suppressor from the thread. He pocketed the suppressor. Lastly, the agent checked the chamber and then inserted the pistol inside the belt behind his back.

10:52 PM

"ONE thing is for sure," Stewart said on the speakerphone as he scrolled through the pages of email, "she wasn't an advocate for deleting junk mail. I've never seen so much freaking spam in my entire freaking life. Talk about being an email hoarder."

On the other end of the phone, Carol said angrily, "Do you have something or don't you?"

"Oh," Stewart said giddily, "I have something."

10:54 PM

EVER since Bonnie and his two children were tragically swept away in the 2006 flood, the doorbell never rang, especially at this hour of the night. Bonnie had lots of friends, girlfriends who would stop by; and the children had babysitters as well, whenever Nicky and his wife decided to hit the town for a little adult time.

When the doorbell rang for the first time in years, Nicky thought the worst.

"Quiet, boy," he said to his dog, Smiley, who was throwing a fit. Biscuit darted from his kennel in the kitchen and joined Smiley in the uproar. He sprang from the La-Z-Boy, *muted* the crime drama on television, and grabbed a shotgun from the bedroom closet.

Both Smiley and Biscuit followed Nicky through the hallway. Biscuit was making so much ruckus that, even if the worse waited for Nicky at the door as he suspected, he or she had to deal with the little bullet, Biscuit first, then Smiley, then Mr. Smith and Wesson, and *then* Nicky.

In the foyer, he peeked through the curtains but didn't see a car in sight.

With his heart racing, Nicky switched on the front porch light, only to find a dark-suited man hunched over with dirt stains on his face as well as his clothes, both sleeves of his shirt rolled up his forearms, his tie loosened.

As soon as Nicky cracked open the front door—the chain still hooked around the lock—Agent Karp, who was breathing heavily, suddenly threw both hands in the air.

"What'd you want. . . " Nicky said over the barking.

Agent Karp's hands got as high as his shoulders before Nicky pumped the shotgun.

"Please," begged Agent Karp as he pointed across the driveway, "my car. . . it. . . the damn thing died on me about six miles from here. . . "

"Not my problem."

"Please," Agent Karp said, his breath labored. He reached into his pocket and pulled out a flip phone. "Please," he said once more, displaying the phone in his hand. "I'd use my cell, but I can't get a signal out there. Please help me, sir. All I'm asking for is to use your phone, if it's no trouble."

Nicky looked over the strange man's current condition, the stains of dirt on his fancy suit, the beads of sweat racing down his forehead, the mud caked on his leather shoes.

"Please," Agent Karp said again, "and some water, if it's no trouble."

10:55 PM

STEWART came across an email sent from Renny on Monday, October 20, 2014.

The subject was titled "*SENSITIVE INFORMATION.*"

He skimmed through the entire email.

Below were attachments—at least twenty from what he could count—mainly Word docs, mp4s, waves, and QuickTime mov. files.

"Carol. . ."

"Yeah," Carol said, slurping from a glass of melted ice cubes. "I'm here."

Then, there was a heavy silence.

Finally, Stewart said, "You're not going to believe what I just found. . ."

11:08 PM

THE last thing Nicky thought before that bullet from the Beretta 92FS went directly through his head: *I told you so.* . . And to die right here in the Hall of Death while sipping on a cup of Joe with a man named Ashley—if that was even his actual name. Ah hell! Irony is a bitch with one helluva sense of humor. Whatever happened to being neighborly? The one time I help out a fellow, I get shot for it. *And* whoever said that your life flashes before your eyes right before you die is full of shit.

In those final moments of death, Nicky didn't see anything at all. No flashes. Instead, Nicky heard the social commentary of his own stream of thoughts.

Then, that *thing with the string*. . .

11:53 PM

AFTER Stewart ended the conversation with Carol, he spent around an hour listening to each wave file and reading through each entry.

He mostly skimmed through Renny's journal entries and skipped through the interviews, except one that had piqued his interest the most.

Red-eyed from staring at the computer screen for hours, Stewart rewound the recording and turned up the volume to the max. There was static at first.

Then. . .

MR. HOPKINS [DISTORTED]: *There. . . was once. . .*

(MR. HOPKINS' *voice finally clarifies.*)

. . . a young girl named Agatha. . . grew. . . up in a place called Alimos, Greece, east of the port city Pireas and south of Athens. Agatha's father was a fisherman. Her mother, a weaver. Agatha also had two sisters, Stheno and Euryale. On some days, Agatha's father would take her out to sea with him. Agatha didn't have much interest in her father's work. She was more interested in the view, mainly one view in particular: a hill that sat in the middle of Athens. That hill was called Acropolis; and on that hill sat a temple, Athena's temple. Ever since she was a little girl, Agatha had always dreamed about leaving Alimos and traveling to Athens, to that one temple, *not* because it was so pleasing to the

eye, but because, like every sixteen-year-old, she was curious. She spoke of the temple to her father, who had specifically warned her to never go near the temple—it was [QUOTES] Off limits, [END QUOTES] which, of course, gave Agatha even more motivation to visit the temple.

RENNY: Why?

MR. HOPKINS: Teenage rebellion, I suppose.

(He *coughs and clears the phlegm from his throat.*)

One day when her father was at sea and her mother had slipped away from the house with Agatha's two other sisters, Agatha decided to run away. The night before, she had gotten into an argument with her two sisters who thought her dreams of traveling to Athens were absurd. Despite her father's strict orders, Agatha visited Athena's temple at night. There, she was ambushed from behind and raped by the god, Poseidon. Traumatized and haunted by the recent event, Agatha sneaked onto a cargo vessel, which sailed through the Alboran Sea and the Strait of Gibraltar. While sailing through the Atlantic, there was a terrible storm. The vessel capsized, forcing Agatha into the violent waters. Agatha wound up on the island of São Vicente, Cape Verde. Most of the crew died in the wreckage, but Agatha survived and was *lost*. . . again, wandering the land of the São Vicente until one day she fell into a cave filled with hundreds and thousands of poisonous snakes. The goddess Athena came to Agatha and told her that this was her punishment and that she would be forever cursed and every time a man set his eyes on her, that man would be turned to stone. Athena turned Agatha into the most repulsive creature, turned her hair into snakes, her skin into scales, and branded Agatha with a new name. *Many* centuries later, after she was beheaded by the great warrior, Perseus, my father discovered the head buried deep in the Black Sea, surrounded by a school of box jellyfish.

(RENNY *turns away from the two statues of Isabel and Dominic and leans closer to* MR. HOPKINS.)

RENNY [CURIOUSLY]: The girl, Agatha, what was her new name?

(A *long pause in the conversation.*)

Leon, what was her name?
MR. HOPKINS [CLEARLY]: . . . Medusa. Her name was Medusa.

Stewart didn't have any response to the story, except an involuntary *hmm*. He tapped the spacebar on the keyboard, which immediately paused the wave file. Again, Stewart let out a quiet *hmm*. That was all Stewart had to say, really, *hmm*, which was highly unusual coming from a guy who knew everything about everything.

He pulled himself away from the computer screen and forced himself into thought, deep thought.

Under his breath, he asked himself, "Is it real?"

If it is, then. . . Stewart listened to the story of Medusa one more time, googled that one name, *Medusa*, and read the contents on the Wikipedia page. Again, Stewart was left speechless, alone in his own thoughts. He ended up listening to the story four more times, following every sentence, every word, every syllable that rolled from the edge of Leon's lips. At the end of each and every listen, Stewart was *still* as confused as he was the first time around.

IN-DEPTH

An Exclusive Conversation with Ellis Kross

by Daniel Murphy

Meet Ellis Kross

ELLIS KROSS is a multi-genre author and graphic designer. He is the author of numerous novels, including the coming-of-age story, *Joshua'z Tree*, the Hitchcockian crime drama, *The March to Sundown*, the blockbuster, *FRANKIE*, along with the psychological thriller, *A Tear That Ripples Across The Pale Sky*. Ellis was born and raised in Sinclair Leprieur, Louisiana, the setting for his debut novel, *The Shadow Player*, which was later developed into a three-part series known as "V" (The Fifth).

Meet Daniel Murphy

DANIEL MURPHY is a journalist and editor-in-chief at *AfterThoughts* magazine. Daniel was born in Doyle Sounds, Michigan. After working as a column writer for a local newspaper, *The Singing Sandman*, before working for several notable magazines, Daniel documented his time spent on tour with the rock band Mona's Arc. He eventually settled in Silver Gates where he currently resides with his sprightly blue heeler named Lucky.

Daniel Murphy: How did you come up with the title, *Freeze: A Week With Mr. Hopkins*?

Ellis Kross: The word *freeze* happens to be the name of one of the main characters in the story. The word has multiple meanings. Cops use it when trying to catch criminals. When I was a kid, watching movies or TV shows with cops in it, I remember hearing that word a lot and was always captivated by it whenever I heard it coming from someone's mouth, more than likely, a cop with a drawn gun, ready to open fire after a long foot chase. Why that one particular word? Why not use the word *stop*? Or, *pause*? The word *freeze* carried more weight, like a warning. In the story, the presence of the character, *Freeze*, was not only a warning, but also perhaps the last face criminals saw before they were either hauled away or worse. As far as the other meaning, computers do it when they're overloaded with too many commands. The character, Anne, spends a lot of the story on the computer. I wanted to incorporate those two meanings of the word *freeze*, how they were used or applied. *Freeze: A Week With Mr. Hopkins* being two stories told in a span of two weeks. Two stories, two weeks, each story weaving through one another. ▸

DM: When you first begin writing a story, are there any specific scenes you create, opening lines, or do you just wing it?

EK: Most of the time, I have a general idea of where the story should go—always a beginning and an end, and from there, it's up to the imagination to fill in the middle section, that meaty stuff. There are times when a story grows entirely into something else. With *Freeze*, there were two scenes that stood out the most. From there, the story revolved around those scenes even though one of the scenes—the one with Red Strike—isn't really talked about in the book. The first one came from Mr. Hopkins' dialogue when he mentioned what happened in Rural. I had an image of this mysterious man and his family living in a small border town in Texas, on a ranch perhaps. Hot outside. Summer. Two paths: one, a man spending time with his family; the other, a team of hired guns, ex-military perhaps, on the way to send a message to this family man who has either exposed or left a corrupt organization with a debt that could only repaid in blood. 'An eye for an eye,' says Mr. Hopkins. Soon, these two paths were going to meet and the fallout would be swift. And that was the very first thing I wrote for *Freeze*—of a sick old man sitting in a wheelchair in front of a window, talking about a tragic event to a young journalist, who would later be known as Renny Jacobson. I ended up shaving off a lot of detail from the scene because I felt it was better told through Mr. Hopkins' POV, *not* the author's. I think from that point forward the reader can use his or her imagination and picture how horrendous it might have been for Leon and what he did to the people he loved more than the world itself. The second scene took place prior to the massacre in Rural, but it was written as a dream sequence from Leon's glory days as *Freeze*, mainly one day in particular called The Red Strike. It took place in the heart of downtown. Police are camped outside a courthouse. Inside, there is a judge being held hostage by a nasty group of Russians wearing red bags over their heads. The leader carries a sword. His minions, assault rifles. The captain of the police makes a call. The man on the other end is this enigmatic character, *Freeze*. He's in bed with a woman, a beautiful model. Captain tells *Freeze* he needs his 'services.' As usual, *Freeze* arrives late in a sports car. Cops are nervous. They're wearing silver retro-futuristic visors over their faces to pro- tect themselves from this character, *Freeze*. It ends with *Freeze* taking out the Russians. He rescues the judge. Walks out of the courthouse with the judge by his side— camera flashes glimmering around him. Then, he wakes up from his butler (who'd be later known as Diego) cracking open the blinds to a bedroom—rays of sunlight over his scarred face. It's about twenty years after those glory days. There's this sick old man lying on a bed, but you can't ex- actly see his eyes. He covers them with his hands before you learn that this man is, in fact, blind, and that he has *no* eyes. Then, he tells Diego, 'We're running out of time.' Two scenes, one of great tragedy, heartache, while the other, one of fame and glory. However, each scene ends the same: with an old man living with a heavy burden. In time, you realize what that burden is through a collection of interviews.

DM: Why did you turn the attention on Renny more so than Mr. Hopkins?

EK: I deliberately wrote more about Renny, obviously. Not only did I want the reader to get to know Renny a little more (after all, he was a pretty interesting character who grew up like any all-American boy), but I also wanted to build more sympathy for him before I killed him.

DM: Do you go into a story knowing who's going to die, or do you come up with it as you go along?

EK: Before I write a story, I know all the players involved and who is going to die or who is going to live or who is going to be the protagonist or antagonist or both. There are certain characters who stay on the fence throughout most of the story. I usually ask myself, 'Should this particular character live? What makes them likable? What makes them worthy? Will the story be better off with them in it or not in it? What ripple effect will happen if I kill this certain character?' Sometimes, I just sit back and let the story write itself.

DM: In the story, Freeze carries around Medusa's scales in a can of Zigzags. Why did you decide to use a fictional candy?

EK: Zigzags is a peppermint candy inspired by Altoids. I'm fascinated by the idea of opening a lid and unveiling, not candy, but in this case, snake scales, more slowly, rather than having them shoot out from, say, a Pez dispenser.

DM: If you had to come up with a tag line for Zigzags, what would it be?

EK: 'Life's too short to play it straight and narrow.'

DM: What was your process like while coming up with the follow-up to *A Week With Mr. Hopkins*? And what are your thoughts on sequels?

EK: When I first started writing *Final Days*, I had a lot of directions I could take the story, ones that strayed well beyond the original thread. I decided to stick to the initial core of the story. It's sort of a rough blueprint for what's to come. There are many ambiguous ideas in *Final Days*, ones that may need further explanation. The answers may come to light in the future—or not. The more time I've spent with these characters, the more I've gotten to know them. And I'm amazed by their evolution. I also enjoy the style of *Final Days*, short and concise, leaving it up to the reader to connect the dots. As far as sequels, if there's a story there to be fleshed out, one that couldn't be told the first time around, then why not tell it?